Dedicated to my Nana and Aunt F

CONTENTS

BOW STREET SOCIETY:
The Case of The Lonesome Lushington
by
T.G. Campbell

All characters in this novel are fictional. Any resemblance to persons living or dead is purely coincidental.

ACKNOWLEDGEMENTS

Thank you to Karen McDonald for her proofing skills and unending levels of patience during many a late night Skype rant. Thank you also to my sister, Bronia, for her proofreading skills and support. Also to Pashen and Thayne for their continued support in this endeavour.

During the course of researching the historical context for this novel, I had assistance from certain individuals and organisations. The assistance they gave me, and the information they provided me with, was both invaluable and appreciated beyond measure. Those individuals who assisted me included: Paul Robert of The Virtual Typewriter Museum who, for a second time, was generous enough to answer my question. It was thanks to him I could describe the brand, and history, of the typewriter used by Doctor Weeks. Also, Julie Mathias, head of learning at the Old Operating Theatre & Herb Garret Museum in London. The advice and information she graciously granted to me, in answer to my question, enabled me to form a more historically accurate description of the dissection tables used by Doctor Weeks. Furthermore, she supplied me with the name of an additional source of reference which shall undoubtedly prove invaluable as I write more *Bow Street Society* books.

I'd also like to thank artists Heather Curtis and Peter Spells. Heather designed the Bow Street Society logo on the front of this book (which also appears on my website and social media). Peter created the amazing central illustration on the cover. Peter also designed the central illustration of my first book *The Case of The Curious Client.*

Finally, I'd like to thank all my family and friends for their patience and support while I've been writing this book.

PROLOGUE

BLAGGARD OF BOW STREET HANGED read the evening's *Gaslight Gazette* headline. It had come as a relief to all those who were involved in the case; the unexpected entering of a not guilty plea at the trial had caused quite the ruckus, both within the courtroom and beyond. As he looked upon the headline, Inspector John Conway could well recall the roasting Thaddeus Dorsey had received on the witness stand by the defence. Then the independent doctor's testimony submitted by the Crown had successfully argued Dorsey suffered from the same thing a bloke called Charles Bonnett had first identified years back—hallucinations caused by severely deteriorated sight. In the end, the jury hadn't fallen for any of the prisoner's lies and they were found guilty. A month of appealing later and they had finally met their maker on the end of a rope. Yet even as darkness descended upon London this cold, February day, the grizzled policeman suspected the next sensation to grab the public's consciousness was already unfolding on one of its streets.

"This so-called 'Bow Street Society,' what do you make of them?" a deep, baritone voice enquired. Small eyes peered out from under unkempt, black brows over the top of the newspaper, looking to Conway for a response. John's voice was rough when he spoke—which was only natural for him. "They're a group that wanna do good."

"Hmpf. A group of *amateurs,* who're not even retired coppers, but bloody members of the public. Reading this though, you'd think the sun shone out of their backsides." A large hand reached around the side of the newspaper, picked up a pint of ale, and pulled it out of sight for a sip. "The hanging was welcomed by the clerk of the Bow Street Society, Miss Rebecca Trent, who is quoted as saying it was the members' hard work which exposed the murderer of Mr Arthur Perkins in the home of Mr Thaddeus Dorsey."

"She would though," Conway pointed out as he had some of his own pint. The newspaper was lowered and the head of the Mob Squad was gifted with a glare. "*You* were the investigating officer; *you* brought the blighter in, not her and not *them.*"

"Yeah, but they got the rope, Woolfe, and now it's done," Conway replied and emptied more of his pint down his throat. Now in his early forties, John Conway had been born in the East End district of Stepney. As such, he'd kept his accent even whilst working up the ranks of the Metropolitan Police. The wearing of his facial features, from years spent out in all weathers both as a constable and inspector, made him look far older than his years. It didn't mean he hadn't taken care of himself though; his well-maintained, dark-red beard, hair, and moustache were all testaments to the fact.

The tension in the frame of his drinking companion eased as he conceded to the truth and rose to his feet. "Another?" he enquired, his shadow enshrouding Conway and his shaking head.

"Nah. Thanks."

"Suit yourself." Inspector Caleb Woolfe was older than Conway, about forty-eight or forty-nine. He was much taller too—six feet four inches to Conway's five foot nine. Both men were well built with broad shoulders but Woolfe was solidly so. His height, build, and broad chest—along with his unkempt black hair, bushy eyebrows, leather-like skin, and red nose—had earnt him the nickname 'Big Bad Woolfe,' given by copper and criminal alike. No one wanted to be running away from him; the long stride afforded to him by his height meant he could swiftly catch up to his prey with very little effort. Similarly, he'd soon disappear from the sight of officers who were trying to match his pace.

As Woolfe stepped away from the table to procure his drink, Conway's view of the *Ship & Anchor*'s interior became unobstructed. Given its name, and location upon the promenade of the River Thames' Victoria Embankment, a newcomer would be forgiven for expecting to find washed-up, old fishermen and retired Royal Navy sailors within. Instead of the Metropolitan Police officers—some uniformed, some plain-clothed—who occupied it. This ironic twist in clientele—all of whom enjoyed a smoke and drink—could be explained by the presence of Scotland Yard a mere mile south down the river. The pub was geographically closer to the embankment's end at Blackfriars' Bridge than its counterpart at Westminster Bridge.

The pub was accessed via a singular set of double doors, opening out onto the embankment's promenade, leading one straight into the main bar area. The promenade itself being a hundred feet wide, thus setting the pub some ways back from the bank of the River Thames. The half-hexagonal-shaped bar occupied the back-left corner of the spacious, open-plan room. Serving behind it was the pub's landlord, Arnold Fairchild, and his long-serving barmaid, Pearl. A door at the back of the bar led to both the cellar and the stairs up to Fairchild's private rooms. Unlike some public houses of the day, the *Ship & Anchor* didn't let out rooms to guests.

Two immense oak-framed windows to the right of the front doors looked out onto the promenade. Small, framed panels of navy-blue and frosted glass check occupied the lower half of these windows, thus preventing any pedestrians traversing the promenade's footways from seeing whoever occupied the low-backed bench beneath. Upholstered with well-maintained, navy-blue fabric to match the stools' cushions, many favoured the comfortable bench. Innumerable tables, covered with glasses and used ashtrays, littered the bar area. Their round, wooden tops were dull and only as wide as the black, cast-iron, three-legged frames they were affixed to. These frames had wheat sheaf motifs upon their sides and Queen Anne-style curved legs. In the centre of this frame, fixed just above the point where the inward curves of the legs were closest, was a flat, circular, cast-iron motif of flowers. No doubt to keep the frame intact, well balanced, and sturdy. The oak stools surrounding the tables, though not as ornate, had been specially built to complement the tables' height. As a result, almost all who sat upon them had to do so with knees bent and feet flat upon the floor.

A uniformed sergeant idly played a piano against the far wall, on the right side as one entered the pub. An immense hearth, with cast-iron surround and fire crackling within, stood in the centre of this same wall. The walls throughout the pub were decorated with navy-and-light-blue-striped wallpaper, whilst the exposed floorboards were oak with a light covering of sawdust. Despite the Thames Embankment having electrical street lamps since 1878, the *Ship & Anchor* still very much relied upon gas to illuminate its rooms, including the one filled with vast clouds of tobacco smoke. It was this kind of smoke that had made the Royal Navy vessels in the old oil paintings adorning the walls difficult to make out; years of exposure had caused a thick, yellow film to accumulate upon their surfaces.

The Victoria Embankment was but one of three divisions which made up the Thames Embankment and which were the work of Sir J. W. Bazalgette. The second being Albert Embankment, from the south end of Westminster Bridge to Vauxhall, and another from Millbank to Battersea Bridge being the third. Costing over a million and a half pounds, construction commenced in 1864 and ended in 1870. Many customers of the *Ship & Anchor* therefore took the yellowing of the paintings as evidence it had occupied the spot since 1870—twenty-six years in all by 1896!

Conway's dark-blue hues ran over the many bodies sitting, standing, and walking around the interior; every conceivable inch of the place was occupied. Yet, despite this, the crowd at the bar—which was easily three deep—parted like the Red Sea when Woolfe approached. He wasn't difficult to miss, after all, easily being a foot taller than the majority of men there. Conway lit a cigarette and tossed the spent match into the ashtray on his table. He watched through the dissipating cloud exhaled from his lungs as his friend ordered ahead of the others and waited for his drink, his fingers strumming impatiently upon the bar. No one complained; no one even spoke to Woolfe. Instead, they gave him a wide berth, literally, and only returned to their former jostling and chattering once he'd gained his pint and was on his way back to his table.

"You put the fear of God into 'em lads, Woolfe." Conway remarked, the corner of his mouth lifting slightly, when his fellow inspector plonked himself back down on his stool. After this, Conway's view was once again blocked but he didn't mind.

Disappointed, Woolfe replied, "It doesn't take much, unfortunately."

"Takes more than you think, mate," Conway retorted, taking another mouthful of his pint and returning to the enjoyment of his cigarette once more.

ONE

"It's a disaster, the absolute *worst* that could've happened," Miss Rebecca Trent, clerk of the Bow Street Society, stated coldly. The possibility of feeling hot from moving furniture had led her to abandon blusher for the day and only wear lipstick, a true anomaly for her. Chestnut-brown hair was pinned up with a fair number of its shorter strands hanging loose. The mauve skirts she wore were plain but practical. Sturdy boots adorned her feet and a light-cream, closely fitted blouse completely covered her bust and arms. She had foregone her corset for the day. At twenty-eight years of age, she would've been considered 'old' but others' opinions of her rarely caused her consternation. Her hands were upon her hips as she glared at the two men. "All you had to do was move five pieces of furniture from Endell Street to here. *Five*! From *one* street away and *you* have somehow managed to perform a trick even the Great Locke would be envious of! You have achieved the impossible and *lost* my typewriter between *there.*" Her outstretched arm pointed to the right. "And *here*. Do you have *any* notion of its cost?" The two men turned their caps in their hands. Worried wouldn't even begin to describe what they felt. Only one of them was brave enough to shake his head.

The three of them stood in the hallway of Mr Thaddeus Dorsey's former home, now the legal property, and new headquarters of the Bow Street Society. Though all furniture apart from the wall-mounted telephone had been removed, the room itself was finely decorated. Black-and-white-checked tiles covered the floor whilst the walls boasted an embossed, repetitive, burgundy, flock pattern on a light-red background. Directly opposite the front door, and behind the group, was a grand staircase. It had rounded oak balusters holding up highly polished, smooth, oak handrails on both sides. The balusters had cubed tops inlaid into the underside of the rail, wide rotund middles, and cubed bases embedded into the stairs, around three balusters per step. The stairs themselves were covered in a burgundy carpet and led up to a narrow landing where another closed door, also of oak, could be seen. The landing seemed to continue to the left and right, back towards the front of the house, though only part of this could be seen from the front door.

Meanwhile, back on the ground floor, the hallway continued to the left and right of the stairs and led to two further oak doors. It was from the open oak door on the right the rough, East End voice of Mr Sam Snyder came. "It'll prob'ly be back in the old place." The middle-aged man's face was weathered and framed by bushy sideburns. Deep-set, brown, beady eyes held no malice as they beheld the movers. His broad shoulders almost touched the door frame whilst he wiped dust from his hands; his hands calloused from years of driving a two-wheeler hansom cab. At approximately five feet six inches tall, he didn't strike an imposing figure, even if the size of his hands threatened a devastating punch should one be required. More accustomed to wearing a heavy, black cape during the bulk of his waking hours, Sam enjoyed the much lighter weight of his indoor clothes.

"We'll find it, Miss Trent," the first mover volunteered.

"Then go and find it!" she ordered, pointing again. Needless to say, the men didn't need to be told twice. They hurried outside like rabbits bounding from a warren.

Rebecca sighed and rubbed her forehead in frustration. She remarked, "If they don't find my typewriter, I swear there shall be another murder here."

Sam chuckled, paying no heed to the scolding glance his amusement had earnt him. "You don't mean that, lass. Come on, let's ge' a cuppa." He held the door open for her and allowed her to head into the kitchen first. The room certainly looked a great deal different than it had when Mr Thaddeus Dorsey had 'resided' there.

Rebecca briefly admired the newly acquired, yet battered, table before moving to the back door and, easily, turning its knob. "The garden still needs a lot of work," she commented. Closing the door, she slid across its three bolts and turned the key in the recently installed lock.

Sam reminded her from behind, "It's only been a month."

"A month without any new cases." Rebecca went to the stove and hung a cast-iron kettle above it to boil. Sam meanwhile set about bringing second-hand chairs in from the hallway to put around the table. He'd kept the kitchen door open, however, so he heard Rebecca continue. "We're relying wholly on member contributions to keep the Society afloat."

"Sumin'll turn up, lass," Sam reassured as he put the last of the chairs in place and sat down.

Rebecca didn't join him; instead, she checked the stove's coal levels and cleaned the soot from her hands with a cloth. Through a sigh, she replied, "Probably our eviction notice."

"Hello?" a third voice suddenly called from the hallway. It didn't yell though, merely raised its pitch. "Is anyone here?"

Rebecca met Sam's questioning gaze, "I've already deposited this month's mortgage repayment."

The cabman turned his head toward the door in curiosity and suggested, "Best go see who it is."

"Hello?" the voice called again, this time with a definite edge of distress.

"Wait here," Rebecca instructed her friend. Sam gave his assent and she departed from the kitchen to politely greet their visitor. "Good morning, madam. May I help you at all?"

"Is this the Bow Street Society?" the visitor enquired upon seeing Rebecca's approach. She was a petite, perfectly proportioned woman, around thirty-five years in age. Virgin skin, almost translucent in its paleness, embraced the soft contours of her face. Though they were shaded by a pale-yellow straw hat's wide brim, Rebecca was struck by her visitor's intensely desperate chestnut-brown eyes. The fit of her dark-brown tweed, long-sleeved jacket, marginally higher calibre of material used in the ankle-length, light-brown bustle skirts, and flawless posture, all suggested a restricted wealth.

Having come to her conclusions within moments, Rebecca's attention was next drawn to her visitor's slight tugging of her leather glove's fingertip—despite her still wearing it. She replied, "It is. I'm Miss Rebecca Trent, the Society's clerk—" She paused as her visitor gave a curt nod and, intensifying her glove tugging, cast her gaze downward. Venturing to continue, Rebecca said, "I'm also responsible for deciding whether or not our Society accepts a commission set before it—"

"But you are a woman," the visitor interrupted, astounded, as she lifted her head sharply. A reaction which, though typical of the time, Rebecca detested.

"And perfectly capable of making such a decision, I can assure you. Mrs—?"

"Suggitt, Mrs Diana Suggitt." Mrs Suggitt pursed her lips together momentarily. "The Society *must* accept this commission, Miss Trent, without question," she insisted, her despair intensifying further. Seeming to have forgotten her initial surprise regarding Rebecca's gender and role, Mrs Suggitt now continued, "The most dreadful thing has happened and only the Society can see to its resolution." Her lips trembled, her voice was strained with emotion yet not a tear had been shed. Instead, the glove tugging ceased and, with a look cast squarely at the clerk, she stated, "I immediately thought of the Bow Street Society upon hearing the news…" She paused for a moment to purse her lips again and added. "…They shan't investigate her death properly, Miss Trent."

"Who shan't? And who has died, Mrs Suggitt?" Rebecca watched her mouth as it shook, betraying the great sadness lying beneath the mask.

"The police," Mrs Suggitt replied, after yet another moment was taken, this time to compose herself. "And my sister. Maryanna. Roberts. She…" The glove tugging resumed and, as Mrs Suggitt closed her eyes, she went on, "Murdered… She has been murdered… *Brutally* so. Yet she was a fallen woman, Miss Trent. If they wouldn't find the monster of Whitechapel, why should they find the fiend who slayed my sister?"

"When was she murdered?" Rebecca enquired, intentionally ignoring the question.

"I'm afraid I don't know. I spoke to my husband, Clement—on the telephone—but fifteen minutes ago and came straight here."

"Where is your husband?" Rebecca was reluctant to hope this lady was the potential client she seemed.

"I assume he is with the police. He told me he would find out what was happening but I mustn't, under any circumstances, go to my sister." Mrs Suggitt swallowed. "Yet, how can I not? At this moment, as we speak, my sister is lying in Oxford Street for all of London to gawp at."

"Mrs Suggitt, if your husband *is* with the police, they will already be—"

"*Please,* Miss Trent! I ask not for myself, or my husband, but for my sister." Mrs Suggitt half-turned away, her voice trembling as she continued, "What you see before you is not what I have always been. I am that rarity of a poor woman whom has married well but my sister—my whole family in fact—has remained where I started." She refaced the clerk. "Yet *I* have money and can pay whatever fee you deem appropriate so, please, I ask you to heed my sister's call as you have heeded others."

"Mrs Suggitt…" Rebecca began with a sigh yet paused as she felt the other woman's hand suddenly grip her own. The desperate look she gave her—the pleading of someone facing utter condemnation otherwise—would have abolished all reasons against taking on the case even if Mrs Suggitt hadn't uttered her next words. "I ask only for justice." Rebecca smiled and, placing her other hand upon her client's, gave it a firm squeeze of reassurance.

"Then both you and she shall have it." She allowed Mrs Suggitt to pull her hand away from hers while she enquired, "You said your sister lies on Oxford Street; where, exactly?"

"The *London Crystal Palace Bazaar*."

"Thank you. I shall allocate some members to your case and send them to Oxford Street. If you do wish to join your husband, I can arrange for our cabman, Mr Samuel Snyder, to take you free of charge."

Mrs Suggitt was still showing clear signs of distress yet there was sincere gratitude when she replied, "Yes, please. Thank you, Miss Trent."

"If you'd like to wait here, I shall ask him to prepare the cab."

"Of course." Mrs Suggitt moved away to compose herself. Rebecca meanwhile headed back into the kitchen. A few moments passed and she returned, having completed her task. She paused momentarily, however, upon seeing how adrift Mrs Suggitt's solitary figure seemed in the hallway's vast emptiness. It wasn't often Miss Trent felt her heart ache for another's plight.

Slowly, she approached the woman and softly informed her, "Mr Snyder shall be with you shortly, if you could wait here still?"

"Of course," the grief-stricken woman agreed. Yet her words were soon swept away on a fresh tide of sorrow and the clerk felt her ache return. She could do nothing to ease its symptoms but she could certainly do something about its cause.

Again excusing herself, Rebecca entered her new office which had formerly served as Mr Dorsey's bedroom. A desk, filing cabinet, and two chairs were the only items in the space; the desk in the centre faced the door with the chairs on either side, and the filing cabinet against the back corner to the right of the window. She went to the filing cabinet, pulling from it index cards and copying the address onto each of the small envelopes. Next, she instinctively sat behind the desk, intending to type the envelopes' contents, but gave an angry sigh at the offensive space.

She muttered, "By hand it is."

* * *

Mr Joseph Maxwell scratched his head and hummed. A man of average stature, but of slender form, he had broad shoulders, freckle-covered sunken cheeks, high cheekbones, and highly distinctive red hair he kept neatly combed and in a slight parting on the left. He also had a hint of lavender-and-carbolic soap lingering about him. Long, ink-stained fingers absently rubbed his pale chin as he contemplated a solution to his current problem; a clump of four typewriter arms jammed together against the paper with a pencil wedged beneath. He opened several drawers in his desk but, alas, could find nothing suitable.

"Where's your article, Maxwell?!" Mr Morse, his editor, bellowed from the door of his office.

"C-coming, sir!" Joseph cried. He stood and wiped his palms upon the skirt of the black frock coat he wore over a dark-green waistcoat, high-collared white shirt, and black, silk cravat. The last had its tiny bow tied over his Adam's apple.

"Well, hurry up!" Morse growled, adding, "We've not got all bloody day!"

"Yes, sir!" Joseph, panic-stricken, yanked at the jammed piece of paper with one hand and the misbehaving arms with the other. The former tore in half whilst the latter relented for a mere moment before jamming Maxwell's fingertips instead of the pencil. An almighty yelp filled the *Gaslight Gazette's* office as the journalist pulled his arm back and brought the entire typewriter with it. Notebooks, papers, pencils, a half-eaten sandwich, and even a cold cup of tea all came toppling off the desk while Maxwell frantically tugged at the arms with his free hand. "Argh!" he yelled as, finally, his poor fingers were freed from the wretched device.

"Still a clumsy fool, I see," a disdain-filled voice remarked. Yet it didn't belong to Morse or even the other journalists around Joseph who ignored his antics. Instead, it was a voice he'd never expected to hear at his place of work. He looked up in astonishment as he cradled his poor fingers. A considerably older gentleman glowered back. "F—Father, I—I wasn't—"

"Get the words out, man!" Thin lips contorted into a scowl. "Only idiots stutter." His voice, nasal in character, dripped with disapproval.

"Sorry, Father," Maxwell managed to get out before the other continued.

"I still live in hope you'll one day show me you're *not* an idiot, Joseph, but my hope fades each time we meet. *Sit* down!" Though his father was only of average height, Joseph still felt intimidated by him. He therefore dropped down without even thinking to check if there was a chair beneath him first. Luckily there was. Joseph's father remained looming over his son's desk.

Mr Oliver Maxwell was in his mid-fifties with defined cheekbones and jaw, high forehead, slanted salt and pepper eyebrows, and a receding hairline. The retained hair had been parted off-centre with its natural black colour remaining at the sides of his head. Small salt and pepper patches were still visible though not only above his ears but at the edge of his hair line and parting. He continued, "You are to come to dinner with your brothers tomorrow night, Joseph. Your mother wants to see you."

"Yes, Father. But—"

"This is *not* up for debate."

"Murder on Oxford Street!" a messenger boy yelled across the office. Maxwell looked past his father at the young male and knew it would be a matter of time before another of the journalists took the assignment. He'd intended to ask his father why he hadn't simply sent him a written invitation but now this rare opportunity to claim a story, rather than be assigned a dull one by his editor, had distracted him. He swallowed hard under Oliver's scowl but nonetheless slowly rose from his chair. "Father, please excuse me but I must—"

"And what exactly is it you *do* here, Joseph? Other than peddle lies and cause scandals. This newspaper has ruined many a man." Oliver's eyes widened and narrowed upon catching his son reaching for his coat. "*Where* are you going? *Sit* down!" Yet Joseph didn't, infuriating Mr Maxwell, Snr, further. "You always were an insolent little wretch. Why couldn't you have been more like your brothers? Both successful, and both married well."

"I want someone on Oxford Street, *now!*" Mr Morse simultaneously bellowed above the din of the office. Catching sight of Joseph preparing to leave, the editor pointed at him and demanded, "Maxwell! Where's your *bloody* article?!"

"When are you going to find some stupid, wealthy woman to marry you?" Oliver continued, oblivious to Morse's angry interjections. "Dowry, Joseph. That's what you need, a decent dowry."

"C-coming, Mr Morse!" Joseph called as he attempted to step around his father. The elder Maxwell easily blocked his path, however.

"You've never shown any inclination toward women or mentioned any women on the rare occasion you deign to grace your mother and I with your presence. Do something about it."

"Yes, Father," Maxwell replied through a sigh as he saw Mr Baldwin, another of the journalists, grab his coat and hurry from the office.

"*Don't* you sigh at me, boy," Oliver growled. "Arrive promptly at eight."

"Yes, Father," Joseph repeated, deflated. It was only after the weight of his father's presence had lifted did he realise he could still reach Oxford Street before his rival. Pulling his coat on, he turned toward the door, only to walk straight into the corner of his desk. He grunted loudly. As his thigh throbbed though, he plucked up the torn article from the floor, deposited it upon his editor's desk, and hurried from the office before Morse could bite.

TWO

One of the most famous of London's thoroughfares, Oxford Street is over a mile and a half long, and is one of the main arteries between the fashionable residential quarter and the counting house of London's vast city. It is used by the never-ending stream of traffic travelling from east to west and vice-versa. Included within it is New Oxford Street while its central point is Oxford Circus, also known as Regent Circus because it also sits at the top of Regent Street. This circus not only marks the crossover point of the east and west and north and south communication lines, but is also the location of the first ladies public lavatory erected in 1884. A welcome addition no doubt when one considers in 1896, as in modern times, Oxford Street was brimming with shops dear to the hearts of country and city ladies alike. One such establishment was the *London Crystal Palace Bazaar*. Located upon the east side of Oxford Street, just past the circus, it sat opposite Argyll Street with entrances on both Oxford Street and at 9 Great Portland Street. This bazaar was built of glass and iron to the designs of Mr Owen Jones. One of its most striking features was its roof of coloured glass. Commodities for sale there included toys and the "cheaper kind of fancy goods."

Usually the bazaar's sellers would've been preparing for a new day of trading but, as the clocks within chimed eight thirty, all was calm. The bazaar's Oxford Street entrance had been cordoned off by a line of Metropolitan Police officers. The opening of the Portland Street entrance had also been blockaded. Thus, all the sellers within could do was hopelessly watch the gathering of a large crowd upon the street outside. The necks of the external gawkers stretched as they tried to catch a glimpse of the grisly scene mere metres away. Among them was Mr Joseph Maxwell who, with pencil and notebook in hand, was jostled this way and that. He had no idea where Mr Baldwin was, a good thing, too!

"P-Pardon me?!" he called over to a constable attempting to keep the crowd back. "What's happened here?!"

"A murder," the constable bluntly replied before shouting to the crowd at large. "Stay back! There's nowt to see here!" Maxwell seriously doubted it, a view shared by the crowd as no one even considered stepping away from this potentially macabre piece of excitement.

"Is it true the body's been mutilated?!" Mr Baldwin's voice yelled from somewhere. Maxwell frantically glanced around but couldn't locate his rival.

"Wh-who was murdered?" Maxwell meekly shouted before clearing his throat and attempting to repeat it a little louder. "Who was-oof!"

A particularly hard shove from a fellow gawker sent the poor journalist hurtling to the ground. He put his hands down but was too late. He hit the wet, horse filth-covered cobbles while his pencil and notebook hurtled from his grip. The visage before him of several feet both snapping his pencil and kicking his notebook away forced him to abandon any hope of retrieving either. Maxwell sighed and heaved himself up onto all fours. He didn't stand fully though for, through the fleeting gaps between people's legs, he could see the familiar face of someone, crouched down, in the bazaar's doorway. Unfortunately, he couldn't see what they were looking at from this angle.

"Doctor Weeks!" Maxwell yelled, poking his head through the first gap and using his shoulders to force his way forward. As he repeated this method to reach the front of the crowd, still upon all fours, he yelled, "Doctor Weeks, sir! Doctor!" When he finally did emerge from the crowd, a constable grabbed the surplus material of his jacket and roughly 'helped' him to his feet.

The constable demanded, "'Ere, what's your game?"

"It's all right, Constable. I'm a journalist," Maxwell stated once he'd been released, straightening his frock coat. This honesty was rewarded by a second shove, back into the depths of the crowd, by the unimpressed officer. "And a friend of Doctor Weeks!" Maxwell managed to cry as he stumbled backward. The Canadian turned hazel-brown eyes toward him, upon hearing his name, but simply muttered a curse under his breath and withdrew the lit cigarette from the corner of his mouth. He rested it against the top edge of a book while he rose to his feet and wrote some notes. Grey, woollen, fingerless gloves, a knee-length, black overcoat, and a grey, woollen scarf, protected him from the cold, but he still looked worse for wear. Dark circles were under his eyes, his usually slicked-back, jet-black hair was a little unkempt, and no wax at all could be seen on his small moustache. The only neat parts of him were his short-haired sideburns but, due to their length, it was nigh-on impossible to make them messy.

While Maxwell was watching Weeks, he missed the fact someone else strode toward him. It wasn't until this person completely blocked his view and he stared at their chest, he realised he'd garnered some unwanted attention.

"What's your name?" a voice enquired from above. Maxwell lifted his chin slightly, then some more, and narrowed his eyes against the sun peeking out from behind the other's head.

"Mr Joseph M-Maxwell, sir, journalist with the *Gaslight Gazette.*"

"You're not a friend of Doctor Weeks' then," the man retorted.

"W-well, y—yes, I am. That is to say, we, um, we have worked together—" Maxwell stopped himself and, smiling weakly, corrected, "Not *worked* together, but… we have a mutual friend." He swallowed hard, "M-May I speak with him, Mr…?"

"Woolfe. *Inspector* Woolfe, E Division, and, no, you can't." Woolfe eyed the smaller man suspiciously and Maxwell tried to think of another reason why he should be permitted access to the Canadian. Yet no sooner had he thought of one did Maxwell see Woolfe wandering back to the crime scene. There, Maxwell noticed another plain-clothed officer, presumably a sergeant, taking notes and speaking to a wealthy gentleman in a tan, knee-length coat. Needless to say, the journalist was disappointed he wasn't any closer to either Weeks or the would-be witness. However, he was also surprised to discover he'd been holding his breath the entire time.

"Better luck next time, Maxwell," Mr Baldwin's voice commented from behind. Maxwell looked over his shoulder and saw his rival's smirking face.

"At least I spoke to someone," Maxwell pointed out, much to Baldwin's annoyance.

"And what good did it do you? *None!*"

"What do you *mean* I cannot visit Messrs Drysdon and Drysdon? I have an order to be collected for my dear nephew's birthday; it must be collected today or his special day shall be ruined, *ruined*! And after the tragic loss of his parents in the bicycle accident, I shall hold the Metropolitan Police *personally* responsible if I do not collect my order today!" A rather offended, high-pitched, female voice demanded further along the crowd's front. Both Maxwell and Baldwin looked to see a woman, no older than fifty, speaking to a constable.

She had a fair complexion and warm, chestnut-brown hair styled in tight curls upon her head and pinned up beneath a fantastic headdress of small, black ostrich feathers. The latter, in addition to the court (or 'Louis') shoes she wore, made her seem taller despite her being only five feet. Her slender, though wide-shouldered, form, wrapped in a black, fur coat hanging about an inch off the ground, complemented the contours of her face.

Standing at her side, though behind, was another woman who was no older than twenty and no younger than seventeen. While the older woman was adorned in fur, the younger wore an open, cropped, black jacket. It followed the V-shape silhouette of her torso and flared out into two, small points at the back. Its sleeves meanwhile sported the fashionable "leg-of-mutton" shape (tight on the lower arms, puffed out on the upper). Worn under this was a loosely-fitted, burgundy, cotton blouse (or 'waist') ending just below her bust. Here the blouse tucked into a dark-brown, small, brass-buckled belt to accentuate her naturally narrow waist. Below this were minimal bustle skirts which had burgundy panels on their front and dark-brown, pleated layers cascading down their back. Yet, despite all of this, the overall beauty of the young woman's appearance was underwhelming. Even her chocolate-coloured hair was plain, devoid of curls and wrapped into a bun nestled against the base of her skull. Meanwhile, the right, front side of her hair was covered by a narrow hat pinned, unfashionably, at an angle. The remainder of her appearance comprised of brown, cotton-clad hands lying upon the handle of an immense, closed, black umbrella positioned, vertically, against the front of her skirts. Though she could never be considered beautiful in a traditional sense, her broad, squared shoulders, perfect posture, locked elbows, and hard scrutiny gave her an unignorably attractive air of strength.

The young woman—as if feeling eyes upon her—glanced in Maxwell's direction and stepped closer to her wealthier companion. When she did, however, another woman was revealed to accompany them. Maxwell's eyes widened, "Georgina…" At only five feet tall, Miss Georgina Dexter had been completely hidden by the taller, plainer lady. Despite her shortness, her petite form was nevertheless perfectly proportioned. Fair-skinned with red hair, she had a subtle beauty about her, considered admirable by most men. Her hair was always tightly pinned and half-hidden beneath a bonnet as a matter of course. Today's bonnet being dark-turquoise, with slightly ruffled edging, to match the dark-turquoise and black panelled non-bustle dress she wore. The entirety of her chest and half of her neck were covered by the dress under a black jacket ending at her high waist. Finally, a satchel sat against her hip, its strap over her head and resting on her opposite shoulder.

She was several feet away, with many a person in between, but the journalist resolved to reach her nonetheless. Pushing his way, quite roughly, through the crowd therefore, he soon came close to accomplishing his mission. The final barrier of people proved resistant to his efforts however. After much shoving, with no success, he pushed his fingers into the gap between shoulders and, slowly, outstretched his arms. Just as his bent elbows were about to unfold though, one of the people moved and Joseph was sent hurtling forward, narrowly missing his fiancé. Yet even as he caught himself, he cried, "Georgina!"

"Mr Maxwell!" she exclaimed, startled. She lowered her camera and gripped his arm to steady him. "Are you all right?" she enquired and gently brushed the dirt from his frock coat as he did the same.

"Yes, yes. It was just a tight squeeze—through the crowd," he explained.

Georgina glanced behind him, "You need to be more careful; you'll hurt yourself." Noticing his sore fingertips, she held this hand without thinking and added, "Your poor fingers!"

"Typewriter." He felt his cheeks burn as she gave him a questioning look. Deciding to change the subject though, he smiled and added, "I had to see you. It's been a long time since we last spoke." Her confusion morphed into sadness and she bowed her head. Maxwell's smile died, "I want to make amends, Georgina, for the night at your parents' house when I—"

"I'm glad you're all right, Joseph." She turned her head away as her lips trembled. "I… I really must take these photographs for Lady Owston." Fully facing the bazaar's entrance again, she lifted the rectangular prism-shaped, wooden camera to her chest and pressed a button atop it. A click sounded, followed by a second and a third. Looking ahead of her, Maxwell saw the crime scene—namely the ghastly mutilated body of a naked woman slouched in the doorway—

and realised she was documenting it. Due to the shadows cast by the entrance porch's walls, it was difficult to see exactly *how* the poor woman had been mutilated. There was certainly a great deal of blood on her chest, stomach, and shoulders. Her chin rested on her chest and... a cap was upon her head? Maxwell squinted but soon wished he hadn't. *Not a cap,* he thought, his stomach turning. *It's her skull!*

He slowly turned away from both the scene and Georgina, but the damage had already been done. A violent retch overcame him, forcing him to clap both hands over his mouth. All thoughts of documenting the scene were forgotten—he'd lost his notebook anyway—as he gave another retch and added to the small amount of vomit already in his mouth. Unable to hold it in any longer, he bent over and emptied the contents into the gutter beside the curb.

"Are you well?" Georgina's voice enquired as a gentle hand rubbed his back. Needless to say, several in the crowd's front row had moved back to avoid getting their shoes soiled.

"Yes..." Maxwell replied, spitting out the remnants. Slowly, he straightened and, nodding at her, allowed the artist to continue with her work. It surprised him she could bear to look at such things. Then again, the more he watched her, the more he noticed how she repeatedly swallowed back her disgust.

He didn't dare look back toward the bazaar. Instead, he shifted his weight from one foot to the other and, in an awkwardly nervous voice, began, "Georgina..." His last shred of courage deserted him, however, and he cast his eyes downward. Unable to find his strength, or the answers he needed to remedy the rift between them, he instead took a deep breath and offered. "I tried calling to Doctor Weeks but he couldn't hear me." He paused, "Is the Bow Street Society investigating this murder?"

"Haven't you received a letter from Miss Trent?" Georgina enquired. Holding the camera away from her body, to get a closer shot of the scene, she again pressed the button. Remembering Maxwell hadn't been given such a correspondence last time though, she explained. "She sends letters to everyone she wants to give a case to."

"Oh." Maxwell frowned, "In that case, no, I haven't."

"I can't talk to you about it, then, Joseph," she replied. "I'm sorry." The sadness those two simple words carried though suggested far more than their surface meaning. "Speak with Miss Trent. I'm sure it's just a mistake?"

Joseph nodded slightly and said, "I will make it right." Yet Georgina turned her back upon him at this, the movement too quick for him to see the tears which threatened to overwhelm her.

"Do you have *any* idea who I *am*, Constable?" the wealthy woman meanwhile challenged. "I am Lady Katheryne Owston and this is my secretary, Miss Agnes Webster. Where is the investigating officer? I *demand* to speak with him."

"I'm he, what's going on?" Inspector Woolfe enquired as he approached. The deepness of his voice never failed to make even the simplest of questions a demand; such was the case here.

Yet Lady Owston gave the odd-looking man a disapproving once-over with her eyes and announced, "I wish to collect a most important gift for my nephew from Messrs Drysdon and Drysdon."

"You can't."

"I know *that*, Inspector—I assume you *are* an inspector? Otherwise I *demand* one be brought to me."

"I am; Inspector Caleb Woolfe from E Division."

"How unfortunate for you," she replied with distaste. "I want to know *why* I can't collect my order."

"There's been a murder, Lady Owston. The poor girl's body's in the doorway of the bazaar so we can't let anyone in or out until we've done what we need to do and moved her," Woolfe explained. Lady Owston covered her mouth to stifle a loud gasp at the revelation.

"Oh, how *very* awful! The *poor* girl!" She twisted her body to ask the younger woman, "Agnes, my smelling salts," before again addressing Woolfe, "Did she have a name? Any family? I would like to send them a monetary gesture of support." She took a small bottle from her companion, uncorked it, and deeply inhaled the strong scent emanating from it.

"Why would you want to do that?" Woolfe enquired with confusion and suspicion.

"Why would I *not*, Inspector? We are all Christians here; charity is the responsibility of us *all* who can afford to give it. Will you deny me such a Godly deed?" Her tone was quite serious, her expression stern.

Sighing softly, Woolfe replied, "Fine. Her name's Mrs Maryanna Roberts. She's got a husband, Abraham Roberts, and a daughter."

"How did she die, Inspector?" Maxwell interjected, stepping forward. Lady Owston and Agnes both turned toward him in unison, the former aghast and irritated, the latter mildly curious. Georgina meanwhile discretely slipped her camera into a fur hand muff.

"We don't know yet," Woolfe replied, his voice as annoyed as Katheryne's face.

"Will the family know she is dead?" Lady Owston enquired, sympathetically. "If she's only just been found, I don't wish the news of her demise to be in the form of my gesture."

"They do. She was found at six o'clock this morning by Constable Fraser when he was on patrol. Now, if you'll excuse me, Lady Owston, I've got a job to do." Woolfe cast one last warning glare toward Maxwell before he returned to Weeks. Maxwell watched him but could feel three sets of eyes burning into him.

"Exactly who *are* you?" Lady Owston demanded but lifted her hand to cut him off. "*Never mind*! I do not have time for this. Agnes, Miss Dexter, this way." She stepped around him and headed for a cab parked some distance down the street, with Sam Snyder sitting in its driver's seat. Agnes followed, taking a small, leather-bound notebook and pencil from Lady Owston as she did so. The umbrella's handle was hooked into the crook of her arm before she set about making short-hand notes on what had occurred.

Georgina meanwhile told Maxwell, quietly, "Please don't follow us, Joseph."

"When will I see you again?" he enquired but the female artist turned, began to follow the others and stopped. She stood, her back to him, for several moments.

He watched her, hopefully, but this hope faded as she bowed her head and replied, through a sad sigh, "I don't know." She lifted, and turned, her head to bid him goodbye before hurrying to catch up with Lady Owston and Miss Webster. The further away she got though, the more adrift Maxwell felt. When she reached the cab, and climbed in, a thought came to him. He swallowed hard and took up pursuit.

Yet, as Joseph reached the cab, Sam glanced around and the journalist was forced to duck down below Snyder's elevated driver's seat. Keeping low, Maxwell pressed his palms against the smooth, slanted, back wall of the cab and listened intently. "Mrs Suggitt, I'm Lady Katheryne Owston, an independent journalist for the *Women's Signal* and *Truth* publications. Miss Agnes Webster is my secretary and Miss Georgina Dexter is a most talented artist. Miss Webster shall be taking some short-hand notes during our discussion but, rest assured, these shall remain confidential." The higher-class lady's voice was markedly quieter, and lower in pitch, than it had been outside.

A second voice he didn't recognise, but he assumed to be Mrs Suggitt's, enquired, "And you are all members of the Bow Street Society?"

"Yes," Katheryne confirmed. "Miss Trent's correspondence gave us the facts you've already disclosed, Mrs Suggitt, but we must know absolutely everything if we are to discover the identity of your sister's murderer."

"I understand."

"When was the last time you saw your sister?"

"About a week ago but I…" Mrs Suggitt's voice faltered. "I almost saw her yesterday."

"Almost?" Miss Dexter enquired, curiously.

"Yes." Mrs Suggitt replied. "She visited *The Queshire Department Store* in search of me but I wasn't there."

"I know *The Queshire Department Store* well," Katheryne replied. "But why would she think to search for you there? Had you arranged to meet her?" There was a long pause during which Maxwell felt the first spots of rain land upon his hands and unkempt, red hair, causing the former to cool within moments.

"No, I hadn't. My husband is the store's assistant manager."

"Ah yes, of course. Mr Clement Suggitt. I assume your sister also knew of his employment there?"

"Yes. And how I often meet my husband for lunch. Yesterday though I was late—I can't remember why—and, when I arrived, I was informed by Mr Queshire himself my sister had caused a most despicable scene with the husband of one of his wealthier customers. She'd *propositioned* him with his wife standing there! I was mortified and, naturally, understood utterly when Mr Queshire informed me he'd had to escort her from the premises. Yet, when I enquired if he knew where she'd gone, he replied he didn't know, but it was more than likely the nearest pub."

"A surprisingly flippant remark from Mr Queshire," a fourth monotone voice stated, assumedly Miss Webster's.

Lady Owston hummed, adding. "He's usually a most accommodating man—to women of all social classes."

"Oh, he is," Mrs Suggitt agreed. "But even Clement was surprised by how angry he was."

"I'm quite certain he was. I have met your husband on several occasions, Mrs Suggitt, while conducting research for my *Women's Signal* articles. In fact, I saw him only minutes ago speaking to the police outside of the bazaar."

"Clement knows I'm here?" Mrs Suggitt enquired.

"Not presently, but if you wish him to, Miss Dexter may accompany you to him."

"Yes, I…" Mrs Suggitt's voice broke a little. "…I would like to see him."

"Did Mr Queshire give any reason as to why he thought your sister would go to a public house?" Lady Owston continued but only after allowing Mrs Suggitt a moment.

"No, he walked away after stating such to me." Another pause and Maxwell glanced upward upon hearing the slight creaking of Sam's seat as the cabman shifted his weight. Eventually Mrs Suggitt continued, with the deepest of sighs. "Drink was my sister's demon, Lady Owston; it took her under its spell several years ago following the deaths of her other children in infancy. She couldn't come to terms with them. She blamed herself even though we all reassured her there was nothing else she could've done."

"We?" Miss Webster enquired.

"Clement, Abraham—Maryanna's husband, her only surviving child, Regina, and I. All the children died of disease, polio, cholera. We were all as heartbroken as she but she took it the worst. Neglecting her duties as a wife and mother and finding solace in the arms of a gin bottle. Her husband stood by her until he could no longer keep her in the house. He said she needed to sober up before coming back. Regina and I have tried to give Maryanna the help she so desperately needs—" Mrs Suggitt's voice faltered as she corrected, "Needed. But my sister continued to drown in the liquor."

"She remained close to her daughter, though?" Miss Dexter now enquired.

Mrs Suggitt replied, "As much as her husband would allow, yes."

"I'm sure you can appreciate, Mrs Suggitt, why we will need to speak to Mr Roberts," Lady Owston carefully stated.

"Yes," their client replied, softly. "I shall see to it you have his address."

"Can you think of anyone who would want to see harm come to your sister?" Georgina's sympathetic voice sounded next.

Mrs Suggitt took in a deep, shuddering breath but answered, "When she wasn't under the influence of drink, my sister was the kindest, most considerate woman you could ever hope to meet. Under it, she could be vile, vulgar, and erratic but not to the degree anyone would want to see her *dead.* Not even Abraham and he had been shamed by her actions the most."

"Forgive me, Mrs Suggitt, but I *must* ask this: where were you last evening and the early hours of this morning?"

"At home."

"Thank you, Mrs Suggitt," Lady Owston said. "You will need to speak to Inspector Woolfe about what you have told us. Feel free to inform him you have hired the Bow Street Society if you so wish. If you don't, we shan't reveal the fact either. We do recommend you be as honest and open with the police as you can though; none of us wish to be arrested for perverting the course of justice. Do you have an address where we may reach you?"

"Yes... here," Mrs Suggitt's voice sounded strained as, Maxwell presumed, she gave Lady Owston the address in note form.

Yet another pause followed—only to be abruptly ended by Katheryne announcing, "I believe a visit to *The Queshire Department Store* is in order, Agnes. Miss Dexter shall take good care of you, Mrs Suggitt. Agnes will take dictation of Mr Roberts' address from you before we depart, however." A softly spoken 'thank you' from Mrs Suggitt was Maxwell's cue to depart, carefully creeping away while still bent over so as not to alert Sam's attention.

Despite his precautions though, the journalist was alarmed to hear the cabman's voice call, "Be seein' you, Mr Maxwell." Joseph straightened, and turned upon his heel to find Sam looking over his shoulder at him. The journalist gave a curt nod and, tugging down his frock coat, quickly strode away feeling thoroughly embarrassed.

"There he is again," Lady Owston remarked, half-turning toward the rear of the cab.

"Who?" Miss Webster enquired though looking to her employer rather than the retreating figure.

"The pale fellow who kept asking questions," Lady Owston replied, not noticing the way Miss Dexter, perturbed, stepped forward and parted her lips as if to call him back.

"Mr Joseph Maxwell," Sam explained, smiling. "Journalist with the *Gaslight Gazette.*" Miss Dexter was grateful the cabman hadn't alluded to her engagement or the fact Joseph was a fellow Bow Street Society member. It would've only caused awkwardness.

"A fine thing he had the sense to depart," Lady Owston remarked. "Come, Agnes!" She took off down Oxford Street with Miss Webster who took large, swift strides to fall into step beside her. As soon as the two were out of earshot of Mrs Suggitt, Lady Owston added, "Let us test our client's account."

"Do you think she's lying?" Miss Webster enquired, surprised.

"No, but we mustn't accept all she tells us as Gospel either."

The secretary agreed, not having thought to take such precautions.

Meanwhile, Miss Dexter had mouthed a 'thank you' to Sam as she'd given him her camera for safe keeping; unless the police line had dispersed, there was little point in any further attempts to capture the crime scene. She'd accompanied Mrs Suggitt back toward the bazaar in spite of her own heart pounding in her chest at the thought of encountering Inspector Woolfe again. She could well imagine the inspector confiscating her camera should she begin capturing Mr and Mrs Suggitt's likenesses in front of him. Such was in the best-case scenario, she shuddered to think of the worst—a night in a police cell! *Newgate Jail!* She swallowed hard. *Yes, best to leave it there*, she thought.

THREE

Magnificent structures, awesome in their size, lined Oxford Street as testaments to the religion of capitalism and consumerism. Like preachers in a pulpit, the store owners called forth their flock through strategically placed signs and alluring window displays. All promised, without explicitly doing so, an unobtainable state of utter completion, a state only attained via the purchasing of their goods. Many a female worshipper, cocooned by private carriages from the offensiveness of city life, could be seen waiting outside her chosen temple. Time and again, offerings would be brought forth, by store employees, for her silent approval or loud rejection. Only once she was satisfied with her state of completion would she make a glittering 'donation' and claim her prize. Such women had been discouraged from doing this outside the bazaar and surrounding stores for obvious reasons. Yet the two Bow Streeters saw more and more of them as they walked further along Oxford Street.

Neither paid any heed, however, choosing instead to scan the plethora of signs above their heads for the familiar dark-red and gold one belonging to *The Queshire Department Store.* Lady Owston, a veteran "wor-shopper" of that temple, caught sight of its advertisement first. "There it is!" she announced without breaking the rhythm of her swift stride.

Miss Webster, who had been walking at her side, couldn't see the sign at first so enquired, "Where?" She held her hat against her head—for it had become quite windy—and slowed her pace to scan the signs more thoroughly. As a result, she quickly fell behind, soon becoming cut off from Lady Owston by the many bodies which seemed to multiply by the second. "Lady Owston!" she shouted, waving as highly as possible, and sidestepping those rapidly coming from the opposite direction.

One such person was a gentleman who'd just ignited his cigarette, holding the still lit match in his hand. Agnes' breath caught in her throat at the sight of the flame despite having only seen it for a moment. The deafening noises of Oxford Street became muffled against the backdrop of her racing heart and tightening chest. She gasped for air but none came. "I cannot breathe…" she uttered, her voice overpowered by those around her. Though she kept on walking, her pace was a great deal slower. One hand tightened its grip upon the umbrella handle whilst the other reached out. "Lady Owston!" she cried desperately though she'd long since lost sight of her employer. Her fellow pedestrians continued to swarm past her, hurrying to flee the rain now falling with a vengeance. Yet all Agnes could see were dark, indistinguishable shapes flying past her, rendering her dizzy and disorientated. She knew this dizziness would soon lead to a faint, as it had done many times before. The secretary therefore headed for the nearest wall to lean upon, which she reached without issue. Her heart continued to pound and her lungs still refused to take in air whilst her head swam with black shapes and golden flames. She swallowed several times but it alleviated nothing, so she pressed the umbrella's tip against the pavement and lent heavily upon its handle.

"Deep breaths," Lady Owston's voice finally reassured and Agnes felt a hand gently rub between her shoulders. A small sob escaped the secretary's lips instead of words; nothing needed to be said, though. Calming as the fear dissipated, Agnes felt her chest loosen enough for her to fill her lungs. Afterward, her panic had subsided further and she was able to straighten.

"How did you find me?"

"You found me, child." Katheryne slipped her fingers around Agnes' arm and turned her toward the impressive façade of *The Queshire Department Store*. Miss Webster was amazed, for she was certain she'd become lost. Yet there was the dark-red and gold sign swinging from a pole above her head. Its top and bottom edges had black diamonds in their centres and upward curves on their left and right-hand sides. A thick, golden line followed the sign's internal contours but left a half-inch gap between it and the edges. In the centre of the landscape-orientated sign was an oil painting depicting a beautiful woman sitting side on and looking outward over her shoulder. She wore a golden headband with a veil of fine, translucent cotton resting against her back, the top of the veil having been wrapped around wavy, brown hair pinned into a mound upon her skull's crown. Her flawless face, hair, and shoulders were bathed in heavenly light while the plain, red, sleeveless dress and golden armbands she wore were tainted by brown shadows. The remainder of the sign included the name of the store, painted in gold, in four parts shared between the top black diamond and the left, right, and undersides of the goddess-like vision.

Agnes felt the corners of her mouth lift as her amazement became amusement. "So I did." She placed her own hand upon Lady Owston's. "And I'm now ready to continue."

"*Excellent,*" Lady Owston replied, beaming. The two ladies simultaneously faced the department store. The establishment was a good two storeys shorter than its neighbours which, in addition to being set back a good couple of feet, could've easily driven its dark-brown, brick façade into obscurity. Yet the ignited, glass-covered gas lamps, mounted above the horizontal *Queshire Department Store* sign, lifted the establishment from the shadows of its surrounds. The gaslight within the store, shining onto the pavement through tall, wide, and curved windows on either side of the door, also helped to achieve the same effect. Beyond these same panes of glass, one could see the torsos of four dummies, each stood upon a wide shelf. Fashionable shirts and blouses, coupled with accessories such as ties or costume jewellery pearls, adorned the dummies' forms. Set dressing around the dummies, in the form of leather-bound books, highly decorative perfume bottles, and a program to the popular play currently performing at the *Theatre Royal* Drury Lane, all enhanced the fantasy being suggested. The store's main door was painted in the same burgundy as the sign and had a central pane of red and gold stained glass diamonds in a repetitive pattern. Though beautiful, glittering in the candlelight of a single lamp hanging from the doorway, the glass prevented a clear view of the store beyond. Thus, giving the curious shopper no choice but to venture within—and this is exactly what Lady Owston and Miss Webster did next.

The interior was larger than one may have expected following the dwarfed façade. Not one but *three* glass display counters filled the first ten feet of the ground floor; the first two stood on the left and right-hand sides looking inward toward a third in the centre. The left counter was filled with wooden stands displaying a vast array of different styles of ladies' hats, most reinforced with wire to ensure they maintained their characteristic shape. From the broad-brimmed, black-straw Olympia, with its chipped edging and upturned back edge pinned into a flourish, to the popular staple of a Murray Hill Ladies' Leghora flat straw hat. The hats were available to purchase in plain or readily decorated forms. Those which were already adorned showcased complex and elaborate arrangements of pleated chiffon, silk ribbons, steel buckles, velvet, nets of silk or lace, and even wild flowers. Each element of decoration was displayed at various heights to increase the overall drama of the headpiece.

Free-standing mirrors, tilted upward, stood on the two front corners of this millinery department's counter, ready for a customer's admiring glance. Within the counter were the trays of steel, brass, gold, and silver hat pins, some plain, others adorned with faux glass or even real gems. Hairpins, made from brass, steel, or even rubber were also to be found upon the shelves of this counter's interior. Among them the most popular hairpin purchased from the establishment, made of brass and carefully bent into a daisy shape at one end. Gas-lit chandeliers, suspended from the ceiling, made the entire display positively shimmer and shine.

Even Miss Webster, who wasn't the shimmering and shining kind, was attracted to the spectacle at first. Yet it was the boxes of leather and cotton gloves, neatly stacked in small pyramids at each corner of the central counter, which truly piqued her interest. While Lady Owston headed for the right-hand counter, Miss Webster enquired from a shop assistant to see inside one of the boxes. When Agnes saw the gloves within, and smelt the unmistakeable aroma of new leather, she could hardly resist reaching for them. Lady Owston's sudden command to follow her, however, put an end to Agnes' plans. "I'll return," she informed the shop assistant and hurried across to Lady Owston, standing by the haberdashery department.

The department had a multitude of both plain and patterned materials. Displayed in the form of four-foot-long rolls which could be easily measured and cut to order, the material was wrapped around paper tubes which were, in turn, threaded along horizontal, brass poles with a length of material hanging down. The brass poles were permanently mounted on the wall behind the counter, at one end, in rows of ten and columns of five. Carefully folded, fine silks and lace were laid out on the countertop for customers to inspect their quality. Finally, a cluster of three dummies' torsos, each mounted upon narrow, three-legged, wooden tables, stood to the right of the counter. One wore a pale-pink, puffy-shouldered, cotton blouse coupled with a cream-and-pale-pink polka dot cravat. Its table was hidden from view by a dark-brown, straight-lined skirt ending just above the floor. Around the dummy's 'waist,' where the blouse and skirt met, was a leather belt with a small buckle. The second torso wore a more traditional, black-cotton bustle dress that also hid the table. The dress was accompanied by a black, lace veil to firmly associate the attire with the act of mourning. The third torso was adorned in a lightweight, pale-yellow, bustle dress made from cotton. Cut-out flower detailing in the skirts' layers complemented the yellow daisy decorations in the otherwise forest-green, hand-crocheted shawl draped around the dummy's shoulders.

Beyond the haberdashery department was a set of stairs leading upward toward the shop's front. As a result, Miss Webster couldn't yet see what was at their summit. To their left, however, was the perfumery department, followed by a plain, wooden door, and the hosiery department. From what she could see, hosiery had a whole host of stockings, various types of corsets (from plain to nursing), and undergarments tastefully displayed in their boxes within its counter and on shelves behind it. The perfumery meanwhile had soaps, wrapped in brown paper bearing the store's stamp, in neat pyramids on the counter top and intricately blown glass perfume bottles displayed on the counter's interior shelves. Every one of the store's departments had its own cash register for convenience.

"Mr *Queshire*," Lady Owston said, happily, at Agnes' side as the store's proprietor approached. This prompted the secretary to not only refocus her attentions for a second time but to also retrieve her notebook and pencil. When she caught sight of Mr Queshire, however, she was, quite frankly, taken aback. *Surely this couldn't be the Mr Queshire we are seeking?* She inwardly questioned. His physique and boyish facial features placed him no older than eighteen and yet, when he spoke, his voice came from someone beyond those years.

"Lady Owston, good day to you." He smiled at both women but waited for Lady Owston to make the formal introductions.

"This is my secretary, Miss Agnes Webster. Agnes, this is Mr Edmund Queshire."

"Good day to you, too, Miss Webster. And welcome to *The Queshire Department Store.*" To both he added, "Are you looking for something in particular today or merely browsing?" He half-turned to indicate the perfumery department. "I perfected a new soap only this morning. I think you would approve of it, Lady Owston. Rich, creamy, and excellent for the skin."

Agnes hadn't replied to Edmund's greeting, instead preferring to hold her tongue and further inspect the man's curious appearance. She also knew her employer would relish the opportunity to hold a prolonged conversation with him. She therefore paid close attention to the style of suit he wore first. Frockcoats had become associated with the older, or more conservative, gentleman but Mr Queshire wasn't wearing one. Instead, he had chosen the more fashionable three-piece suit in dark forest-green cotton. Underneath the suit's buttoned-up waistcoat was a white shirt with a turned down, starched collar. In its centre was the large knot of a long tie, matching the colour of his suit, with its end tucked into the waistcoat. She moved onto his face; fair, clean shaven skin lay over mildly defined cheekbones and a soft jawline. Her scrutiny continued upward— momentarily meeting his olive-green hues—and took in the side-parting of his short, fine, chocolate-brown hair.

"The Bow Street Society, of which we are members, has been commissioned to investigate a most hideous crime," Lady Owston's voice continued, Agnes having missed whatever had preceded it. Deciding she should perhaps listen more closely from then on, she refocused her attention. Katheryne added, "A *murder*, Mr Queshire."

"Of course…" Mr Queshire replied after a significant pause, during which his cheerful expression had descended into a sombre pit. The tone of his voice had also become a great deal heavier. "I trust you refer to the slaying of Mrs Maryanna Roberts," he stated rather than enquired, the knowledge it could, logically, be no other at the forefront of his mind. Lady Owston's simple nod was still enough to draw a thick, sad sigh from the store's proprietor nonetheless. "Naturally news reached us here soon after the poor woman was found. The constable who made the discovery recognised her as a customer of ours and, of course, sister-in-law to my assistant manager, Mr Suggitt, who went immediately to the police upon being told the news when he came to work this morning." He paused as another thought occurred to him, one which confused him. "Why are you here, then? I assume it was he who commissioned the Society?"

"I'm afraid we can't divulge such sensitive information, Mr Queshire," Lady Owston explained. "But it is actually you to whom we wish to speak." Mr Queshire was still, overtly, confused so Lady Owston went on. "I understand Mrs Roberts was here yesterday and caused an incident of a *most* regrettable nature." Mr Queshire's lips parted, and his brows lifted a little, in surprise.

He replied, "She did, but how did you know of it?"

"Our client said you'd witnessed it and told them of it afterward. Is that correct?" Lady Owston enquired, keeping her own tone non-judgemental and gentle.

Mr Queshire, seemingly satisfied with the explanation, replied, "I can't confirm the last part without knowing who your client is, but I did see the end of the incident, yes." He paused as two ladies approached the haberdashery department to admire and inspect the lace. A small glance, and slight, side-long hand gesture, from Mr Queshire had him, Lady Owston, and Miss Webster moving deeper into the store. "One of our shop assistants, Miss Rose Galway, saw the beginning."

"May we speak to her? I promise it shan't take long. If it's more convenient, we could even talk to her together?" Lady Owston enquired, glancing toward Agnes who was still note taking but didn't voice any objections to the idea.

Mr Queshire also seemed agreeable to it, judging by the return of his charming smile. "Of course," he replied, moving deeper still into the store as four or five women hurried out of the rain on Oxford Street and toward the perfumery department. "Let's retire to the storeroom, however, where it's quieter and more discreet." He indicated the single, wooden door Agnes had seen earlier and the two women accented. "Follow me, ladies, and I'll invite Miss Galway to join us along the way."

* * *

"Your husband's identified the body, Mrs Suggitt," Inspector Woolfe informed her. The *London Crystal Palace Bazaar's* doorway was only six feet away from them, but it was Woolfe facing it. Furthermore, a camera, mounted upon a wooden tripod, blocked the ghastly view as a photographer, brought thence by the police for the purpose, captured the sight. Fine droplets of rain had soaked Woolfe's coat, unkempt hair, and face during the course of his initial investigations, but he showed no sign of being perturbed by it. Mrs Suggitt on the other hand was huddled underneath an umbrella held aloft by her husband standing at her side. Mr Clement Suggitt was marginally taller than this wife so both were being, for the most part, kept comfortably dry. The edges of Mr Suggitt's tan coat were a little damp while his polished, brown-leather shoes were half immersed in a dirty puddle. A double-breasted, dark-brown, two-piece suit was worn under the coat; the jacket of which was fastened with two rows of three, light-brown buttons. In the pocket of the tan coat was a dark-brown, cotton handkerchief to complement the suit. Rather than a long tie, Mr Suggitt had opted for a light-mustard cravat tucked into his jacket and resting over a white, starched-collar shirt. His brown moustache, though bushy, was neat and was the only facial hair he had. Large ears and nose were the most striking of his features. Finally, his wavy, brown hair was neatly combed and centrally parted whilst his small eyes were hazel in colour. His wife held his arm and her grip tightened upon it at the news.

"Thank you," she said softly, gazing up at him, with a hint of appreciation in her otherwise melancholy face.

Prior to imparting this news, Inspector Caleb Woolfe and Mr Suggitt had settled the issue of Mrs Suggitt's unexpected presence at the scene. Woolfe hadn't been best pleased by the revelation the Bow Street Society had been hired by the victim's grieving sister. The glare he'd shot Miss Dexter's way, when she'd been introduced as a member, had made clear how displeased he was. Naturally, the imposing policeman gave a short lecture of the shortcomings of members of the public investigating a murder, alongside a recommendation he and his officers be permitted to do their duty. Mr Suggitt had agreed but, so far, Mrs Suggitt had held back her thoughts on the matter. This did *not* make Woolfe at all happy, but he resolved to keep a close watch on the Bow Street meddlers and continued with his interview.

"Do you know why your sister would've been at the bazaar this morning?" he enquired without any acknowledgement of her grief. Like he'd told her though, he had a duty to fulfil. Rather than concern himself with comforting the woman—something her husband was already doing—he was interested in her reactions and answers. So far, she was acting every inch the mourning relative but he'd been deceived before.

He watched her throat move as she swallowed. The request for guidance from her husband, in the form of a glance, wasn't unusual in itself. When Mr Suggitt's reply was a shake of the head, however, Woolfe became suspicious.

Mrs Suggitt replied, "No, I'm afraid not." The inspector knew of *two* reasons why Constable Fraser had recognised the victim when he'd found her this morning and, going by the Suggitts' reluctance to speak, they did too. She'd been a regular customer of *The Queshire Department Store* on account of her familial connection to its assistant manager. He decided to test his theory of the extent of the Suggitts' knowledge regarding the second reason Constable Fraser had given him.

"Was she living with Mr Roberts?"

"No," Mr Suggitt replied, curtly yet didn't elaborate upon it.

Mrs Suggitt meanwhile took in a deep, shuddering, breath and added, "Mr Roberts is a good man."

"Where does he live?" Woolfe enquired, reserving judgement on Mr Roberts' character for when he met him. Mr Suggitt, unlike his wife, didn't look to his spouse for guidance before giving the address. Miss Dexter, who had been standing a little behind the three, bit her lip. She hoped Mrs Suggitt wouldn't reveal the Society had also been given the address. From the little she'd already seen and heard of him, she thought Inspector Woolfe rather frightening indeed. *She* certainly couldn't dissuade him should he choose to demand the address from her. Fortunately, Mrs Suggitt didn't make such a thing necessary. Miss Dexter released her lip and stepped closer to her client, practically hiding behind her.

"They've got a child between them, a daughter—" Woolfe began as he finished making a note of the address but Mrs Suggitt interrupted, with a sharp gasp.

"*Regina!*" She pressed her closed hand to her mouth to stifle a sob threatening to overwhelm her. "She'll be so upset."

"Was she close to her mother?" Inspector Woolfe enquired though he'd intended to put the question to the couple a moment ago. The Suggitts looked at one another for a second time, this time both were uncertain.

"There were tensions within the family, Inspector," Mr Suggitt finally replied, hoping it would be enough.

Yet the Big Bad Woolfe wanted more, "What about?"

"Maryanna's drinking," Mr Suggitt retorted harshly and sighed. "I've already gone over this with your sergeant, Inspector. What more—"

"Did you ever give Mrs Roberts money?" Woolfe enquired of Mr Suggitt directly since it would have been he who was in command of their finances.

The assistant manager stared at him. "I *beg* your pardon?" he enquired, affronted.

"Mrs Roberts was a fallen woman, wasn't she, Mr Suggitt?" He looked to Diana. "Mrs Suggitt?" Addressing Clement, he continued, "Addicted to the gin and giving out 'favours' to pay for it. Constable Fraser, who found the body, knew her not just because she was your sister-in-law but because he'd arrested her numerous times for prostitution. Now, it's obvious you both knew this, so it makes sense you would have—maybe in the past—given or offered her money, Mr Suggitt. You'd not disowned the family, after all."

"*My* financial affairs are my *own* business, *Inspector.* Diana, we are leaving." He attempted to guide his wife away but Woolfe's voice caused them to pause.

"You told my sergeant you were at home all evening. Am I correct, sir?"

"You are," Mr Suggitt replied without hesitation. He wasn't the one Woolfe was watching though. Mrs Suggitt had sharply turned her head toward her husband, upon hearing his answer, with definite surprise.

This, naturally, intrigued the policeman so he enquired, "And were you with him?"

"Yes," she answered, startled.

Yet her husband soon came to her rescue. "She was, Inspector. We have no reason to want Maryanna dead."

"Just routine, sir. Mrs Suggitt, when was the last time you saw your sister alive?"

"About a week ago." She looked to her husband. "But you saw her yesterday, didn't you, Clement?"

"*Did* you, Mr Suggitt?" Woolfe enquired. This was certainly news to him, especially since his sergeant had filled him in on Mr Suggitt's interview, given prior to his wife's arrival, and nothing of the like had been mentioned. "Did you neglect to tell my sergeant that, sir?"

"He never asked," Mr Suggitt retorted, bluntly. Upon seeing Woolfe's suspicious glare though, he added, "And I didn't think it relevant since it was at *The Queshire Department Store* and *not* here." He put his arm around his wife's shoulders and continued, "I'm sorry, Inspector, but my wife and I are very

39

distressed by this whole business. As unwell as she was, Mrs Roberts was still part of our family. I'm also finding your line of questioning *very* offensive, not to mention intrusive. So, if you'd excuse us, we would like to visit our niece."

"I will," Woolfe replied. Both Mr and Mrs Suggitt visibly relaxed. Their tension returned, however, when the inspector added, "When I've finished asking what I need to know." Mr Suggitt's face contorted with anger but Woolfe didn't provide him with an opportunity to protest. "As you saw Mrs Roberts yesterday, sir, you can tell me what she was wearing."

All anger drained from Mr Suggitt's face, along with its colour. He glanced toward the doorway, recalling the sight he'd been forced to witness up close earlier, and replied, "Yes... of course." He swallowed hard, "Erm, I believe it was... a green dress—"

"Long or short, sir?"

"Long, past her knees, boots, and a shawl. I *think* it was the shawl Diana gifted to her." He looked to his wife for assistance.

"It's crocheted, Inspector. Dark green with yellow flowers on it. If she was wearing it." She said.

"Thank you," Woolfe closed his notebook and looked between the two. "That's all for now, but I'd like to continue this discussion tomorrow, Mr Suggitt." The policeman eyed the man with great suspicion; he was *certain* his sergeant would've enquired about the last time Mrs Roberts was seen. Alas, it would be his sergeant's word against Mr Suggitt's, so there was little to gain from pressing the point.

Mr Suggitt wasn't best pleased. He enquired, "Whatever for?"

"New information comes our way all the time in these sorts of cases, sir. There might be something I need to ask you about." Mr Suggitt sighed but, reluctantly, agreed. Woolfe didn't smile, however. Instead, his perpetual glare remained firmly in place as he replied, "I'll come by tomorrow morning around ten o'clock, if it suits?"

"It does," Mr Suggitt replied, great concern evident in his face. He gently guided his wife away from the terrible scene and down the street toward Mr Snyder's hansom cab.

Miss Dexter followed but only to ask, "Mr Suggitt, would you be so good as to visit the Bow Street Society's headquarters later today? I'm an artist by profession; if you, again, describe Maryanna's missing clothing to me, I can draw it. I may then make minor adjustments, under your guidance, so we may distribute the sketch to locate her clothes."

"Very well," Mr Suggitt replied. Miss Dexter agreed on an appropriate time and Mr Suggitt assisted his wife into Mr Snyder's cab. Without thinking, he gave the Bow Street Society member Mr Roberts' address and climbed inside. Part of Mr Snyder's remit was to drive suspects (or witnesses) to wherever they wished to go—sometimes without their knowing he was part of the group investigating them. He therefore accepted the commission, waited for the two to become settled, and geed his two horses into motion.

Within moments, the cab was out of sight and Miss Dexter was left to risk a peek at the inspector. She slowly turned, relieved, when she saw he was distracted and not preparing to arrest her. Deciding she could do nothing more there, she started on her way to *The Queshire Department Store…* only to hear Inspector Woolfe yell, "Get the bloody photographs taken and the body away from here! I'm going to *The Queshire Department Store!*" Miss Dexter stopped in her tracks and looked over her shoulder. Woolfe was coming her way. *Lady Owston*! She thought, realising neither she nor Miss Webster were anywhere in sight. Having no cab now to jump into, Georgina knew she'd have to hurry to beat Inspector Woolfe to her friends. She therefore walked as briskly as she could, but soon found this to be inadequate when Woolfe passed her.

"Inspector!" she shouted after him. He didn't stop, however. "Um, *Inspector Woolfe!*" she shouted again, this time running to catch him up. Already he was several metres away so she had to run very fast indeed. As luck would have it for her, he'd heard her swift footfalls, stopped, and turned to face her. When she finally reached him, she found him to be glaring down at her—at least it looked like a glare. She couldn't be sure since he towered so highly over her.

"Yeah?"

"Miss…" she began, utterly out of breath. "…Miss Georgina Dexter." She took a few gulps of air. "Mrs Suggitt's friend?" She straightened, still trying to catch her breath. Of *course* Woolfe remembered her—the *Bow Streeter*. His eyes narrowed, but, from somewhere, Georgina found the courage to continue, "Please, sir, may I ask... do you have any idea where Mrs Roberts' clothes could've disappeared to?"

A deep, guttural growl sounded from the policeman as he pointed at her. "Look, Miss Dexter—or whatever your name is—I'm not John Conway. I *don't* help amateurs who think they're better than us coppers—"

"But will you help her poor sister—Mrs Suggitt? She will naturally want to know." Miss Dexter feared Inspector Woolfe would gobble her up, like the wolf in the fairy tale, as he continued to glare at her.

A moment or two later and Miss Dexter was *certain* he would do as she feared; his glare was so *very* fierce! Yet, unexpectedly, he admitted, "No." He enquired, "Was that all you wanted?"

Miss Dexter was quite surprised; she hadn't expected him to agree for Mrs Suggitt's sake—she thought she'd been clutching at straws. Now at a loss as to what else she could ask to stall him, she began to consider faking a faint. She certainly felt lightheaded enough after her run. "Well..."

FOUR

The storeroom to which Mr Queshire took Lady Owston, Miss Webster, and Miss Galway was dimly lit. Though small, there was sufficient space for a square table, four wooden chairs, a pot-bellied stove, and at least four piles of boxed stock. The window, positioned above the table and to the left of the stove in the corner, looked out onto a bland yard backing onto a service alleyway—the two being separated by a high, brick wall. The stove heated the room so, along with the brown, stripped wallpaper, it was rather cosy. It was made all the more so—at least for Mr Queshire and Mr Suggitt—by the pot of French Breakfast coffee on the table, the books upon a shelf, and the morning's *Gaslight Gazette*. Prepared twice weekly, the coffee was left to cool and only heated on the stove when required—usually midmorning or lunch time; as per the habits of the English middle classes at the time. Due to the expense of the pre-roasted, pre-ground coffee kernels, only the managers were permitted to partake in this beverage—usually. That day, Mr Queshire made an exception by not only serving Miss Galway a cup but also offering one to his Bow Street Society guests—both of whom politely declined.

Lady Owston added, "I'm more of a tea drinker myself."

"I'm sorry, Mr Queshire," Miss Rose Galway mumbled, head bowed, as she took the cup.

"Whatever for?" he enquired, somewhat mystified.

"Whatever it is I've done, sur," she retorted, keeping her head down. Her accent was unmistakeably from the East End of London, albeit disguised, but the store's uniform of a plain, cream-coloured blouse, ankle-length, brown skirt, and belt hid her poverty well.

"*Have* you done something, Miss Galway?" Lady Owston joined in. The shop assistant meekly looked up from her stool. Her petite build would have made her childlike if it had not been for the crow's feet laughter lines, and wiry, dirty-blond hair she attempted to tame into a loosely pinned bun at the back of her skull.

She mumbled, "I dunno, Milady."

"Then what reasons have you for your apology?" Lady Owston enquired, more intrigued than perplexed by the woman's need to repent.

"None, Milady." Miss Galway looked to Edmund. "I just thought I had because you asked me in here, Mr Queshire."

"No, Rose."

The shop assistant again bowed her head, "Sorry, Mr Queshire."

This seemed to annoy the proprietor a little for he retorted, "Stop apologising, Rose—" He interrupted himself and forced a smile, having realised he'd inadvertently raised his voice. "You have nothing to worry about." He again smiled but this time more sincerely. He continued, "Lady Katheryne Owston and her secretary, Miss Agnes Webster, here wish to know what happened yesterday between Mrs Roberts and the customer."

"She didn't do her in," Miss Galway stated bluntly in disbelief. Mr Queshire's smile faltered but he retained his composure nonetheless.

He replied, "No one is saying she did; Lady Owston and Miss Webster just want to know because they've been commissioned to investigate the poor woman's murder."

Miss Galway's head shot up and she looked to first Lady Owston and Miss Webster. "What, you two are police? Didn't know they let women in."

"They don't," Miss Webster retorted in her usual monotone. "Lady Owston and I are part of the Bow Street Society."

Miss Galway's face positively lit up at the news. "I read all about your last case—with the old, blind boy? Hung onto every word the newspapers printed, I did. You couldn't have gotten better people to get Mrs Roberts' killer, Mr Queshire."

"*I* didn't enlist their services," he pointed out.

Lady Owston quickly added, "And the Thaddeus Dorsey case was investigated by my fellow members, not Miss Webster and I."

Miss Galway's shoulders dipped, disappointment momentarily filling her face, but she said, "You're still gonna get them, though, yeah?"

"We shall do our best," Lady Owston reassured. Yet Miss Galway's next comment would startle her at first but also please her once she'd realised its significance.

"Mrs Holden didn't do her in though; she's too much of a lady for that."

"*Rose!*" Mr Queshire cried, flabbergasted, which made the shop assistant jump.

"*What'd* I do, sur??" she pleaded, clearly frightened by the proprietor's outburst.

"I wasn't intending on giving the Society our customer's name," Mr Queshire explained, annoyed. Lady Owston had previously assumed as much so she cast a discrete, triumphant smile at Agnes upon hearing it.

Rose sat bolt upright, "I—I didn't know, sur!"

"It's fine, Rose," he replied. Yet the shop assistant continued to apologise.

"Rose," he interrupted, giving her a firm look. She stared at him, however, still frightened. "It's fine," he continued, this time softening his voice. "No harm is done."

"We shall treat the information with the utmost confidence, Miss Galway," Lady Owston also reassured, further easing the woman's alarm. Miss Webster, on the other hand, retained her stoicism while writing a shorthand transcript of their conversation.

"Tell Lady Owston and Miss Webster what happened with Mrs Holden," Mr Queshire prompted once Miss Galway was convinced all was well.

"Well… I was serving Mrs Holden in the haberdashery department when Mrs Roberts got in the middle of us and asked where her sister was. I told her she wasn't there. Mrs Roberts walked a little ways and I got on with serving Mrs Holden. The next thing I hear is Mr Holden saying, 'I beg your pardon?' His wife and me look over and see Mrs Roberts trying to hold the poor man's hand. She was telling him she could keep him warm at night, too. Mrs Holden was mad when she heard this and told me as much. She announced she was leaving, got alongside her husband, and started walking out."

"This is where I come in," Mr Queshire interjected. "I was in the millinery department when I overheard Mrs Holden announce she was leaving. Naturally, I was dismayed by what I heard so I intersected Mrs Holden at the door. I enquired if all was well and she informed me she'd expected more from my establishment and intended never to set foot here again. I apologised, profusely, and enquired what had happened. She pointed directly at Mrs Roberts, still standing at Miss Galway's counter, and exclaimed 'her!' Still somewhat dumbfounded by the whole matter, I at once went to the haberdashery department only to see Mrs Roberts swaying quite markedly. I don't like to speak ill of the dead but Mrs Roberts had a very particular scent about her person."

"Hence your explanation to Mrs Suggitt when she enquired after her sister's whereabouts," Miss Webster stated as she continued writing.

Mr Queshire nodded and sighed heavily. "An uncharacteristically callous remark on my part. I was, I'm ashamed to say, angry and embarrassed by Mrs Robert's conduct—both toward Mr Holden and myself. When I'd approached, she'd made lewd, and *very* false, suggestions about our acquaintanceship. She forced me to take action." He frowned. "I'm not proud of myself."

"What did you do?" Miss Webster enquired bluntly. She'd also paused in her writing to look squarely at the man, thus driving home the challenging tone of her voice further. Mr Queshire didn't pull her up on it, though.

Not even as Lady Owston interjected, "Whatever it was I'm *certain* you were justified, Mr Queshire. Especially given the *outrageous* behaviour of Mrs Roberts."

"Thank you." He smiled appreciatively at Lady Owston. His hues returned to Miss Webster, becoming colder in the process, as he replied, "She was removed from the store. We don't have any security officers here, so I had to remove her myself. I tried to do it discreetly but her drunkenness kept her tongue sharp. My strength was greater than her own so she was outside within moments but, in between, she drew the full attention of the other customers with her foul language. Furthermore, the Holdens decided against remaining and left the store."

"Was a constable not summoned?" Miss Webster enquired.

"The woman was already miserable," Mr Queshire stated. He then paused, however, and added in a more subdued tone, "I didn't want to make matters worse."

"Could Mr Suggitt not have intervened on your behalf?" Lady Owston enquired, trying to keep her tone casual as she didn't want to insinuate Mr Queshire had acted poorly. Rather than give an immediate answer, however, Mr Queshire instead turned to Miss Galway and requested she fetch a bar of the new soap. The shop assistant didn't hesitate in doing so either; she was keen to make amends for her earlier blunder. "As you've witnessed, Miss Galway has trouble holding her tongue," Mr Queshire explained once she had gone. "I didn't want her to hear this for that reason."

"You may speak freely with us," Lady Owston said. Though both her curiosity and excitement were piqued at the prospect of the impending revelations, she nevertheless kept them well hidden. Mr Queshire's emotions were plain to see, however, and it was clear he was fighting against himself.

"Mr Suggitt didn't intervene…" he began, uncertain. "But nor did I ask him to." He frowned deeply but seemed to reach a point of resolution wherein he continued, more confidently, "He would always distance himself from Mrs Roberts whenever she came to the store."

"Did Mrs Roberts realise he was doing so?" Lady Owston enquired but Mr Queshire shook his head.

He replied, "No, but it was never him she wanted to see."

"Who, then?"

"Her sister, Mrs Diana Suggitt. Mrs Suggitt comes here every day, without fail, to escort her husband to lunch. When the store is—very often—busy and I require all assistants to forego their break to meet demand, Mr Suggitt usually does the same even though, for him, it's not mandatory. Mrs Suggitt still comes, even then, and asks after her husband. He'll eventually be brought to her, but in the meantime, she'll browse the departments and discuss the store's apparent level of busyness with the assistants. And, when Mr Suggitt does join his wife, she'll speak with him for half an hour while customers fill the space around them." He momentarily pursed his lips into another frown, "It can be rather irritating."

"Presumably Mrs Roberts has come seeking her sister prior to yesterday's incident?"

"Yes, many times, and, I'm sorry to say, many times inebriated. As I said, Mr Suggitt would distance himself from Mrs Roberts, though he has never denied his familial connection to her when directly asked. His wife, on the other hand, would speak openly with her in the store. Admittedly, Mrs Roberts had never behaved so incorrigibly before yesterday. The particular scent I spoke of always lingered around her, however." He frowned slightly. "He's never spoken to me of this. So, I'm afraid I don't know the reason why he'd distance himself. After having observed how much of a concerted effort he'd made to do so in the past, I felt reluctant to ask him to break the habit during the incident yesterday." He sighed.

"And yet you say Mrs Suggitt spoke openly with her sister *in* the store? Despite her husband avoiding her?" Lady Owston enquired and Mr Queshire's frown deepened.

"I know how my words may make things appear, Milady, but Mr Suggitt is a good man; he would never deny his wife the reassurance of speaking to her sister."

"Of course," Lady Owston smiled, softly. "Was Mrs Suggitt very worried about her sister's welfare?"

"Yes, and with very good reason."

"Did Mrs Roberts acknowledge her sister's concern at all?"

"It's not my place to say, but she did always become calmer whenever Mrs Suggitt spoke to her."

"Did Mrs Suggitt ever give her sister money?" Miss Webster interjected, lifting her head once more with her pencil poised over the notebook.

Mr Queshire stared at her, stunned, and retorted, "I don't know. Besides, *Mr* Suggitt is the one you should ask, not I."

"Mr Queshire," Lady Owston began, attempting to distract him from Agnes' poorly worded line of enquiry. Her ploy worked—for his mild annoyance dissipated—and she could ask, "Was Mrs Suggitt there when you removed her sister from the store yesterday?"

"No, she arrived about half an hour later, which was unusually late."

"Did she say why?"

"She spoke to her husband, who told her of the incident with her sister, and she enquired of me if I knew where Mrs Roberts had gone. That's when I made the awful, awful remark. I was still angry about the whole thing." He sighed again. "I'm sorry, I don't know if she gave a reason for her lateness or not. I wish I could be more helpful."

"I'm *sure* the Suggitts would be *most* appreciative of the help you've already given us, Mr Queshire." Lady Owston gently patted his hand and he gratefully thanked her. She continued, "After you had removed her from the store, did Mrs Roberts return at all? Perhaps still seeking her sister? Presuming you were at home all evening, of course."

"I was, and no, she didn't. After shouting obscenities at my store, she walked away. I wasn't paying attention to the direction she went; I was happy to be rid of her." He sighed deeply. "If she had returned though—even after the store had closed—I could've kept her safe and sent for her sister. She wouldn't be…" Regret weighed down his features, ageing him in a moment. "Her poor family."

"I got it, sur," a meek Miss Galway uttered upon suddenly re-entering the storeroom. She hadn't thought to knock since they expected her return. Both Lady Owston and the store owner allowed this minor breech of etiquette, however. He accepted the soap with thanks and offered it to Katheryne. "A gift from *The Queshire Department Store*."

"*Oh!* I couldn't *possibly*—!" Lady Owston exclaimed with delighted amazement, her hand going to her chest.

Yet Mr Queshire's hand moved closer and he urged, "I *insist*." His charming smile and relaxed demeanour returned. "I'll be *very* offended if you don't."

"Very *well!*" she cried, chuckling softly. "If you *insist*." She took the soap and stuck it under her nose to inhale its scent. "*Oh*, Mr *Queshire*! It's *divine*! Agnes, smell this." She promptly stuck it under the nose of her secretary who, after jerking her head back a little, took a reluctant sniff of the bar.

"Hmm, very nice," she remarked, unconvinced.

"*Agnes,* you didn't even smell it properly. *Here—*" Lady Owston went to again shove the soap under Miss Webster's nose but stopped. Her eyes were fixed upon the stairs, now made visible by the open doorway. "How very peculiar…" she mused, much to the perplexity of those present. Mr Queshire was the first to reply, however.

"Is there something wrong with the scent?"

"No," Lady Owston replied, forcing herself to look at the store owner. "The soap is *lovely*, but I'm certain I just saw one of your customers entering the room at the top of the stairs."

"It's the hairdressing salon, Milady," Miss Galway pointed out since there was another open doorway when one turned right upon reaching the top of the stairs. The light coming from the windows of the salon illuminated the very small landing there. Yet Lady Owston shook her head, lifted her gloved hand, and briefly closed her eyes.

"No, you misunderstand. I saw her go through the door marked *Staff only.*" She let her hand drop, sighing, but froze upon seeing the alarmed stare Miss Galway gave Mr Queshire. "Is everything well?"

"Absolutely," Mr Queshire replied, not having noticed Miss Galway's reaction. "I'll go up there and make sure no one is lost." He excused himself and left the three women alone, closing the storeroom door behind him as he went. Yet Lady Owston's curiosity regarding Mrs Galway's reaction was far from sated.

She placed a gentle hand upon Miss Galway's arm and enquired, "Are you well?"

"Yes, Milady," the shop assistant swiftly responded. Lady Owston cast a glance at Miss Webster who, like her, was unconvinced.

"It's just you seemed—" Lady Owston began but Miss Galway interrupted her.

"How does somebody become a member, then?" Lady Owston blinked, having not expected such a question from a woman who had seemed so very frightened mere moments before. Nonetheless, she decided to humour Rose in the hopes of getting some more answers.

"You have to be interviewed by the Society's clerk, Miss Rebecca Trent. I could put you in touch with her and… put in a good word for you, if you'd like?"

"You'd do that for me?" Miss Galway enquired, stunned.

Lady Owston's smile broadened, "Of *course*, Miss Galway. The Society would be enrichened to have someone with your talents as a member. Being a member does mean you have to share information with one another, however. Sometimes *very* confidential information…"

"But I don't know anything."

"Why were you so alarmed when I spoke of the customer entering the *Staff only* room at the top of the stairs?" Lady Owston enquired and, again, Miss Galway became alarmed.

"I can't say, Milady. I was being foolish, that's all." Miss Galway's hand reached for the door as she continued, "I must be getting back to work or Mr Queshire *will* be angry at me."

Lady Owston was naturally disappointed but still she allowed Miss Galway to heed her innate instinct to run. "Thank you, Miss Galway, you've been most helpful. And my offer still stands if you wish to take advantage of it."

"Thank you, Milady. I will, Milady," Miss Galway replied and practically ran from the storeroom, leaving the door ajar behind her. Lady Owston waited a moment before opening the door wider. She scanned the stairs, and the ground floor area, but could see no sign of Mr Queshire.

"How *very* curious…" she mused aloud. "Come, Agnes," Lady Owston called and left the room to head for the stairs. Miss Webster, having finished her writing and put away her notebook, duly followed. Yet no sooner had the two ladies climbed halfway up the stairs did the door marked *Staff only* open and Mr Queshire stepped out. He paused upon seeing them but soon gifted his charming smile.

"Lady Owston." He descended the stairs toward them. "It was a misunderstanding; the poor lady thought she was going into the salon. May I assist you with anything else?"

"No, thank you, Mr Queshire," Lady Owston replied, adding, "You've been *most* helpful." She looked behind her. "Let us go, Agnes!"

"Yes, Milady." The secretary obeyed, descending the stairs and waiting at the bottom. When she joined her, Lady Owston paused to wave up at Mr Queshire and led the way past the perfumery, haberdashery, and millinery departments to leave the store. There were many more women by then, so the journey took some doing.

"Excuse me," Lady Owston politely requested to a blond-haired lady blocking the walkway. She obliged the independent journalist by stepping aside long enough for her to pass. At which point she placed a shawl on the counter and stated, "Mark the loosening of the weave, miss."

"I can assure madam none of the items in the store are second-hand," an assistant calmly replied. Katheryne didn't catch the customer's response as she pulled open the door, however.

"Something isn't quite correct, Agnes," she remarked once they were outside. Yet before Miss Webster could respond, her employer strode off down the street, exclaiming, "*Inspector*

Woolfe! What *are* you doing to Miss Dexter?" The large man twisted his body to look behind him upon hearing his name, revealing the much smaller Miss Dexter in the process. Miss Webster meanwhile hurried to catch up with Lady Owston who was now saying, "I've heard of police intimidation, but *really!*" She gently took hold of Miss Dexter's arm and pulled her closer, asking, "Are you well?"

"Y—Yes, Lady Owston. I—I was feeling faint and Inspector Woolfe assisted me." She offered a small, nervous smile to the man. "Thank you, Inspector, I feel much better now."

Lady Owston looked between the two, her hand over her mouth. "Oh, I *do* apologise, Inspector! I quite misunderstood the situation."

"Forget it," Woolfe half-grunted and, stepping around the two, passed Miss Webster on his way into *The Queshire Department Store.*

"I believe it's time to leave, ladies," Lady Owston stated, wrapping her arms about Miss Dexter's on the right and Miss Webster's on the left. Neither lady had any objection to the suggestion so Lady Owston led their retreat.

"I have Mr Roberts' address but Mr Suggitt took Mr Snyder's cab," Miss Dexter explained when some distance had been put between them and the store. "I think he may have taken his wife to Mr Roberts' home to see their niece."

"Then we wouldn't want to impose," Lady Owston replied.

Yet Miss Webster stated, quite seriously, "Unless they are discussing their stories."

"Even if they are, it shall do them no good. We shall *still* find the truth of it," Lady Owston declared.

"Inspector Woolfe was also given Mr Roberts' address," Miss Dexter continued. "He's arranged to speak to Mr and Mrs Suggitt again tomorrow morning."

"*That* is when we shall speak to Mr Roberts and his daughter. We also have the Holdens to speak to," Lady Owston decided for them.

After informing her fellow members of the Suggitts' answers with regards to Maryanna being at the bazaar, Miss Dexter enquired, "Do you think we should find out if Mrs Roberts knew anyone at the bazaar before leaving?"

"We shan't get near it with all the police around, my dear. Alas, I suspect poor Mrs Roberts wasn't there to see *anyone* at the bazaar when one considers she was found so early in the morning. Though I have known women who loved shopping so much, they have had their servants sleep in the doorways overnight so as to be the first to make a particular purchase, I think it *highly* unlikely this was the reason for Mrs Roberts' presence. No, *first* we shall return to Miss Trent and divulge our findings thus far. *Onwaaard*!" Both Miss Dexter and Miss Webster looked at one another; this would be an adventure indeed with Her Ladyship investigating! Yet neither was at all perturbed by the thought.

Miss Webster said, "I'd like to look at Miss Trent's copy of the *Post Office Directory* when we reach Bow Street."

FIVE

Miss Rebecca Trent cradled a cup of tea as she crossed the room to its window. The rain was getting heavier; its violent beating amplified by the absence of soft furnishings which would've otherwise absorbed it. Dark-grey clouds blanketed the sky and made the room incredibly gloomy. All the rooms above the ground floor were the same. There were gas lamps but she'd decided against lighting them, citing lack of necessity. Aside from the sounds of rain, occasional rumble of thunder, and horse hooves hitting the cobbled street below, the house was quiet. It wasn't difficult then for the knocking at the front door to reach her ears and cause her to vacate the room, traverse the landing, and descend the stairs. She moved at a faster pace than usual, not wishing to risk the loss of *any* potential client. Thus, she slid across and turned the door's bolts and key in no time at all. No sooner had she opened it was she charged by Lady Owston. Miss Trent had excellent reflexes, so the necessary swift back peddling was easy.

"*Well*!" Katheryne exclaimed as she passed the clerk, turned upon her heel, and slapped her gloved hands together. "What a *most* intriguing morning *we* have had, Miss Trent!"

"Where shall I place this?" Miss Webster enquired, holding up her soaked umbrella. Miss Trent took charge of the item and rested it between two of the stairs' rounded, oak balusters. Meanwhile, Miss Dexter, having followed the others inside, gave the door a gentle tug to ensure it was closed properly.

"Was this where the poor man was murdered?" Lady Katheryne enquired as she took hold of the bannister and ascended the stairs. Yet she stopped at the third stair, twisted her body toward the others, and cried, "*Never mind*! It's *irrelevant*!"

"*What* was intriguing, Lady Owston?" Miss Trent sternly enquired with one hand upon her waist. She didn't try to hide her disapproval either; it couldn't have been more blatant on her face if someone had written it there.

Lady Owston, who had now climbed to the top of the stairs, hadn't noticed. Instead, she replied, in a rather sing-song voice, "A brother-in-law who not only distanced himself from his wife's sister in spite of said wife's closeness to her, but also became irate when the possibility of his giving said sister-in-law money was mentioned, information being held back from the police, shop assistants becoming alarmed over allegedly trivial matters such as customers entering storerooms." Her extended hand made a circle. "The usual detective fare." She turned toward the others and remarked, "It is *rather* spacious here. You *must* give Agnes and me a tour sometime."

"Was Mrs Roberts where Mrs Suggitt claimed she'd be?" Rebecca enquired, ignoring the irrelevant request. She approached the bottom of the stairs and looked up, expectantly, at the aristocrat.

Lady Owston didn't seem to be in much of a hurry, however. She instead removed her gloves before, eventually, replying, "She was."

"I was able to take some photographs of the body," Miss Dexter interjected. "But my camera is with Sam and he has taken the Suggitts to Mr Roberts' home to see Maryanna's daughter, Regina." Another knock sounded and all four women looked at one another.

"Are you expecting anyone, Miss Trent?"

"I never *expect* people, Lady Owston," Rebecca remarked as she returned to the front door, adding once she got there, "except clients." When she pulled back the door however—momentarily hiding Georgina in the process—it wasn't a client at all, but Mr Snyder. Like Miss Webster's umbrella, his ankle-length cape and broad-brimmed hat were soaked. Yet both were designed for such weather so, when he stepped inside and removed them, his clothes underneath were bone dry. With the absence of a hat stand to hang them upon, the cabman was forced to utilise the stairs' highly polished, smooth, oak handrail. He smoothed down the sleeves of a cheaply made, brown-tweed jacket that had been ripped, and sewn, here and there. Beneath this was a shirt, greyer than white, and a long, black tie whose tip rested on a slightly rotund belly. Black trousers were tucked into the tops of heavy, scuffed, well-worn, black-leather boots. Slung over his shoulder was the leather strap of a satchel and it was from there he retrieved Miss Dexter's camera.

"Kept it as dry as I could," he explained as she took it. Georgina swiftly turned it over in her slender, yet dexterous, hands several times so she could inspect it. Both relief and gratitude were in the smile she gave the cabman once she was done.

"It's perfect, Sam. Thank you," she said as she carefully slipped it into her own satchel and explained, to no one in particular, "I'll develop the photographs this afternoon."

"Did the Suggitts go to Mr Roberts' residence?" Lady Owston enquired as she descended the stairs behind Mr Snyder and stepped around his broad-shouldered frame to face him.

The working-class cabman wasn't at all perturbed by her obvious wealth, but he still knew his manners. He therefore moved to give her more space and replied politely, "They did, Milady. Woz the same address Mrs Suggitt gave Miss Webster."

"Ah, so you *were* paying attention?" Lady Owston remarked, impressed.

Mr Snyder chuckled softly when others may have been offended. "A cabman sees and hears more than you'd think, Lady Owston."

"May I see your copy of the *Post Office Directory*?" Miss Webster suddenly enquired, addressing the Society's clerk. "Mrs Roberts offended a Mr and Mrs Holden at *The Queshire Department Store* yesterday; I would like to check if they're listed."

"Do you have Christian names?" Miss Trent enquired as she went to the hallway's telephone, mounted upon the wall in its wooden box casing, and retrieved the required directory from the floor underneath. Miss Webster shook her head but Miss Trent gave her the directory nonetheless. Agnes flipped swiftly through its pages, as familiar with it as if it were her own diary.

Within mere moments, she announced her success. "Here they are," she said, walking past both Sam and Katheryne, and resting the directory upon a carpeted stair.

Miss Dexter, intrigued by this miraculous deduction, slowly approached and enquired, "How can you be sure they are the Holdens from the store?"

"Mrs Holden was described as being too much of a lady to commit murder by the store's shop assistant, Miss Rose Galway, ergo Mrs Holden is wealthy—either upper middle class or upper class. We know her husband was with her as it was he who Mrs Roberts propositioned. So, we know they reside together. Due to my accompanying Her Ladyship to various balls, dinner parties, and afternoon teas at wealthy ladies' homes to discuss the latest fashion trends, I have come to know which addresses are the more affluent. Those Holdens who reside in these areas are the ones we should be searching for in the directory. Fortuitously, there is only one: Mr and Mrs Bartholomew Holden who reside at 200 Hill Street in Mayfair."

Miss Webster took a note of the address as Lady Owston, beaming with pride, remarked, "Agnes is *very* clever." Miss Dexter was certain Miss Trent could've come to the same conclusion, with Sam's assistance, but at least Miss Webster and Lady Owston had personal experience of these places. Agnes closed the directory and, turning to Lady Owston, gave the address to her to read. Katheryne's face lit up as she said, "Not too far from the *lovely* Mrs Braithwaite in Berkeley Square, either!" She paused, considering an inner thought. "I wonder if she knows the Holdens? Ah well, *never mind*!"

"You'll be going to question them now?" Miss Trent enquired as she retrieved the directory and returned it to its usual place. When Lady Owston confirmed they would be, Miss Trent enquired, "And what of Mr Roberts? Have you already spoken to him?"

"Inspector Woolfe intends to speak with Mr Roberts this afternoon," Miss Dexter explained. "And the Suggitts again tomorrow morning."

"I thought it best we not risk the inspector's wrath by attempting to speak to Mr Roberts today," Lady Owston interjected and ushered Agnes toward her umbrella before asking Sam, "Would you be so kind as to take us to the Holdens residence, Mr Snyder?"

"Yeah, I'll jus' ge' the cab," he replied.

Lady Owston's hand lifted. This time to indicate she wished him to wait a moment. Looking to Miss Trent she said, "As wealthy as I am, I am still a woman. We are not weak but— some, not all—men still believe us thus. Therefore, I request a gentleman to speak to Mr Holden whilst Agnes and I speak to his wife."

"I'll arrange for one to meet you there," Miss Trent replied, her earlier annoyance at the woman having eased when Sam arrived and Miss Webster did her trick with the directory. It had disappeared completely when Lady Owston had, at least, *requested* a gentleman instead of demanding one.

This politeness continued with the next question— much to Rebecca's satisfaction. Katheryne enquired, "May we have his name?" Yet before the clerk could reply, there was another knock on the door.

"He'll make himself known to you if you wait in Mr Snyder's cab for him," Miss Trent explained while, again, making the journey across the hallway and opening the door for a third time. This time, Miss Dexter was nowhere near the door so neither she, nor anyone else, was hidden behind it. This didn't stop Rebecca from releasing a deep sigh upon seeing her latest visitor. With one hand on the door and another on her hip, she enquired, "Yes, Mr Maxwell?"

"S-Sorry for bothering you, Miss Trent, but—" He stopped as he caught sight of the artist over Rebecca's shoulder. "Georgina?" he enquired, surprised. Miss Trent half-turned to glance at Miss Dexter and Maxwell saw it was truly her. Rather than be reassured by this fact though, the *Gaslight Gazette* journalist instead panicked. He stuttered, "I—I didn't know y— you were here. I came to speak to Miss Trent." He pointed at the clerk. "About the murder of Mrs Roberts and why I wasn't assigned to investigate it—" He again stopped himself but this time to wipe his sweaty palms down his frock coat. "I—I didn't follow you here, I swear."

"I didn't think you had," Miss Trent replied, somewhat dryly.

Yet it was Lady Owston who next spoke up behind her, "Had you not heard enough whilst you were eavesdropping?"

"No," Maxwell replied but quickly corrected. "Yes, I mean-no, which is to say I—"

"*Save* your excuses, *sir*!" Lady Owston interrupted, stepping past both Rebecca and Maxwell and starting her descent of the external stairs to the street. "Good day to you, Miss Trent, Miss Dexter," she added as she turned back toward the house to wait for Agnes, who quickly caught up. It had stopped raining so neither required the use of Agnes' umbrella. Mr Snyder, having put his hat and cloak back on, joined them a couple of moments later. He opened the cab for them, held each lady's hand as she climbed inside, and carefully shut the doors over their knees. After paying a street urchin he'd hired to watch the vehicle, he climbed up and settled into his seat mounted at the back of the hansom cab, giving him a clear view over its top. His hands once again found the reins and geed the two horses into motion, sending both the cab and the Bow Streeters on their way.

Back at the house, Mr Maxwell continued his feeble attempt to explain himself. "I was in the *Gazette's* office when the story came in." He rested his hand upon his cravat. "And I decided to cover it but when I arrived, I saw Georgina—" He flinched, "Miss Dexter… and so I went over to her and, naturally I was surprised to find she had been assigned, by you, to investigate the case for the Society when *I* had received no such note. I thought, perhaps, it was a mistake so I came here."

"Not all members are assigned to investigate all cases, Mr Maxwell," Miss Trent replied calmly. "This was explained to you at your initial interview."

"Yes, I remember, Miss Trent," Maxwell answered, smiling weakly. "But I'd thought—I'd *hoped*—after the success of the Dorsey Case, you would've thought to assign me to *this* case. I-you're not leaving already, are you?" he suddenly enquired of Georgina as he realised she was passing him on the porch.

The artist halted at its edge and, looking over her shoulder, frowned as she stated, "I must return home and develop my photographs."

"Then allow me to accompany you to the omnibus stop," Maxwell said, happy for the chance to spend some time alone with her. He was keen to cut short his conversation with the clerk. He said, "Obviously I misunderstood, Miss Trent," and bid her farewell. Stepping alongside Georgina, he offered his arm and she looked from it to Rebecca, and finally Maxwell's face.

Her lips parted but she didn't speak to him. Instead, she addressed the clerk, "I've arranged for Mr Suggitt to pay a visit here later today, Miss Trent, to describe Mrs Roberts' missing clothes to me so I may draw them. I will return in time for his arrival, if these arrangements are acceptable?"

"They are." Miss Trent smiled. "Good afternoon, Miss Dexter, Mr Maxwell." The young artist nodded and, after bidding farewell in return, descended the stairs but without taking Mr Maxwell's arm. The *Gazette* journalist retracted it as a frown formed on his features. "I'd follow her if I were you," Rebecca told him and closed the door, leaving him alone on the porch.

Thankfully, Miss Dexter wasn't walking fast. "Father has invited me to dinner tomorrow evening," Maxwell announced once he'd fallen into step beside her. As he continued talking, despite her silence, Miss Dexter fought the urge to return to whence she came. She didn't feel unsafe in Maxwell's presence—far from it—she just wasn't sure she wanted to act as if nothing had happened as he was clearly doing. Something *had* happened; something truly terrible, in her mind, and it couldn't be swept away by a nice walk and idle chatter. "…Will you meet my parents?" Maxwell's voice suddenly penetrated Georgina's thoughts—and with an alarming question indeed! She abruptly stopped and stared up at him (for he was a good seven inches taller than her).

Stunned, she enquired, *"I beg* your pardon?" Confusion entered her features as she enquired, honestly uncertain of the fact, "Did you *truly* ask what I thought you did?"

"Erm, I'm not sure." Mr Maxwell frowned, perplexed himself. "What did you think I asked?"

"To meet your parents."

"Oh," he smiled, relieved. "Yes, you did." Georgina's lack of enthusiasm caused his smile to disappear and her utter bewilderment brought a deep concern to his heart. "I've met yours," he pointed out, feebly. He added, "We *are* engaged, Georgina."

"Without the proposal," she retorted, her voice breaking at the last despite the angry bewilderment it held. Unable to even *look* at him for the moment, while she attempted to compose herself, she turned her back on him. Maxwell, increasingly alarmed by her reactions, moved closer to her.

A pale, slender hand moved as if to rest upon her shoulder but closed its fingers and lowered once more. "I'm trying to make amends, Georgina," he told her quietly. She didn't respond however but he could see she was now holding a handkerchief to her lips. This only made him feel worse. "I'm sorry for the way I did it," he continued sadly, as he moved closer to her still. "But I'm not sorry for being engaged to you." He looked to his feet as speaking to the back of her bonnet became too much to bear. "I… I love you." Georgina's bonnet dipped forward at this but he didn't see it. A long, excruciating few moments passed before her very soft reply.

"I'm very fond of you, too, Joseph, but what you did… you trapped me in an engagement I neither wanted nor asked for. And in so doing, you have planned a future I never wanted for myself, the future of a housewife and mother when all I've ever wanted is to be an artist. To be independent, doing what I love."

"You can still be an artist, Georgina," Maxwell reassured, adding, "I'll do whatever it takes to make you happy." Georgina's head rose and she turned back toward him, surprised by his words. Yet a part of her was also hopeful that he was sincere. Not for his sake but her own. She scrutinised him for any hint of deceit but could find none.

"You do not know the brevity of what you say." Her voice broke a little as she continued, "Of what you *offer* me, Joseph—"

"I do," he replied but she interjected.

"Then promise me… give me your word what you say shall come to pass with both your support and blessing."

"I promise, Georgina," he replied, reaching for her hand without thinking and holding it in both of his own. Lifting it to his chest he continued, "With all my heart and word as a gentleman, I'll do whatever it takes to make you happy, to make you the successful—independent—artist you want to be."

She again searched his face for any hint of deviousness but, again, found none. Hope blossomed in her bosom as she shortened the gap between them and rested her other hand upon his.

"I believe you," she admitted softly, much to Maxwell's relief. "So yes," she continued. "I shall meet your parents." Maxwell had honestly forgotten about his request so was pleasantly surprised by her answer.

"Thank you, Georgina," he replied, grateful for so much more. They each squeezed the other's hands and, turning, linked arms. "I think you'll really like my mother," he remarked as they walked side by side toward the omnibus stop.

Georgina smiled, saying, "If she's anything like you, Joseph, I'm certain I shall."

* * *

A cream ceramic bowl, with hand-painted Chinese decoration, had the surface tension of its cold water broken by a dunked flannel. The cloth was next shaken to cleanse it of lavender-scented carbolic soap residue before it was raised and placed upon warm skin. Circular motions were made with it across the man's well-defined abdomen muscles, the tip of his covered finger brushing the waistband of his trousers.

Yet another, more feminine, hand appeared and caressed the flannel's wet trail on his skin. The corner of Percy Locke's mouth elevated as he watched their reflection in the immense, real gold gilt mirror mounted upon the plain, dark-blue papered wall directly above the desk. A slender shaped face, high—yet delicate—cheekbones, and an unadulterated, perfectly formed nose were just some of his features being reflected. Though he had been washing, the unchecked, small, golden-blond curls atop his head were dry; so too was the closely cut hair and sideburns directly underneath—the latter of which ended at the corners of his jaw.

He smiled. "I thought the door was locked."

"It was," the dark blond-haired lady stood behind him, replied softly into his ear. At six feet, she was only an inch taller than he but the high pinning of her naturally wavy hair upon her head's crown made the deficit all the more pronounced. The usually waist-length hair had been folded in several places. It had been pinned to create a sculpted style that continued to the nape of her neck. She wore a white, long-sleeved blouse with a pale-blue flower print and dark-blue buttons down its front. Its material was loose fitting on the body and arms, but tight against the wrists. Her skirts, made of plain pale-blue cloth, hung down from her hips and ended at her ankles. The blouse had been tucked into the high band of her skirts, serving to accentuate her narrow waist further. Over her blouse, and ending mid-way down her thigh, was a dark-blue, cotton jacket with mutton-chop sleeves. A brooch, inlaid with a single blue sapphire at its top and a real gold cone underneath, was pinned to the jacket's lapel.

While her right hand explored Percy's abdomen, her left rested on his shoulder. She leant closer to him and kissed his neck as his smile broadened.

"I see," he replied before gripping her wrist and pulling her around to face him. A sharp gasp escaped her lips as she became pinned against the desk's edge. Yet there was no fear in her blue-green hues. In fact, her chest rose and fell quickly as she reached behind her to grip the item of furniture.

With a lust-laced voice, she enquired, "I suppose you are amused?"

"But of course, darling," he replied with a definite twinkle in his emerald-green eyes. An arm, as muscular as his abdomen, tossed the flannel into the bowl behind her, his lips moving tantalisingly closer to hers. Her lips parted slightly but she knew it improper to succumb to her innermost desires. She was therefore relieved when he, knowing her as intimately as he did, gave her exactly what she wanted by putting his arm gently around her waist and pulling her into a kiss. The parting of his lips spurred her into, again, parting her own, the caressing of her tongue by his caused her hands to rest upon his back, and the pressing of her body against his made her want so much more. She had to accept, with his breaking of their kiss, her physical desires would remain unsatisfied. She didn't mind however; as she moved her hands to the crooks of his arms, she saw her heart's own desire within her husband's eyes.

"You are a dangerously attractive man, Mr Locke."

"A fact I cannot deny," he replied with a smile. She moved her head and shoulders back a little as she parted her lips in mock surprise and laughed.

"Is that so?" Her hands slowly slid down his forearms as she continued, "Let no woman say modesty is one of your virtues, darling—" She stopped as her fingers found something she'd not been expecting. Upon seeing what it was, she demanded, "*What,* pray tell, is *this*?"

"I believe it is called a needle mark, darling."

"A *fresh* one," she retorted, her anger rising. "I thought we had come to an agreement over this, Percy." The illusionist sighed deeply, moved away from her across the dressing room, and pinched the bridge of his nose.

He replied, exasperated, "I do not wish for a lecture, Lynette."

"And *I* do not wish for a dead husband!" she exclaimed, pure fury eclipsing the passion she'd felt mere moments before. "When did you poison yourself with it?" Yet Percy was already turning away from her and retrieving his shirt from behind a five-panelled, oak folding screen with Chinese dragons, lotus flowers, and bamboo carved into it. Aside from his shirt, an immense trunk with iron frame, wooden side panels, and curved lid occupied the space behind the screen. A dark-blue chaise lounge was set further back, against the wall, opposite the desk which Mrs Locke still stood in front of.

The desk took up the entire length of the wall with three deep drawers at either end. Its surface was highly polished whilst its edges and drawer fronts depicted hand-carved stars, moons, and other signs from the zodiac. Tubes of grease paint, boxes of talc, and bottles of black hair dye lined the back edge of the desk at either side of the previously described bowl. A jug, matching the bowl in decoration, stood at the back. Lined up to the bowl's left were combs, hair scissors, nail scissors, and nail files. A bar of lavender-scented carbolic soap, a box of powdered talc, chalk dentifrice in a round, ceramic pot, and a wooden toothbrush with horse hair bristles were meanwhile lined up to the bowl's right.

Yet none of these items were of any interest to Mrs Locke who waited expectantly for an answer. When none came, and her husband's intention to continue with his day regardless of her opinion became plain, she pointed out, "You cannot rehearse with such *filth* in your body, Percy."

"Is that a challenge?" he enquired sardonically. Her glare was anything but, however.

She strode away from the desk and penned him in between herself and the screen as she replied, "It is the advice of your doctor *and* your wife." A gentle tapping sounded from the door behind her. "Will you not hear me?" she questioned as her husband reached for the key. Their eyes met briefly but it was his which broke away first. Indeed, his entire head turned away while the lock clicked open.

"Come in," he called and stepped behind the screen. Doctor Lynette Locke was given no choice but to surrender her blockade, therefore, as her husband's personal valet, James, stepped into the dressing room. He silently joined his employer and assisted him with dressing. Lynette folded her arms across her chest but it was clear the conversation was over as far as Percy was concerned.

"Good day to you, *Husband*," she stated, spitting out the last word.

A moment later and Percy heard the loud shutting of the door. He was relieved, certainly, but also marginally ashamed for reneging on their verbal agreement.

"Two notes have arrived for you, sir," James informed him while smoothing down the back of Percy's shirt and assisting him in putting on his black waistcoat.

"I will read them presently," Percy replied, grateful for the distraction. Reaching into his own pocket, the valet retrieved a heavily perfumed envelope and a more formal one, adorned with a familiar 'B' stamped into its corner. Percy accepted both and, while James put on his white-cotton cravat, examined the first. He gave a wry smile upon reading the words, but didn't share them. Instead, he cleared his throat and slipped the note into the inside pocket of the frock coat hanging on the wall. Next, he turned his attention to the second correspondence. "It would appear my services are requested by the Bow Street Society once again," he remarked as he carelessly discarded the note onto the chaise lounge. "Is my carriage ready?"

"Yes, sir," James replied, taking the frock coat from the wall and holding it up behind Percy.

"Excellent." The illusionist slipped his arms into those of the garment and permitted his valet to lift it onto his shoulders. "If my wife returns, inform her I have departed on Bow Street Society business."

"Yes, sir." James, having smoothed out any creases in the frock coat, now stepped back to allow his employer to remove himself from behind the screen. A momentary check in the mirror followed before the Great Locke made himself disappear from the dressing room—as swiftly as he had made his wife do the same.

SIX

Running southwest from Berkeley Square toward Park Lane, Hill Street was named after a slight rise in the ground that existed when it was farmland. Developed in the first half of the eighteenth century, Hill Street, and its Mayfair counterparts, quickly became the fashionable choice of residence among lords and admirals. One notable resident, in the second half of that century, was Mrs Elizabeth Montagu who, alongside Elizabeth Vesey and Frances Boscawen, hosted a group of artists, writers, and thinkers in her home. This group became known as the Blue Stocking Circle, deriving its name from a decision made by scholar Benjamin Stillingfleet to obey Vesey's call to "come in your blue stockings," thus abandoning formal evening wear.

Mrs Montagu died in August of 1800—almost a century before Lady Katheryne Owston and Miss Agnes Webster set foot upon Hill Street's pavements, but her fame hadn't dwindled. In fact, the two had discussed their knowledge of the Blue Stocking Circle on their journey from Bow Street, each having previously encountered talk of it at the *Writer's Club*.

"Perhaps *I* should host such similar salons?" Lady Owston remarked as she carefully climbed down from Mr Snyder's cab and thanked him for his assistance. He had been holding her hand to enable her to steady herself. The cabman touched the wide brim of his hat as he gave a nod. He gave Miss Webster the same assistance during her alighting before he returned to his driver's seat.

"You practically do already, Lady Owston," Miss Webster pointed out. She lifted, and turned, her hand to check for rain. Feeling none, she returned her umbrella to the cab's interior seat.

"Perhaps, but giving our gatherings a *name* would give them an added level of credibility, do you not think?" Katheryne replied, but at once enquired, "Are we here?" She pressed her hand against her ostrich-feathered headdress and peered up at the five-storied building with basement, this lowest level being accessed by way of stone steps. These were barricaded by a gate hung on the far right of some wrought-iron, spear-headed railings. Below street level, immense, smooth, white stones formed the building's foundations. Above it, red bricks, blackened over the years by soot-laden air, provided a somewhat muted stateliness.

A solid, dark-green door stood silent guard upon a single, stone step. Anyone considering an attempt to "slip past" it would've been discouraged by the sharp spikes of an iron ring affixed to the frame of a plain-glass window crowning the doorway. The spikes pointed to a tiny gap in the ring's centre, thus making the unwanted entry of a pint-sized burglar much harder. Such a deterrent would've been acceptable to any Englishman of the time who wanted to protect his castle. The door was set back from the pavement and sheltered from the elements by a Greek-style porch with two pillars—lifted by podiums—supporting a triangular pediment. The pillars, podiums, and pediment were all stone.

Sash windows, approximately four feet tall, framed the porch. Their frames were wood, painted white, and each boasted a red brick fan at its top and a wide, stone ledge underneath. The second, third, and fourth storeys of the building had identical windows in lines of three. Finally, the fifth storey was housed in the roof of the building; these windows were at the front of brick 'box' casings which jutted out from the roof, enabling the windows to align against the guttering. The bright glow of electrical lighting only shone through the windows on either side of the porch, but this was enough to signify the building was at least occupied.

"Yes, we are here," Miss Webster replied.

"*Good*!" Lady Owston beamed, clasping her hands together. "All we need now is Miss Trent's gentleman," she remarked and released a contented sigh. She remained beside Mr Snyder's cab but kept her back to it as she waited… for all of thirty seconds. "Mr Snyder, are you able to see any vehicles approaching?" she enquired.

"Nah, Milady," he replied, sniffing against the cold chill of the day. His nose was already bright red but, accustomed to such temperatures, the seasoned cabman didn't complain. This was more than could be said about Lady Owston.

"Where *is* he??"

"Perhaps if we had been told the gentleman's name…" Miss Webster's monotone commented. Though it may seem rude to some, the secretary's intention hadn't been such.

"You'll know him when you see him, miss," Mr Snyder remarked knowingly. Both ladies looked up at him in astonishment; it hadn't occurred to them to ask Sam if *he'd* ever met their quarry. Yet before they could do so, the sounds of horse hooves clip-clopping along cobblestones, accompanied by the crunching of carriage wheels, announced themselves at the entrance of Hill Street. "'Ere 'e is," Sam confirmed the ladies' suspicions with a smile. Both Lady Owston and Miss Webster stepped away from his cab to gain a better view of the approaching carriage. Its middle-aged driver was attired in a high-grade, black-leather cloak and impeccable, black top hat with plain, cream band. The vehicle meanwhile matched the servant's cloak in colour but gold-plated detailing upon its doors, handles, and edges denoted the vast difference in class. As the carriage came to a stop behind Mr Snyder's cab, a golden, intertwined 'P' and 'L' within a square border could be seen upon the passenger door's central panel.

Lady Owston was the first to venture forward. However, she'd only traversed a few steps before the sight of a slender, black, leather-clad hand, slipping out from behind a red-velvet curtain, stopped her. The hand reached downward, lifted the door's external handle, and gave it a gentle push. Immediately after the door had silently swung open, the top of Mr Locke's top hat emerged from the vehicle while his polished shoe dropped down onto the metal, external step. His other hand kept a firm grip upon the leather strap within the carriage until he'd successfully alighted.

"Mr *Locke*!" Lady Owston cried, excitedly, as she strode toward him with outstretched arms. She didn't embrace him though; instead, she momentarily lifted her hands and allowed them to drop back down in a gesture of happy disbelief. "What an *absolute* pleasure it is to make your acquaintance! Miss Webster and I are *tremendous* admirers of yours, aren't we, Agnes?"

"Yes, Lady Owston."

"I am pleased to hear it, ladies." To the third Bow Streeter, he added, "Mr Snyder."

"Mr Locke," the cabman replied, touching the brim of his hat while bowing his head as a mark of respect. The illusionist, pleased with the greeting, turned upon his heel and graced his companions with his charming smile. "Miss Trent's letter briefly outlined the ghastly goings on at Oxford Street but, without having witnessed them myself, I must place myself into your hands." He looked to the building and continued, "The Holden residence, I presume?"

"You presume correctly, sir," Lady Owston replied. "Miss Webster discovered it in the *Post Office Directory*. We were awaiting your arrival before we made our presence known. Are you familiar with the Holdens, Mr Locke?"

"Only by name." He gestured toward the door. "Ladies first." Being *most* impressed with the handsome young man, Lady Owston eagerly accepted the invitation, strode across the pavement, and stood under the porch. Miss Webster hurriedly followed her with the illusionist coming last, but then taking his place between them. It was he who, with the silver grip of his ebony cane, rat-a-tat-tatted on the door.

"Good morning," greeted the middle-aged butler. He wore his morning uniform of dark-grey trousers, a high, double-breasted, black waistcoat (devoid of any watch chain), black tie, and black dress coat. Neatly trimmed sideburns—tan in colour—framed his face but his chin and upper lip remained clean shaven. His posture was perfect as green eyes, flecked with brown, looked to each of the visitors in turn. His enunciation was also faultless as he enquired, "May I help you?"

"Indeed, you may," Mr Locke replied, stepping forward to offer the butler his calling card. "I am Mr Percival Locke, a member of the Bow Street Society, and these are my associates: Lady Katheryne Owston, an independent journalist, and her secretary, Miss Agnes Webster. We would like to request an audience with Mr and Mrs Holden—if it isn't too inconvenient? Please pass on our apologies for the unscheduled visitation but circumstances have forced us to forego the etiquette of polite society in this instance. We have been commissioned to investigate a murder, you see." The butler's stoicism was momentarily broken at this news—but soon returned.

He answered, "I shall make enquiries."

"Thank you," Mr Locke said. "Perhaps it would be appropriate for us to await our answer inside?"

The butler parted his lips to refuse but paused as he, again, looked to them all standing on the porch in plain view of the neighbours. Apparently deciding to make an exception in this case, he stepped aside and moved a slightly raised hand toward the first white door on the left of the hallway, "If you would be so kind as to wait in the library."

"Of course," Mr Locke replied, removing his top hat and gloves, and placing the latter into the former. After putting both into the butler's waiting hands, Percy next led the ladies inside and through the indicated door. Lady Owston had also removed her hat and surrendered it to the butler alongside her coat. While Miss Webster had passed over her coat, she had declined the servant's offer to take her hat, instead choosing to keep it pinned upon her head.

Though allegedly a library, the furnishings of the room beyond also portrayed a dual function of a study; a flat-top desk was set before the window and only the wall to one's right, as one entered, had bookcases.

The desk was two feet wide by five feet long, yet ample walking space still surrounded it nonetheless. Its top was highly polished—the window being easily reflected in it—and the superior carpentry skills which had gone into its construction could be read in its joins and even the quality of oak chosen. Mr Locke walked behind the desk the moment the butler had closed the door. Stepping back from the piece, the illusionist bent forward to visually inspect the piece. *Automatically locking drawers,* he thought and ran a finger over the top lock. If it had been necessary, Mr Locke knew he could've broken the lock in seconds rather than minutes. Yet only his curiosity had led him to this line of ponderings and, currently, his curiosity wasn't a sufficient enough reason to damage their host's property.

Mr Locke straightened and stepped around the office chair, which was tucked underneath the desk, to gently nudge the lace curtain aside. He had a clear view of Mr Snyder's cab, his own carriage, and the houses opposite. Nothing of note struck him about the view.

The two bookcases along the one wall were utterly identical in design. Each shelf was filled with volume upon volume of expensive, leather-bound books. The bookcases were also constructed from oak and, like the desk, showed all the hallmarks of an expert hand.

A gigantic, iron hearth framed by brown and cream-checked tiles mounted onto an oak surround occupied the wall opposite the door. Lady Owston headed to this upon entering the room—not to warm her hands, however. Instead, she picked up a fire guard made of a turned, oak frame with a thick, hand-stitched tapestry panel hanging in its centre. This she moved in front of the fire before returning to Miss Webster, who faced the bookcase without digesting any of its titles, and gently touched her arm. The young secretary, upon hearing the guard was in place, quietly reassured her employer she was well.

"We should have sent word ahead of ourselves," Katheryne remarked as she crossed the room. This time, as she approached the fire, she indeed warmed her hands. Miss Webster meanwhile had begun to stroll around the outer edge of the library, admiring the impressive amount of illumination given off by the electrical lights. Lady Owston, seeing Mr Locke walking around the desk to join her at the fireside, enquired, "Would you not agree, Mr Locke? After all, they only have our word we are who we claim to be."

"Provided we do not give them reason to doubt our honour, Lady Owston, I suspect we shall be well-received," Percy replied with confidence. Both ladies glanced at one another, not entirely convinced, but neither pursued the point.

Several minutes had passed when the butler eventually returned. He opened the door wide with one hand, causing those within to simultaneously turn toward it, and stepped inside. Only then did he announce the answer they had been patiently waiting for, "Mrs Holden shall see you now."

"And Mr Holden?" Mr Locke enquired.

The butler responded, "Away from home, sir." He paused for the acceptable amount of time required for such news to be sufficiently absorbed. It wasn't long, five seconds at most. "However…" He again paused but this time to allow the visitors to draw their attention away from one another and back onto him. "I have Mrs Holden's authority to inform you he is to be found at *The Royal Coachman Public House* located on the far end of Hill Street. Now, if you would like to follow me, the mistress is awaiting your introductions in the lounge."

"She shall have to be introduced to Lady Owston and Miss Webster, only," Mr Locke replied, stepping around the servant with all the grace of a ballet dancer. He reclaimed his top hat and gloves from the hall table as he continued, "Ladies, we shall reconvene at Bow Street in…" He checked his pocket watch. "An hour. Good day to you all." Without slowing for an answer, he strode back down the hall and left, effectively seeing himself out of the house.

"To the lounge…?" Lady Owston gently reminded the somewhat speechless butler who simply stared at the now closed front door in disbelief.

However, upon realising he was being addressed, the butler straightened and, momentarily pressing his heels together, replied, "Yes… apologies, ma'am, this way."

"Thank you." Katheryne followed, with Agnes at her side, across the hall to where they were instructed to wait beside an oil painting depicting an English countryside scene. The grandfather clock nearby ticked loudly in the intervening moments between the servant leaving them and their being invited into Mrs Holden's presence.

"Lady Katheryne Owston and Miss Agnes Webster of the Bow Street Society, ma'am," he announced as they stepped around him—for he stood with his back against the open door—and walked but a few paces into the room.

"Thank you for agreeing to speak with us, Mrs Holden," Lady Owston began, the gratitude in her voice utterly sincere.

Mrs Ruth Holden couldn't have been a day younger than sixty. Grey skin, which would have once been firm and fair, hung from her chin and neck. Loose, and thin as paper, it rested in two folds—not rolls—upon the neckline of her dress. The dress was underwhelming; plain, dark-grey material bagged around Mrs Holden's limbs and hips and covered every inch of her form. A white blouse could be seen marginally peeking out from underneath the dark-grey at Mrs Holden's neckline and cuffs. Long, wiry, grey hair was scraped back under a white, cotton bonnet whose ribbon tied below her chin, its large, white bow rested on her covered bosom. Faded-blue eyes followed the two ladies as if they were mice invading a cat's territory.

"Only my curiosity permits your presence here." Mrs Holden's voice was strong despite her advanced years. "That will be all, Wolston."

"Yes, ma'am." The butler gave a slight bow and departed. Lady Owston and Miss Webster had no choice but to remain standing.

"I was told there would be three of you," Mrs Holden remarked. "Mr Locke has departed in search of my husband, I presume?"

"He has," Lady Owston replied. She didn't apologise for him, however. Having only met the gentleman a few minutes prior, she didn't feel it was appropriate to make such a presumption.

"He shan't have far to look," Mrs Holden commented, prompting Lady Owston to glance at her secretary.

"I believe he was travelling to *The Royal Coachman Public House*?" She enquired.

"My husband's favourite pastime; he has not permitted a drop of liquor to pass his lips these twenty years... but he enjoys the 'atmosphere' of the place." Mrs Holden said, both her tone and body language betraying the disdain and disapproval she held about the notion. As if suddenly noticing the two ladies were still standing, Mrs Holden invited them both to sit upon a low-backed, leather sofa identical to the one she herself sat upon.

The two sofas stood facing one another on either side of a fireplace, twins of the one in the library. Miss Webster was most thankful indeed to find a fireguard, as plain as Mrs Holden's attire, already positioned in front of her foe. Though the cracking, snapping, and popping of the fire couldn't be muffled by the guard, Miss Webster could distance herself from it—both emotionally and literally—by taking the end of the sofa furthest away. At least she would have both her employer and Mrs Holden's voices between herself and it. The task of carefully recording the conversation in shorthand in her notebook would also serve as a distraction to her fears. No sooner had she begun this though did Mrs Holden enquire, "What is she doing?"

"If you consent, Mrs Holden, we would like to take a written record of our conversation so we may refer back to it if necessary during the course of our investigations," Lady Owston explained.

"Whatever for?" Mrs Holden demanded.

"Scotland Yard, specifically an Inspector Woolfe, is investigating the matter about which we have come to speak with you today," Lady Owston answered. "And you know how *intrusive* the police can be, not to mention *incompetent* and *corrupt.* They will come here, Mrs Holden—"

"Let them come! They shall speak only to the door."

"Consider the scandal the mere presence of a policeman could cause, though, should your neighbours catch sight of him. It is a scandal our client wishes to avoid also, which is why she has commissioned the Bow Street Society to investigate. To achieve this, though, we need a record of the conversations we have with *all* witnesses—so we may read, and reread, what was said in case an important clue has been missed. A clue you yourself could be in possession of but not realise it. I think it unlikely though since you strike me as a highly intelligent and shrewd woman, Mrs Holden."

"Thank you, Lady Owston," the older lady replied, her tone softening a fraction. "I must confess I have heard your name spoken among my acquaintances; they speak highly of you and now I see why." She glanced at Agnes. "Very well, young lady, you may take your record."

"I can assure you it shan't be passed on to anyone beyond the Bow Street Society without your explicit consent, Mrs Holden," Lady Owston informed her.

Yet the elder lady retorted, with vigour, "Which I shall never give." Her tone suggested she didn't want to hear any more on the matter, and this was further backed up by her next words, "What is the matter you wish to speak to me about? Wolston spoke to me of a murder."

"Yes; Mrs Maryanna Roberts," Lady Owston replied, pausing to watch Mrs Holden's reaction to the name. The older lady's face didn't show even a glimmer of recognition, however. "You met her, I believe, at *The Queshire Department Store* yesterday?" Lady Owston encouraged, again waiting for any sign Mrs Holden knew of whom she spoke. However, none came. Cautiously, Katheryne ventured, "There was an incident between Mrs Roberts and your husband—?"

"Oh *her*!" Mrs Holden interrupted, her face contorted as if she'd tasted something rotten. "An *awful, awful* creature! Straight from the slum and the gin house, there can be no doubt about it! Absolutely no idea how to behave, though one should not expect manners from those of *that* class; the *criminal* class is what they call them, do they not?"

"I have heard the terminology used before, yes," Lady Owston replied, able to hide the inner revulsion she felt at the wealthy woman's attitude due to many an hour spent with women of a similar ilk. Miss Webster also drew upon these same experiences to find the strength to hold her own tongue—at least as far as this matter was concerned. Lady Owston nevertheless soldiered on with her current train of thought. "Mrs Roberts was, unfortunately, found murdered this morning—"

"Nothing unfortunate about it! The *creature* propositioned my husband, in *public*, and became violent and abusive when Mr Queshire escorted her from the premises." Mrs

Holden glanced up toward the heavens. "We are told we must be Godly and sympathetic toward the plight of the poor, but I couldn't be either when she did *that*."

"There is some belief Mrs Roberts was murdered last night. Her body being found on Oxford Street this morning. Naturally, you were not on Oxford Street last night, were you?"

"I was not. Mr Holden and I were at the *Theatre Royal*, Drury Lane until nine thirty. We arrived home at ten o'clock. Mr Holden wished to read in the library so I retired to bed without him."

"Could you recall what time he eventually retired to bed?"

"No; Mr Holden knows not to disturb me when I am sleeping," Mrs Holden stated absolutely. Miss Webster continued to make efficient notes meanwhile.

"And this morning, did either of you have need to visit Oxford Street?" Lady Owston enquired though, as soon as she realised how her question had come across, she quickly added, "To collect an order from *The Queshire Department Store*, perhaps?"

"We both rose at seven thirty. My maid dressed me and my husband's valet dressed him. We breakfasted together in the morning room before he retired to the library and I took the bureau here to write some letters." She turned her head toward the item of furniture standing against the wall to the left of the window. "It was only a half hour ago he departed for his favourite pastime."

"Thank you, Mrs Holden," Lady Owston said, smiling in both relief and gratitude.

Yet the old woman's face seemed to take on a different expression, first one of suspicion and then of conviction as she replied, "Neither Mr Holden or myself would have ended the wretched creature's existence. Aside from it being utterly against *God's* Commandments, neither of us would waste our time or strength on such a foul human being."

"I believe you," Katheryne answered wholeheartedly. Mrs Holden was a "wretched creature" herself but, strangely, it was the wretchedness which convinced Lady Owston of the older woman's innocence. A glance at Agnes told Katheryne the secretary felt the same. As for Mr Holden, they would have to wait and see what Mr Locke would return to Bow Street with.

* * *

Miss Trent entered the *Water Lily House* and allowed its only door to naturally fall shut behind her. Warm air had fleetingly kissed the icy chill of outdoors as she'd done so but then wrapped itself about her like a long-lost relative. Slowly, she ventured further down the narrow path bordered by immense, ceramic pots. Her hand pushed aside a length of vine dangling from the white-painted, wrought-iron beams above her.

One of the most attractive greenhouses in the *Royal Botanic Gardens* at Kew, the *Water Lily House* was, and still is, found adjacent to the awesome *Palm House*. The *Palm House* being, arguably, the most widely recognised pieces of architecture at Kew. With its almost acre of glass in its sloped walls, incredible 362-foot length, hundred-foot breadth, and impressive sixty-six-foot height, the *Palm House* accommodated full-sized tree ferns, date palms, betel nuts, coconut trees, upas trees, bamboo, cotton plants, coffee shrubs, tamarinds, and even the clove. As a result, visitors in 1896 could, as they may now, easily imagine themselves being in a tropical forest. If the *Palm House* was such a fair land of exoticism therefore, its neighbour, the *Water Lily House*, was a hidden oasis of serenity. In the centre of the much shorter, domed structure was a tank thirty-six feet in diameter containing rare varieties of water lilies. Rising from its middle was a very fine papyrus plant. Chest-high iron railings surrounding the tank's circumference prevented any curious horticulturalists from simply reaching across and touching it, however. Other exhibits of interest, to both enthusiasts and ignoramuses alike, were the Sacred Bean of Egypt, the Telegraph Plant of India, and the Sensitive Plant— among other curiosities.

Happily for the Bow Street Society clerk, these plants also provided an excellent wall of greenery to block the view of anyone curious enough to glance in while passing by. The mammoth leaves of some of the exhibits also served to partially obstruct one's line of vision as one strolled around the tank. Visitors could therefore conceal themselves amongst the foliage without being seen until the last moment; such was the reason she'd been drawn to this particular greenhouse. Certainly, the *Palm House*'s exhibits would've had the same effect but Rebecca had suspected it could've been too crowded for her purpose—a suspicion confirmed upon her passing through it a few minutes prior. The *Water Lily House*, on the other hand, was deserted.

She ran her hand across the top railing as she began a slow circuit around the tank, her attention very much upon the palm in the centre. When she reached the halfway point, she heard the house's door opening and closing and the sound of footsteps soon after. She refrained from lifting her head, however. Instead, she chose to open the penny guide book she'd purchased upon entering the Gardens. The footsteps came closer, paused, walked away, and paused again. Still she didn't look up. Finally, after what felt like a lifetime, the footsteps returned to the door. *Bloody Hell,* she thought as she looked up and saw a man step aside to allow the previous visitor, a woman, to leave. Of course, she recognised him but this recognition was hidden by her turning away from him and continuing her stroll around the tank.

"A nice-looking fern," the man remarked as he came up alongside her and gestured toward the plant in the centre.

Rebecca stopped in her walking, looked toward the tank, and replied. "I believe it is a papyrus, sir."

"Ah," Chief Inspector Jones replied. "So it is." He cleared his throat while Rebecca bowed her head toward her guide.

"There is much more to see at the Gardens than this," she remarked and offered the, now closed, guide to him. "I think you'll find it an interesting read, sir."

"Indeed." He took the booklet and, opening it, saw the typed report concealed within. Closing the guide, he discreetly slipped it into the inside pocket of his overcoat. In a much quieter voice, he enquired, as he looked out across the pond, "Who have you chosen for this case?" For the time being, they were alone in the greenhouse, but each knew this could change in a heartbeat should another visitor arrive. Besides, he hadn't wanted his voice to travel *too* far. The clerk, well versed in such subterfuge, matched his tone precisely.

She said, "Lady Katheryne Owston, an independent journalist with the *Women's Signal* and *Truth* publications, her secretary, Miss Agnes Webster, and artist, Miss Georgina Dexter."

"Not Mr Maxwell?" Jones questioned.

Rebecca again turned away from him and recommenced her stroll. She was silent until she was certain he was following, at which point she explained, "His clumsiness and ineptness make him a liability."

"And it in no way has anything to do with the fact he and Miss Dexter are in the midst of a disagreement?" Jones challenged though good naturedly.

Rebecca stopped and, meeting his gaze across her shoulder, replied, "Personal feelings have no place in an investigation, Richard." She smiled. "You taught me that."

"I did?" he enquired, surprised, as the two continued their circuit of the tank, him behind her at a respectable distance. After some time to reflect though, he recalled the incident to which she referred and nodded. "What did they find when they went to Oxford Street?"

"Mrs Roberts' badly mutilated body and the usual circus of gawkers of the macabre being held back by police. Mr Suggitt, Maryanna's brother-in-law, was there and Mrs Suggitt was taken to Oxford Street by Mr Snyder." Rebecca appeared to admire the Sacred Bean of Egypt and continued, her voice remaining quiet, "Mrs Suggitt told Lady Owston, Miss Webster, and Miss Dexter her sister had been last seen alive, by Mr Suggitt, at the *Queshire Department Store.* The owner, Mr Edmund Queshire, was interviewed by Lady Owston and Miss Webster about an incident which happened between Mrs Roberts and one of Mr Queshire's wealthier customers, the Holdens. Lady Owston, Miss Webster, and Mr Locke are questioning the Holdens as we speak while Miss Dexter has returned home to develop the photographs she took of the scene in readiness for tonight's meeting. Mr Suggitt has been invited to spend time with Miss Dexter, shortly before the meeting, to describe Mrs Roberts' missing clothes to her so she may draw them."

The door of the green house opened and a rather serious-looking young man—presumably a botany student— entered with notebook and pencil in hand. The poor man's glasses steamed up from the rapid change in temperature. While he fumbled to retrieve his handkerchief, Jones walked past Rebecca and removed the guide she'd given him to make a show of checking a plant against one of its entries. "Almost at the week's end," he stated loud enough for both Rebecca and the student to hear. "Soon we shall be meeting another week, shan't we?"

"We shall, sir," Miss Trent replied, politely, but without being overly familiar. She, of course, had guessed the chief inspector had resorted to code to refer to a mutual acquaintance.

"At such close quarters, the Weeks don't know the impact their passing so swiftly has on our lives, do they?" Jones next enquired.

Rebecca shook her head. "They don't, sir, but nonetheless we must appreciate what each week brings us."

"And be cautious of their gifts at the same time," Jones warned, glancing at the student who concentrated upon his sketch of the papyrus. When he turned back toward Rebecca though, he saw she'd begun to retrace her steps to the door. Lighting his pipe, he calmly followed, looking at the plants as he passed. Fully aware of his walking behind her, Rebecca had nodded in polite understanding and moved slowly enough to ensure he would catch up with her just as she left the greenhouse—which he did.

Only once they stood outside, on the empty step overlooking an equally empty path, did Jones give her his actual warning, "Doctor Weeks needs to be careful, as always, but so do you and the other Bow Streeters." Seeing a couple approaching, he stepped aside to allow them to pass as he remarked to Rebecca, "It's cold outside, isn't it?"

Miss Trent nodded, replying, "It is, sir, but I am well versed in guarding against turbulent weather."

"Inspector Caleb Woolfe is a determined police officer and a cynical man," Jones continued after the couple had entered the greenhouse and the door had fully closed behind them. "He doesn't let anything lie, no matter what the consequence," he informed her, his voice surprisingly grave.

"We will be cautious," she reassured in earnest. The tension in Jones' face dissolved and he offered a small smile.

He tapped his breast pocket twice and replied, "Thank you for the guide, miss. I shall enjoy reading it as I stroll around the gardens."

"You're most welcome, sir." She paused. "Be sure to guard against the weather, also." Jones nodded his assurance at this statement before stepping past her, descending the three steps, and casually walking further into the gardens. Miss Trent meanwhile didn't linger to watch. Descending the steps at a much brisker pace, she strode toward the gardens' main entrance. *Why can't every case be investigated by John Conway?* She mused though the answer was one she already knew. Still, it didn't ease the irritation she felt at the prospect of having an annoying fly of an inspector buzzing around, asking irrelevant and uncomfortable questions. *Or worse,* she thought, the warning Richard had given her mere moments before drifting to the forefront of her mind.

SEVEN

With a history dating back almost two hundred years, *The Royal Coachman Public House* had once served as a coaching inn where travellers, weary from their time on the road, could lay their heads and fill their stomachs. In 1896, its days of renting rooms were over and its main function was to quench its patrons' thirst. Constructed from brown brick, it had tall windows on the ground floor and smaller on its first. The cellar was accessed via a hatch at the building's rear while its main door led directly into the small bar room. Its interior walls were white-washed plaster, while oak beams, supporting the floor above, were fully exposed against its ceiling. Freshly applied virgin sawdust was sprinkled across the oak floor to catch any dirt or spills. The bar's panelling and countertop, both constructed from the same wood, were highly polished and pristine. The burgundy fabric of the stools, and rounded tops of the squat tables, were clean and undamaged.

Mr Bartholomew Holden slowly lowered his pipe and rested his withered hand upon his knee. White smoke toppled from his pale lips like a waterfall. Pale-green eyes, nestled beneath a stern brow, surveyed the relaxed goings on of the pub in which he sat. He'd always enjoyed watching others completing their daily business; it was why he'd taken to sitting in *this* chair, in *this* corner. A lead-latticed window on his right overlooked Hays Mews, *The Royal Coachman* being located on the corner where it and Hill Street met. Any chill the sixty-three-year-old man may have felt from it was combated by the heat of the large hearth, positioned diagonally from him, on the other side of the cosy room. From this little patch of England, he would observe the subtle shifts in his habitual environment without feeling obliged to be a part of them. That particularly irritating responsibility was the foundation of his dreary working life. Repetitive questions, repetitive meetings, and repetitive correspondences all demanded his undivided attention on an hourly basis—despite his tireless input never having any tangible impact on the workings of the wider business. Nevertheless, it kept him in bread and water. He smiled as he, once again, reminded himself there was 'none of that here.' Today was his day off, too. His smile broadened.

Mr Holden had spent the entirety of his adult years working in the City of London's financial district. Luxuriant, russet locks, which had once upon a time covered his head, now hung as limp, white/grey strands from a dramatically receded hairline. Many of his peers had chosen to retain full beards, moustaches, and sideburns but he had chosen to do away with the first two; they added too many years otherwise. What remained were cheeks which almost drooped past his chin, swollen bags under his eyes, and a jawline bearing a closer resemblance to a lacklustre oil-painting than a chiselled sculpture. His nose, with its broad bridge and pointed snout, exaggerated the harshness of his brow. Yet he wasn't an angry man by any stretch of the imagination. Even his dark-grey frock coat, black waistcoat, black cravat, and dark-grey trousers hung upon his frame without any strictness. He was a man who, from the outside, appeared comfortable in both his own skin and clothes.

The pipe was hooked onto his bottom lip and puffed away upon. Around the corner from where he sat, the front door opened and, shortly thereafter, a stranger crossed Mr Holden's line of vision. It was a rarity for the old man not to recognise a patron of the establishment but, whenever it occurred, it had always unnerved him. Familiarity was security and peaceful familiarity was bliss; this young gentleman approaching the bar had shattered it all. Mr Holden frowned, causing his cheeks to droop all the more. *Was my name uttered?* He enquired of himself as the gentleman made enquiries with the landlord. *Damn my ears!* He cursed, poking a finger into one as if it would miraculously improve his hearing. In doing so though, he failed to see the landlord point toward him and the gentleman approach his table.

"Mr Bartholomew Holden?" a voice enquired from above. Mr Holden looked up sharply in surprise but replied, "I am he; to whom am *I* speaking?"

"Mr Percival Locke. I am a magician who—"

"*Not* interested, young man. Take your parlour tricks elsewhere."

"Pardon me, but you misunderstand, sir. I *am* a magician but I am here in my capacity as a member of the Bow Street Society. Perhaps you have heard of them?"

Mr Holden reflected on the name. Somewhere, from the depths of his mind, he pulled forth a memory of a newspaper article. "Dorsey Trial?"

"The Society was involved in the investigation of that case, yes. I myself was among those members. May I join you?"

Mr Holden appraised the gentleman stood before him; curls which looked adorable on a child but utterly amiss on a grown man, and an arrogant air that betrayed a lack of years lived... *A dandy,* Mr Holden concluded. Yet he was curious; he didn't know this man but he wished to converse with him—why? Finally, he assented, "If you so wish."

"Thank you," Percy replied and removed his top hat and gloves. Following the placing of the former into the latter, he carefully put both on the vacant chair adjacent to the one onto which he now settled. "Your wife informed me of your whereabouts," he went on to explain. "My associates—Lady Katheryne Owston and her secretary, Miss Agnes Webster—are currently visiting upon her. I therefore wish to beg both of your pardons for the unscheduled, and uninvited, intrusions upon your time and your home."

"It is given," Mr Holden replied with a small nod. Mr Locke smiled, showing a relief on his face the older man didn't believe for a moment. *Charmers, the lot of them!* He thought. *Insincere charmers.* He was glad this Mr Locke was speaking to him, however, and not his wife. *Though, on second thoughts, attempting to charm a statue in Trafalgar Square would probably yield better results,* he inwardly admitted. "As you are no doubt already aware, Mr Holden," Mr Locke's voice cut through his ponderings. "The Bow Street Society is a group of lawfully minded individuals who work to solve cases on behalf of their clients. Its current client is Mrs Diana Suggitt, sister of Mrs Maryanna Roberts—a lady who, we have been led to believe, made your acquaintance under less-than-respectable circumstances at *The Queshire Department Store* yesterday."

"If I did, it is no business of yours, Mr Locke."

"Even if I were to tell you Mrs Maryanna Roberts was murdered last night?"

"*Are* you telling me?"

"I am," Mr Locke responded and Mr Holden broke eye contact with him to tap the side of his pipe's bowl. "When did it occur?" he enquired. Rising, he shuffled across to the hearth where he deposited the remnants of his spent tobacco. He kept his back to the illusionist while he ran his finger around the inside of the pipe bowl and flicked out the stubborn fibres. Mr Locke had always been under the impression the intermingling of new tobacco with old in a pipe assisted with enriching its flavour. Perhaps he had been wrong? He wasn't Sherlock Holmes, after all. He didn't have a paper on the different types of tobacco.

"Last night."

"Dear God," Mr Holden muttered, aggrieved, as he looked to the brickwork above the hearth. The sadness which had weighed down his words wasn't the kind one human being expressed while instinctively lamenting the death of another, however. "What is the world coming to?" the older man enquired hypothetically despite his looking to the wall for answers. Slowly, he refaced Locke and shuffled back to his chair. He said, "Mrs Suggitt has my condolences."

"I am certain she shall appreciate them," Mr Locke replied, allowing Mr Holden his moment to deposit his pipe back into his pocket once he was seated. "The incident at the department store yesterday, and after…?" the illusionist continued to gently nudge the conversation toward what he needed to know.

Mr Holden, seeming to be again in control of his emotions, hooked his thumb into his waistcoat's watch pocket. "An unfortunate one, but resolved nonetheless."

"Resolved how?"

"My wife and I left the store," Mr Holden stated. "Truly, there is no need to rake it all up again."

"Mrs Roberts has been murdered; you do not think the incident in the department store could bear some relevance?"

"Absolutely not."

"Even if someone, who had witnessed the altercation, had possibly taken it upon them to confront her about her behaviour?"

"I do not see *who*; as I told you, Mr Locke, the matter was resolved."

"And you did not see Mrs Roberts again?"

Mr Holden shook his head and, with a convincingly perplexed expression, enquired, "Should I have done?"

"I do not know; should you?" Mr Locke tossed the question back at him, which took the older man aback somewhat.

Rather than demand an explanation from the illusionist though, Mr Holden instead took a few moments to organise his thoughts. Eventually he enquired, in a lower tone of voice, "May I rely upon your discretion, Mr Locke?"

"You may."

"Thank you." Mr Holden cast a glance toward the landlord and other patrons, all were engrossed in their own mundane lives, however. "A gentleman has certain needs, you would agree?"

"I would."

"Needs a wife cannot satisfy for the sake of propriety," Mr Holden continued.

Percy slowly nodded but leant forward to reassure, "I know to what you refer; may I assume Mrs Roberts... dealt with these needs?"

"You may," the elder man answered. "Naturally, she was paid for services rendered."

"Naturally," Mr Locke repeated and Mr Holden stared at him, annoyance in his features.

"Do you mock me, sir?"

"I do not, Mr Holden. I myself do not limit myself to my wife alone." He smiled softly. "Though for reasons perhaps different to your own."

"Indeed," Mr Holden replied, frowning. He didn't agree the two of them were in any way alike but an ally was an ally nonetheless—even one who was a dandy. *At least he can appreciate the sensitivity of the matter,* he concluded. "Our marriage was one of convenience, Mr Locke. When our son was born, we at least had his welfare in common but, now he has a family of his own..." Mr Holden, realising he was revealing more than was proper, trailed off. "Maryanna was one of my regulars. Yesterday wasn't the first time I had met her, but it was the first time she'd met my wife." He sighed deeply. "Ruth of course knows I am not always here when I go out on an evening but it isn't for her to say where I take my pleasure, is it?"

"Indeed, it is not," Mr Locke agreed and not entirely without sincerity. "It is a gentleman's prerogative to do as he wishes."

"*Precisely,* Mr Locke."

"So, you left Oxford Street, returned home, and departed company from your wife to seek out Mrs Roberts?"

Percy enquired, slowly, as he tried to get a clearer picture of last night's timeline as far as Mr Holden was concerned.

The older man shook his head and replied, "My wife and I visited the theatre after dinner and returned home at around ten o'clock. Once she had retired to bed, I slipped from the house and sought out Maryanna—not to harm her, you understand, but to remind her of her place." He paused. "Naturally, I took advantage of the service she offered following our discussion. Afterward, I gave her only half of what I do usually, partly because she was inebriated at the time and partly because I wanted her to understand she couldn't approach me in such a manner in public again. I warned her she would get no more coin from me in future if she did."

"At what time did you locate Mrs Roberts?"

"It was around ten forty-five, I believe."

"And when did you part company?"

"Only a short time later," Mr Holden leant over the table to whisper, "Services were rendered verbally, you understand." Percy merely nodded knowingly. No further explanation was required.

Recalling a point mentioned in Miss Trent's note to him, Mr Locke enquired, "Can you recall what Mrs Roberts was wearing?"

"A dress—hanging a long way past her knees, some heavy boots, and a scarf; all dirty and tattered."

"When you parted ways, did she tell you where she was going?"

"No. We merely bid good night. I returned home and retired to bed."

"May your wife corroborate your account?" Though Percy wasn't entirely certain the question was necessary; as a married couple, Mrs Holden couldn't give evidence against her husband in open court. It would nonetheless help to verify the man's story, however.

Mr Holden shook his head, "I very much doubt it, Mr Locke. It was quarter to midnight by the time I crept under the blankets and she was asleep. I am always careful not to wake her."

"Then you could have murdered Mrs Roberts," Mr Locke stated, bluntly. The colour drained from Mr Holden's already grey face though no other sign of fear surfaced upon his features.

"I couldn't, Mr Locke. Despite what I am, and what I did with Mrs Roberts, I'm not a heartless or unfeeling man. Murder isn't a vice I indulge in." Percy watched Mr Holden intently as he analysed every facet of his face and every movement of his eyes. He picked up his top hat and, taking his gloves from it, stood.

"I'm aware you only have my word to support my claim of innocence," Mr Holden continued. "But I shall tell you again, Mr Locke. I couldn't have murdered Maryanna Roberts. Fumbled pleasures in darkened streets? Yes. Deceiving my wife for the sake of propriety? Indeed. But *never* murder."

Yet Percy didn't answer him until his hat and gloves were both in place. When he finally did, he stated, "I am inclined to believe you, Mr Holden." He watched as the older man sat back against his chair, the relief evidenced by the colour returning to his cheeks. Taking a calling card from his pocket, he placed it on the table in front of Bartholomew. He said, "Should you recall anything further. Good day to you, Mr Holden."

"Yes, of course…" Mr Holden pulled the card toward him with a stubby finger. "Thank you, Mr Locke—and good day."

* * *

"A darker shade of green, I believe… Although, perhaps, it was lighter but made darker by the dirt?" Mr Clement Suggitt mused aloud as he keenly studied Miss Dexter's drawing. It was within her sketchbook, propped up on the easel she usually reserved for George Dexter's oil paintings. Mr Suggitt had been describing his last recollection of Maryanna's clothing to Georgina for almost an hour. Yet the young artist had been the embodiment of kindness and patience, being silent when he'd procrastinated and giving gentle encouragement when he'd expressed frustration.

"I can sketch it again for you, Mr Suggitt, but with a dirty dress so you may compare the colouring?"

"No…" He leant back in the chair borrowed from the kitchen. The two sat adjacent to one another, but at an angle to the easel, with sufficiently respectable space between. No other furniture occupied the barren parlour on the ground floor of the Bow Street Society's headquarters. Thus, both of their voices, and the fire in the hearth, sounded much louder than they were.

"…I don't think it will be necessary." He clasped his knees as he straightened. With confident resolution, he continued, "Without seeing the items in the flesh, so to speak, I think your depiction is as close a one as we shall get to what I remember."

"Thank you, Mr Suggitt." Miss Dexter picked up the sketchbook and offered it to him. "Would you like to take a closer look?" He duly accepted but nodded upon absorbing the full detail of the image; a pair of black-leather ankle boots which were scuffed, faded, and caked in mud and a forest-green dress whose skirt, ripped and tied in many a place, hung loosely like an apron around the shins. The features of its top half were made mysterious by the fact a dark-brown, tweed jacket, which had only one of its four buttons intact, covered it. The sleeves of this jacket ended midway down the forearms and the stitching on its left shoulder had been ripped open on the front, thus revealing its dirty, yellow, cotton lining. The button, located in the centre of the jacket, had been fastened and a forest-green, ragged, woollen scarf lain over the top. This scarf was threaded through itself via a loop created by it being folded in half and wrapped around the neck. Over the jacket, but resting in the crook of the elbows, was a dark-green, almost black, shawl with yellow flowers dotted here and there within its crocheted structure. Finally the hat was made of worn, dirty straw adorned with even dirtier, white-cotton posies. The front edge of its brim had folded upwards into a point from innumerate tugging down of the hat's sides to shield one's ears. Georgina felt a mixture of hope and sadness at this; hope they could find Mrs Roberts' murderer and sadness that she was now looking at the very last thing the poor woman had worn. What Maryanna had *always* worn, at least according to Mr Suggitt. "Begging your pardon, sir," she began in the midst of another silent spell between them. "But do you know why anyone would want to steal Mrs Roberts' clothes?"

"I'm afraid I don't," Clement answered without hesitation. He passed the sketchbook back and Georgina rested it upon her lap. "They certainly weren't valuable—at least not in a monetary sense."

"The shawl was a gift from your wife," Miss Dexter recalled aloud, her voice soothing in its unobtrusiveness. It had certainly succeeded in putting Mr Suggitt at ease when they'd commenced the session.

With a wistfully nostalgic smile, the man nodded, "Yes, she crocheted it herself last spring. I'd offered to pay for one to be made, and to even purchase something similar from the store, but Mrs Suggitt wouldn't hear of it. She told me she wanted to be sure her sister would be warm enough during the coming winter. She used the thickest wool she could find. It wasn't as expertly finished as it might have been, had a seamstress created it, which was probably for the best in hindsight."

"It sounds beautiful," Miss Dexter complimented, inclining her head to again look upon the sketch.

"Charming, yes, but not beautiful." He had mimicked Georgina in the inclination of his head but, unlike her, his expression was now one of cynicism rather than admiration. When he continued, he spoke distantly, "If it had been, it would've been sold to procure monies for gin."

Miss Dexter hummed before recalling another question she wished to ask, "May I enquire what colour Mrs Roberts' hair was?"

"Yes… a mousey brown, I believe. Long, possibly to her shoulders." Pulling forth his pocket watch from his waistcoat, as freely as if he were awaiting the arrival of a train, he popped its lid open with his fingernail. "And now I must take my leave, Miss Dexter," he announced, rising to his feet. "The doctor gave my wife a sedative this afternoon and I want to be there when she wakes."

"I understand," Miss Dexter returned, also standing. Having closed her sketchbook, she rested it on the easel. "I will inform you at once if the clothes are found, sir."

"Thank you." He snapped his watch shut and, depositing it back into its usual place, pulled his tan coat closer about him. "Miss Dexter, my wife and I greatly appreciate all you and the Bow Street Society have done for us, and Mrs Roberts, in this matter. However, after some consideration, I feel it best we all take a step back and allow the police to do their work without being hindered by our meddling." Miss Dexter must've looked surprised by this statement as he added, "You've done nothing of the kind—far from it. The truth is though my wife shouldn't have hired your group in the first place. I had told her over the telephone I had everything in hand; there was no need for her to come here—" He stopped himself as he realised he was babbling. "She was upset and shocked, as we all are, and she wasn't in her right mind. Please, by all means, attempt to locate my sister-in-law's missing clothes—if only to put my wife's mind at ease on the point. As for the murder though, I think it would be better all-round if we forget about trying to solve it ourselves." He moved toward the door but the artist remained where she was, albeit turning on the spot to continue facing him. Just before he was about to leave though, he turned back around and added, "If you could pass the news of our decision on to Miss Trent and your associates, I'd be most grateful. Good day, Miss Dexter, and thank you."

"Good day, Mr Suggitt," Georgina replied, watching him leave. She waited until she heard the click of the front door before lifting her skirts with both hands and hurrying to find Miss Trent.

EIGHT

Lady Owston touched Miss Webster's wrist. "Thank you, dear," she said, looking up at her. The steaming cup of tea she'd poured was most welcome after their cab ride in the wind and rain.

Agnes' muttered "You're welcome" was accompanied by a meagre twitching of her mouth. Anyone else would've considered her rude, Lady Owston was habituated to her small quirks. After all, she'd practically raised the child since the tragic loss of her parents all those years ago. Thus, she'd felt grateful for the repaid affection, as slender as it was, and permitted her ward to step away unchallenged.

When Agnes reached for the pot, she noticed an additional cup to her own. Perplexed, she glanced about the table and saw all present were not lacking in tea. All being Miss Rebecca Trent, Mr Samuel Snyder, and Miss Georgina Dexter. The last being the one who had filled their cups while Agnes had been otherwise occupied with Lady Owston's, a duty borne from a desire to please than a sense of obligation.

"If you would be so kind, Miss Webster?" Mr Locke most politely requested from behind her. If she had been startled by him, she didn't show it as she lifted the teapot from the table and turned toward him.

"I would; if you would be so kind as to apologise, Mr Locke. You shouldn't creep up on a woman." The ghost of affection she'd shown to Lady Owston had been exorcised, supplanted by a cold monotone and emotionless expression.

The illusionist bowed his head slightly while leaning upon his cane, "My sincerest apologies, Miss Webster. I shan't loiter around your person again."

"Apology accepted," Agnes retorted with a terse nod. Bringing both teacups closer to the table's edge, she filled them and added the cream and sugar to each of their tastes.

"Will you not ask me how I was able to enter undetected when the door was so clearly locked?" Mr Locke enquired upon taking his teacup and saucer from the secretary.

Miss Webster merely picked her own up, took a sip, and replied, "No."

"We already read of your exploits in the *Gazette's* coverage of the Dorsey case," Lady Owston interjected while Agnes turned from the illusionist and, in silence, took her place beside her at the table. "I'm curious; is the breaking of locks a skill you learnt for your performances?"

"Call it a hobby of mine," Mr Locke replied noncommittedly. Taking his drink to the vacant chair to the right of Miss Trent, who sat on the end closest to the hallway door, he remarked. "It was worryingly simple. I had assumed you would have had the lock switched for a far superior one following my recommendation regarding the back door's security." He lifted the cup to his lips and added, "But clearly not."

"Perhaps you would care to pay for it?" Rebecca enquired plainly.

Mr Locke placed his drink upon the table, replying, "If it is what it shall take to have it replaced—"

"It is," the clerk interrupted.

The illusionist smiled, "If you would permit me to finish, I was about to say I would be more than happy to put forth the capital."

"I'll expect a cheque in the evening post tomorrow," Miss Trent retorted absolutely. Before Mr Locke could respond though, she went on, "Thank you all for coming this evening. Let's get started, shall we?" Mr Locke held his smile but spoke no further, instead choosing to light one of his fine quality cigarettes. Miss Webster averted her gaze the moment she saw the matchbox in hand, however.

Though gas lamps had been lit inside, outside was an abyss of darkness displayed against a soundtrack of heavy rain. Thus, all one could see in the back door's window was one's own reflection, distorted by the trails of water droplets hurtling down the glass. When the clerk had intimated the commencement of the meeting, all attention was focused upon her. They no longer noticed the dark, the rain, or even the sodden, pale face pressed against the glass as if it were the fourth ghost from Dickens' *A Christmas Carol.* In fact, the first the group knew of its presence was when an almighty bang erupted from the door, shaking it within its hinges. Miss Dexter gasped in fright and pressed her hand to her mouth. Miss Webster's shoulders tensed. Lady Owston almost choked on the tea she'd been swallowing, Mr Locke dropped the hand holding his cigarette to the table, and Miss Trent utterly lost her train of thought. Regardless of their initial reactions, however, everyone turned toward the source of the bang.

Another bang quickly succeeded the first as the ghastly visage yelled, "One of ya wanna let me in?!"

Miss Dexter and Miss Webster were the closest but neither moved. The artist held her chest to calm her racing heart while the secretary wasn't willing to admit a man she didn't recognise. Mr Snyder *had* recognised the 'ghost,' however. Rising from his seat, without a word, he moved around the table and quickly saw to the unlocking of the back door. No sooner had he pulled it ajar though did Weeks attempt to throw all his weight against it. Yet the well-built cabman wasn't so easily shifted.

"*Shit!*" the Canadian yelled as a sharp pain shot down his arm from his shoulder.

He gripped it with his other hand and half-stumbled into the kitchen. "Should've waited," Mr Snyder remarked after shutting the door. Doctor Weeks, who had been hissing and rubbing his sore limb, stopped long enough to give him the kind of look an alcoholic would bestow on a pub landlord who'd called time. The cabman, unintimidated, simply added, "Sit down by the stove and ge' a warm, Doctor."

"I'll give ya somethin' warm alrigh'; righ' where the Goddamned sun don't sh—"

"*Sit* down, Doctor Weeks," Miss Trent said over him. Having stood, she had the flats of her hands resting on the table. Lady Owston, Miss Webster, and Miss Dexter all looked from her to the Canadian and back again. Mr Locke, amused, had continued to smoke. Weeks, still holding his arm, seemed to consider having a confrontation but only for a heartbeat. Instead, he chose to stride over to the vacant chair beside Miss Webster's and unceremoniously tossed his bag onto the table with a tremendous thud and shaking of teacups.

"Do you *want* every constable at Bow Street station to hear you?" Miss Trent demanded in response to this childish behaviour.

"That's the las' thing I want and y'know it," Weeks countered and plonked down onto the chair. Scraping it back, he put his wet, booted feet onto the table in front of him and retrieved a packet of cigarettes from his pocket. The sight of the crumpled, mushy mess solicited a curse from the Canadian and it was discarded upon the floor. Mr Locke rose and offered a cigarette from his case, which Weeks gladly accepted. Putting the cigarette into the corner of his mouth, he ignited it with a match—about the only dry thing on his person—and filled his lungs. He rested the crown of his head atop the chair's back and, as he exhaled smoke in a long, upward stream, gave a deep, guttural groan of satisfaction. "Not as good as sex but sure damn close," he remarked, removing the cigarette momentarily to admire it.

"In case you were wondering, Doctor," Miss Trent began with a measure of sarcasm. "This is Lady Katheryne Owston, an independent journalist who writes often for the *Truth* and *Women's Signal* publications, and her secretary, Miss Agnes Webster."

Weeks lifted his head and looked to the two as if seeing them for the first time. "Evenin', ladies," he said with a smile, the cigarette bobbing up and down in the corner of his mouth as he spoke. He thought he recognised the older one from earlier but he couldn't be sure; it had been chaos on Oxford Street. Realising something, he glanced around, "Where's the fool from the *Gazette*?"

"He's not—" Miss Trent started, only to be interrupted by polite knocking upon the window. Seeing the face of the very man in question pathetically gazing back at them, she sighed, "Here." She gestured toward him with one hand as her other plucked the pocket watch from the table. "Let him in, Mr Snyder."

The door was unlocked for a second time. Mr Maxwell was courteous though in his waiting for it to be fully opened before entering. Like the Canadian previously, he too was drenched from head to foot and coat to skin. His courtesy continued to prevail, however, as he smiled politely at the gathering. Quickly noticing the table was practically full, his smile faded. "You're not holding a meeting, are you?"

"Nah, we jus' thought we'd take turns starin' at each other," Weeks snapped, pulling a silver hip flask from his coat pocket and taking a sharp shot of whiskey.

"Oh," Mr Maxwell replied, somewhat confused. "Why?"

"Mr Maxwell," Miss Trent suddenly addressed him. "This *is* a meeting and *you* are interrupting. *Why* are you here?"

"To see Miss Dexter; she told you earlier she was coming back in time for an appointment with Mr Suggitt," Joseph replied in utter honesty.

Yet Rebecca's glare continued as she waited for a further, more adequate explanation.

Resting his hand upon his chest, Mr Maxwell nervously cleared his throat and continued, "But I saw Doctor Weeks walking down the alleyway and my curiosity got the better of me."

"Jus' like it got the better of ya on Oxford Street?" Weeks challenged, referring to the shouting incident.

"Yes, I mean, no…" Joseph's fingers slid downward to grip the lapel of his frock coat as he felt his heart beat a little faster under the Canadian's scrutiny. "I wasn't there as a Bow Street Society member but as a journalist. You see, my editor, Mr Morse, wanted someone to cover the story and—"

"That damned stunt of yer's could've cost me my job," Weeks growled, pointing at him. "I don't give a shit what yer reasons were." He tossed back another shot of whiskey, it being the only thing to alleviate his anger.

"Didn't you see him following you, Doctor Weeks?" Miss Webster enquired, now speaking of Mr Maxwell's evening exploits.

Yet it was Joseph himself who hastened to explain, "He walks faster than me. By the time I came to the gate, he was already inside, so I followed."

"*Enough,*" Miss Trent ordered resolutely with a loud snap of her pocket watch's casing. "Mr Maxwell, you have no right to be here because you were not assigned to this case. However, since you *are* here and I don't want to waste any more time or effort expelling you, sit down, be quiet, and listen." She retook her seat and made a note of her decision. She added, "Consider yourself assigned." Mr Maxwell beamed with delight at this news. Yet the glare she cast toward him made his blood run cold. "Doctor Weeks," she began, using the intervening moment to regain her composure. "Please give us your findings."

"Whatever ya say, Miss Trent," Weeks replied, putting his flask onto the table beside his legs. With the cigarette still in his mouth, he took a folder from his bag, opened it, and rested it on his thighs. Mr Maxwell meanwhile had wasted no time in retreating to the vacant chair opposite Miss Trent. When he'd done so, Miss Dexter had gently enquired if he'd like some tea, to which he replied in the positive while still trying to maintain a whisper. Miss Webster had opened her own notebook and readied her pencil to record the doctor's findings. Lady Owston on the other hand, who had never heard such a report before, braced herself for the grisly details by gripping the arms of her chair. Mr Locke, who had finished his cigarette some time previously, watched and waited alongside Mr Snyder, the cabman having returned to his seat after ensuring the back door was once again secured. Taking the cigarette from his mouth, Weeks exhaled the additional smoke and rested the heel of his hand on the table's edge. He began, "Meat were sittin' on the ground in the doorway of the *London Crystal Palace Bazaar—*"

"Pardon me," Lady Owston interrupted, the uncertainty in her voice most uncharacteristic. "But… 'meat'?"

"Yeah, the 'meat.'" He flicked the ash from his cigarette into a tray on the table. "Maryanna Roberts."

"Oh, good gracious!" Lady Owston gasped, seriously taken aback by the terminology used to describe another human being.

"He always calls it that," Joseph tried to discreetly inform her. His voice wasn't quite quiet enough, however, for the Canadian scowled at *him* as he continued.

"*Like* I were sayin'; she were sittin' on the ground." He paused to find his place in the report. "She had her back to the door and her head down. She were naked, and her scalp and breasts were missin'."

"Do you think she could be another Jack the Ripper victim?" Mr Maxwell nervously ventured, feeling a pit in his stomach as he suggested it.

Lady Owston, still reeling from the above, gave another shocked gasp and admitted, "The idea had never even *occurred* to me!" She was acutely appalled and horror struck as she begged, "*Please,* Doctor Weeks, say it isn't so."

"It ain't so," he replied without hesitation.

"Oh *thank* God!" Katheryne cried as she fell back against her chair. "Agnes, my smelling salts, please." She feebly fanned herself until she felt the bottle in her hand. At which point she stuck its open neck under her nose and tried to breathe in as naturally as she could. Though they were already taking effect mere seconds later, Agnes knew her guardian wouldn't be fully recovered for several moments yet. She therefore forewent her notes for the time being and instead gently rubbed Lady Owston's arm to comfort her.

Weeks, who had waited, continued, "I checked the body 'gainst the Ripper files myself; he left the clothes with his victims, killed 'em in Whitechapel, and done his last murder eight years ago. Mrs Roberts ain't one of his."

Lady Owston swallowed hard as she pressed the back of her hand against her cheek. "Thank you, Doctor Weeks," she replied, after pausing a moment, and gave the salts back to her secretary. "For being so diligent."

"Are you quite well, Lady Owston?" Miss Dexter enquired, concerned.

"Yes, child," Katheryne attempted to reassure though her voice remained a little unsteady. "Please continue, Doctor Weeks. You too, Agnes; back to your note-taking."

"Breasts and scalp were cut from the body with a blade blunter than a surgeon's or butcher's," Weeks coolly went on. Lady Owston, though clearly disturbed by what she was hearing, remained strong. "The wounds had jagged edges and there weren't s'much blood 'round 'em as I'd expect to find if the heart had still been beatin' when they were cut. So, I reckon they were cut off after she died. No blood on the ground under or 'round the meat in the doorway. Also found hessian fibres in her hair." He took a deep pull from his cigarette, "What it gets us is this: she were killed someplace else, put in a sack, and dumped at the bazaar."

"She was put into a *sack* to be moved?" Miss Webster enquired, breaking the rhythm of her rapid note taking.

"That's what I said, weren't it?" Weeks countered.

"I only ask, *Doctor,* because I'd imagine such a feat would be quite difficult. I run the household accounts for Lady Owston and therefore arrange the purchase and delivery of sacks of potatoes every month. I couldn't imagine trying to get a body into one of those."

"D'pends on 'ow many bushels' worth you ge'," Mr Snyder interjected, thoughtfully, while he rubbed his cheek and chin. Since the cabman had been rather quiet, his speaking now was quite the surprise to most. "I've seen several bushels worth being loaded up with coal from ships at the docks. Farmers hire the big sacks from the sack hiring companies, too. They've got depots at places like railway stations and coal merchants."

Miss Webster hummed as she considered this. "Yes, you are right, Mr Snyder. We only tend to get the smaller amounts as there are so few of us in the house." She looked around at the others. "So, the sack could've come from any number of places, including from the kitchen of anyone who knew her."

"We've gotta ask Mr Queshire, the Suggitts, Mr Roberts, and Miss Roberts if they can ge' those sacks," Mr Snyder stated.

"If it *was* one of them who murdered her," Mr Maxwell commented dejectedly.

"Clearly, whoever murdered Mrs Roberts couldn't afford to leave her body where the deed had been done," Miss Webster mused aloud. "Possibly due to it being likely it would be discovered."

"It was discovered on Oxford Street, however," Mr Locke pointed out. "In plain sight of anyone walking past."

"Precisely," Miss Webster agreed. "*Anyone* could've walked past or even placed her there. Not *someone* who could be linked to the crime by where her poor body was found."

"Maybe the murderer was so sickened by his, or her, own act." Lady Owston paused to take a large swallow of tea. "He, or she, wanted her to be found for his, or her, own feelings of shame to be alleviated?"

"I would have cause to doubt such a notion," Mr Locke admitted. "In addition to leaving the body where it could be found, a feeling of shame would also encourage smaller, more subtle, acts to further assist with the easing of the murderer's guilt. For example, ensuring Mrs Roberts' body was covered to protect her modesty. Yet Mrs Roberts' body was devoid of clothing, correct?"

He looked to Doctor Weeks for confirmation, which he received in the form of a curt, "Yeah."

"Which suggests to me not only a measure of arrogance in our murderer but also a desire to humiliate our victim; he wanted to expose her to the world by presenting her in the most vulnerable state possible."

Lady Owston, who reached to pour another cup of tea, replied, "Foulness, utter, utter foulness."

"D'ya mind if I fuckin' continue?" Doctor Weeks growled, and resumed. "Rigor Mortis starts takin' hold after 'bout thirty minutes or so but can take several hours to finish doin' its shit to the point where a body can't be manipulated. It had to have been put in the sack before it happened. There were some bruisin' on her face, chest, and arms but not enough to say it were done before she were killed. Small scratches on her skin—forearms and thighs—which ain't what I'd call defensive. I reckon the sonofabitch beat her after she died and tore her clothes off. They're missin'. All of that would've taken a good slice of time. I reckon the bastard that done this didn't know the body would stiffen up like a penis in a whorehouse so ya'll ain't lookin' for a medical man.

"There were traces of semen in her mouth, on her lips, in her throat, colon, vagina, and stomach." He scratched his cheek. "Not to put too finer point on it, ladies and gentlemen." He calmly removed the cigarette and steadily exhaled the smoke. "But I've stroked the snake inside enough ladies' mouths to know what trace it leaves on their lips." Lady Owston made a small, disgusted noise and visibly shuddered. Yet Weeks simply went on, "Our lady were covered in it. She fucked a lot of men before she died and didn't give a shit about disease." The shaft of ash, dangling precariously on the cigarette's end, was discarded into an ashtray with one tap of his finger.

"When I cut open her belly, her stomach were inflamed, makin' me think of some kinda poison bein' what killed her. There were the smell of gin but, on testin' some of the juices, found only a small amount. There were no food but there were coffee—'bout half a pint's worth." He paused to crush out his cigarette in the ashtray. "'Cause of the gin, I checked her liver; were showin' disease but not enough to kill her and, 'sides, her skin weren't yellow as yer'd expect to find with liver failure. So I went back to my theory on the poisonin'. Dunno if yer've seen cases of long term poisonin's in the 'papers but it's fuckin' hard to prove poison in the hands as a murder weapon. Now, I'm talkin' *arsenic,* ladies and gentlemen. I tested s'much as the coffee in her belly as I could usin' somethin' called the Marsh test. Got some traces of arsenic at the end of it and even the smell of garlic."

"Garlic?" Mr Maxwell enquired, confused.

"S'what arsenic smells like when ya heat it, and there were enough to kill her after I weighed it—'bout three teaspoons worth. Ya'll remember I told ya'll 'bout the semen in her throat? There were some vomit, too; there and in her gullet. I tested some of the vomit usin' the Marsh test; were arsenic in it. I tested her stomach tissue, skin tissue, and muscle tissue; no arsenic. So that tells us she weren't poisoned by someone over a long period. I reckon the arsenic were what the murderer had to hand but it weren't a murder done when havin' the mother of all fuckin' arguments as folks've knives and shit for them times. Nah, the murderer were actin' on a thought put in his head shortly b'fore he killed her but he chose to do it with arsenic and watch her die. The vomit were her initial reaction after swallowin' the poison. arsenic, in a big-ass dose like that, can start workin' in as little as one minute. Sonofabitch could've held her down or locked her in to stop her gettin' help to make sure she died."

"You said proving arsenic as a murder weapon is very difficult, however," Miss Webster reminded him. "Yet it sounds to me as though you have done an excellent job at proving it."

"Thanks for your vote of confidence, Miss Webster, but this is jus' a theory of mine based on what I know. But even that has been called bullshit by others in the past."

"How so?" Miss Dexter interjected, her tone one of surprise as she assumed the Canadian was referring to his own work. Yet, as Weeks continued, it became plain he was speaking of the toxicology field as a whole.

"Arsenic is one of the most commonly used metals; it's used in farmin', wallpapers—Hell, it's even fuckin' used to make the apparatus the Marsh test relies on. That and the sulphuric acid and zinc ya gotta use could have arsenic in 'em if ya don't make sure they're free of impurities first. Then yer've got 'normal arsenic' to think 'bout."

When he saw the obviously confused expressions around the table, he sighed. Pressing his fingertip against his report, he explained, "We've all got arsenic in us; least that's what a fella called Orfila found out— 'im and his associate, Jean-Pierre Couerbe. Orfila were also the one who gave folks suggestions 'bout gettin' rid of impurities in the Zinc and Sulphuric Acid in the Marsh test. Couerbe had been testin' dead folks who they reckoned hadn't been poisoned with arsenic— rotten dead folks. He found arsenic so took it to Orfila. They worked on it together." Weeks took in a deep breath. "Cuttin' a damned long story short, Orfila's work showed how 'normal arsenic' ain't soluble in boilin' water whereas yer poisoner's arsenic is." The Canadian paused to have a fourth shot of whiskey. "So, I done a Reinsch test on the coffee from her stomach; it showed arsenic, too. Only thing with that is ya gotta make sure the copper ya use is pure 'cause that, too, can fuck up yer findings. Like I said, damned hard provin' arsenic as a murder weapon in the hands of a poisoner."

"Yet you believe Mrs Roberts *was* killed by the arsenic?" Miss Webster enquired, curiously.

Doctor Weeks nodded. "Yeah; I know I made my tests as damned near accurate as I could fuckin' get 'em and I know in my gut that Mrs Roberts were killed by it. Ya'll and Woolfe are gonna need more than that if this shit gets to court though."

"Yes, well, we will deal with it when—or if—it comes to it," Miss Trent stated, making notes of her own.

"Do you know when Mrs Roberts was murdered?" Mr Maxwell enquired, addressing the Canadian.

"Wondered when ya'll were gonna bring that up," Weeks glanced over his report. "I reckon it were sometime between midnight and four o'clock this mornin'."

"You can't be any more precise?" Miss Webster enquired.

Weeks shook his head, "Nah, I can't. And that's jus' an informed guess as it is. Take it or leave it."

"And she was discovered at six o'clock this morning, correct?" the secretary enquired while recording the Canadian's previous answer.

Weeks glanced at his report, "Yeah, by Police Constable Fraser, but how the fuck did ya know that?"

"Inspector Woolfe himself told us this morning," Lady Owston clarified.

Mr Locke's brow lofted and he enquired, "If the latest she was murdered was four o'clock, why was she not discovered until two hours later?"

"Maybe it was too dark to see?" Mr Maxwell suggested.

The illusionist shook his head, "As I have told you previously, patrols are conducted at least ten minutes apart. If Mrs Roberts' body was in the doorway prior to six o'clock, she would have been found. Ergo, her body wasn't placed until at least ten minutes prior to Constable Fraser passing. In which case, it would be necessary for our murderer to have had somewhere secure to store the body, furthermore a reasonable knowledge of the area." Since Joseph merely hummed, contemplating the scenario, Mr Locke once again addressed

Weeks. He enquired, "How did you reach the conclusion it was the coffee and not the gin which was poisoned?"

"Cause the coffee weren't digested and I found it in the vomit in her throat and mouth—along with the damned arsenic. 'Sides, a murderer ain't gonna give the lush a poisoned bottle of gin and, as she lay fuckin' dyin', pour coffee down her throat."

"A 'lush'?" Lady Owston interjected.

"Short for Lushington," Mr Snyder replied, smiling softly. "Someone addicted to the drink."

"It's what's called a 'slang' term," Joseph further clarified triumphantly.

"Yes, I'm quite familiar with the notion of 'slang,' Mr Maxwell," Lady Owston retorted. "It is a vulgar butchering of the English language." She turned her attention back to the illusionist, "Mrs Suggitt informed us her sister was a fallen woman and her drinking was to blame. I would therefore be inclined to agree with Doctor Weeks; coffee isn't the usual beverage of choice for someone who wishes to become inebriated. The fact she drank it at all also leads me to suspect she was offered it by someone she both knew and trusted. I know *I* wouldn't accept a drink from a complete stranger."

"Took a lot of comparin' but I got it down to the French Breakfast kinda coffee, too," Weeks added, choosing to take the last swig from his flask.

"We need to find out who close to Maryanna had this coffee, as well as access to arsenic and hessian sacks," Lady Owston pondered aloud.

"If they're guilty though, they're not going to admit to owning arsenic, are they?" Maxwell enquired, frowning.

Weeks, having put his now empty flask back in his pocket, said. "Ya'll gotta check the poison books of pharmaceutical chemists 'round where them folks live to get that kinda information. Since the Pharmacy and Sales of Poisons Act of 1869, no one can sell the stuff without bein' one of those. People can't buy it if they ain't known to the chemist either, and they gotta give their name and address. If the chemist knows yer murderer they'd sell the arsenic to 'em—or if they knew someone who introduced 'em to the chemist. So, yeah, chemists 'round where they all live is a fuckin' good place to start."

"I can do it," Mr Maxwell volunteered with a lifting of his hand. "And maybe Miss Dexter would like to…?"

"Miss Dexter would be better suited to speaking with Mrs Roberts' daughter," Miss Trent recommended. "Miss Webster, given your experience with ledgers, you shall accompany Mr Maxwell." The secretary nodded her assent while a small glance of apology was cast Joseph's way by the meek artist. Miss Trent, having made a note of the arrangements, enquired, "Was there anything else, Doctor Weeks?"

"Yeah; this." He tossed a photograph onto the table. The others rose from their respective seats slightly to take a closer look at it. It was of Maryanna Roberts, very much alive, sitting against a plain background with her hands against her chest. Her fingers were spread wide as her hands framed a rectangular piece of slate hanging from string about her neck. Written on the slate, in white chalk, were numbers and the date. Maryanna's hair was intact in the photograph, but the fact it was in varying shades of brown made its colour hard to distinguish. It was clearly shoulder length, however. The glazed look in her eyes, and pronounced leaning of her body to the right, suggested she was drunk at the time the photograph was taken. Indeed two hands, one gripping each shoulder, appeared to be keeping her upright. The owners of these hands were out of shot but Mr Locke knew who they would be.

"Her photograph from the Convict Supervision Office," he remarked, leaning back in his chair and lifting his teacup for another sip.

"May I capture it with my camera, Doctor?" Georgina requested meekly.

The Canadian shrugged his shoulders. "Do what the hell ya like, s'long as I get it back."

Miss Dexter offered an appreciative smile and a softly spoken thank you. She next retrieved her camera and took several shots.

Lady Owston meanwhile, though pleased to have an image of a breathing Maryanna Roberts to hold in her mind, couldn't help but feel the harsh reality of what had befallen the poor woman. "I presume Mr Suggitt's identification of the body was correct? This photograph is of the same woman found in Oxford Street?"

"Yeah; Inspector Woolfe asked me to check. He also said she'd been arrested for prostitution when I told 'im about the semen in her different holes." Suddenly pulling his feet off the table, he snatched the photograph and stuffed both it and his

103

report back into his bag. "Yer've seen enough." He tossed the bag under the table and put his feet on it.

"The fact she had a criminal record as a prostitute certainly gives credence to Mr Holden's account," Mr Locke revealed nonchalantly. He'd be lying if he said he wasn't thrilled when everyone looked to him with synchronised inquisitiveness.

"You speak of the incident at the department store?" Lady Owston hazarded a guess first.

"Though it *is* a consequence of her behaviour then, it isn't the incident to which I refer." Percy paused, simply for dramatic effect. "Following a respectable night at the *Theatre Royal,* Drury Lane, the Holdens returned home. After waiting for his wife to retire to bed, however, Mr Bartholomew Holden departed again, this time to seek out Mrs Roberts."

"Did he find her?" Mr Maxwell enquired, undoubtedly, on everyone's mind.

"He did. He told me his intention was not to harm her but to remind her of her place. He admitted to me he paid for 'services rendered' following their discussion, but he had only given her half of his usual amount. In parts, he said, to her being intoxicated and to his wish for her understanding behaviour, such as she had displayed at the store, could not be repeated should she ever meet him in public again. He said he found her at around ten forty-five and they parted company a short time after." He paused, but to consider how he should verbalise his inner thought. "The way he put it, Doctor Weeks, is the 'services' were 'rendered' in a 'verbal' sense." He cleared his throat, "Ergo it would explain why you found that particular substance not only in her throat and mouth but also in her stomach." Weeks merely grunted, however. "Mr Holden could not present his wife as a witness to the time he returned home for she was asleep when he slipped into bed and he did not dare wake her. Personally, I have severe doubts of Mr Holden's guilt. If nothing else, he was saddened to hear of her demise; his marriage is, by his own account, one of convenience and loneliness."

"We were given much the same story by Mrs Holden," Lady Owston stated. "Aside from the account of her husband visiting Mrs Roberts for…" She smiled politely, "you-know-what."

"Maybe they concocted the whole story to prevent the truth from being exposed?" Mr Maxwell put forth not only to Katheryne but the others as well.

Yet it was she who responded without hesitation, "No; *too* improbable. Mrs Holden spoke so vilely of Mrs Roberts, I think murdering one so far down the social ladder would be positively beneath her in her mind. She even told us as much." Katheryne lifted her hand slightly, "No, I have to concur with you, Mr Locke. Neither Mr nor Mrs Holden were responsible for Mrs Roberts' murder."

"So, we're ruling them out as suspects?" Mr Maxwell queried, looking at the independent journalist and illusionist in turn.

They answered with a simultaneous, "Yes."

Very well," Miss Trent agreed. "Unless we come by new evidence which makes us question our stance, we should all consider the Holdens as irrelevant. Miss Dexter, will you show everyone the sketch of Mrs Roberts' missing clothes you did under Mr Suggitt's direction?"

The artist, who had retreated to her chair to avoid the Canadian's wrath, softly cleared her throat and reached behind her to take the sketchbook from the shelf. "Mr Suggitt had some difficulty resting on a final depiction," she explained as she opened the book and placed it in the table's centre for all to see. "After an hour of trying, and some gentle encouragement, he declared these to be Maryanna's missing clothes. He was also able to tell me her missing hair was mousey brown in colour."

She looked troubled for a couple of moments before adding, "Mr Suggitt doesn't want us to continue with our investigation." She held tightly clasped hands against her skirts. "He said his wife wasn't in her right mind when she hired the Society and he thought it best if we let the police do their duty. Inspector Woolfe told the Suggitts the same when he questioned them outside the bazaar. There was something else, too. When Mr Suggitt told the inspector they were both at home the night Mrs Roberts died, Mrs Suggitt was surprised." She frowned deeply, "Perhaps I am seeing things which weren't there." She lowered herself onto her chair, her head bowed.

"Go on, Miss Dexter," Mr Maxwell encouraged.

Georgina looked to him, offering him the weakest of smiles, but he didn't dare attempt to take her hand. Instead, he returned the smile, by way of reassurance, and she continued,

"By his behaviour, and his responses, I couldn't help but feel he was hiding something; what, I know not."

"Ya didn't ask 'im when ya were takin' the drawin'?" Weeks challenged.

Georgina's frown returned, "We spoke only of the clothes, Doctor."

Miss Webster meanwhile consulted her notes of the day's interviews. "Mr Queshire told Milady and me of Mr Suggitt's habit of distancing himself from Mrs Roberts. Furthermore, this was the reason why he'd not been requested to intervene when she'd behaved so deplorably with the Holdens. Given what we now know about Mrs Roberts 'other' activity, isn't it possible Mr Suggitt was also paying her for sex?" Mr Maxwell dropped his teacup at this, spilling its contents all over the table. He at once shot to his feet and, taking a handkerchief from his pocket, made a feeble attempt to mop it up. "Well? Isn't it?" Miss Webster pressed; her voice a perfect monotone despite her frankness.

"Sure it is, darlin'," Doctor Weeks replied, grinning.

"We shall speak with the Suggitts again tomorrow," Lady Owston stated after she'd briefly directed a look of disappointment at her secretary. "Once Inspector Woolfe has finished his interrogations in the morning and Mrs Roberts' daughter and estranged husband have been spoken to." She passed her own handkerchief to Mr Maxwell to assist him with the mopping up. "It's equally possible Mr Suggitt distanced himself from his sister-in-law due to her drinking so we shouldn't leap to any conclusions."

"Yes, Milady," Miss Webster replied, turning the pages of her notebook back to where she'd been recording the meeting.

"*Now,* back to your absolutely *fantastic* sketch, Miss Dexter," Katheryne complimented. The young artist felt her cheeks grow hot.

"Thank you, Lady Owston."

"Credit where credit is due, child," Katheryne reassured. However, upon giving the sketch her full attention, she felt the flicker of familiarity in her mind. "I do believe I've seen this garment before." She tapped the portion of the sketch depicting the shawl. "*Yes, I have!* Agnes, do you recall? In the *Queshire Department Store*, on the dummy in the haberdashery department?"

"I do, Lady Owston." The secretary flipped back in her notebook yet paused as she too recalled something. "It can't be the same garment, however. Don't you recollect, as we were leaving, one of the assistants explained to a customer none of the items in the store were second-hand?"

"*Pish-posh!*" Lady Owston retorted. "I can assure everyone here the *Queshire Department Store* does sell second-hand goods for *I* have, in the past, purchased garments displaying minute signs of wear. Mr Queshire simply doesn't wish for the fact to be known due to the negative connotations associated with such garments." Katheryne took a sip from her tea. "While it *is* true garments which pass hands in the Rag Fair *are* of a questionable quality, those I've purchased from the *Queshire Department Store* would be acceptable to *anyone* who couldn't recognise the less obvious signs of it having been previously owned."

"What's the Rag Fair?" Mr Maxwell queried.

"A dark, dirty street that's got more in common with the Thames than a place to do business," Weeks piped up as he poured some coffee from a pot on the counter behind him.

"I'm surprised you've heard of it, Doctor," Lady Owston replied. "Very few in London—even those who have resided here for years—have."

"I had the misfortune of havin' to visit the hellhole once to look at some poor sonofabitch who'd been murdered there." Weeks took a swallow of the coffee. "Crouchin' in ankle-deep, muddy water ain't fun."

"Quite." Lady Owston smiled sympathetically. "Nonetheless you are mistaken." She looked to Joseph. "The Rag Fair is held in the vicinity of Houndsditch. It begins at the end of Cutler Street, leads out of Houndsditch, and proceeds about seventy or eighty feet in an eastward direction. It then embraces a narrow street called White's Alley, and extends about a hundred feet towards the north. There it takes an eastward turn and proceeds in a direct line to extend as far as Petticoat Lane, where it turns to the north and south. Probably the entire length of the area wherein the patrons of the Rag Fair may be found is nearly a quarter of a mile of the vicinity; while the width of the space the Fair itself occupies varies with the breadth of the streets and lanes on which it is held. The lane, of which you spoke, Doctor Weeks, is the largest, I believe."

"And people can buy second-hand clothes there?" Joseph enquired.

"Buy *and* sell, Mr Maxwell. It is frequently members of the Jewish population who do the buying, usually behind the closed doors of the sellers' residence." Lady Owston rested her hand upon the sketch. "But Mrs Roberts didn't sell her shawl in the Rag Fair, if this is indeed the same item. I'd have to inspect it in person to be certain."

"Mr Suggitt told me she couldn't have sold the shawl as it wasn't nice enough," Miss Dexter said in the hope of being helpful.

Miss Webster once more paused in her note taking to ponder the sketch. She mused, "A donation, perhaps?"

"One which would have had to have been made between Mr Suggitt's seeing her at the store and Mr Holden's rendezvous with her last night," Mr Locke pointed out. "For I asked Mr Holden if he could recall what Mrs Roberts had been wearing when he had last seen her; a shawl was never mentioned. Of course, it could merely be the weakness of memory preventing him from recalling such a garment yet he was able to tell me she was wearing a scarf, dress, and boots. If Mr Suggitt did indeed distance himself from her at the store, and her sister was nowhere to be seen, Mrs Roberts could have donated the shawl from some sense of spite."

"Or whoever killed her," Weeks stated, tilting his chair back and again putting his muddy feet on the table. Hands resting in his lap meanwhile cradled the steaming cup of coffee.

The young artist, perplexed, enquired, "But wouldn't Mr Suggitt have recognised it?"

"Another question only Mr Suggitt knows the answer to," Mr Maxwell said, frowning. Not only were his clothes soaking but his handkerchief and Lady Owston's, too. He'd abandoned trying to mop up the rest of the tea; it was a losing battle with so much liquid and so little absorptive material.

"I will pay another visit to the *Queshire Department Store,* take a closer look at the shawl, and speak again with Mr Queshire. He may be able to shed some light on the matter," Lady Owston suggested. "Such a *charming* man he is—and generous, too. He gave me a bar of soap he'd made only this morning and didn't charge."

As Katheryne rifled through her bag to find said toiletry, Miss Trent pointed out, "As charming as he may be, we must not remove him from our list of suspects without just cause; aside from her rendezvous with Mr Holden, the last place Mrs Roberts was seen alive was his store."

"I would beg to differ," Lady Owston replied while still searching. "But nevertheless, I shall *bow* to your experience, Miss Trent."

The corner of Rebecca's mouth twitched. Taking a moment, she then clarified, "So Mr Maxwell and Miss Webster will visit the chemists in and around Oxford Street, the Suggitts' address, and the Roberts' address. You, Lady Owston, will meanwhile speak with Mr Queshire." Those concerned nodded their agreement. "Miss Dexter, you will be speaking with Miss Regina Roberts. Mr Snyder." She looked to the cabman. "Given your working-class background, I think Mr Roberts would feel more at ease in your presence than anyone else at this table."

Sure," Sam replied, happy to help in whatever way he could.

"Meanwhile, I'll contact Mr and Mrs Suggitt and arrange for them to meet Lady Owston, Miss Webster, Mr Locke, and Mr Snyder tomorrow evening. Somewhere Inspector Woolfe wouldn't expect to find you all."

"If they are indeed hiding something, I think speaking to the two Suggitts separately would be an excellent tactic," Mr Locke remarked. "They may reveal information they are otherwise hiding from even one another."

"Ensure you all return to me with your findings following your investigations in the morning, however," Miss Trent gently reminded the group.

"*Here* it is!" Lady Owston cried happily, as she finally withdrew the bar of soap from her coat pocket. She held it in one hand as she rested the other on top. "He makes *all* of his own soap on site; his father would be proud."

"His father?" Mr Maxwell enquired, intrigued, thoughts of his own father lingering about the edges of his conscious mind. Which reminded him, he needed to purchase a new shirt in time for tomorrow evening's family dinner.

Lady Owston hummed, "His father owned the store—it was a simple haberdashery back then—prior to Mr Queshire. When Mr Queshire Senior was tragically killed by a horse and carriage, the business was passed to his son and heir. Mr Queshire Junior's hard work has made the department store into the success it is today."

"You seem to know a lot about it," Mr Locke observed.

"I've covered the *Queshire Department Store* and its many delights in several of my articles for the *Truth* publication—in addition to being a loyal customer of theirs." She smiled wistfully at the soap as if it were a precious gem. "It's truly a remarkable story. With so much tragedy in his life, one would think Mr Queshire would be bitter but one couldn't hope to meet a *nicer* man!"

"Who else died?" Mr Maxwell enquired, turning in his chair to face Lady Owston, and inadvertently leaning his elbow on the wet table in the process. Lifting it, he frowned but rested his hand on his lap instead.

"Well, there was his sister—she was only fifteen when she died. Then his father, as I've already explained, and, many years later, his poor mother. Oh! I *almost* forgot! While we were at the store, there was a *most* peculiar incident concerning the room at the top of the stairs." She pointed upward and continued, "One of the customers entered a room marked *Staff only.*" She dropped her hand and looked about the table. "I remarked upon it to Mr Queshire and one of his *many* assistants, Miss Rose Galway." Lady Owston breathed in sharply. "Oh *my,* she turned as *white* as a sheet, didn't she, Agnes?"

"She did."

"Mr Queshire investigated and reported to us a customer had simply become lost. Yet Miss Galway's reaction was *most* strange, wasn't it? Even when Agnes and I tried to encourage the reason for her fear from her she refused to reveal it. She practically fled the room. I think I may speak to Mr Queshire of her odd behaviour tomorrow." She paused. "Something about the way the customer entered the room, however…" She frowned. "…I may attempt to see for myself what is in there during my visit."

"Nothing illegal unless you have good reason, Lady Owston," Rebecca gently reminded her.

Lady Owston made a dismissive gesture with her hand and replied, "*Perish* the thought, Miss Trent!"

"Miss Galway also enquired about becoming a member," Miss Webster prompted.

"Of *course* she did," Lady Owston agreed, recalling the conversation, too.

"A member of what?" Miss Trent probed.

Both Katheryne and Agnes glanced at one another but it was Lady Owston who replied, "Why the Bow Street Society! Yes, Doctor Weeks, take a *sniff*!" she exclaimed as the Canadian had reached over and picked up the bar of soap to take a closer look. "Have you *ever* smelt anything *more* divine?"

Yet before Weeks could give his answer, someone started braying, violently, on the front door. Everyone turned to look toward the hallway. Mr Maxwell enquired of Miss Trent, rather foolishly, "Are we expecting anyone else?"

"Open up! This is the police!"

NINE

"*Shit!*" Doctor Weeks cursed through clenched teeth, having recognised Inspector Woolfe's voice. A sharp nod had accompanied the bitter exclamation, followed soon after by the dragging of his bag toward him by his feet. The deep squeak of his chair scraping against the stone floor came next. As soon as his knees had cleared the table, he lifted his bag, stood, tossed the soap back to Lady Owston, and fled the same way he'd arrived.

Miss Trent had risen to her feet but made no effort to prevent his departure. In the mere minute that had passed, the other ladies had remained seated. Mr Maxwell, however, had unintentionally mimicked the doctor in the abandoning of his own chair, but hadn't left. Instead, he stuck to the spot with the air of a startled rabbit about him. "Wh—what's he doing here?" he stuttered, resting his thumb and fingers on either side of his cravat.

Woolfe's voice boomed again, "*Open this door or I'll kick it down!*"

"I'll be right there!" Rebecca answered and left the kitchen. Joseph gripped his chair's backrest as he slowly sat, all the while staring at the hallway. Though Weeks had taken the autopsy report and photograph, Miss Dexter's intricate sketch remained. Noticing it was still in the table's centre, Georgina realised the inspector would recognise it for what it was. She reached across, plucked it up, and deposited it into her lap where it was turned face down. Just in time, too, for the kitchen door opened and Miss Trent returned with Woolfe.

"Inspector Woolfe of Scotland Yard," Rebecca introduced and moved to stand at the table's other end. "Inspector, this is Lady Katheryne Owston, her secretary, Miss Agnes Webster, Miss Georgina Dexter, Mr Samuel Snyder, Mr Joseph Maxwell, and Mr Percy Locke. You already know who I am so, with those formalities dealt with, what do you want?"

Recognising several of those present from earlier in the day, the policeman didn't hesitate in singling them out. Firstly, he locked his harsh scowl upon Lady Owston. "You've been questioning *my* witnesses." He next addressed Miss Dexter, "I *told* you to let me do my duty."

He strode toward Miss Trent, only to turn his back on her and stand behind Maxwell. His large hand squeezed Joseph's shoulder. "And *you*," Woolfe snarled. "First you tell me you've worked with Weeks and now I find you *here*?" Still gripping his shoulder, the inspector pulled him onto his feet and spun him around. When he stepped forward to pin the poor journalist against the table's edge, he completely blocked him from Miss Trent's view. The clerk, enraged, stepped around the inspector to half-place herself between them.

"Step away," she warned, fearlessly glaring at him. Caleb, briefly taken off guard, looked to her. His conviction quickly returned, however, and he sidestepped from Joseph to tower over Rebecca instead. "Don't think you can intimidate me, Inspector," she said, her defiance unwavering. Woolfe set his shoulders back, thereby making himself even taller. The air in the room was heavy as the others watched with a mixture of tense anticipation and quiet confidence in Miss Trent's abilities. Joseph hadn't moved, his gaze darting between the pair. Miss Trent went on, "Continue as you are and you shall get no cooperation from us."

"I'm not getting any as it is," Woolfe coldly pointed out. Miss Trent didn't respond, however. Instead, she folded her arms across her chest and, turning her head away slightly, lofted one brow in stern expectation. Though the immense policeman wasn't afraid of the clerk, he wasn't a fool either. If there was any chance of their doing as he demanded, he wasn't about to let his pride destroy it. Taking a half step back, he barked at Joseph, "Sit down."

Maxwell dropped down like a sack of potatoes.

"Whatever Mr Maxwell may have said to you has nothing to do with either this Society or its client, Inspector," Locke said while Rebecca stepped behind the policeman and rested her hands on her hips in disapproval.

"A client who, until now, has cooperated with the police on account of the advice I gave her," Lady Owston added, her nerves beginning to calm as the tension slowly faded.

Mr Locke nodded and, rising himself, approached Caleb to offer him a cigarette. As he did so, he said, "She may have a change of heart upon hearing of your treatment of Lady Owston's associate and friend."

"Are you trying to blackmail me, *magician*?" Woolfe growled and took a step toward Locke.

"Blackmail is a dirty trick played by crude criminals; I do not endorse either." The illusionist's open case still rested in his palm as he'd calmly spoken. Seeing they were finer than the cigarettes he was accustomed to, the inspector pulled one out and sniffed it. Finding it to his satisfaction, he put it between his lips and allowed the Bow Streeter to use his match. Mr Locke smiled and shut his case. Returning to his chair, he glanced back at Caleb and enquired, "How did you discover Lady Owston had spoken to a witness?"

"The witness told me," Woolfe replied, his anger fading. Miss Trent remained close to him, ensuring she was between him and Joseph at all times. The journalist, feeling somewhat on edge, remained silent.

Mr Locke meanwhile enquired, "And which witness was this?"

"I'm not telling you."

"Inspector, please." Locke smiled with mock frustration. "You cannot play judge, jury, and executioner without permitting us to put forth a case of defence. Furthermore, you have not fully enlightened us as to the charge."

"Attempting to pervert the course of justice for your own gains," Woolfe stated, beginning a stroll around the room simply to satisfy his curiosity. Reaching the hallway door, he caught sight of the sodden cigarette packet. Everyone followed Woolfe's line of vision; hoping he hadn't recognised the brand. The inspector picked it up and turned it over. A heavy atmosphere once again descended.

"Her Majesty's British Empire does not restrict the exchange of conversation," Mr Locke continued but paused when Woolfe discarded the packet onto the table without remark. "Shall you pay a visit to all of London's citizens? For the brutal murder of Mrs Maryanna Roberts will undoubtedly be discussed among them."

"They've not been commissioned by her sister to investigate!"

"Inspector Woolfe," Lady Owston said, smiling sweetly, as she approached him. "You were kind—so *very* kind—when you told me of Mrs Roberts' family. Then..." She half-turned toward the artist. "When *dear* Miss Dexter felt faint. I mistook your good deed for a foul one and I, again, apologised to you for it. Please, do not make a mockery of my apology by behaving like the beast I know you are not. You are a good man, a *just* man." She blocked his path and offered a larger smile. "Miss Rose Galway is the witness, isn't she?" Woolfe smoked some more as he took time to both calm himself and contemplate his answer.

Unexpectedly disarmed by her sincere words, the policeman replied, "Yeah, she is."

"And did she tell you I had instructed her *not* to speak to you or the police?"

"She didn't."

"Then you already have the truth of it, Inspector," Lady Owston beamed.

Miss Trent further explained, "We don't want to assist Mrs Roberts' murderer any more than you do. The Society has been hired to investigate her death and we intend to honour our commitment." She paused and, in a softer tone, continued, "We aren't against you or the police, Inspector. If you're willing to permit our pursuing our own lines of enquiries, we'll be sure to let you know what we discover."

"No," Woolfe barked. He crushed out his cigarette. "You've got no jurisdiction over this case, in the eyes of Scotland Yard or in the eyes of the law." He turned toward them, his back now to the hallway. "You say whatever you want to Mrs Suggitt; if she's guilty, I'll see her twitching on the end of a rope regardless." He cast a hard glance over them all. "And you'll all find yourselves breaking rocks at Dartmoor if I find out you've been questioning my witnesses again. This is your final warning."

* * *

From the address given by their client the previous morning, Mr Maxwell and Miss Webster knew the Suggitts to reside in Reeves Mews, a small street located between South Andle to the east and Park Street to the west. To the north was Upper Grosvenor Street leading to Grosvenor Square while to the south was Mount Street, eventually leading to Berkeley Square. These other streets were the habitual surroundings of, as Booth's Poverty Map of 1889 classified them, the "upper middle and upper classes wealthy" and "well-to-do middle class." Reeves Mews, on the other hand, housed those who Booth termed the "fairly comfortable" with "good, ordinary earnings."

At the end of the Society's meeting, both Miss Webster and Mr Maxwell had discussed the Suggitts' local area with Mr Snyder, who had agreed to bring them this day. He had been the one to confirm the social class of Reeves Mews to the pair—much to Miss Webster's surprise—in addition to informing them of available omnibus and tram routes from that location. Though a good many omnibus routes included Oxford Street, their stops required walks of varying distances from the Suggitts' residence to reach. Given the relatively short distance between Reeves Mews and Oxford Street, however, and the apparent wealth of the couple, the three Bow Streeters had decided it was most likely Mr Suggitt took a hansom cab to work. Especially as Mr Suggitt's hailing of Sam's own cab in Oxford Street hinted at a lack of private transportation. They had presumed Mrs Suggitt to use the same method whenever she travelled, for she hadn't called upon a domestic driver to take her from Bow Street either.

The immediate vicinity of the Suggitts' home comprised largely of residential properties. Beyond, to the west, was the vast expanse of Hyde Park and to the north, Oxford Street. The possibility of the Suggitts purchasing arsenic from a chemist further afield had occurred to the three. After all, murderers had been known to charm chemists in the past whenever a purchase of poison was required and the two were strangers. Though not entirely dismissed, they'd nevertheless decided this to be unlikely, simply because visiting a chemist far away could be construed as more suspicious than visiting one's local. In the Suggitts' case, their numerous local chemists were on Oxford Street, a location they already had ample reason to visit. This fact was therefore at the forefront of Miss Webster and Mr Maxwell's minds when, the next day, they parted company from Mr Snyder and Lady Owston at the *Queshire Department Store*.

The closest chemist was approximately a five-minute walk away—twenty when the pavements were so overcrowded, one's nose practically nudged the back of the person in front. Thankfully, the day favoured the shorter duration because of torrential rainfall—something neither Miss Webster nor Mr Maxwell preferred, huddled as they were beneath the secretary's immense umbrella. Worse still, as they soon discovered, their intended destination was on the opposite side to themselves. Now, attempting to cross any major thoroughfare in 1896 London was almost akin to a modern-day adrenalin sport.

Attempting to cross Oxford Street in 1896, London could therefore be considered a death wish. This didn't perturb Miss Webster, however, who, channelling her guardian's characteristic determination, stepped from the pavement the instant she saw a gap in the traffic. Even while she eluded an oncoming coach and horses, she yelled, "Come on, Mr Maxwell!"

"I don't think we should—!" the *Gaslight Gazette* journalist began before his view of her was obscured by a dustman and his cart. Deciding he must follow suit, Joseph closed the umbrella and gave chase, narrowly avoiding the back end of an omnibus as he did so.

"*Get outta the road*!" the Cad cried, twisting his upper body to shake a fist at him while gripping the omnibus' back and perching on his narrow ledge.

"I'm trying to!" Maxwell threw back despite having already lost sight of the vehicle—and Miss Webster. He whirled around, greatly fearing for her wellbeing, and came face to nose with a shire horse pulling a brewer's cart. The animal nodded its head and snorted, startling Joseph and sending him, reeling, into the path of a hansom cab traveling in the opposite direction.

"Mr Maxwell!" Agnes cried, prompting the journalist to turn toward her and thereby discover the imminent danger. She stood but a few feet from him on the pavement, whereas the cab was even closer. Without pause for thought, he threw his entire body weight, quite literally, forward and felt the pavement under foot just as the cab reached him. Its driver, having seen him, had yanked on the reins at the last moment. The two horses' heads were pulled back and their front legs lifted clear off the cobbles, their hooves kicking the air. Mr Maxwell ducked sharply but, thankfully, was already out of harm's way.

"Watch where you're bloody goin'!" the cabman hollered once the horses' hooves made contact with the ground.

Straightening his frock coat, Mr Maxwell looked more than a little sheepish. "Apologies, sir!"

"Where is my umbrella?" Miss Webster enquired as he was safe. Joseph lifted and examined first one arm and then the other in search of it. Realising he no longer had it, he turned back toward the road and saw it, lying, in its middle.

He intended to point it out as he said, "There—" but the horrifying sight of a coach running over it caused his hand to freeze and his voice to fail. Miss Webster, having witnessed the same as he, turned toward him. If she was angry, she hid it beneath a cold mask.

Nonetheless, her voice sounded heavier in its flatness as she said, "We have a task to complete." Mr Maxwell, feeling incredibly guilty at the loss, frowned but didn't reply—what *could* he say? An apology seemed hardly sufficient given Miss Webster's stiff exterior.

Drummond's Pharmaceutical Chemists was quintessential of the period; displayed within its single, rolled plate window, were glass bottles containing varying amounts of coloured water. These bottles, known as carboys from the Persian word 'Quarabah' for a wine or rose-water holding vessel, would've been originally used to hold the tinctures and extracts prepared by an apothecary. The bottles would've been placed in the window so as to enable the sun's heat to assist with the process. By the nineteenth century, however, the containers used for this purpose were moved behind the counter and given the alternative name of a shop round. The popular 'onion,' 'pear,' and 'swan neck' shaped carboys were used in place of these in the window displays. The reasons behind the specific colours used to change the appearance of the water within are uncertain. Some have suggested they may be a representation of bodily fluids, while others think a vague symbolism of chemicals to announce the presence of a chemist's' shop is more probable. Whatever the purpose, the colours' lovely hues—formed when the shop's interior gaslight illuminated the carboys—were alluring to customers. Even during the darker evenings of winter months, one could see the spectacle from afar.

The top shelf of the *Drummond's* display housed the pear-shaped carboys. On the shelf beneath were two taller swan-neck carboys—one at each end of the shelf. They were approximately an inch taller than their pear-shaped counterparts. Between the swan-necked carboys was a third style of glassware called a specie jar. Specie jars were used as decorative display pieces without any practical value as vessels. The example in *Drummond's* window had large dimensions and a label of MAGNESIA painted on its inside; the background colour of the label being white to denote the jar's contents.

In the bottom-right corner of the window was a white sign announcing *Medicines Dispensed with PURE DRUGS ONLY* in thick, black print.

Miss Webster entered the establishment ahead of Mr Maxwell and at once discovered a rumpus of customers, each one waiting but for different reasons. Those on the far side appeared to be facing some scales standing upon the counter. Troy weights, which were utilised for prescribing and dispensing of medicines despite the Avoirdupois weights and measures being favoured in the Medicinal Act of 1858, were stacked both beside and on the scales.

A male, no older than thirty, tried to measure a dosage of powdered medicine while a stern-faced governess looked on. She held the handle of a large pram positioned flush against the counter, despite the fact the ten-foot squared space couldn't accommodate it. The customer attempting to be served by a much older gentleman, at the opposite end of the counter, had to therefore stand back and lean forward to be heard. The din of the remaining people—queueing behind either the governess or the leaning customer—was almost unbearable in the small space.

Miss Webster and Mr Maxwell exchanged glances through the gloom, for only two pairs of gas lamps illuminated this side of the shop. To their immediate left was a supporting wall, shared with the neighbouring establishment, covered in polished-mahogany panelling and advertisements. These latter were for medicinal goods such as: cod liver oil emulsion, food products to supplement the normal meals of invalids and infants, liver pills, and pain-relieving embrocation. Unfortunately, neither Bow Streeter could get close enough to recognise them as every inch was occupied by bodies. Although the tumultuous weather had caused the day to be cold, the combined bodily heat within *Drummond's* had transformed it into a veritable hothouse. This, combined with the thick mustiness of damp clothing and the malodorous aroma of chest-infected coughing, served to make the establishment thoroughly unpleasant.

Having no choice but to wait their turn, Miss Webster and Mr Maxwell sidled along the wall to the end of the queue for the older gentleman. Admittedly the queue for the younger was longer, no doubt due to his reduced pace of working. Agnes and Joseph heard snippets of conversations as they waited; some about the weather, some about friends and relatives, but mostly about the body found on Oxford Street. They couldn't hear all being said but everyone's expressions displayed varying degrees of shock and confusion nonetheless.

"Do they think it's another one of his?" a man, standing with his back to Maxwell, enquired of his associate. The *Gaslight Gazette* journalist couldn't fathom the reply, however. He could only assume they were discussing a comparison to the Whitechapel Murders.

As time passed painfully by, the shop steadily emptied. Eventually, Miss Webster and Mr Maxwell could see the counter fully. It occupied the full length of the shop with the younger man on its far left and the older man by the window on its right. While the first ran the scales, the second operated an impressive, brass cash register to take the monies from customers in both queues. Cylindrical jars lined the counter's front edge and contained a variety of lozenges and other products.

The queue moved forward again and both Bow Streeters could see beyond the counter. A set of small, square, wooden drawers stood atop a solid, mahogany unit. Each drawer had the name of the chemical it contained handwritten upon a card inserted into squared, brass frames. Above the set of drawers were shelves holding a multitude of highly decorative shop rounds. Wide-mouthed, bulbous-stoppered bottles contained powders, narrow-necked, pouring-lipped bottles contained liquid preparations, and glass-domed, collared bottles with sharp-pouring, spouted stoppers contained oils—to name but a few. The blue bottles, perhaps most familiar to us, with their tin-capped necks, contained syrups. Yet the Bow Streeters weren't interested in any of these; their focus lay purely upon those bottles which contained the more dangerous substances.

Heavy, close-fitting domes were fixed over the stoppers of ether bottles. When they came across this style next, Miss Webster and Mr Maxwell could see the difference between them and the other shop rounds. Yet neither of them held the pharmaceutical knowledge required to recognise the reasoning behind these bottles' designs. It was therefore fortuitous that all the bottles on the shelves had paper labels, each with either the full name or an abbreviated version of it written upon them. The ETHER label was therefore plain to see on the domed bottles. So too were the ARSENIC ones on the pair of green, vertically ridged bottles, the ridges being an obligatory design feature for all poison bottles to ensure a chemist could differentiate them from other substances using touch alone.

"Good morning and welcome to *Drummond's Pharmaceutical Chemists*. I am Mr Drummond. I sincerely apologise for the wait. How may I be of assistance?" greeted the older gentleman as Agnes and Joseph finally reached the front of his queue. He wore a black waistcoat, black cravat, and a white shirt whose sleeves were rolled up to his elbows. An apron covered most of his chest; only his cravat's top and edges of his waistcoat's arm holes were visible. Tied in a knot at the man's front, over his stomach, the apron hung down to his ankles. He was in his mid-forties with ebony-coloured hair, short sideburns, and moustache. His lower teeth and jaw jutted out slightly from beneath his top, thus giving his chin a pointed appearance. His five-foot-eight frame was thin but nevertheless healthy while his complexion was pale on account of his spending his waking hours tucked away in his shop. Unusually large hands rested against his sides as he leant forward with his shoulders to peer pale-blue hues at first Agnes and then Joseph. His voice matched his overall demeanour in its pleasantness which put them at ease.

In contrast, the younger man was much shorter—at approximately five feet—with scrawny arms and legs, a dry, pale complexion, and dark rings under his eyes. His apron, being identical to Mr Drummond's in design, was much too big for him. As a result, the dark-grey jacket he wore underneath was practically hidden from view. His pallid, blond hair was neatly combed while his face was clean shaven. Unlike Mr Drummond, his chin was small and unremarkable and, by the way he kept sniffing, it was obvious he had caught a cold.

"Good morning, Mr Drummond," Miss Webster replied, stepping forward since the inconsiderate governess and pram had long since departed. "We would like to purchase some arsenic, please."

Joseph glanced at her but nodded nonetheless, his voice surprisingly calm as he added, "For some rats."

"Cook almost leapt out of her skin when she saw one scurrying across the floor."

"Dear, dear me," Mr Drummond muttered, shaking his head. "I would like to assist but neither of you are known to me. As such, I couldn't *possibly.*" He lifted his heels from the floor at the last, "sell you arsenic." The Bow Streeters exchanged glances for a second time. They well recalled Doctor Weeks' description of the legal parameters set down for chemists with regards to the sale of poisons. They'd almost hoped Mr Drummond would be one of those chemists who didn't follow these as strictly as they should.

Perturbed, Miss Webster replied, "I understand. Perhaps something else—"

"We're willing to sign your poison book," Mr Maxwell purposefully interrupted.

The chemist gave him something akin to a scowl as he replied, "I should think so, too, sir." To Agnes he said, "I have lozenges for coughs—syrups, too, if you prefer." He turned toward the shelves. "We are in the midst of the sneezing season, after all. Perhaps a meal supplement if you are unable to swallow your food?"

"If you'd be so kind as to sign the poison book, sir," the younger gentleman directed his own customer while placing a small, narrow, brown paper-wrapped parcel upon the counter.

Mr Drummond, having overheard his assistant, turned toward him and tutted upon seeing the parcel. "Dear, dear, me, Mr Collins." Mr Drummond plucked up the dosage. "This isn't four grams, this is *eight*." To the customer, he added, "Apologies, sir, but I'm obliged to measure it again before you can sign the book." The customer sighed but, reluctantly, agreed and stepped away. Mr Drummond closed the poison book and slid it across the counter to the register. Mr Collins meanwhile stood on a stepping stool and retrieved the bottle of arsenic from the shelf.

Seeing both chemist and assistant were preoccupied, Mr Maxwell neared the book but didn't yet reach for it. Instead, he glanced at the few remaining customers to check no one was within a foot of them. Miss Webster, to his right, followed his gaze but cast a questioning countenance at him after when she couldn't fathom what his intentions were. The journalist rested the heel of his hand beside the book and, looking from it to the secretary, gave a small cough. His head completely faced the chemist and assistant while his body rested at a 180-degree angle to them, against the counter. Agnes only had to see where his hand was to comprehend his idea.

She moved closer to Joseph, to use his body as a shield, and tentatively picked up the book. Mr Maxwell kept his back to her while he put on a show of lifting the lid of a nearby jar with his other hand as if to inspect its contents. Neither Drummond nor Collins so much as lifted their heads, let alone noticed what they each were doing. Joseph decided against putting his hand in and replaced the lid.

He heard Agnes turning a page and gave another cough to disguise the sound. Still facing the proprietor and his assistant, Joseph turned his head, but not his body, toward the shelves to browse. A quiet hum came from him while his fingers took turns to tap out a tune on the countertop. Inevitably, the song's words were sung under his breath—until Agnes turned another page and he coughed louder. Both Drummond and Collins stopped their work this time. Drummond said, "One moment, sir, and I'll dispense some syrup for your cough."

"Thank you," Joseph replied, balling up his hand and thumping his chest a little too hard. He winced but managed to disguise it with another, more abrupt, cough. "Terrible… I've had it for weeks." He rubbed his chest now and, dipping his chin, coughed for a fourth time. The other customers, having overheard his comments, discreetly stepped further away from him.

Mr Drummond had meanwhile finished measuring the dose and searched for the poison book. Joseph felt a knot in his stomach, a knot which unfurled as he heard Agnes put down the sought-after item. Turning fully toward the counter, Mr Maxwell picked and held the book up, asking, "Is this what you're looking for?"

"*Yes,* thank you, sir," Mr Drummond happily replied, accepting it from the journalist. "Syrup, wasn't it? However, I would recommend a visit to a physician if you've had the cough for several weeks."

As if on cue, Joseph coughed again. Mr Drummond stepped back, the book held tightly against him. "If you think it's for the best," Mr Maxwell replied. "That's what I'll do. Thank you, Mr Drummond, and good day."

"Good day, sir, miss," the chemist replied, none the wiser as the secretary stepped back outside and waited for her associate to join her.

When he did, she didn't hesitate to tell him, "We must return to the *Queshire Department Store* and speak with Lady Owston at once."

"Why? What did you find?"

"A name I hadn't expected to see."

TEN

Lady Owston faced a blockade of feminine forms at every counter within *The Queshire Department Store.* Modest headwear of governesses and ladies' maids ebbed and flowed among pockets of middle class ladies' elaborate hats. Whenever a gap appeared, another body filled it. Given her vantage point from the door, one would think Katheryne protected from the chaos. Yet on each side, she had streams of ladies both arriving and leaving, their elbows, boxes, and umbrellas nudging her. Acting upon an instinct to safeguard her personal space, Lady Owston kept side and back-stepping until, quite unintentionally, finding herself at her desired destination.

More ladies departed and the dummy appeared in her line of vision. Yet Katheryne's heart sank; the shawl wasn't anywhere to be seen. She considered searching for it among the many customers but quickly dismissed the notion as impractical. Enquiring with the department's assistants was out of the question, too, since she was already behind a crowd at least two deep in places.

"Good day to you, Lady Owston," Mr Queshire's voice greeted from her left.

Emitting a great sigh of relief, she faced him with a smile. "*Mr* Queshire, thank *heavens.*"

"Are you well?" he enquired, concerned.

"Yes," she replied with a broad smile of relief. "You would do well to add telepathy to your many talents, for I was just contemplating how I may seek you out in this commotion."

"You flatter me; I merely caught sight of you as I was passing. I hope my soap was satisfactory?"

"Of *course* it was. Admittedly, I've not had the opportunity to sample it but I have *every* confidence it shall be *sublime.*" She gestured toward the dummy. "I saw a shawl I'd hoped to purchase but it's gone…?"

"Remind me of which shawl you are referring to?" Mr Queshire enquired as a gap formed to allow them to approach the counter, its assistant already serving another customer. Lady Owston took Miss Dexter's sketch from within her coat and smoothed it out upon the glass.

"*This* one." She tapped the depiction of the forest-green, hand-crocheted shawl. "It was draped over the shoulders of your dummy only yesterday."

"Then I'm afraid it must have been sold," Mr Queshire replied apologetically.

Lady Owston frowned and enquired, "Would you know to whom?"

"We don't keep a record of who purchases which garments unless they require delivery." He looked to his now freed assistant and pushed the sketch toward her. "Please check the delivery ledger for this shawl, Miss Lemon."

"Yes, Mr Queshire." The delivery ledger was retrieved from a shelf, hidden by fabric, and the assistant worked her way through its entries.

"If it's not too inconvenient, I'd like a private word with you afterward," Edmund requested, addressing Lady Owston.

The independent journalist beamed as she replied, "You have again read my mind, Mr Queshire."

"There's no record of it having been delivered, sir," Miss Lemon revealed and closed the ledger.

Mr Queshire gave a small bow of his head. "Thank you. If I'm required, I'll be speaking with Lady Owston in the storeroom."

"Yes, sir," the assistant acknowledged and, picking up the ledger, returned it to its home. Katheryne meanwhile reclaimed her sketch and accepted Mr Queshire's request to follow him. He forged a path through the crowds surprisingly quickly, his gentlemanly manners fully utilised as he went.

"Please, sit," he invited and closed the door on the chaos. "Inspector Woolfe of Scotland Yard came here yesterday," he began once they were seated. "He enquired about a crocheted shawl also, one worn by Mrs Roberts. I presume your sketch is of the same garment?"

"It is, in addition to the other garments she was last seen wearing by Mr Suggitt here in this very store. I'm surprised you didn't recognise them immediately."

"Though I'm a connoisseur of clothing, I didn't pay much heed to her apparel. As I explained yesterday, I allowed my emotions to get the better of me." His demeanour became a little sheepish. "I was forced to admit such to Inspector Woolfe, too."

"The inspector is only doing his duty as an officer of the law," Katheryne reassured, her words echoing Caleb's own from the night before. She added, "He was *frightfully* angry at the Society being hired to investigate the matter."

"I had no choice but to tell him of your visit here yesterday," Mr Queshire explained with much regret in his voice.

Lady Owston momentarily placed a gloved hand upon his arm, however. "I would've asked you to have done so anyway. We've no interest in keeping information from the police." Retracting her hand, she continued, "But I apologise for deceiving you earlier. I wanted to look at the shawl to satisfy myself that it was indeed Mrs Roberts'."

"I can at least ease your mind in that respect," Edmund replied, his features being lit up with a smile. "There's no possibility the shawl you saw on the dummy yesterday could've belonged to Mrs Roberts for none of the items we sell are second-hand."

"Come, come, Mr Queshire," Katheryne teased with a playful wagging of her finger.

Yet the owner's smile had vanished and, in an unexpectedly hard voice, he enquired, "Do you call me a liar, Lady Owston?"

She was utterly speechless at his sudden, dramatic metamorphosis, needing to take several moments before she could reply. "In actuality, Mr Queshire... I do." The corner of Edmund's eye twitched but his scowl remained. "I've purchased goods from your store that have clear signs of previous wear," she continued. "Clear to those with an eye for these things anyway."

Mr Queshire abruptly thrust back his chair and, standing, glared down at her. She held her breath. A mere moment passed but it felt to her as the longest she'd ever known. "You have found me out," he finally stated. "And now have me at a disadvantage." Putting his weight upon his knuckles on the table, he leant forward. "What do you intend to do with your... newfound information?"

"I shan't be making scandalous revelations in the *Women's Signal*," she assured without hesitation.

Edmund straightened but the air of suspicion remained, "Many would be interested in publishing such a story, however, given my store's reputation. Do you say such monetary incentive isn't appealing to you?"

"I have enough money already, thank *you*!"

"So, the knowledge has no value to you?"

"On the contrary, Mr Queshire; it's *highly* valuable as far as Mrs Roberts' murder is concerned."

The last of Edmund's suspicion dissipated as he nodded his understanding and enquired, "If I should tell you all I know about the shawl, may I rely upon your utter discretion regarding how I came to own it?"

"You may," she replied.

Mr Queshire lifted his hands from the table and, giving a weak smile of relief, thanked her.

"Unnecessary," she said with a slight lifting of her hand. "Now, when did the shawl come into the store's possession?"

"I don't know, but I came across it among the donated garments in here." He pushed aside two stacked boxes to reveal a large, wicker basket behind. Its lid was closed and secured with a thick, dark-brown, leather strap. "Two nights ago, I believe."

"The night Mrs Roberts was murdered?" Katheryne felt a sudden chill.

Mr Queshire seemed to feel it, too, as he half-turned toward her. "You're right… it was." He stepped around his chair and dropped onto it. With wide eyes, he muttered, "Dear God."

"When did you put it on the dummy?"

"I…" He glanced over the table, frowning, as he tried to recall. "Inspected it for faults, as I do with all the garments we receive, and mended any flaws. Sometimes I have to make additions to garments to lift their overall quality, but I don't recall… no, I didn't need to with the shawl. I put it on the dummy once I was finished—the same night I found it in the basket. It's remarkably easy to sell on worn garments as new with a few adjustments. You're the first to notice the deception." He briefly met her gaze. "New fabric is so expensive…" A deep, sad sigh followed. "I honestly had no idea it was Mrs Roberts until you pointed out the connection."

"Inspector Woolfe didn't notice the shawl at all?"

"No; he asked me if I could recall what Mrs Roberts had been wearing when I saw her last. I couldn't."

"Do you know who donated it?"

"We don't keep a record." Mr Queshire shook his head. "For obvious reasons."

"Who else has access to the basket?"

"Mr Suggitt. We've kept it a secret from even the assistants for fear of loose lips fuelled by greedy hearts."

"Has Mr Suggitt ever told his wife about its existence? Could she have put something in there without your knowledge?"

"I suppose she could have… I would be disappointed if Mr Suggitt *had* told her of the basket, though."

"Why?"

"Betrayal of professional trust, naturally. Do you believe her to be involved in her sister's death, then?"

"I'd prefer not to speculate at this point in our investigations, Mr Queshire," she explained. "May I ask you to check the basket now? For her other items of clothing."

Edmund swivelled sideways in his chair and stared at the piece of furniture in question. "Of course," he replied and rose to his feet. Katheryne followed and the two simultaneously peered into the mound of fabric. He shifted garments aside several times and even delved deeper and pulled out those from the lower layers. After ten minutes, the lid was replaced and Katheryne sighed. "Nothing." She said with a frown. "And you were here *all* night?"

"Yes; my rooms are upstairs, as you know. I worked in the store until eleven thirty and retired to bed."

"Did you not eat at all?"

"Only a cold supper which I ate here in the storeroom."

"And *no one* came to the store after it had closed?" Lady Owston enquired, the frustration clear to hear in her voice if not plain to see in her eyes.

"No one whatsoever," Edmund confirmed with a shaking of his head. His voice was again laden with regret as he added, "I wish I could be of more help."

A sudden knock caused both to divert their attention. Without waiting for either occupant to give permission to do so, their visitor opened the door and stepped inside. Upon seeing Miss Galway, Edmund scolded her for her rude behaviour and explained the importance of waiting to be invited into a room with a closed door. Lady Owston, on the other hand, had become distracted by a glimpse of a lady she knew exiting the *Staff only* room at the top of the stairs. Neither Mr Queshire nor Miss

Galway had noticed her observation though so, on this occasion, she kept her own counsel on the matter.

"Miss Webster is here, Sur," Rose related, meekly. "She and her friend want to speak to Lady Owston."

"Ah yes," Katheryne smiled. "I asked them to meet me here. Thank you, once again, for your precious time, Mr Queshire."

"You're most welcome, Lady Owston," Edmund replied, having simultaneously risen to his feet. "Rose, you can make amends for your behaviour by escorting Lady Owston to her friends," he ordered the assistant.

Rose bowed her head, "Yes, sur."

"Good day to you, Lady Owston," Mr Queshire said and, upon leaving the room, went to the perfumery department where a customer beckoned him over. Miss Galway meanwhile waited for Katheryne to leave the storeroom first before walking ahead of her to where Miss Webster and Mr Maxwell waited at the millinery department.

"If that is all, madam, I must return to my counter," she explained after Lady Owston, Miss Webster, and Mr Maxwell had greeted one another.

"Actually, Miss Galway," Agnes began, as she looked to her. "There is something further, required not by Lady Owston but myself." Rose glanced among them, confused. Nonetheless the secretary went on, "May you explain why your name appears in the poison book at *Drummond's Pharmaceutical Chemists* shop?"

* * *

"You'd better have a bloody good reason for waking me," an angry voice threatened as its owner pulled open the door and stood in its stead. Burnt umber-brown eyes sought out Mr Snyder and then Miss Dexter in the gloomy corridor; she stood to the right of the cabman. A gaunt, weathered face covered with thick stubble aged the observer beyond his thirty-five years. His was a life hard lived, malnourishment having stunted his growth at a young age—as evidenced by his mere five-foot height. Yet he'd overcome the accompanying physical weakness to forge a trade as a manual labourer and developed large biceps and broad shoulders. Still half asleep, he retrieved a thin cotton coat from behind the door and put it on.

He enquired, "Who're you?"

"I'm Mr Snyder and this 'ere's Miss Dexter. Can we talk to Mr Roberts?"

"You don't look like peelers," the man countered, having noticed straightaway the cabman's own weathered face and calloused hands. Even the middle-class girl beside him lacked a policeman's bark—if women had been allowed to join their ranks, that is.

Mr Snyder replied, "That's 'cause we're not. I'm a cabman and Miss Dexter's an artist. We're also Bow Street Society members. Are Mr Abraham Roberts and Miss Regina home?"

"I'm Mr Roberts. Regina's out working." Having assured himself of his own respectability with the coat, despite still wearing old trousers and darned socks, Abraham stepped aside. "Maryanna's sister said you'd be coming by. Come in."

The home was a single room dominated by a coal-burning stove. The bed, for everyone's use, was a straw-filled mattress shoved into a cubby hole opposite. A faded, ochre-coloured curtain was pushed aside to expose disturbed blankets. Mr Roberts crossed the room, which was approximately fifteen feet long by ten feet wide, and drew it back into place. In the centre of the room was a squared table, which had seen better days, and three chairs. Abraham invited his guests to sit and began to prepare some tea for them all. Mr Snyder, having closed the door behind him, took the chair facing the stove while Miss Dexter occupied the one to his left.

With their host distracted, the young artist made her observations of the room. It was cramped and quite obviously overcrowded; clothing of all shapes and sizes hung above the stove to dry, and in cupboards whose broken doors didn't close completely. She enquired, "Do you live here alone with your daughter, Mr Roberts?"

"Yeah; we had another family sharing with us but they left for America last week," he said and made a line of three mugs on the table. Georgina returned her attention to the clothes; two of the dresses were markedly different in both style and size. It was as if they belonged to two different women. She'd already assumed the housework had been done by Regina Roberts, since the place was tidy and well swept, but those dresses caused her to question not only herself but Mr Roberts, too. The kettle on the stove suddenly gave a shrill whistle, however, and disrupted her ponderings. Assuming any accusations of falsehood would be ill-received so soon after their arrival, she decided to tuck away her suspicions in her mind and await her tea. Having taken the kettle from the stove, Mr Roberts poured the hot water through a meagre clump of leaves as he held a tiny tea strainer over each cup in turn.

"You drink French Breakfast coffee, Mr Roberts?" Sam enquired and pointed a stubby finger at the shelf to the stove's right.

Abraham glanced at it from over his shoulder, "No, Diana bought Maryanna that last Christmas; forgot we even had it." Even from where they were sitting, Georgina and Sam could see the coffee wasn't covered in the same dust as the remainder of the shelf's contents. Abraham's informal use of Mrs Suggitt's first name had also piqued their curiosity.

When he'd joined them, Miss Dexter took a delicate sip of weak tea and enquired, "Are you close to Mr and Mrs Suggitt?"

Mr Roberts warmed his hands on his cup as his eyes glazed over. He said, "They've treated us well. Despite all that Maryanna done."

"They were here yesterday, weren't they?" Miss Dexter enquired further, her voice quiet but confident nonetheless. "Mrs Suggitt loved her sister dearly."

"So did I," Abraham countered, meeting her gaze for the first time. "It was the drink what made Maryanna the way she was. I done my best, we all did, but she wouldn't have any of it. In the end, she was drinking away the housekeeping money. I couldn't let her do that." Pain crossed his features while he tried to refocus his mind by starting at his drink. "Regina's the only one I got left now."

"You said she woz workin'?" Mr Snyder enquired, thinking a change of subject would be best.

"Yeah, she helps sell flowers at Covent Garden Market," Mr Roberts took a mouthful of tea. "Any way she can, really. Anything to make ends meet."

"Was she working the night her mother died?" Miss Dexter reluctantly enquired, her heart holding great disdain for the insinuation the question posed.

It wasn't a question completely unexpected by Abraham who replied, "Only until it got dark then she came home and we had supper together."

"Did either of you go out again after that?" Mr Snyder probed next.

"No, Regina and I got knocked up at four o'clock. I then left to sleep outside the dock gates and she went to the Market."

"When will your daughter be home?" the artist enquired but Abraham frowned. Miss Dexter thought, for a moment, he couldn't tell them. Then he came back with a question of his own, one Georgina couldn't even begin to answer.

"Depends on the selling, don't it? Regina's the wandering sort, too, if there's no work to be had. Picks up bloody railway ticket stubs and brings them home." Realising he'd been rambling, Mr Roberts took a swig of his tea and said, "When it's dark is when she comes home."

"Do you sleep outside the gates every night?"

"You've got to if you're not a Royal; only way you give yourself a good chance of being picked by the ganger is to be at the front," Abraham explained. Yet Miss Dexter was none the wiser. It must've shown on her expression, too, for the labourer continued, "Royals are the blokes on the ganger's list; you get on that and you can be all but sure you'll be picked to unload the goods." He rubbed his neck. "The rest of us've got to take our chances."

Georgina gave a meek smile of thanks as her cheeks burned. She took a small sip of her tea to hide her embarrassment while the cabman enquired, "Woz you picked this mornin'?"

Mr Roberts shook his head, "Nah. All the Royals got picked but the quay-gangers didn't want any others. Sometimes a ship comes in late so I waited around but nothing."

"What time did you leave?"

"Was about two o'clock this afternoon, give or take a few. When I got home is when I was told about Maryanna—found an inspector here."

"Where woz your daughter?"

"Gone to stay with Diana and Clement, he told me."

"Mr Roberts, I know this may sound a queer question," Georgina tentatively began. "But do you own any hessian sacks?"

"What?" Abraham glanced about, after his initial confusion, and shook his head.

132

The same check by Miss Dexter confirmed the validity of his answer. Yet nonetheless, she knew all possibilities had to be explored so therefore enquired, "And you haven't had any in the past few days?"

"Maybe when Regina got a bushel of potatoes?" Sam interjected.

"We can't afford them by the bushel," Mr Roberts replied and waited for any further questions from the two Bow Streeters. When none came, he gripped his cup and said, in a much quieter and emotionally strained voice, "Police told me she was found on Oxford Street... cut up. That right?" Miss Dexter gave a small swallow but couldn't even look at him as she nodded. The ensuring silence forced her to face her fears, however, and she could've cried when she saw his tightly clasped hands pressed against his brow. Her heart then ached further when she witnessed them trembling, and his shoulders shaking, from his silent sobbing. She wanted to reach out to him, to reassure him all would be well. Yet Mr Snyder's large hand upon her own stayed her. She looked to his kind face, as sorrow filled as her own, and heeded his unspoken warning. As much as it distressed her, she agreed with it; they mustn't get too close, mustn't be drawn in by emotion which could be a lie. She bowed her head and felt the room become darker despite the daylight coming through the window.

"Please go..." Mr Roberts suddenly said through a harsh sob. Rising to his feet, he then retreated to the stove where he hid his tears from their view behind a turned back. Mr Snyder and Miss Dexter didn't hesitate in their ensuing departure. He held her close as she leant upon him, struggling to keep her own cheeks dry.

"His grief was sincere, Sam," she half-whispered while they descended the stairs. "Whatever the cause of it... his grief was sincere."

* * *

Rose Galway had an intense feeling of déjà vu as she again found herself in the storeroom. Lady Owston sat opposite her while Miss Webster and Mr Maxwell stood behind their associate. The din from the department store was muffled by the closed door but its sound nevertheless jolted Miss Galway's mind into realising someone was missing. She straightened to stand and said, "I'll fetch Mr Queshire."

"No, Rose," Katheryne replied, halting the assistant in her tracks. Her voice was then surprisingly subdued as she continued, "It's time for you to speak freely, and openly, with us."

Rose fell back against her chair in dismay, "But I've already been doing that, Lady Owston."

"You didn't tell Miss Webster or me the truth of the room at the top of the stairs."

"But there's nothing to tell—!" Rose exclaimed as she pressed down with her palms to lean over the table. Katheryne had abruptly cut her off, however.

"*How* can I trust you, Miss Galway? To risk my own reputation with Miss Trent when you *still* refuse to cooperate with me?"

"Please, Milady," Rose said, slouching with a disheartened expression on her face. "It's nowt to do with Mrs Robert's murder." The assistant sniffed deeply and pressed the cuff of her blouse to the underside of her nose. A hushed request from Katheryne had Miss Webster offering her handkerchief to the young woman.

While doing so, Agnes enquired, "Why was your name written in Mr Drummond's poison book the day before her murder?"

"I bought it for Mr Suggitt, didn't I?" Rose retorted, frustrated both by her tears and the insinuation. "Said Mr Queshire wanted it for rats in the cellar." She wiped her nose, rather indelicately, upon the silk handkerchief. "None of us killed her."

"Where were you the night Mrs Roberts died?" Mr Maxwell enquired as he sat down beside her.

Rose crumpled the handkerchief in her hands and dabbed at her eyes, "At the lodgings 'round the corner with all the other assistants. Ask anyone; I've got no reason to murder the bloody woman."

"None of that now, Miss Galway—" Lady Owston scolded.

The assistant, bolstered by her increasing level of anger, snapped, "Why bloody not? You're all saying I killed her… or suggesting it was someone here. Why don't you ask her mum? She was the one who disowned her."

"Oh?" Miss Webster enquired, casting a reassuring glance at her employer who was a little riled by the young woman's rudeness.

Rose continued, "Yeah. You heard what Mrs Roberts did here the other day; she was a nasty piece of work. Pulled the wool over her sister's eyes, and her daughter's, but not Mr Suggitt's and definitely not Mrs Yates'."

"Her mother?" Mr Maxwell clarified.

Rose nodded and went on, "Her mum hated the way she treated her husband and always told her she'd abandoned her daughter when she'd chosen the drink. Maryanna was her dad's daughter, that's what she used to call her. He died from the drink, leaving the family destitute."

"How do you know all this?" Mr Maxwell enquired, somewhat impressed at the detail she gave them.

Rose shrugged one shoulder, her anger weakened by Joseph's reaction, and replied, "Hear things, don't I? Said by Mr Suggitt and his wife when they think no one's listening. Her mum told Mrs Suggitt that her sister was squeezing her for all she was worth and she was a fool for letting her. That Mrs Roberts was past all hope and she should worry about Regina and Mr Roberts more. Mrs Suggitt couldn't take that though, could she? Was always in here, complaining to her husband about how it wasn't fair and how Mrs Roberts just needed help. From what I saw of her, the only help she needed was directions to the nearest pub."

"So you liked Mrs Roberts as much as her mother did," Miss Webster coolly remarked.

Rose, having stopped crying, put the crumpled handkerchief upon the table. "Doesn't matter what I thought of her. I'm just telling you what I've seen and heard." Agnes, Katheryne, and Joseph all exchanged glances. "I didn't kill her!" Rose yelled, a mixture of panic and anger both in her voice and on her face. "I got the poison for Mr Suggitt like I've done loads of times! Ask him! Ask Mr Drummond! Ask Mr Queshire!"

"Calm yourself, Miss Galway," Lady Owston ordered. The assistant again fell back against her chair, but this time clutched a tight fist to her mouth. A gentle smile slowly formed upon Katheryne's face though and she repeated, in a softer tone, "Calm yourself." Rose swallowed several times and, using her blouse's cuff, wiped her eyes before nodding.

"Who drinks the French Breakfast coffee?" Mr Maxwell suddenly enquired, pointing to a shelf behind Rose.

The assistant turned within her seat to see what he was referring to while the others followed his finger. "Only Mr Queshire and Mr Suggitt are allowed to," Miss Galway explained, sniffing.

Miss Webster enquired, "Who else has access to this room?"

"Anyone, I suppose. The door isn't kept locked."

ELEVEN

The remaining chemist shops within a ten-minute walk of *The Queshire Department Store* failed to yield any further results for all their persons of interest. The time it had taken Miss Webster and Mr Maxwell to gain access to each establishment's poison book meant they'd diminished two-thirds of available daylight without departing Oxford Street. Fortunately, it was still with them when they'd arrived at Queen Street. Adjacent to Moore Street—where Abraham Roberts and his daughter were purported to reside—Queen Street counted Booth's "fairly comfortable" among its residents. Edgware Road to the east largely housed the "well-to-do" middle class while Nutford Place to the south mirrored Queen Street's population. Moore Street, with its "vicious, semi-criminal" class of person— the "lowest class," was a marked contrast to its surroundings.

The chemist shop closest to Moore Street was *Eastleigh's,* a photographer which also dispensed medicine. From the outside, the store looked altogether unappealing; paint peeled from the grubby sign hanging above the equally grubby window, while the contrasting streams of income suggested poor health in the store's finances. A bell shook above their heads as they entered but there was no ring, the clapper having been broken and lost long ago. The store's interior echoed the façade in its drabness; gas lamps which were barely lit cast a glow onto the dusty, dirty floor while the walls displayed advertisements yellowed and curled over the years. Unable to see much by the inadequate light, Miss Webster and Mr Maxwell had to practically feel their way to the counter. The first signs of dusk, despite it being only four thirty, didn't help matters either.

When they finally reached their destination, however, they were surprised to find no one there. Granted the distance was too great for one to simply lean across and steal one of the many aged bottles from the shelves. All the same, it was rather disturbing to think anyone could lift the hatch, walk behind the counter, and take a bottle of arsenic without the chemist ever laying eyes upon them. Precisely how Mr Maxwell then demonstrated—much to Miss Webster's unease. Needless to say, the bottle was replaced and a small card plucked up in its stead, which the *Gazette* journalist read aloud: "Photographic session in progress. Please ring bell for assistance." Joseph put the card back where he'd found it and added, "We shan't be doing *that*, Mr Eastleigh."

"It nonetheless means he is nearby," Miss Webster pointed out. Noticing another door on her side of the counter, she walked toward it and pulled it ajar as quietly as she could. Beyond, she found a set of narrow, deep stairs which spiralled upward to a closed door. Muffled voices reached her ears but she couldn't make out what they were saying. When she looked to her associate to inform him of this, she discovered him flipping through the pages of a ledger, presumably the poison book. She crossed the floor, leaving the door ajar, and took it from him. "Listen for any sound of Mr Eastleigh or his customer approaching the stairs," she ordered as she turned the ledger around and found the date of Mrs Roberts' death. Joseph, bending to her superior expertise in the area of records, moved out from behind the counter, closed its hatch, and went about doing as she'd asked.

Carefully, and slowly, Agnes ran her index finger down the column of names. The day prior to Mrs Roberts' murder contained no familiar names, nor did the day before that or the day before that. Beginning to think they'd encountered yet another dead end, she suddenly caught sight of a name she knew: *Mrs Sarah Yates.* She frowned, "Miss Galway didn't tell us Mrs Yates' first name."

"Pardon?" Mr Maxwell enquired, confused, as he began to move toward her.

At that moment though, the door at the top of the stairs opened and a man's voice could be clearly heard to say, "Bring your wife and children back tomorrow, Mr Fields, and I'll capture their likenesses as well as I have yours."

Miss Webster ran her finger along the row in the entry to garner further information—of which there was considerably little in comparison to some she'd looked at this day.

The thudding of feet upon the stairs finally convinced her it was time to relinquish her prize. Closing it, she slid it back to Maxwell who, in turn, slid it across the counter and into the waiting drawer on the other side. He'd managed to reach over, while standing on his tiptoes, close the drawer, and return to a standing position just as the other door opened and a large-set man stepped into sight. Following him was an equally stout man with thick, unkempt, blond hair, a bulbous, red nose, and beady, green eyes. Noticing Agnes and Joseph by the counter, he bid his current customer goodbye and turned toward them. "Can I help you at all?"

"No, thank you," Mr Maxwell replied, much to the owner's surprise.

Luckily, Miss Webster had the presence of mind to add, "You don't appear to have the lozenges we're after. Good day to you."

"Good day…" the chemist replied, with a scratch of his head, as Mr Maxwell followed her. The two walked briskly along Queen Street toward Edgware Road where they'd arranged for Mr Snyder and Miss Dexter to meet them. The intended rendezvous point for the Society's meeting with the Suggitts that evening, *The Turk's Head Public House*, was situated on the corner of Queen Street and Edgware Road. It was far too early to wait there, however; especially as none of them were at all familiar with the establishment.

"What did you find regarding Maryanna's mother?" Maxwell enquired once they'd arrived and couldn't see Mr Snyder's cab approaching.

"If it is the same Mrs Yates, she purchased arsenic four days prior to Mrs Robert's murder. The reason given was an infestation of mice." Agnes retrieved her notebook and pencil and began writing. She added, "I'd be interested to hear how Mr Snyder and Miss Dexter's visit to the Roberts' residence went, too."

"Why?"

"Because the address belonging to the Mrs Sarah Yates in the poison book is the same as Mr Abraham Roberts. It may simply be two families share the same living space but, if this is so, it would be an incredible coincidence."

* * *

Founded in 1892 by journalist Frances Low, the *Writers' Club* aimed to assist female authors who, in the main, devoted themselves to writing pieces for the press and/or magazines. Occupying the ground floor of Hastings House on Norfolk Street, its close vicinity to the Strand and Fleet Street provided convenience for those wishing to leave copy of their work at the newspaper and magazine houses on their way home. There wasn't any accommodation for club members but other excellent facilities, including a dining room, kitchen, cloak room, and two reception rooms, could be enjoyed. Additionally, a writing room, furnished with tables and writing materials, was set aside for members' use and wherein a strict policy of absolute silence was enforced. For those ladies who wished to spend the entirety of the day at the club, a plain dinner, tea, and supper could be had at a very moderate cost. Every Friday, members' guests could also be entertained with an afternoon tea, something Lady Owston had taken advantage on many occasions with her friends.

She was presently in the first reception room reading the latest membership applications pinned to the bulletin board above the mantel. The *Writers' Club* honorary president was the Princess Christian while among its many vice presidents were Lady Seton, the Duchess of Sutherland, and the novelist Mrs. G. Linnaeus Banks. Yet none of those distinguished ladies were the one Katheryne waited upon this eve. *They* hadn't been the customer she'd seen leaving the mysterious room at the *Queshire Department Store.* That had been Mrs Peter Gromwell, a long-time member who was a creature of habit. Every Thursday, she'd dine at the *Writers' Club* while her husband dined at his own—and today just happened to be Thursday.

Lady Owston faced the doorway when she heard Mrs Gromwell's voice in the main hall, complaining about the inconsideration of a British winter. Another of the club's members passed the reception room first, followed by Mrs Gromwell who stilled the moment she glanced within. She was a woman of average height in her late fifties. Wiry, washed-out, brown hair was pushed beneath a modest, beetroot-purple, square-brimmed bonnet with loose-cloth back. The brim easily cast her face's top half into shadow, while its strings were tied *behind* the flaccid roll hanging from her chin. Her dress followed tradition in its style and fit—wide skirts, narrowed shoulders, and a marked bustle at the rear. Her corset, though shapely, wasn't as tight as it may have been in her youth. Wide, light-olive eyes regarded the independent journalist over extraordinarily defined cheekbones.

Katheryne offered an inviting smile but Mrs Gromwell, having a startled look about her, swiftly hurried from sight.

"Mrs Gromwell?" Lady Owston called, trying to catch her up. Finding her not too far away, still in the Hall, she approached.

Mrs Gromwell turned upon her heel and gave the most forced smile Katheryne had ever seen. "Lady Owston," she said. "I didn't see you there."

"Well, we are *all* getting *rather* short-sighted in our old age, aren't we?" Katheryne replied, her voice sickly-sweet. "I thought I saw you at the *Queshire Department Store* earlier."

"You did…?" Mrs Gromwell enquired, her voice shaking ever so slightly.

Lady Owston maintained her joyful demeanour, however. "Yes, coming out of the room at the top of the stairs," Katheryne feigned a confused expression as she enquired, "Now *what* is that department called again?"

"The salon?"

"No, no, the *other* door at the top of the stairs."

"I really do not know what you mean," Mrs Gromwell replied, evidently worried.

Lady Owston stared at her with mock disbelief before giving a coy smile, "Surely you know which department you were in?" She gestured toward the second reception room, "Perhaps if we ask one of the other ladies—?"

"*No!*" Mrs Gromwell cried in distress. "I *tell* you I do not *know,* Lady Owston. Now, *please,* leave it be." She tried to make a sharp retreat but Katheryne effortlessly blocked her path with her own body.

"I cannot," she told her, speaking with a far more serious, yet quieter, tone. "A woman was murdered on Oxford Street two nights ago. Whether the room at the top of the stairs has some bearing on the matter or not, I *must* know what is in it. Quite honestly, I'm losing my patience with it, for everyone is hiding its contents as if it were the Ark of the Covenant." She put a hand on Mrs Gromwell's arm, "Whatever it is, please know you may rely upon my absolute discretion."

"Peter doesn't even know," Mrs Gromwell admitted, her voice near paralysed with fear. This both surprised and intrigued Katheryne in equal measure.

Moving closer still, Katheryne enquired, "Know about what?"

"My shame," Mrs Gromwell replied, her voice barely above a whisper.

It sent Lady Owston's mind whirling with all manner of possibilities and, for a moment, she was truly at a loss as to what to say. Finally, with tremendous trepidation, she enquired, "Mrs Gromwell... what have you done?"

"I've deceived you all..." she replied just as the dining room door opened behind her and two other members entered the hall. To allow them enough room to pass, Katheryne was obliged to release her hold on Mrs Gromwell but, in so doing, she lost sight of her. By the time her view became unobstructed, her companion was gone.

"Oh, *bother*," Katheryne muttered under her breath before checking the dining room. Finding no sign of Mrs Gromwell within, Lady Owston searched both reception rooms, cloak room, kitchen, and writing room but none sheltered the panic-stricken woman. Reluctantly surrendering to the obvious, Katheryne returned to the dining room.

"Mrs Gromwell didn't stay for her supper," one member remarked to another as she entered.

"How queer," the second replied, concerned.

"Perhaps she was unwell? She did look *frightfully* pale when she passed me in the hall," a third added.

The first smirked and said, "I do not know how you could tell under that bonnet of hers. I've never seen her without it."

"You know... neither have I," the second admitted with a half gasp. Katheryne was only marginally listening, however. Realising she would be late for dinner with her secretary before attending the appointment with the Suggitts, she prepared to leave.

"Good evening to you all!" she cried once she was ready. The three ladies simultaneously bid farewell and their conversations died away as Katheryne made her way from Hastings House and hailed a passing hansom cab.

* * *

"Very handsome, dear," Mrs Maxwell said, her arthritic thumbs fumbling to straighten the tiny bow of her son's midnight-blue cravat. Smoothing over his white shirt next, she tugged down his waistcoat, and checked his watch chain hung as it should. The waistcoat was black with midnight-blue flowers embroidered into it using silk. His everyday frock coat had been exchanged in favour of another which complimented his cravat.

Mrs Maxwell stood up on her tiptoes to brush his shoulders with her fingers and finally stepped back to admire him.

She was a petite woman with genial, dark-green eyes and impeccably pinned, auburn hair which was greying at the edges. In her late forties, her face showed no signs of weathering or tanning. In fact, it was as pale as porcelain and had only a handful of wrinkles at the corners of her eyes and mouth. In preparation for the evening, her maid had helped her into an emerald-green, silk bustle gown with simple embellishments. Cream-coloured, silk, elbow-length gloves completed her outfit. Yet her fussing over Joseph wasn't for the same reason.

He swallowed hard and looked past her to his father's study door. "Will you accompany me, Mother?"

"I will, but only for as long as he tolerates my presence," she replied. Taking each of his hands in hers, she used her handkerchief to wipe away the sweat from his palms. "Deep breath now," she smiled. "You know how your father detests any form of weakness."

"Yes, Mother."

"Good boy." She momentarily rested her hand upon his cheek while she gazed lovingly into his eyes. When she allowed her hand to drop, she took her own advice while she turned toward the door and knocked.

Immediately, they heard Oliver's stern voice beckoning them to "Come!"

"Forgive me for disturbing you," Mrs Maxwell began once she was inside and her son stood behind her. "But Joseph is here; he wishes to speak with you."

"He's early," Mr Maxwell, Snr, muttered from where he sat in an immense chair behind his desk. Nevertheless, he finished the line in the correspondence he'd been writing and held both ends of his pen between his respective thumbs and index fingers. As he cast a cold gaze over his child, he enquired, "*Well*? Out with it."

"I—I simply wanted to tell you that I've invited a lady to dine with us this evening," Joseph replied and moved around his mother to stand directly in front of the imposing piece of furniture.

Oliver's gaze hardened. He put the pen down and, standing, replied, "I don't recall authorising such an invitation."

"You didn't, Father, which is why I wanted to speak with you before she arrives—"

"Who is she?" Oliver barked.

Joseph, who had flinched at the noise, felt his heart race in fear. Yet the mere thought of the artist had his nerves weakening and his cheeks flushing. He could smile, therefore, when he replied, "My fiancé, Father: Miss Georgina Dexter."

"Isn't it wonderful news, Oliver?"

"*Leave* us, woman."

Mrs Maxwell bowed her head and hurried from the room. When he heard the door close, Joseph suddenly felt trapped and vulnerable. His mother's presence could never guarantee his father's calm, but the *Gaslight Gazette* journalist would nevertheless feel protected whenever she was there. With her gone the room seemed all the larger and Oliver all the taller.

Maxwell Senior walked around his desk toward his son. "The Dexter's are not a family I'm aware of. How did they come into their money?"

"Um, they d—didn't. Mr Dexter is a—a clerk, I believe."

Oliver's fierce scowl in reaction to this news forced Joseph's gaze to the floor. "You *snivelling*, foolish *wretch*. You *dare* come to me and speak of a *wench* you have invited to *my* home and to *my* table?"

"She's not a wench, Father—"

"*Don't* lie to me! *You* are not *valuable* enough, or *charming* enough, to find a fiancé in a *day*!"

"I didn't—"

"You will cancel her dinner invitation and nullify your preposterous engagement. Do I make myself clear?"

"I thought you'd be happy—"

"This family will *not* be shamed by your *vile, filthy* habits, Joseph!" The *Gaslight Gazette* journalist's lips and hands trembled as he fought to control his fear. "*Stop* quaking and do as I say!" Oliver retraced his path around his desk.

"Y—Yes, Fath—"

"*At once!*"

Joseph instinctively ducked at his father's yell and half-ran, half-stumbled from the room with a plethora of stuttered apologies and goodbyes.

TWELVE

Aficionados of fine cask ale, appreciated while lounging in a comfy chair before a roaring fire, didn't count among the patrons of *The Turk's Head Public House*. A dilapidated establishment, its nightly entertainments included knife fights fuelled by drink. Due to its corner location, its interior was cramped and potentially dangerous if one risked a wobbly stool without first taking the necessary precaution to hold it down. Sparse, stale alcohol-soaked sawdust was still sprinkled across the floorboards, perhaps the same sawdust as several weeks prior. Two dirt-covered windows, at right angles to the door on the corner, ironically promised 'fine ales' in chipped, peeling white paint whilst, on their inside, sun-faded pews offered an uncomfortable alternative to the stools. Despite its convenience to wealthier neighbourhoods, the pub was frequented by residents of Moore Street and the lane to the rear of Molyneux Street and south of John Street. Both the lane and Moore Street were identical in their Charles Booth Poverty Map classifications.

Lady Owston and Miss Webster, being the first of their group to arrive, observed the dark, smoky, crowded interior from the proportional safety of the street. "And you are *quite* certain *this* is it?" Katheryne reiterated her disbelief. The light cast out by the street gas lamp behind them was absorbed by the window's grimy surface, thereby highlighting every disgusting facet of filth.

"I passed by earlier today," Agnes explained for a second time.

Katheryne turned toward her, for they had been stood shoulder to shoulder, and enquired. "*Please* do check again?"

The secretary fought her urge to sigh and once more retrieved the folded note from her bag. "*The Turk's Head Public House,* corner of Queen Street and Edgware Road."

"Evening, ladies," a deep voice greeted at their backs. They turned inward to see the most welcomed visage of Sam standing beneath the lamplight.

"*Mr* Snyder," Lady Owston beamed, offering him her gloved hands. "We appear to have become confused in our unerring enthusiasm to assist the Suggitts. Agnes is convinced *this* is where we shall be gathering." She gestured toward the pub. "But *I* have reason to doubt her conviction—purely on the basis of what is inside, you understand. Agnes isn't *usually* wrong."

"Nah, this 'ere's the place." Sam nodded. Katheryne's face fell, but Agnes' lifted with an air of triumph. "I hope you didn't mind my not bringin' you 'ere," Sam continued. "But the Missus had my supper on the table and I'd not seen the little ones since this mornin'." He thumbed behind him. "I've got the cab tonight though, so I'll take you back."

"How very kind you are," Lady Owston flatly replied.

"Not me… Miss Trent," Sam corrected.

The independent journalist cast a dirty look toward him and, with more conviction, enquired, "Shall we go inside?" Yet she didn't wait for their answer, instead choosing to stride forward and commandeer a vacant pew to the right of the door.

A twinkle of jest played within the cabman's hues as he invited the secretary to enter next while one side of Agnes' mouth lifted at his having outwitted her employer. Taking her place beside her, she rested her hand upon her bag and held it close against her thigh. From their vantage point, they could see the entire room—and all the suspicious expressions being cast their way.

Mr Snyder enquired, "What are you ladies drinkin'?"

"*Drinking*? In *here*?" Katheryne scoffed, firmly gripping her own bag with both hands as it sat on her lap. Sam merely waited for her to realise the absurdity of her objection and give him an answer. After glancing at the drinks standing on nearby tables, Katheryne did indeed do just that. "A sweet sherry, Mr Snyder. Agnes?"

"The same, please."

"Wait a moment," Katheryne hastily bid to the cabman as he turned toward the bar. Opening her bag to retrieve her purse, the shaking of his head stopped her.

He replied, "Keep your coin. I've got money enough."

"Oh… very well," Lady Owston surrendered and graced him with a grateful smile. "Thank you, Mr Snyder." Agnes repeated the pleasantry and cast a cursory glance of her own about the place once he'd left them. The only fireplace she could see was on the opposite side of the room with many bodies between her and it. So dense was the crowd she could see neither flame nor ember.

The only employee behind the paltry bar was a haggard woman with dirty-blond hair; loosely pinned with several strands hanging about her face. Probably in her late fifties, she had permanent, large, dark rings under her puffy eyes and creased skin riddled with wrinkles. Sunken cheeks and a narrow, flat nose gave her an almost witch-like appearance. She wore a straight-lined, plain, dark-grey woollen dress underneath a long, white-cotton apron. A knitted, light-grey shawl was draped about her shoulders, its ends folded by the crooks of her elbows. There were two customers already at the bar, in addition to Mr Snyder, but Agnes couldn't be sure if they were queuing or had been served already.

"My wife's note from Miss Trent," Mr Suggitt suddenly stated from the door while holding an envelope before the ladies' faces. It had the unmistakeable Bow Street Society mark in its top right corner.

Entering the pub behind him was Mr Queshire who, standing to the right of Clement, explained, "I'm here at Mr Suggitt's request."

"Mrs Suggitt was too distressed by the note's arrival to attend this evening," the assistant manager went on while Katheryne motioned for them to take the vacant stools opposite. Both gentlemen accepted her invitation yet each instinctively touched the stools' torn fabric for dampness prior to committing their behinds. "She, as well as me, had assumed your enquiries to be over."

"Why? Because you'd asked them to be?" Agnes challenged.

Clement inhaled deeply and answered, "I'm quite certain the police are capable of identifying, and arresting, Mrs Roberts' murderer. My wife agrees she should not have hired the Society at all."

Lady Owston and Miss Webster exchanged glances. "Miss Trent shall require Mrs Suggitt's formal withdrawal of her commission in writing," Agnes stated. Katheryne couldn't recall such a clause having ever been mentioned, however. Upon reflection, she suspected Miss Webster's words were precisely the ruse they appeared to be.

The same cynicism wasn't behind Mr Suggitt's words, though, as he replied, "I'll have her write Miss Trent first thing in the morning."

"I may, inadvertently, be responsible for some of this confusion," Mr Queshire confessed with a regret-riddled voice. "I told Mr Suggitt of your discovery regarding Mrs Robert's shawl, of it having been unwittingly… 'passed on' by my store."

"Diana takes much comfort from knowing it's found a good home, Edmund," Mr Suggitt replied, smiling half-heartedly, as he attempted to ease his friend's emotional burden.

A thank you was softly given before Mr Queshire continued, "After you'd left, Lady Owston, I naturally considered the other clothing depicted in your sketch. I checked our stock again and the remainder of the storeroom but there was no trace of them anywhere."

"I have no recollection of the mannequin from that morning," Mr Suggitt admitted through a beleaguered sigh.

Miss Webster, having commenced a written record of their conversation, paused to enquire, "You were not the one who procured the shawl and placed it into the store's 'possession,' then?"

"Pardon?" he enquired, confused.

"Perhaps on behalf of Mrs Roberts herself?" Agnes probed further, "Or your wife?" Delving into the earlier pages of her notebook she stopped, at a particular passage. "You told Miss Dexter the shawl was of little monetary value. Being her brother-in-law though, you could've gifted a generous sum in exchange for it, correct?"

"Absolutely not," Edmund interjected. "The items are donated, not purchased."

"Perhaps to others, Mr Queshire," Miss Webster replied. "Mr Suggitt, your wife had always held a deep-seated concern for her sister, and you knew of the arrangement at the department store. If Mrs Roberts had approached you—possibly the very night she died—and asked to sell the shawl, would you have not granted her request? If only to appease your wife's troubled mind? Or, perhaps, you have broken Mr Queshire's trust and told your wife of the arrangement concerning donated stock? *She,* in that case, could've been the one to place it in the—"

"*Enough!*" Mr Suggitt cried, simultaneously leaping to his feet. Lady Owston gave a startled gasp and pressed herself against the pew. Miss Webster's reaction, on the other hand, had comprised of a mild flinching of her mouth and a reflexive blink of her eyes. Nevertheless, her heart pounded as he loomed over her.

Mr Queshire slowly rose, saying, "Clement, please sit down—"

"*No*," he snapped. "I don't have to stay here and be accused of such dastardly things—and by a woman no less!"

"Why is it you become irate whenever the possibility of you giving Mrs Roberts money is mentioned?" Agnes enquired, her voice retaining its resolution despite her immense trepidation.

Mr Suggitt's expression hardened. "Because my financial affairs are precisely that, *MY* financial affairs!"

"Oi!" the barmaid barked and Clement spun around instantly. The other patrons, having had their peace disturbed by the wealthy man already, watched the unfolding spectacle. The barmaid repeatedly thrust her finger in Mr Suggitt's direction as she warned, "You being my daughter's husband, don't stop me from getting the landlord to toss you out on your ear." Clement's back visibly stiffened and his hands clenched at his sides. His eyes held a glower that challenged the woman to remember her place, but it wasn't verbalised. Instead, he left her unchallenged while fighting to calm his indignation. A heavy pause followed, during which a patron's cough was the only sound made.

Clement eventually drew in a slow, deep breath and carefully exhaled. With it went the tension from his hands and a curt nod toward the barmaid. He turned 180 degrees and, granting himself another nod, sat with all the decorum of a true gentleman—albeit an angry one. The remaining occupants of the room, seeing the show had ended, gradually resumed their conversations. Beside Clement, Mr Queshire remarked, "Such *unnecessary* behaviour."

"How did you know my mother-in-law worked here?" Mr Suggitt enquired, quietly.

"We didn't," Lady Owston admitted. "Miss Trent simply chose this location as, she thought, it was unlikely Inspector Woolfe would find us here. I presume she was already familiar with the establishment. *Personally,* neither I nor Agnes has *ever* set foot within its walls before tonight. Good evening, Mr Locke!"

"Forgive my lateness, Lady Owston, but I was delayed at the Palladium," the illusionist explained. He looked to the, now standing, department store owner and removed his glove to accept the offered hand. Allowing Edmund to introduce himself first, Percy replied, "Mr Percival Locke."

"Mr Clement Suggitt," the man introduced, also standing to offer his hand.

"My sincere condolences to you and your wife," Mr Locke replied.

Mr Queshire, having sat, returned his attention to the barmaid, who had begun serving Mr Snyder. Experiencing no recognition of the cabman, on account of having never been introduced, Edmund disregarded him.

Having already paid for his order, it was a mere matter of Sam waiting for his drinks to be poured. The two sweet sherries had been procured from a dusty bottle claimed from an equally dusty shelf. Two barrels stood side by side upon a counter beneath the shelf, and it was from a tap inserted into the right of these the barmaid poured his pint. He swept his thumb across his nostril as he enquired, "You'll be Mrs Sarah Yates, then?"

"How'd you know?" She put his pint on the bar and wiped her hands upon her apron. "You're not one of the regulars."

"I've been workin' for your daughter, tryin' to find out who done in her sister. Me and the other Bow Street Society members."

"Waste of bloody money," Mrs Yates scoffed, wrapping her shawl about herself. Sam thought he caught a glint of gold on her marriage finger but the light was dim and she was already elaborating, "Was probably one of her customers who did it. I told Diana that but, like always, she wouldn't take a blind bit of notice of what I had to say. Was the same when Maryanna was alive, the devious beggar. All she cared about was the drink, sod everything, and everyone, else."

"Is that why you're livin' with your other son-in-law?" Sam enquired, keeping his voice casual. Nonetheless, Sarah seemed a little taken aback by his apparent knowledge. Truth was he'd only been guessing the other dresses drying above the stove at Abraham's place were Sarah's.

"Yeah," she replied. Moving closer to the bar, she gripped the corners of her shawl and, folding her arms across her chest, held them against her sides. "Did Abraham tell you that?"

"Nah." Mr Snyder smiled.

Sarah eyed him, "How'd you know, then?"

"Saw your dresses hangin' 'bove the stove when I woz there talkin' to Mr Roberts today. Thought 'e would've told you we'd been."

"I've been here all day, ain't I?" She relaxed, "Anyway, someone had to take care of him and her daughter when she walked out on them."

"I thought 'e told her to leave?"

"Only because he caught her stealing the housekeeping," she pointed out. "And that was her choice, weren't it? Take the money to get the drink or keep it to put food in her daughter's belly. She chose the gin. Was her father's daughter all right, bloody drunks. I hate 'em."

Sam tasted his pint but left the sherries untouched. He said, "But you work in a pub."

"Never let 'er come in 'ere, did I? She was barred for running her mouth off—as usual. Anyway, we've all got to do what we can to make ends meet, don't we?"

Sam hummed in agreement and once more partook of his pint. He could feel her eyes boring into him, however. Returning his drink to the bar top, he said, "Only havin' the one."

"I prefer lemonade myself," she retorted and poured herself a glass from a jug on the beer-barrel counter.

When she'd re-joined him, Sam enquired, "Woz you workin' the night she died?"

"Yeah." She took a sip. "Wouldn't of made a difference to her if I'd not been."

"Why's that?"

"We wasn't talking on account of her drinking, and of her pulling the bloody wool over Diana and Regina's eyes." She waved her hand, "I tried telling them she'd only break their 'earts but…" She sighed. "What can you do?"

"What time did you work to?"

"Half past ten." She paused. "If you don't believe me, I can fetch the landlord; he won't talk to the police but he'll talk to someone from Bow Street. You done right by that blind fella."

"Nah, I don't think we'll need that," Sam smiled.

Mrs Yates watched the cabman a moment. "Good." She moved closer to him. "I'm s'pposed to work until eleven but I had an old friend come in on one of the ships. Sailed back out this morning, he did." Sam didn't need any further explanation;

if her words weren't enough, the wistful look in her eyes certainly was.

"You don't think much of him?" He thumbed over his shoulder toward Clement and added, "Your other one?"

Sarah peered around the cabman to watch Mr Suggitt interacting with those at his table. "He loves Diana right enough but still likes to lord it over the rest of us." She took a second sip of lemonade. "But he doesn't know I know he was in here asking after Maryanna the night she died."

"How come?"

"Asked Mr Ratchett if he'd seen her, didn't he?" She smirked. "And he told me he'd been in. God knows why he was wanting her at that time of night."

"What time woz it?"

"Dunno, but it was before I left because Mr Ratchett told me about half past nine. I was upstairs seeing to Mrs Ratchett then; poor blighter's been sick for days." She drank some more lemonade. "When he told him she wasn't 'ere, he asked if she'd been in at all that night. When he told him she hadn't, he got all agitated and left again." She finished her drink and put the empty under the bar.

Sam enquired, "You bought arsenic from *Eastleigh's* chemist shop, yeah?"

"Yeah; Mr Ratchett wanted it for the mice he got upstairs." Mrs Yates eyed him. "I read what they're saying in the 'papers. Killed with arsenic, wasn't she? I'll save you the trouble and tell you now." She held up a slanted hand. "I might've wanted to throttle her at times, but I didn't do my own daughter in."

"Thanks for the drinks," Sam replied, hooking two fingers around the sherry glasses and picking up his pint. Returning to the table, he carefully put the ladies' drinks down and set his own in a small space at its edge. He retrieved a nearby vacant stool and, putting it between Lady Owston and Mr Locke, sat down.

"This is Mr Samuel Snyder," Lady Owston introduced, addressing Mr Suggitt and his employer. "The Society's cab driver and, I must say, *invaluable* expert on London's transportation networks."

Sam, having tucked his broad arms against his sides to squeeze into the small space, had to twist his body sideways to shake their hands. Once the formalities were over, he said, "Had a good little chat with your mother-in-law, Mr Suggitt. How come you and your wife never told us Mrs Yates is livin' with Mr Roberts?"

"I didn't think it was relevant," Clement answered. "And I am supposing Diana thought so, too."

"Even though she and Maryanna didn't get along?" Sam pressed, his tone betraying his curiosity.

"The root of their dispute was Maryanna's drinking, not Mrs Yates living with Abraham." Clement replied.

Mr Snyder hummed. Shifting on his stool to become more comfortable, the cabman scratched his cheek. He then pondered aloud, "What woz it you told the inspector about where you woz when Mrs Roberts was done in?"

"The truth; that I was at home," Clement replied, unconsciously shifting his own weight.

"Why'd your mother-in-law tell me you woz in 'ere askin' after Mrs Roberts, then?" Sam enquired.

Clement stared at him a moment, "I…" He looked to Edmund at his side, and then at the others as his lips parted.

"If I recall Miss Dexter's account correctly," Agnes began, checking her earlier notes as she did so. "Your wife was surprised by you telling the inspector you were home all evening. She naturally confirmed your story but was startled when Inspector Woolfe enquired if she was with you."

Mr Suggitt's gaze had darted about the table while she'd spoken and, when she'd finished, he was undoubtedly at a loss for an explanation.

"Perhaps it's time you told us the truth," Katheryne encouraged.

Clement again sought out assistance with his eyes but no one spoke up in his defence; not even Edmund. He, like the others, waited for him to explain. "I didn't murder her," Mr Suggitt finally pronounced. "I *was* looking for her that night, yes, but I never found her."

"Why were you seeking her out at all?" Mr Locke enquired as he held his open cigarette case to the man. With trembling fingers, Clement slipped one out and held it aloft as Percy snapped the case closed. Upon striking a match and igniting Mr Suggitt's cigarette, the illusionist caught sight of Miss Webster's flinch from the corner of his eyes. As he shook out the flame and discarded the match, he looked toward her, intrigued.

Mr Suggitt meanwhile had pressed the cigarette to his lips and, after inhaling the smoke, had steadily exhaled it downward. His hand continued to visibly shake even as he went on, "I'd presented Maryanna with a proposition only the day before." He paused for another hit of tobacco to steady his nerves, "A rather generous sum of money in exchange for leaving London." He leant upon his elbow as it rested on the table and, with cigarette held near to his lips, added, "She was making our lives a misery."

"Whose?" Mr Locke enquired, tapping his own cigarette against his case.

"Her daughter's, her husband's… but mostly my wife's. She cared a great deal for her sister, too much, in all honesty. Too many times, she would offer assistance, which her sister would take with promises of giving up the gin, and too many times her heart was broken. I couldn't bear to stand idly by and see her in pain any longer. If Maryanna wished to drink herself into the grave, then so be it." Mr Suggitt claimed another pull from his cigarette and withdrew his elbow from the table. Seeming to regain a degree of composure, he continued, "But she refused. Two hundred pounds I offered her to leave London and that *Lushington* wouldn't accept it." He drew in a deep breath, "After her usual vile insults, she threatened to tell Diana everything. I knew she wouldn't understand *why* I had done it, all she'd see was an attempt by her husband to rid himself of a parasitic relative who he despised. I'd never made a secret of my dislike of the woman."

"We know," Lady Owston remarked, momentarily meeting Mr Queshire's gaze as she recalled his telling her of Clement distancing himself from Maryanna whenever she visited the store. "You thought you could persuade her not to tell your wife," she continued. "So you resolved to find her the night she died, having presumed she'd come to the store that day to tell your wife, correct?"

"Correct…" Mr Suggitt came to the end of his cigarette and crushed it out. "I didn't know *how* I would persuade her; more money, probably. I checked the usual doss and public houses Diana had told me she frequented. Even when I came here, I had doubts I'd find her. She and her mother haven't spoken since Maryanna spent her housekeeping money on gin." He paused long enough to glance over at Mrs Yates to satisfy himself she hadn't overheard, "I spoke to Mr Ratchett, the landlord here, but he'd not seen Maryanna all evening. It didn't even occur to me he would tell her mother of my visit."

"Where was she?" Miss Webster enquired.

"Upstairs, he told me. His wife is unwell and she was tending to her, a sickness of the lungs—or something."

"When did you arrive here?" Mr Locke enquired, steadily making his way through his own cigarette.

"It was around quarter past nine, I believe. I left home at eight thirty—after dinner. Diana *was* at home when I left so, *yes,* she lied for me but, at that time, didn't know where I'd gone or why. I cannot say I'm proud of myself for allowing her to do so." Clement took in a deep, shuddering breath, "I stayed here for only a few minutes and continued my search. I gave up around ten thirty and arrived home just after eleven thirty."

"Was your wife still at home when you returned?"

"Yes; she was sound asleep when I retired to bed at around a quarter to midnight. I... made every effort not to wake her. I didn't want her knowing I'd returned so late."

"Does she now know the reasons for your leaving home?" Mr Locke enquired.

Clement nodded and replied, "I told her during the cab ride to Mr Roberts' home. She wasn't best pleased but she understood why I did what I had." The Bow Streeters all knew it would be pointless to ask if Mrs Suggitt would confirm her husband's story; she'd already lied once for him so, undoubtedly, she'd do the same again.

"Does the police know?" Mr Locke enquired.

"We told Inspector Woolfe this morning. He threatened to arrest me should Mr Ratchett not confirm my whereabouts. I have not had another visit from the inspector since, so I assume he must have."

Deciding to take a different tact, Lady Owston addressed both Mr Suggitt and Mr Queshire as she revealed, "Mrs Roberts was murdered using French Breakfast coffee laced with arsenic, a tin of which is in the *Queshire Department Store's* storeroom. Miss Galway's name was also found in the poison book of *Drummond's Pharmaceutical Chemist's* on Oxford Street. She had purchased arsenic for, she claims, an infestation of rats."

"That's correct," Mr Suggitt replied. "I'd sent her to fetch some as I'd forgotten to do so and the store was particularly busy that day. As for the coffee, it's well known among the assistants it's there as its consumption is restricted to Mr Queshire and me alone. The door is also never locked; the assistant's regularly replenish goods from the stock we hold in there."

"Your easy access to the method by which the poison was administered does place you both under suspicion, however," Mr Locke pointed out to both Clement and Edmund.

They gave one another an incredulous glance, and Clement replied, "But I have a tin of it at home, too. Diana and I developed a taste for it while we were honeymooning in Paris. I wouldn't even *think* to lace it with *arsenic* and I would *certainly* not serve such a deadly drink to *anyone*. Who, on God's green Earth, *could* do such a thing?"

"Most *certainly* someone known to her," Mr Locke retorted. "Whether the coffee used was attained from the storeroom, Mr Roberts' home, your own home, or elsewhere, the fact remains she accepted coffee—far from her usual choice of beverage—from her murderer and, without any hint of hesitation, drank enough of it to be struck down by the poison." He tapped his cigarette to dislodge its excess ash while the colour drained from Clement's face before their very eyes. He slowly rose but then stumbled in a half faint. It was only Mr Queshire's quick thinking, in grabbing his arm and pulling him back down onto his stool, that prevented him from falling and striking his head on the table behind him.

"No... I can't believe it..." Mr Suggitt said. "She was murdered by a madman... a stranger in the street."

"Would you accept coffee from a stranger?" Mr Locke enquired.

Mr Suggitt, gripping the edge of his seat, leant to the side as he frowned deeply. His face was contorted with pain and confusion but, nevertheless, after a moment of consideration he shook his head and muttered, "No... I would not."

"Why did you think the inspector would wish to arrest you if he didn't think someone she knew had murdered her?" Locke queried.

"He accused me of the deed but didn't enlighten Diana and I as to the method used to administer the arsenic." Clement explained.

"Do you have any hessian sacks at the store?" Mr Snyder enquired.

Both Mr Queshire and Mr Suggitt looked to him, surprised, at the unusual question.

"I don't recall…" Clement replied.

"Why?" Mr Queshire added,

"Her body was carried in a hessian sack to where she was discovered outside the bazaar," Mr Locke revealed, scrutinising the men's reactions as he did so.

Mr Queshire swallowed hard while Mr Suggitt looked all the more ill.

"They are not something the store usually utilises," Edmund explained. "But I'll check nonetheless."

"And at home?" Miss Webster inquired, adding. "Perhaps a sack of potatoes or coal?"

"You'd have to ask my wife about that," Mr Suggitt replied.

"I have a small sack of potatoes, but I use a scuttle for my coal," Mr Queshire admitted and Miss Webster made a note of their answers.

Lady Owston meanwhile smiled at the assistant manager, "Mr Suggitt, I'm certain Mr Queshire shan't mind my asking this: what is at the room at the top of the stairs in your store?"

"Another storeroom; chairs and stock for the salon." Clement replied.

"Lady Owston, I do not know *why* you are fixated upon a mere storeroom." Mr Queshire, offering a feeble smile, added in a voice hinting at an erosion of patience.

"I am fixated, Mr Queshire, because I do not believe it to be such. Why would many ladies leave it, on several different occasions, if it was as you say?"

"Because our customers know the salon to be at the top of the stairs, and presume the first door they come to is it," Edmund said "They don't think to look to the open doorway where the salon actually is."

"Oh my God," Clement whispered. Yet his eyes weren't on Lady Owston, but another standing behind Mr Snyder. When his line of vision was followed, they all saw a blond-haired woman at the door wearing Maryanna's shawl.

"Darling?" Mr Locke enquired, rising to step out from the table and face his wife.

"Good evening, husband," she greeted, not at all surprised to find him there among strangers. In her hand she carried a black-leather Gladstone bag.

"My wife, Doctor Lynnette Locke," Percy introduced but everyone seemed stunned at what they had seen draped around her shoulders. "Darling, this is—"

"I thought women were not permitted to become doctors," Mr Queshire stated. "Where did you train?"

The illusionist, whose brow had lofted, looked to his wife who gave a sardonic smile and explained, "The *London School of Medicine for Women* and, before you ask, that institution is legally approved to train women doctors. Furthermore, my training's respectability is equal to that of my male colleagues." She rested her hand upon her husband's chest, "Introductions shan't be necessary. Contrary to the whisperings of your ego, darling, I'm not here in pursuit of you. Mrs Ratchett has been unwell and I'm here to see how she's faring."

"Another of your charitable causes," the magician remarked.

"Indeed," Doctor Locke replied and, looking to the others, explained, "Forgive my rudeness but I hadn't expected to find my husband here and duty draws me elsewhere. Good evening to you all."

As she attempted to depart for the bar, however, her husband gently took hold of her arm and said, "One moment, please, darling. May I ask where you procured your delightful shawl from?"

"*Queshire's,* of course," she responded, offering a smile of acknowledgement to that establishment's owner, a gesture which wasn't returned.

"When? Are you able to recall who sold it to you?" Her husband enquired,

"Yesterday, and it was one of the assistant's. I didn't take her name." Her head tilted slightly as she enquired, curious, "Why?"

"It was my sister-in-law's," Mr Suggitt stated in a subdued voice.

Mr Locke, seeing this had only served to confuse his wife, explained, "The lady who was discovered upon Oxford Street."

"Truly?" Doctor Locke challenged, somewhat taken aback.

"Truly," her husband confirmed and Lynette ran her eyes over the garment.

"My wife crocheted it for Maryanna." Clement informed her,

"She must therefore have it back," Lynnette replied with great resolve and removed the garment. Giving it to the assistant manager, who carefully folded it and rested it on his lap, she said, "With my sincerest condolences."

"Thank you."

"Until tonight, my husband," Lynette said, looking back to Percy. The magician placed a delicate kiss upon her cheek and watched as she went to the bar. Mrs Yates, upon seeing her, opened a door at the back and called for Mr Ratchett. While Percy returned to his seat, the landlord appeared and accompanied Doctor Locke from the room.

A heartbeat after they'd left though, the pub's main door was thrown open and a girl of seventeen marched inside. She had naturally wavy mouse-brown, shoulder-length hair, fair skin, and dark-brown eyes. An old, russet, ankle-length skirt and tattered, forest-green woollen shawl, which covered her entire torso, denoted her poor financial status. Going to the bar, she threw her open hand against Mrs Yates' cheek and yelled, "*Bitch*!"

"Regina!" Mr Suggitt exclaimed as he leapt to his feet for a second time that evening. The young woman spun around, startled, and he crossed the room toward her. He enquired, "What are you doing?"

"She's gone wild, that's what!" Mrs Yates screeched, holding her red face.

Regina's rage was reignited by this remark, however, and she cried, "You killed my mother!" The young woman moved forward, as if to jump over the bar, but Mr Suggitt took hold of her shoulders and turned her to face him.

"None of that, now!" He said.

"*Lemmie go*!" Regina screamed, struggling within his grip. Trying to look over her shoulder at her grandmother, she continued, "You won't get my dad! I won't let you!"

"I don't *want* your dad!" Mrs Yates threw back.

"Then how come you came to live with us soon as he threw out Mum?! You wanted her gone from the start, you *witch*! You turned my dad against her!" Regina retorted.

All the while, Clement struggled with her to try to move toward the exit. When he reached the table where the Bow Streeters and Mr Queshire were, he said, "I must go home. Come on, Regina!" With one, carefully timed shunt, he successfully got her through the door and said, "Do not give her the satisfaction. Your aunt and I will take care of you for tonight."

The young woman jerked her shoulders away from his grip and looked from him to her grandmother and back again. Everyone in the pub gawked at her but she didn't care. As she tugged her shawl back onto her shoulders, she growled at her grandmother, "I won't let this lie."

"An eventful evening," the department store owner remarked as the girl finally allowed her uncle to lead her away. Rising to his feet, he added, "and a late one. Please forgive me but I, too, must be taking my leave. Good night to you all."

While he also departed, Lady Owston finished her sherry and encouraged her secretary to do the same. Upon seeing Mr Locke preparing to leave though, she enquired of him, "Shan't you wait for your wife?"

"Lynette is accustomed to visiting less-than-reputable establishments along the poorer thoroughfares; she feels it her social duty to provide free care to those who could not otherwise afford a doctor's fee." He smiled, "She is also my wife and therefore capable of protecting herself." He picked up his cane and, swinging it outward to press its tip upon the floor, bowed slightly to his associates. "Good night to you all," he said and, turning upon his heel, silently left the pub.

"I do believe it is time for us to leave as well," Lady Owston remarked as she stood with much relief. Miss Webster and Mr Snyder followed suit and the three left together. "We should visit Mr Roberts again tomorrow morning," Katheryne went on as she stepped out into the cold night. "To ask him why he lied about his mother-in-law living with—Miss Galway?"

"Hello, Lady Owston," Rose greeted, pulling her coat further about herself as she approached them. "Didn't know you was here."

"I see." Lady Owston frowned. "Is that why you were watching us through the window?"

The assistant's eyes widened as she cried, "I wasn't!"

"Come now, Miss Galway. I saw you standing at the window overlooking our table."

Rose glanced back and, realising she couldn't deny it, replied, Fine, I was watching—but only because I wanna help the Society."

"You've already been a tremendous help to us," Lady Owston pointed out. "Go home, child. Aside from it being *far* too cold to be loitering outside of pubs, there is *still* a murderer walking around. In addition to the ne'er-do-wells and ruffians one may usually expect to find stalking the streets of London."

"I'll take you," Mr Snyder offered and gestured to his waiting cab.

"Nah, that's okay," the assistant replied with a shake of her head. "Think I'm gonna go inside anyway; get something hot to eat."

"*Miss* Galway," Lady Owston said. "*Go* home." She then strode forward without further ado and climbed into the cab. Agnes followed while Sam indicated the vehicle in a silent re-offering of a ride. For a second time, the assistant refused and the cabman, albeit reluctantly, accepted her decision and went about taking the two ladies home.

THIRTEEN

"We came as soon as we heard," Lady Owston uttered in an unsteady voice as she approached a grief-stricken Mrs Suggitt in the arms of her husband. "When did it happen?"

"A few hours ago," he replied. Miss Webster and Miss Dexter stood at Lady Owston's side but Mr Snyder had erred on the side of caution by remaining with his cab. Regardless of the early hour—four thirty, to be precise—a band of gawkers had congregated upon Queen Street. A cordon of four Metropolitan Police constables carrying lamps had been formed on this end of Moore Street. A Black Maria had been set astride the street's other entrance, the glow from the streetlamps illuminating both it and its driver. A miniscule dot of light, emitted from the vehicle's lantern, also cut through the vast darkness. It had been raining heavily so all the officers were clad in their thick, heavy coats. The air was also dense with a mustiness caused by filth being disturbed by the water.

Miss Dexter gripped the lapels of her ankle-length, midnight-blue cloak as she shivered straight to her core. It wasn't simply the cold of the night which had chilled her, however. From their position, she could see the tenement building she had visited mere hours before; a sorrowful place made all the worse by a second tragedy. "To *think* we only saw her this evening," Lady Owston's voice broke through the artist's thoughts. "Perhaps we could've prevented this from happening."

"There was no suggestion she was in any danger," Miss Webster pointed out.

Lady Owston, accustomed to her secretary's hardy exterior, felt offended by it now. "Oh, *Agnes*, show some emotion for *once!*"

"Forgive me, Lady Owston, I—" Miss Webster answered, shocked. She had interrupted herself, uncertain as to what to say. What could be said? *Mrs Yates is dead...* She thought and bowed her head. She took a step back and half-turned from the group. Miss Dexter, all too keenly aware of the weighty tension that hung between them, instinctively cast her gaze to the ground.

"She's right," Clement murmured eventually. "None of us could've guessed she would be…" He held his wife closer to him as her previously quiet sobbing intensified. "Where *is* that *blasted* inspector?"

"Was he the one to summon you here?" Lady Owston enquired to sharpen her focus.

"No." Clement's hand gently rubbed his wife's trembling back. "We received a telephone call at around two thirty this morning. A Mr Trowel, a neighbour of Mr Roberts, called from the *Turk's Head*. Mr Trowel had been leaving for work when he'd noticed Abraham's door was ajar. Thinking he'd forgotten to lock it, Mr Trowel investigated to check all was well. When he—" Clement's voice shook, "When he pushed the door wider, he saw… *oh God,* I cannot speak it. It is too horrific!"

"She was mutilated," Inspector Woolfe finished for him. He growled, "Who told the meddlers?"

Mrs Suggitt broke down, violently howling into her husband's chest.

Having already struggled to retain his composure, Clement's strength of will was tested further by his wife's unadulterated display. He hissed, "Have a *heart*, Inspector! My wife has just lost her mother to this fiend."

"And we'll catch him," Woolfe retorted in his usual tone. "But until then there's nothing you can do, Mr Suggitt." He scowled at the Bow Streeters, "or you. Go home—all of you."

"What a *foul*-tempered individual," Lady Owston commented when he had walked away and she was positive he wouldn't hear.

"*Why* are they doing this?" Mrs Suggitt enquired through a harsh sob. "What have any of us done to *them*?"

"I think I should take her home," Mr Suggitt told the Bow Streeters yet his wife shook her head.

"No, Clement, we can't go home without Regina and Abraham."

"Where are they?" Miss Webster enquired.

"Inside," Mr Suggitt said. "We brought them here after receiving Mr Trowel's telephone call."

"And they were with you both all night prior to that?" Miss Dexter enquired, her voice gentle. She had been informed of the events of the evening, which had unfolded at *The Turk's Head,* by Miss Webster during their cab journey over.

Mr Clement's next words were therefore not a mystery to the artist. "Yes, after Regina's outburst at the pub, I took her to our home. Mr Roberts arrived at about half past midnight. He woke us from our beds. Mrs Yates had told him of Regina's behaviour and he wanted to confront her about it and escort her home."

Mrs Suggitt was in a clear state of distress as she listened, clutching her handkerchief to her face.

"I took him into the parlour," Mr Suggitt continued, "Where my wife joined us. We spoke to him together and convinced him to stay the night as Regina had already fallen asleep and it was too late to journey back home."

"Mr Roberts had seen Mrs Yates this evening, then?" Miss Webster enquired.

Clement nodded and said, "He told us he'd met her at the pub at closing—around eleven o'clock—and walked her home. Once there, my mother-in-law had told him everything Regina had said and done. He admitted he had been angered by his daughter's behaviour but also shocked. Sarah tried to calm him, he said, but he had wanted to see Regina right away. Since they weren't sure if Regina would return home, and due to my mother-in-law being the focus of her rage, they decided it would be better if Sarah waited at home. I don't think Abraham intended to stay with us but..." He inhaled deeply as his hand again trembled. "...Abraham often sleeps outside the gates of the docks in the hopes of getting work first thing in the morning. We..." His voice shook, "...We thought she'd be safe at home, as she had been so many times before."

"Was she in the habit of leaving the door unlocked?" Lady Owston enquired; her own voice heavy.

"No; they didn't have much but what they did have they were proud of," Clement replied. "Sarah and I rarely saw eye to eye but she was family nonetheless. How could *anyone...*?"

"That is what we intend to find out," Lady Owston soothed. "Could you tell me the address of the lodgings where the store's assistants reside?"

"Why?"

"We saw Miss Galway outside *The Turk's Head* when we left. She told us she would be going inside to buy a hot meal. She may have seen something therefore and I, for one, would like to speak with her before Inspector Woolfe puts the fear of God into her."

"Yes… of course, I…" Clement had to search his mind a moment but was eventually able to dictate it to Miss Webster.

"Thank you, Mr Suggitt," Katheryne said. "We shall be in touch." The independent journalist exchanged glances with her fellow Bow Streeters and the three bade the Suggitts farewell.

"I wonder where Mr Maxwell is," Miss Dexter couldn't help but remark as they neared Sam's cab.

Lady Owston, pausing with her hand upon the vehicle, cast a cursory glance around the gawkers. "I truly have no idea, child," she replied and climbed inside. "Perhaps he is still tucked up in bed?"

"He would have received Miss Trent's note as we did though, surely?" Miss Webster enquired as she sat down beside her employer. The artist took her place last and the three closed the doors over their knees.

After giving Mr Snyder the address, and the vehicle lurching forward, Katheryne replied, "The whereabouts of that journalist, as amicable as he may be, is *not* our immediate concern, ladies. After all, Mr Locke isn't here either."

Georgina hummed, she hadn't even noticed the illusionist's absence. Recalling Joseph's note she'd received earlier in the evening, cancelling her invitation to dinner at his parents' home on account of his mother being ill, she assumed him to have stayed at her bedside. Rather than being comforted by this thought though, she felt all the more concerned. Should she not be at his side if his mother was seriously unwell? Perhaps not; she had yet to meet her so it would be inappropriate. Nevertheless, Miss Dexter gazed at the darkened buildings steadily moving past them and wondered what he was doing at that moment.

* * *

Doctor Lynette Locke turned the latch key and entered her home. The kerosene lamp on the hall table had been left aflame by Mr Lyons, their butler. It had become a regular habit after she'd commenced making night-time house calls to her patients. This eve a particularly difficult birth had forced her from Mrs Ratchett's bedside to a neighbour's home. She relieved herself of her coat and hung it upon the stand by the door. Mr Lyons, having duties to attend to come dawn, wasn't expected to keep vigil until her return.

Given Percy's resounding success as an illusionist at, and owner of, the Paddington Palladium, the Lockes enjoyed the upper middle-class status. As such, they resided amidst Booth's highest classification of wealthy homes on Cleveland Terrace, nestled among Gloucester Terrace, Cleveland Gardens, and Westbourne Terrace. To the east of this area was the then named Great Western Railway Station now known as Paddington.

The house was tranquil and largely in darkness as she placed a policeman's whistle beside the lamp. She'd found it a far more effective defensive weapon than any other for it summoned whichever constable happened to be passing. Her possession of it was kept a closely guarded secret between herself and Percy, he being the one to have procured it. A Chinese puzzle box and finger trap, the latter resting upon a wooden stand, also occupied the table.

Half the ground floor accommodated Lynette's medical practise, her office being at the front and the patient waiting room at the back, each on the left side. Only her wealthier patients visited her home, however. The remainder of the ground floor was occupied by a dining room at the front and a guest parlour at the back. Though their home was on several floors, only she, her husband, and their servants resided there. The Lockes' staff consisted of Mr Lyons, Percy's personal valet, James, her ladies' maid, Belinda, their cook, Mrs Lyons, a scullery maid, Veronica, and a footman, Greenham. James and Greenham had rooms within the basement, adjacent to the pantry and kitchen, while Mr and Mrs Lyons, Belinda, and Veronica were accommodated within the attic rooms. Mr Weatherby, the Lockes' groom and driver, resided above a small stable situated away from the residence.

She moved toward her office, with the intention of putting away her Gladstone bag, when Mr Lyons silently stepped forth from the shadows. He said, "Pardon me, ma'am."

Lynette halted sharply but showed no sign of being startled. Instead, she read the concern on his face and felt a weight drop within her chest, "Where is he?"

"In his study; he retired to it shortly after returning at nine thirty."

"Has he eaten?"

"Yes; a cold supper I took to him at nine forty-five." Lyons paused, "I saw his paraphernalia upon the sofa when I entered but, as per your instructions, didn't remark upon it."

"Very good, Lyons."

"At four o'clock this morning, a messenger boy arrived with this." The butler passed to her an envelope with a 'B' stamped into its top-right corner. Doctor Locke didn't hesitate in tearing it open and reading its contents.

She returned it and said, "Put it aside. He cannot assist the Bow Street Society tonight."

"Yes, ma'am."

"You may also secure the house and retire to bed."

"Yes, ma'am." Mr Lyons dipped his head and went about securing the front door's many bolts and locks. Lynette meanwhile climbed the stairs to the first floor and approached her husband's study. Her singular knock garnered no response so, already knowing of Percy's habit not to lock the door whenever he was inside, turned the knob and entered.

Within, she found the lamp at half strength and the curtains drawn over the only window. A fire, which had once been fierce, now smouldered in the hearth. The window was located on the back wall, overlooking the street, with the hearth on the right and the desk on the left. A collection of egg-cup-and-ball magic tricks was gathered upon the desk alongside sketches and handwritten notes for possible illusions. The lamp stood on the desk's corner adjacent to an opened, narrow, leather-bound box with green-velvet lining. If its indentations of a needle and vial were not telling enough, the sight of Percy upon a sofa to the left of the door certainly was.

Lying on his back with his head closest to the inwardly opening door, he had one shirt sleeve rolled up to his shoulder and a tourniquet tightly tied about his arm. The tourniquet was constructed from a canvas strap which passed through two round bars. A large screw was positioned centrally on the tourniquet and was perpendicular to the plates. This type of tourniquet was specifically for surgical use. The screw would be turned, clockwise, to pull upon the strap via the upper plate rising. The more the strap was pulled upon, the tighter the tourniquet became. His arm with the tourniquet hung over the side of the sofa, its hand resting on the varnished floorboards, while his other lay on his stomach. The box's missing vial lay on its side by his hip so it was to this she went. The label affixed to it

167

stated, as expected, *HEROIN.* The needle was wedged between the sofa's back cushion and her husband. She found both it and the vial to be empty upon retrieving them.

She sighed softly as her hands dropped to her sides, "Oh, *Percy...*" The illusionist, whose eyes were closed, didn't respond. Lynette would've honestly been surprised if he had. Going to her bag, she placed the vial inside and returned the needle to its box. Next, she took her compact from her pocket and held its mirror close to her husband's lips. The steam which formed upon its glass told her he was at least breathing. A careful lifting of one eyelid and then the other confirmed he was still under the drug's influence.

"I suppose I should be thankful you used the heroin *I'd* prescribed," she whispered, knowing the vial had contained very little indeed. Nonetheless, she searched his frock coat, which had been laying across the sofa's arm, for additional vials. When she didn't find any, she crossed the room to his desk and checked each drawer. Again, no further discoveries were made. She walked to the middle of the room as she considered other possible hiding places. Most of his props were secured in an adjacent storeroom but, while it was likely some heroin was hidden there, her immediate concern was the study. She had known him to slip a vial or two onto a hidden shelf within the chimney so her next move was to kneel in front of it and put her arm up. The shelf was found after only a few seconds of feeling around but it was empty. She sighed, partly with relief and partly with concern; either her prescription was his only stash or he'd found a new hiding place. As much as she hoped he'd run out, experience leant her toward him concealing more elsewhere.

Rising, she returned to the sofa and placed a soft kiss upon his forehead. Many questions posed themselves in her mind but she knew none of them would be answered tonight. After gently stroking his head, she took her bag, left the study, and locked its door behind her. Her husband could easily pick it, of course, but she didn't want any of the servants seeing him in that condition. "Good night," she whispered and retired to bed alone.

FOURTEEN

Presumably to eliminate poor punctuality among its employees, the *Queshire Department Store's* assistant lodgings were located on Argyll Street, the same thoroughfare which lay opposite the *London Crystal Palace Bazaar*. The impressive, burgundy façade of Oxford Circus Station which today stands on the northwest corner of the street, where it meets Oxford Street, wasn't built by the Underground Electric Railways Company of London Limited (UERL) until 1906. As a result, only a few people wandered through, possibly going to work, when the Bow Street Society ladies disembarked from Mr Snyder's hansom cab at five fifteen in the morning.

Dawn had yet to break so the cabman dangled a miner's Davy lamp to Miss Dexter. The circumference of light emitted by the tiny flame, housed within the lamp's narrow, cylindrical casing, was sufficient enough to illuminate the path directly ahead. Beyond this, the pitch blackness prevented any structures or obstacles from being discerned. The young artist gratefully accepted the gift and held it aloft as Sam said, "I'll be right 'ere if you need me."

"Thank you, Sam," Georgina replied.

Lady Owston, who had taken Agnes' arm, said, "We shall cry out if we need your assistance, Mr Snyder. Let us press on, ladies." There had been a harsh frost during the night which had made the path a little treacherous. The three therefore approached the lodgings, and ascended its steps to the door with caution, Miss Dexter at the front and the other two at the rear.

Lady Owston reached around the artist to knock, once they'd safely reached their destination. The sash window to the door's right lit up a moment later as a lamp was ignited within. Thin curtains were next pulled aside by a silhouetted individual who proceeded to unlock and lift the window open. When they gripped the ledge and poked their head through the gap, the Bow Streeters could see it was a woman. The glare of the lamp behind her disguised her face, however. Miss Dexter lifted the lamp higher and the young woman at the window blinked and shielded her eyes with her hand. She demanded, "Who are you?! I'll shout for a constable!"

"That shan't be necessary; we're friends of Miss Galway's." Katheryne placed a gloved hand upon her chest, "Lady Katheryn Owston, Miss Agnes Webster, and Miss Georgina Dexter of the Bow Street Society. The man sitting up on the hansom cab is Mr Samuel Snyder; he is also part of our group. Is Miss Galway at home?"

"Yeah; she's in a right state though."

"Oh *dear*," Katheryne replied, concerned. "If you could let us inside, we will bring comfort to her." The nameless woman hesitated. After a moment, she withdrew from the window, slid it closed, and relocked it. The lamp was also extinguished.

"What do you suppose has upset her?" Miss Dexter whispered while they waited.

The sound of approaching footsteps on the other side of the door had Katheryne responding with, "We shall soon find out." A bolt slid back, followed by a key turning, and finally the door opening.

Their friend from the window scrutinised the group, "You'd best not be lying to me."

"May God strike us down if we are," Katheryne retorted and indicated the hallway. The young woman, again, hesitated but stepped aside to permit them entry. "Thank you, Miss—?"

"Smith," the woman replied. She pointed past the stairs and added, "I think she's in the kitchen."

"Excellent," Katheryne lifted her hand, "there's no need to escort us, Miss Smith. Please, you have already done a great deal."

The woman shut the front door and grunted, saying, "If you are lying Rose'll soon sort you out." The three Bow Streeters exchanged glances but Miss Smith returned to her room and slammed its door behind her.

Miss Dexter whispered, "Perhaps Mr Snyder should have accompanied us after all?"

"*Nonsense,*" Agnes rebutted. "We are no weaker for being women."

Georgina smiled, her fear easing under the strength of the secretary's conviction. She replied, "Indeed, Miss Webster." The two women traversed the dark hallway side by side while Lady Owston followed closely behind.

Beyond the door at its end was a modest kitchen warmed by an immense stove. Sitting at a table in the middle of the room was Miss Galway being comforted by a third young woman knelt at her feet. Both women turned sharp eyes toward the new arrivals upon hearing their entrance. "Lady Owston!" Rose cried. She simultaneously leapt to her feet and threw her arms about the independent journalist. "I'm sorry!"

"What's going on? Who're you?" Rose's comforter enquired as she rose to her feet. She looked between Agnes and Georgina.

The artist placed her lantern upon the table while the secretary replied, "Miss Agnes Webster, Miss Georgina Dexter, and Lady Katheryne Owston from the Bow Street Society. Miss Smith let us inside; we are friends of Miss Galway's."

"What*ever* is the matter, child?" Lady Owston probed, half-pulling away from Rose to study her anguished face. "Surely you've not heard already?"

"Heard what?" Rose enquired, perplexed. Katheryne glanced at the other assistant and guided Rose back to her chair. Only once she was seated did Lady Owston break the news.

"Mrs Sarah Yates, mother of Mrs Suggitt and Mrs Roberts, was murdered this night at home." Rose's breath hitched in her throat, her pink complexion paled as if someone had turned a tap, and her form commenced a violent tremble. She attempted to speak but merely succeeded in moving her lips. Katheryne, shocked by the assistant's reaction, placed her hand upon Rose's. She enquired, "Miss Galway? Miss Galway, are you able to hear me?"

"*No!*" Rose's voice abruptly screeched. "*No!* It *can't* be right!" Rose again leapt to her feet but, this time, sought the arms of her friend. "*Tell* them, Annie! It *can't* be right! It *can't*! It *can't...*" Rose collapsed into Annie's arms, forcing her friend to stumble a little, and sobbed uncontrollably. Lady Owston, Miss Webster, and Miss Dexter looked on, stunned.

Annie held her friend close and, rubbing her back, glared at the others. "Look what you've done."

"I don't understand," Lady Owston admitted. "Were Rose and Mrs Yates close?"

"Nah," Annie replied and quietly shushed her friend to ease her distress.

Lady Owston still stared at the two, dumbfounded. She said, "Then I don't understand why—"

"She saw someone, okay?" Annie barked.

Katheryne sighed and, glancing at Agnes and Georgina, replied, "I'm afraid you are going to have to give a far more detailed explanation than that."

Annie scowled at the three Bow Streeters before focusing on calming her friend. For several long moments, there was a tense silence in the kitchen, interrupted only by Rose's shuddering sobs. Eventually, she was passive enough to be guided back to her chair by Annie who, easing her down onto it, knelt beside it and held her hand. She whispered more reassurances to Rose and looked up at Agnes, Katheryne, and Georgina.

"Rose followed Mrs Yates and a Mr Roberts from the *Turk's Head Pub* tonight; told me she was trying to help you lot out with some murder you're working on." Annie's voice held more than a hint of malice as she spoke. "When Mrs Yates and Mr Roberts got to the end of their road though, Rose saw a bloke on the other side of Queen Street, lurking like he was up to no good."

"Did she see who it was?" Georgina enquired, hoping to capture their likeness in a sketch. Rose, who was still crying, managed to at least shake her bowed head.

"He stopped when Mrs Yates and Mr Roberts turned onto Moore Street and then followed. He was like a cat stalking a mouse, Rose said. The sight of it frightened her so; she scarpered back here without stopping once and woke me. Cried in my arms, she did—not as bad as this but bad enough. I'd only just got her calm when you turned up with your *news*. I'd told her the bloke wasn't anything to worry about, said he was probably coming home from seeing some woman and didn't want his wife finding out. Then *you* had to tell her *that*."

"We had no conceivable notion Miss Galway had undertaken a task on behalf of the Bow Street Society," Lady Owston explained. "We engaged in conversation with her outside the *Turk's Head Public House* but *I* told her to come home. Rose isn't a member of our group, although I know she wishes to be." Katheryne sighed, "At what time did she see the man?"

"Around five past eleven, she told me; said she'd sat in *The Turk's Head* until closing time—eleven o'clock—when that Mr Roberts came to walk Mrs Yates home."

"And when did she awaken you?"

"Must've been almost half past midnight."

"We've got to tell Mr Queshire." Rose sobbed and lifted her tear-stained face to her friend.

"Not now, Rosie," Annie soothed. "I told you; he's probably asleep."

"You've attempted to speak with Mr Queshire already this evening?" Miss Webster queried. Her curiosity failed to penetrate her monotonous tone, however.

Annie replied, "Rose wanted to the moment she got back. I told her he'd be asleep but she pushed me, saying he could ask Mr Suggitt to warn Mrs Yates and Mr Roberts. We walked over to the store and spent about ten minutes knocking. Mr Queshire lives upstairs so I doubt he heard us. Rose didn't want to go but it was getting colder and I didn't fancy coming across the bloke that done in Mrs Roberts. I finally got her to come home with me about ten minutes later."

"At what time did you get back?" Lady Owston enquired. Agnes meanwhile had opened her notebook and was writing everything down.

Annie took a moment to consider her answer and said, "Must've been about… half past one?"

"Don't worry, Miss Galway," Katheryne soothed and placed a gloved hand upon Rose's. "*We* shall tell Mr Queshire what has occurred." She straightened. "In fact, we shall do so presently."

* * *

Lady Owston used her umbrella's handle to knock and waited. The *Queshire Department Store's* interior was already lit up by the subdued glow of its gas lamps. She could neither see nor hear any signs of movement but was fairly adamant the owner would've already risen from his bed. At five forty-five in the morning, there was only an hour or so before the assistants were, undoubtedly, expected to arrive. "Mr Queshire?" she called, loudly, through the glass while knocking several times.

A shadow was cast across the door and slowly increased in size as Lady Owston heard someone approaching. When the person reached and unlocked the door, Katheryne stepped backward. Miss Dexter and Miss Webster, who were still with her, did the same. As expected, Mr Queshire opened the door. He was attired in a freshly pressed, white shirt with sleeves rolled up to the elbow, and an apron tied about his waist which covered both his chest and legs. He used the apron's skirt to wipe some white, powder-like residue from his hands as he enquired, "Lady Owston? I wasn't expecting to find you on my doorstep at this hour. Has something happened?"

"Indeed it has," Katheryne replied. "Mrs Yates has been murdered."

"*Pardon*?" Edmund glanced at Agnes. "When? How?"

"We do not know," the secretary admitted. "Have you spoken with Miss Galway at all this evening?"

"*No*, you are the first I've conversed with since leaving the public house last evening. Why?"

"She informed us she'd attempted to speak with you this evening but could gain no answer from her knocking."

"I was no doubt sleeping so wouldn't have heard her. My bedroom is at the back of the building, you see."

"You have not been awake long, then?" Katheryne gently probed.

"A few minutes." Edmund replied. Catching the ladies' looks toward his attire, he added, "I was adding some sodium hydroxide to a soap preparation I've been slowly simmering overnight."

"*Well*, ladies, we can gain no further ground this evening." Lady Owston said, turning toward her associates— only to spin around and cry, "Hessian sacks!"

"Pardon?"

"You said you would check if the store had any," Katheryne reminded him.

The proprietor stared at her. "Yes…" He eventually replied. "It doesn't."

"*Bother.*" She sighed, "Never mind, let us return home, ladies, and have some much-needed rest. We may recommence our investigations in the morning. Good evening to you, Mr Queshire."

FIFTEEN

Strident slurping filled the Bow Street Society's kitchen while Mr Eric Trowel ate a bowl of leek and potato soup. Those of a more delicate disposition may have been offended by his table etiquette—or lack thereof—but Sam didn't have such a problem. Furthermore, it gladdened his heart to see a hungry man fill his belly. The slurping ceased and Eric discarded the spoon into the bowl with a clatter. He settled in his chair with a satisfied smirk, "*Fine* soup, sir. *Fiiiiine* soup!"

"Want more?" the cabman enquired, taking the bowl.

Mr Trowel smiled broadly, "Give me a moment or two, lad, and I just might yet!" Eric Trowel was in his sixties. He bore every second of those sixty-odd years in the wrinkles on his face, the hunching of his back, and the seizing of his knuckles. His fingers had been more akin to talons as he'd held the bowl. Yet, despite the burden of his years, he spoke with joviality many wealthy, young men could only aspire to. Sam was reminded very much of his late dad when he looked upon Mr Trowel, which made it easier for him to speak to him.

"By-and-by, thanks for comin' 'ere, Mr Trowel."

"Thanks for bringing me here!" Eric retorted, referring to the *most* enjoyable cab ride he'd been given. "But any way I can help Abraham and his family, I want to do it. He's a good man, Mr Snyder, and he don't deserve the trouble that's being dealt him." It was obvious the two men enjoyed a long-standing friendship so the cabman decided against fishing for more on that particular point.

"You woz the neighbour who found Mrs Yates, wozn't you?" He enquired.

Mr Trowel leant forward and put his elbows on the table. "I was." He tilted his head and shook it. "The devil himself came to call last night, Mr Snyder."

"We think Mrs Yates woz done in by the same bloke, or lass, who killed her daughter. From what you saw, do you think that's likely?"

"There can be *no* doubt of that, sir." Eric looked straight into Sam's eyes as he spoke, his voice grave. "Cut up here she was." His hand moved in a circle as it hovered over his head's crown. "Hair all gone. And." Eric straightened and, with both hands against his chest, cupped the air. Sam nodded in understanding and Mr Trowel added, "*Gone*." He put his elbows back down on the table, "Dunno what happened to her clothes though. Inspector thought the one who done her in took them. I told him about her ring, too."

Mr Snyder recalled the glint of gold he'd thought he'd seen on her marriage finger the night before. "Gone?" He enquired.

"*Gone*," Eric echoed. He looked to the empty bowl and Sam, picking it up, stood to refill it. Miss Trent had prepared a large pot of the soup in anticipation of Mr Trowel's visit.

As the cabman ladled some into the bowl, he enquired, "What woz the rest of the room like?"

"Table was over and on her waist, like she'd pulled it down on herself." Eric yanked the air toward him. "Chair behind her was resting against the stove with her head underneath." Eric straightened again but this time because Sam had put the fresh bowl of soup before him. Mr Trowel shovelled a spoonful into his mouth and, taking a moment to swallow, continued, "I remember there was this… jar of lemonade on the table and two glasses, one in front of her and one on the other side."

"Woz the glasses empty?"

"No; hers was half-full and the other didn't look like it had had any taken out of it," Eric replied and shovelled more into his mouth.

Mr Snyder rested his own broad arms on the table and leant upon them. He enquired, "What woz you doin' up and about at that time of night anyway, Mr Trowel?" Sam scratched his nose, "What time woz it again?"

"Quarter past two this morning," Eric clarified without hesitation.

Sam gave a curt nod and, briefly pointing at the elder man, said, "Yeah, that's right."

"I'm a knocker-up; first one's at half past three. I don't know about the others until I see what the chalk on the doors or walls say when I get there. I've got to walk to my patch though so I leave at half past two. If it wasn't for Mr Ratchett lending me the money for a cab this morning, I would've missed my first knock-up—and a bloke can't be doing that in a job like that. He's gotta be relied upon, don't he?"

"You called the Suggitts from the *Turk's Head Pub* at about half past two, yeah?"

"Yeah. I told Ratchett to get a constable—which he did because I got one pulling me off my round when I was half done."

Eric lifted the bowl and the slurping recommenced. Sam patiently waited for him to finish. When he had, the cabman enquired, "Then what?"

"Took me off to the station, he did. I thought he was one of them that don't like me doing what they think *they* can do for the same price. I told him where to go at first. Bobby or not, he wasn't gonna stop me earning what's rightfully mine," Eric prodded his chest with his thumb. His left shoulder lifted and fell as he continued, "But then he told me why he was there so I went with him. Wood, or whatever the beggar's name was—the inspector, you know?" Sam nodded so Eric added, "*Him*. He spoke to me and wrote down my statement and got me to sign it."

"Thanks, Mr Trowel," Sam smiled. "You finish that off and I'll get you somethin' to take the rest with you in." The cabman stood, politely accepting the knocker-up's grateful thanks, and left the kitchen. Miss Trent, who had been listening at the door the entire time, waited for him in the hallway. Sam walked past her and stopped at the foot of the stairs. The clerk followed and, when she'd reached him, listened as he told her, "From what he's told me, Mrs Yates woz almost definitely done in by Mrs Roberts' murderer. Woz lemonade, not coffee, but the top of her head woz cut off, so woz her breasts. Her clothes woz gone, too."

"She must've known who it was," Rebecca mused aloud, a grave expression upon her face. "We'll have to wait for Doctor Weeks' findings to be sure, though."

*　*　*

Yea, though I walk through the valley of the shadow of death, Woolfe recited as he strode down the narrow, dimly lit corridor toward a light at its end. Doors were ignored when he passed and forgotten about a moment later. The brass plaque on the closed left side of the last set of double doors announced his destination.

"Doctor Weeks," he greeted as he looked across at the figure huddled over an *Empire* typewriter. Old English style gold lettering spelt out its name on its curved-edge, black, flat

177

cover. First manufactured in Montreal in 1892, this particular example had accompanied Weeks from Canada the following year. Caleb had always admired its simplistic efficiency. He'd been rudely warned about touching it in the past, a request he unquestionably respected when in the owner's domain—even if the desk upon which it sat was unworthy of it.

Case files were misaligned in their pile to the right of the machine. Atop the pile was a tin mug of steaming coffee—undoubtedly 'flavoured' with a shot or two of whiskey. The prior night's coffee, also in a tin mug, stood to the pile's right. Two-thirds smoked cigarette butts had been drowned in the now putrefied beverage. On the opposite side of the machine was a copy of the *British Medical Journal* opened at an article by James Mackenzie, M.D., with the title of *TREATMENT OF ASEPTIC WOUNDS WITHOUT BANDAGES OR DRESSINGS.* The page corner was folded over while tobacco fibres had been dropped into the Journal's central crease. The entire thing had been, like the rest of the room, contaminated by a foul stench of stale tobacco mixed with lime and carbolic. A couple of older, well-thumbed copies of the Journal were strewn across the desk among plain paper sheets, unopened ink wells, pencils, match boxes, and a discarded pocket-watch.

The most striking item on the desk, aside from the typewriter, was the immensely thick thirteenth edition of *Anatomy, Descriptive and Surgical* from 1893. Originally written by Henry Gray with illustrations by Henry Vandyke Carter, Thomas Pickering Pick edited this British edition. Though Weeks' copy was closed, if one were to open it one would find colour plates of the labelled, highly detailed and intricate illustrations depicting the various parts of the human body.

The desk stood against the front-right corner of the room, adjacent to the door. To its left was a set of unpolished, wall-mounted mahogany boxed shelves. A small archive of *British Medical Journals* and (for 1896) the controversial publication, *The Lancet,* from the previous year filled the shelves. A macabre postcard depicting a flayed, decomposing corpse lying on a high table rested against the journals' spines. Behind the corpse were five men in their twenties looking, proudly, at the camera. Each was attired in his everyday clothing and bowler hat. A sixth man, sat at the corpse's head and facing its feet, held a scalpel in an ungloved hand as he, too, had eyes turned toward the camera. *Happy New Year* was printed in large, spiral lettering in the postcard's bottom-right corner.

"My nephew," Weeks stated upon noticing the inspector 'admiring' the postcard. "Third from the right." Picking up his fresher cup of coffee with one hand, he held out a file to Woolfe with the other. The inspector took the file but waited as the Canadian drank the hot beverage. He needed it, too; the dead room's location in the basement meant it was cold enough to prevent the bodies from decomposing too quickly, without chemical-soaked bandages, but also cold enough to bring on hypothermia if one wasn't careful.

"Have you had any sleep yet?" Caleb enquired.

"Nah." Weeks reached upward as far as he could to stretch his arms. Lighting a cigarette soon after, he tossed the packet amongst the mess on the desk. Woolfe's eyes were on the man, however. After visiting the scene that morning, Caleb had returned home for a full stand-up wash and shave. He'd also put on a fresh set of clothes. Weeks, on the other hand, was still wearing the off-white shirt, old overcoat, frayed scarf, and fingerless gloves Caleb had seen him in only a few hours prior. The blood-stained leather apron the doctor wore was a new addition though. Akin to those worn by practitioners of meat cleaving, the apron was what had earnt Weeks the nickname 'The Butcher' among the officers of the Yard.

"Good morning, Doctor Weeks," another medical man, also in his late twenties, greeted upon entering the dead room. There were six marble slabs in total; each one had a squared top, no deeper than four or five inches, supported by strong, straight wooden legs. Three of the six were occupied, so to speak, by familiar-shaped mounds covered by white sheets. The other doctor switched his outdoors coat for a leather apron of his own that hung upon a stand behind the open door. Without uttering another word to Weeks, he crossed the room and uncovered the corpse lying on the slab furthest away from the inspector and Canadian.

"What time did Mrs Yates die?" Caleb enquired of Weeks, lifting the file slightly.

The doctor gestured toward it, replying, "S'all in there." Woolfe remained silent, however, and waited. Sighing deeply, Weeks added, "Between half past midnight and when yer witness found her."

"And the lemonade?" Woolfe enquired.

179

Weeks slowly exhaled the smoke from his lungs. He'd not slept in over twenty-four hours and it showed; his eyelids involuntarily drooped while his movements were slower and more laboured. He wasn't too exhausted to be his usual charming self, however. "Riddled with fuckin' arsenic…" he muttered as he stood and snatched the file back. Putting the cigarette in the corner of his mouth, he opened the file and, turning over its cover, went to a long counter which stood against the entire length of the back wall and sat down on a chair there.

Upon the counter was a cone-shaped beaker with a stopper. Standing vertically in this beaker was a straight tube whose tip almost touched the beaker's base. To the right of this tube was a curved, glass one which, in turn, led through a key-shaped chamber followed by a long, horizontal tube. Approximately two inches to the left of the beaker was a tall, vertical piece of apparatus with a brass base. The base had a nozzle on its side and supported the upper portion of the apparatus. The horizontal tube appeared to pass straight through the apparatus and ended in a point. Woolfe followed Weeks to the counter and looked upon the—to him, at least—complicated piece of equipment. He assumed the liquid within the beaker to be a sample of the lemonade.

The inspector leant over the apparatus for a closer look and the Canadian growled, "*Don't* even *think* 'bout touchin' that, Woolfe."

"I wasn't going to."

"Good." Weeks looked up at him. "'Cause that there's one of the most sensitive tests for arsenic there is and I don't want ya fuckin' it up." Another time, Caleb might have enquired after how the test worked but the doctor's fouler than usual mood convinced him to postpone such curiosities for another time. He therefore stepped back and peered over Weeks' shoulder at the bottles of nitric acid and zinc beside the apparatus. Noticing another piece of apparatus further along the counter, the inspector wandered that way. It was another glass beaker suspended over a flame. This beaker was open-topped and had a bottle of hydrochloric acid and a batch of fine, copper mesh beside it. The liquid in the beaker was, he assumed, yet another sample of the lemonade. Weeks glanced over at Caleb and warned, "Don't touch that either."

"Is this all just for the testing of arsenic?" Woolfe enquired as he returned to the Canadian.

"Yeah; Marsh Test." He pointed at the first set of apparatus. "Reinsch Test," he added, nodding toward the second. Turning the pages in his file, Weeks continued, "The jar of lemonade ya'll found on the table were laced with between three and five teaspoons of arsenic. Only thing in Mrs Yates' stomach—'cept the usual acids—were lemonade. Ain't any arsenic in her tissues and were traces of lemonade and arsenic in her throat, in her mouth, and on her lips. Probably where she vomited so, if ya find her clothes, there'll be some on 'em, too." Weeks stood and, taking the cigarette from his mouth, returned to his desk where he dropped it into the tobacco-saturated coffee mug.

Woolfe, who had followed him, began, "So our killer didn't intend to drink any of the lemonade he—or she— presumably brought with—" He stopped though and plucked up the packet of cigarettes the doctor had previously discarded.

Weeks at once attempted to snatch them back, snapping, "If ya wanted one, ya should've enquired!"

"I saw a packet of *these,*" Woolfe replied as he moved them away from the doctor's hand. "At the house of those meddlers, the Bow bloody Street Society." Percy instantly withdrew his hand and, staring at the inspector, stood perfectly rigid. Woolfe, recognising fear in the doctor, narrowed his eyes. "Have you been telling them things you shouldn't?"

"Nah," Weeks replied.

Caleb closed the gap between them. "Have you, or have you not, been telling the Bow Street Society things you shouldn't, *Doctor* Weeks?" The inspector easily towered over the Canadian, who'd retreated back a couple steps.

"*Nah,*" Percy repeated.

Caleb leant forward, to put their faces millimetres apart, and enquired, "Do you want to try and sound a bit more convincing when you say that?"

"Those damned cigarettes could've been anyone's," Weeks answered without his characteristic bolshiness.

"Yeah, they could've," Woolfe replied, lowering his voice. "But *you* are the doctor working on the Roberts murder case that *they* have been commissioned to investigate by the sister. And *you,*" Caleb paused to adjust the knot on Weeks' scarf, causing him to flinch. "Are the only man I know who smokes *Turkish* cigarettes." The Canadian pursed his lips as he swallowed hard. "If I find *any* evidence that you've been leaking confidential police reports to the Bow Street Society." Woolfe tightened Weeks' scarf. "I'll have your guts for garters—and that'll just be the beginning. Understand?"

"Yeah…" Weeks replied and coughed against the restriction of his throat.

Woolfe smiled, "Good. Now." He ran his hands over the lapels of Weeks' coat and the doctor briefly closed his eyes in a half flinch. A sudden yanking down of the material had him grunting, however, and even sweating. Caleb added, "Get some sleep." Weeks gave another cough and, nodding, let the inspector step away. He then watched him leave and felt his temperature rise as panic began to set in.

SIXTEEN

"There are constables outside your front door," Lady Owston pronounced. The basement kitchen in which she stood had been accessed via a set of stone steps at the property's side.

"The inspector insisted upon it for our protection," Mr Suggitt explained. "Alas I fail to follow his logic; his suspicions firmly point at one of *us* being the devil who's slain our loved ones."

"Perhaps he hopes the murderer will attempt to slay a third?" Mr Maxwell suggested as he moved further inside. Stark realisation struck him, however, and he shot a startled gawp at Clement. "*Oh God,* Mr Suggitt… I—I didn't mean that like it sounded…"

"*Who* are you?" the offended party enquired, perplexed.

The journalist tucked his notebook under his left arm but found its presence too cumbersome when lifting his hand. He therefore moved it to being tucked under his right and wiped his freed hand upon his frock coat's skirt. As he extended it for a second time, he replied, "Mr Joseph Maxwell of the *Gaslight Gazette,* sir." Clement's grip and jaw tightened. "A—And Bow Street Society member," Joseph added.

Mr Suggitt's tension eased at once and he released his hand. "Why have we not met before?"

"I was only recently assigned to investigate the case."

"Are such arrangements commonplace?" Mr Suggitt had addressed Lady Owston, however.

"Miss Trent assigns whoever she deems appropriate for each individual case whenever she decides there is a need for them." She explained.

"I see." Mr Suggitt replied.

Accompanying Katheryne and Joseph were Agnes, Georgina, and Sam, the last having left his cab and horses at a nearby livery.

"Mr Roberts and Miss Roberts are aware of your visit this morning, he being in the dining room and she in the parlour," Mr Suggitt informed them. "Miss Trent stated it was your preference to speak to them separately…?"

"Indeed," Katheryne replied, tugging at her gloves to remove them. "Ladies are more inclined to speak their heart's secrets if their father isn't present to bear witness."

"I also intend to have Mr Roberts describe the clothes he last saw Mrs Yates wearing so I may sketch them," Georgina meekly added.

Confused, Mr Suggitt cast a questioning glance at Sam and enquired, "But surely Mr Snyder would be better suited for such, or Regina? As they each approached her at the public house."

"Yes, but only Mr Roberts was at home with Mrs Yates prior to her death," Georgina said and frowned. "Aside from her murderer that is…" She briefly closed her eyes and dismissed her imaginings with a slight shake of her head. Standing erect, she continued, "If Mrs Yates changed her clothes, Mr Roberts may remember what they were."

"Unless he was the one who—" Mr Maxwell began but was, thankfully, cut short by Lady Owston.

"*Time* is of the *essence,* Mr Maxwell, if we are to hear the answers we require *prior* to the police discovering our presence."

"Y—Yes, Lady Owston…" Joseph replied, his cheeks hot.

Katheryne bowed her head at an angle, "Please *lead* the way, Mr Suggitt."

Yet Clement felt sorely tempted to at once submit Joseph to Inspector Woolfe's mercy. It was only the painful recollection of his wife's precarious emotional stability that stayed his hand. Climbing the set of steep, spiralled, stone steps to the ground floor, he said, "I'd be appreciative if you would refrain from disturbing Diana; she is exhausted and hasn't eaten today. I fear your questions may ignite hysteria within her."

"We shall take *every* care not to do so, Mr Suggitt," Lady Owston said. "But we cannot promise we shan't. If Mr or Miss Roberts share information with us, which requires us to seek clarification from your wife, we are bound by duty to her late sister and mother to speak with her."

"I understand you are in an awkward situation," Clement said upon stepping into the hallway. Facing Katheryne, while she and the others joined him, he went on, "Yet, while I admire and respect your group's dedication, I am fundamentally in agreement with the inspector."

"As is your right, Mr Suggitt," Lady Owston pointed out. "Since Miss Trent didn't receive written confirmation of your wife's intention to prematurely end her commissioning of our services, however, we are obliged to do all in our power to unmask Maryanna Roberts' murderer."

"She would have done such if her mother hadn't been…" Clement rubbed the bridge of his nose between his thumb and index finger. "*Please* understand that I only wish to protect Diana as much as I can from this awful, *awful* business."

"The ultimate, and everlasting, protection you could give her though would be to permit us to discover who killed her sister and mother," Miss Webster stated.

Mr Suggitt's frame drooped and he gave a curt nod. "I know…" He indicated two doors. "The dining room is second on the right and the parlour is second on the left… If you *should* need me at all, pull twice on the bell rope in the corner of each room and my housekeeper shall fetch me." Mr Suggitt half-turned. "I'm placing the welfare of my brother-in-law and niece in your hands against my better judgement. Please do not prove my misgivings are justified."

"You have our words as Bow Street Society members that we won't, Mr Suggitt," Joseph countered, his voice sombre.

Georgina joined him in tone as she added, "You may rely on us."

"Thank you…" Clement said as the weight visibly lifted from him. When he walked away and entered a third, unknown, room, his gait was notably less encumbered.

Lady Owston beamed at Joseph, "Mr Maxwell, *you* shall do me the privilege of joining Agnes and me in speaking to Miss Regina Roberts."

"Privilege?" Maxwell enquired with much trepidation as he gripped the small bow of his cravat.

"Yes, *privilege*," Katheryne repeated.

Realising her compliment was sincere, he stared in disbelief, utterly lost for words. His fingers slid downward to rest on his shirt and a tremendous smile formed. "…Thank you," he uttered, the gravity of his voice echoing Clement's in its appreciation.

"Shouldn't Mr Maxwell assist us with Mr Roberts?" Miss Dexter enquired, casting side the importance of the moment.

"*No,*" Joseph blurted out and turned his head toward the artist. The startled expression he gifted her with was fleeting, yet she noticed it all the same. She was about to bring attention to it and enquire after his reasons when he read her mind, "He has met you and Mr Snyder before, Miss Dexter, and I'd only say, or do, the wrong thing." He pulled his frock coat closed and, straightening his back, puffed out his chest a little. "Ladies first." He looked to Katheryne and Agnes while extending his arm toward the parlour.

Georgina's voice was subdued as she replied, "As you wish, Mr Maxwell." She held clasped hands against her skirts and turned toward the dining room. Joseph's smile faded but, although he parted his lips as if to call her back to him, he remained silent. His fingers also bent to rest their tips against his palm as he lowered the arm he'd simultaneously raised. A once jubilant expression had been replaced by one of regret and sorrow. Yet still he didn't go after the artist. Instead, he gave Mr Snyder a weak smile, when he looked back at him, and followed Lady Owston and Miss Webster into the parlour.

"It's okay, lass," Sam soothed and placed a gentle hand on Georgina's lower back once he'd joined her at the dining room door.

"I know it is," she replied, forcing a meagre smile of her own. Turning upon her heel to face the door, she knocked once. A familiar voice called to them through the wood, prompting Mr Snyder to enter first while Miss Dexter followed closely behind.

Directly beyond the door, standing in the centre of the room, was an oak, extendable table. The table's surface was highly polished and free of scratches or marks. An arrangement of wax flowers and leaves, protected by a tall, glass dome, formed the table's centrepiece.

The remainder of the room consisted of a bay window to the extreme right as one entered, an oak china cabinet against the wall opposite the door, and a sideboard against the wall directly to one's left. On the shelves within the cabinet was the Suggitts' best china dinner service.

Mr Roberts sat to the right of the table's head; his tattered clothes a stark contrast to the opulent surroundings. Though there were still plenty of daylight hours left, the heavy curtains had been drawn across the window to prevent the constables from spying on the residents. The wall-mounted gas lamps had also been lit while a heartily burning fire in the hearth, located to the right of the cabinet, provided comfortable warmth to the room. When he'd heard the door opening, Mr Roberts had lifted his head but hadn't stood, having assumed only Sam was entering. Upon seeing Georgina, however, he rose from his chair and gave a softly spoken word of greeting. His already gaunt features were made all the more haggard by the clear signs of sleep deprivation.

"Please, sit down, Mr Roberts," Georgina said as she took the chair opposite him. Mr Snyder sat to the right of her, avoiding the disrespectful act of sitting in Mr Suggitt's place at the head of the table. Mr Roberts slowly lowered himself onto his chair and, while resting one hand on the table, ran the other through his unkempt hair. He had his head bowed at the same time and, occasionally, tugged at clumps of his hair.

"Diana said you wanted me to tell you what Sarah was wearing last night…" He began as he took a deep breath and straightened. His eyes met Georgina's since she was the one holding a pencil over a sketchbook. Miss Dexter waited for him to continue rather than answer; she found people sometimes felt the need to fill a silence if a pause in a conversation came up. "…She also said you was all at the *Turk's Head* when Regina had a go at her grandmother. So, you must've seen what she was wearing."

"I wasn't," Georgina admitted. "Mr Snyder was, but you accompanied her home, Mr Roberts. If she'd changed her clothes once there, Mr Snyder wouldn't be able to describe them for me to sketch… *Did* she change her clothes?"

"Not while I was there," Abraham replied and leant back in his chair with a deep sigh. "I should've stayed with her." He rubbed his face and, resting his elbows on the table, ran his hands repeatedly through his hair. Stopping when they reached his head's crown on the third sweep, however, he tightly gripped his hair. When he spoke next, the anguish was clear to hear, "*Why* didn't I stay with her? I could've saved her… She could be alive today if I hadn't *left* her!"

"She woz at home; a place where she should've been safe," Sam reminded him. "You wozn't to know."

"But I knew where Regina was, didn't I? I didn't *have* to come here. I should've *stayed* with Sarah." Abraham dropped one elbow off the table and put his head in his other hand.

Miss Dexter placed her pencil on her sketchbook and said, "Your wife was found on Oxford Street where anyone could see her or her murderer." She grimaced, "I know it shall bring you little comfort, Mr Roberts, but it wasn't possible for you to know, or even suspect, what would happen to Mrs Yates." She reclaimed her pencil, "Not even the Bow Street Society had an inclination." She waited a moment to allow Mr Roberts to digest her words before she continued, "But you, and I, and Mr Snyder, may help Mrs Yates now by getting to the truth of her death. Between you both, I'm certain you may recall the appearance of her clothes so I may sketch them and *we* may locate them and, with the greatest of hope, her murderer."

"A grey shawl…" Mr Roberts lifted his head and rested his forearm on the table. "…Knitted. Lightish-grey, you know? With a…darker-grey, woollen dress underneath—or was it black?" He looked to Mr Snyder for help.

"I'll let Miss Dexter know what I remember once you've done yours." The cabman replied.

Abraham considered the possible reasons behind such a decision and, presumably coming up with one that was satisfactory, continued, "Black boots, too."

"Any jewellery?" Miss Dexter enquired as she sketched and shaded the garments.

"Yeah… a ring; gold, it was. Was her wedding ring, given her by her husband's mother. When times got really hard, after Maryanna left, Sarah wanted to pawn it but I told her no. She hated her husband but loved his mother."

"Why didn't you tell us Mrs Yates woz livin' with you when we asked?" Mr Snyder enquired as gently as he could while Georgina finished her depiction of the clothes.

Mr Roberts lifted his hand from the table and, spreading his fingers, replied, "Dunno." He put his hand down, "Nothing was going on between us, despite what Regina says."

"Was the ring plain?" Georgina interjected.

Mr Roberts nodded and leant forward when the artist turned her sketchbook around to show him. "Yeah, that's them," his voice was heavy as he spoke. He stared at the greys and blacks of the sketch. Suddenly he lifted his eyes though and enquired, "How'd you know I walked her home?"

"Mr Suggitt told us," Sam promptly responded.

Miss Dexter recalled the assistant manager's words to them outside the Roberts' tenement building and she shivered. Mr Roberts meanwhile turned from the sketch and stared at the empty chair beside him. His hand once more lifted to grip and tug his hair, this time behind his ear. Georgina closed her sketchbook and, placing it upon her lap as quietly as she could, rested her clasped hands on it while she listened.

"Do you walk her home every night? Did you walk her home the night Maryanna woz done in?" Sam enquired.

"Yeah, but… not *then*. Sarah told me some bloke—some sailor she said—was in London for a couple of days and wanted to spend time with her. She told me she didn't need me walking her home because he would in the morning."

"What time did you walk her home last night?"

"Eleven o'clock, closing time," Abraham replied. "Got back home at quarter past. That's when she told me what had happened with Regina and where she'd gone." Abraham's voice broke as he continued, "She told me to stay at home, that Regina would be back come morning and I shouldn't worry. I was angry though. I wanted to drag her back, to make her apologise."

"Did she bring any lemonade home with her?"

"No, and I already told the inspector we don't keep any in the house."

"So you left there and got 'ere at abou'…?"

"Gone midnight—half past, maybe?" Abraham sniffed hard. He dropped his hand to his knee but kept his gaze fixed on the table's edge. "Clement and Diana told me to stay here, that it was too late to walk back and Regina was asleep besides."

"And woz she?" Mr Snyder enquired.

Abraham turned his head toward him, "Was she what?"

"Asleep."

"Yeah." Mr Roberts' shoulders trembled as he took in a deep, shuddering breath. When he lifted his head, his face was contorted with desperation. "I looked in on her…" His lips quivered while a couple of tears escaped, "…She was safe, cared for." He dropped his head into his hands as he put his elbows back onto the table, "Sarah was alone…" Again, he tugged hard at his hair but his grief couldn't be contained. A single sob burst forth from his throat, followed by many more. His forearms collapsed to lie atop one another on the table with his forehead joining them. Soon, the sound of his uncontrollable weeping filled the room and Georgina felt a terrible ache in her heart for him. She also felt the sting of tears in her own eyes, which caused her to press her knuckles against the underside of her nose.

"Excuse me," she muttered and stood. Unable to address the obvious concern upon Sam's face, she fled the room. Despite her best efforts to stifle it, a harsh sob escaped her, just as she closed the door.

"Miss Dexter?"

* * *

"Miss Roberts?" Lady Owston addressed the young woman lying on a plush sofa standing perpendicular to the fireplace. Regina was on her side, facing the room, with her head resting on her hand. That arm's elbow was in turn perched on the sofa's broader armrest. She gave a mumbled affirmation but resisted, diverting her attention from the copy of *The Bazaar, Exchange, and Mart, The Journal of the Household* she was studying.

First published in 1868, the 'Exchange and Mart' was just one of many catering to the pastime of fireside shopping. Costing 2d per issue, it included goods' advertisements and, by 1896, articles on sport, fashions, etiquette, the management of children, and items for the housekeeper's room among other things. Fireside shoppers could browse the publication and order their preferred goods through the mail—usually directly from the manufacturers. Though some similar publications and suppliers sent free samples, specifically of materials for dresses, linens, etc., with 'carriage paid,' the formal orders were usually made on a cash only basis with no discount. Naturally, Lady Owston had recognised Regina's choice of reading material for what it was and was surprised by its presence, especially when one considered Mr Suggitt's occupation. Unless the *Queshire Department Store* had an advertisement in the 'Exchange and Mart,' it could draw customers away from that establishment.

Katheryne approached the sofa and pointed at the publication, "Have you found something which greatly interests you?"

"I'm just looking," Regina replied and flipped over several of the pages until she reached one which had a large picture. Since she'd not yet pulled herself away from it, Lady Owston decided to take matters into her own hands. Leaning down, she grabbed the corner of the 'Exchange and Mart' and snatched it out from underneath Regina's nose. The young woman instantly shot her hand out but only touched air. She also had to grip the sofa's edge to prevent a fall. She barked, "Give that back!"

"It isn't within my character to be rude, Miss Roberts, and certainly not in the presence of one who has lost as much as you," Katheryne replied. "However, on this occasion, I feel it is my duty to step outside the boundaries of etiquette to tell you to sit up straight, focus your attention, and listen." Though Regina had indeed moved into a sitting position, she had no intention of adhering to Lady Owston's instructions.

Instead, she stood, snatched the 'Exchange and Mart' from Katheryne's hand, and returned to the sofa, saying, "I don't have to listen to you, you're not my mum."

"No, I'm not; your mother is dead," Lady Owston retorted. She'd allowed the woman to take back her precious publication but had then followed her to the sofa where she sat beside her. "*Murdered*, and we—"

"I know she was murdered," Regina snapped, glaring at the 'Exchange and Mart' as she flicked through its pages. She was at least sitting this time so there had been ample room for Katheryne without the sofa becoming crowded. Miss Roberts added, "But the one who murdered her's dead, too, so it don't matter."

"Aren't you sad and afraid about your grandmother being murdered, too?" Katheryne enquired, shocked.

Without hesitation Regina replied, "No, they done us all a favour."

"You do not wish to know who it was?" Agnes interjected. She and Joseph had decided to occupy the armchairs opposite the sofa on their own accord.

Regina hadn't even noticed as she replied, "No."

"Even if it was your father?" Maxwell pointed out. This did grab the young woman's attention, however.

The 'Exchange and Mart' was lowered as Regina glowered at him. "Take that back."

"He was the last person to see your grandmother alive," Agnes said, earning a scowl from Miss Roberts.

The young woman sneered, "You don't know him, or me. He wouldn't do that; he's not got it in him to kill someone."

"Why did you hate your grandmother so?" Katheryne enquired, deciding to use a different tactic.

It seemed to work, too, for Regina looked directly at her and replied, "Because she got my mum out the house, so she could move in with my dad."

"How did she do that?"

"Told my dad lies about my mum. My mum didn't steal the housekeeping money, she wasn't drunk when it was taken and she would've done anything for me when she hadn't had a drink. My dad didn't believe her when she told him she hadn't taken it but that was because Sarah had been filling his head with stones. It was her who told my dad to toss my mum out—and he did! Made her go to *that* life to make ends meet. He made her drinking worse by doing that but Sarah couldn't stop even then. Whenever she got the chance, she was talking my mum down—to me, my dad, even to Aunt Diana. But Aunt Diana's on Mum's side, and mine. She just wanted us all to be back together; even enquired my dad to have my mum back at home."

"Oh?" Katheryne enquired, her curiosity piqued by the last.

Regina frowned and, for the first time since they'd made her acquaintance, discarded her defensive attitude to allow the Bow Streeters to see the vulnerability beneath. She turned the page in her 'Exchange and Mart' but merely stared at the advertisement on the other side. "I don't know if I should tell you."

"Would it be helpful if we told you we were friends of your aunt's? In fact, we have been commissioned by her to investigate your mother's murder. I'm Lady Katheryne Owston and that is Miss Agnes Webster and Mr Joseph Maxwell; we are all members of the Bow Street Society."

Regina briefly bit her lip. "Aunt Diana said you was coming today."

"Your aunt and uncle have been very kind to you, Regina. They told us you and your father stayed here last night," Katheryne informed her. The young woman nodded but continued to frown as she contemplated the positives and negatives of saying aloud what was on her mind. The three Bow Streeters permitted her this time by sitting in silence.

Eventually, Regina closed her 'Exchange and Mart' and set it aside. Turning on the sofa to face Lady Owston, she said, "The night Mum died, Aunt Diana came to the house. She and Dad thought I was sleeping but I wasn't. I was behind the curtain though so they didn't know. I listened…" Her frown faded and she continued, "Aunt Diana was telling Dad how sorry Mum was and how she was gonna get help. Aunt Diana and Uncle Clement was gonna take her in here so she could get away from the gin and stay off it. Dad told her he thought it was good news but said he didn't think it was a good idea for Mum and Sarah to live together. And, anyway, he said…" Regina paused in hesitation.

Lady Owston encouraged, in a soft voice, "What did he say?"

"He told Aunt Diana he loved her, that it was her he'd loved all these years. She wasn't surprised though, or angry. She told him they'd talked about it before and she still loved Uncle Clement. She told him it didn't change things though; she'd still help us as much as she could."

"What time did your aunt arrive and leave?" Agnes enquired, her pencil poised over her notebook. Regina looked to the mantel clock as she cast her mind back.

"I went to bed at about half past nine because I've got to be knocked-up at four in the morning to go to the market. Aunt Diana got there a bit after that. She was there a long time. I don't know what time she left but it was late because I was falling asleep by then."

"Did your father go out at all during the night?"

"No, after Aunt Diana left, he came to bed and we slept until we both got knocked up at four. He walked to the docks to sleep at the gates and I walked to the market at Covent Garden to help sell the flowers."

"Where was your grandmother?" Mr Maxwell enquired.

Regina's hard expression returned as she replied, "Dunno, probably working and out with some bloke. I didn't ask."

"Do you have any lemonade at home, Miss Roberts?" Miss Webster enquired.

Regina, confused, replied, "No. My dad and me don't like it."

"Thank you, Miss Roberts." Katheryne smiled. "You've been most helpful and we *do* appreciate your speaking to us. I'm *quite* certain your aunt does, too. Mr Maxwell." She looked to the *Gaslight Gazette* journalist. "Would you be so kind as to inform Miss Dexter and Mr Snyder we are ready to proceed when they are?"

"Um, yes… of course, Lady Owston," Joseph replied nervously. Standing, he turned toward the mantelpiece and, realising there was no door there, spun around and left the parlour. As soon as he was back in the hallway though, he felt his heart pound and his mind race. He looked in the direction of the dining room and, taking a deep breath, straightened his back. "Come on, Maxwell," he muttered to himself while approaching the foot of the stairs. "You can do this." *It's not as if you have never spoken to her before,* he thought as he rounded the corner. He stopped dead in his tracks, however, when he saw not only Georgina but also her tears. All at once, his fears dissipated and a concern of a different kind filled his heart. "Miss Dexter?"

Georgina's hand fell to her side. Lifting her head, and stepping away from the door, she explained, "Mr Roberts required a moment."

Joseph went to her but stopped short of any reassuring gesture. Instead, he retrieved his handkerchief and held it with both hands. "W-Would he like this?"

"No." She swallowed as her hand came up. "But I would." Maxwell passed it over without hesitation and she thanked him softly.

Feeling the familiar warmth in his cheeks, the journalist replied, "You're most welcome, Miss Dexter."

"How is your mother?" the artist enquired while she dabbed the corners of her eyes.

She'd hardly begun when he responded, "She's well, thank you. Miss Roberts had some interesting things to say." He gestured toward the parlour. "After Lady Owston was forced to pull the 'Exchange and Mart' from under her nose. Apparently, Mr Roberts confessed his love to Mrs Suggitt on the night of Mrs Roberts' murder." Joseph absently toyed with his cravat as he continued, "Naturally, Mrs Suggitt rebuffed his affection."

"How *awful*." Georgina frowned, much to Maxwell's surprise.

"We only have Regina's word such a conversation took place, of course," he returned. Pivoting his waist toward the parlour door, he fell silent. Miss Dexter leant forward a little to peer around him and through the stairs' balusters. She neared them but Joseph humming drew her gaze to his face instead. A half moment later, he spun around and, quite accidentally, their bodies pressed together.

She was as surprised as he but neither pulled away. Instead, the artist smiled and enquired, "What is on your mind, Joseph?"

"Um… well…" He cleared his throat and glanced around. Seeing they were still alone in the hallway, he took her face in his hands and kissed her lips. Though it was a brief touch, and she hadn't withdrawn, the sudden display of affection nonetheless took Georgina aback.

Through the exhalation of the breath she hadn't realised she'd been holding, she said, "Joseph…"

"Forgive me, Miss Dexter," he said, pulling away. Her hand taking his stayed him, however. With a pounding heart, he forced himself to look upon her face; tender happiness waited for him there.

"There is nothing to forgive," she soothed. "We are engaged to be married."

Oliver Maxwell's voice cut through Joseph's mind at once, however, dashing his euphoria like a ship against the rocks. He stepped back sharply and removed his hand from hers. "Please request Mrs Suggitt to join Mr Snyder and I in the dining room." Unable to meet her startled eyes, he kept his own cast downward as he retreated from the hallway. Georgina continued to stare even after the door had closed, utterly dumbfounded as to what had just transpired.

SEVENTEEN

The fire crackled at Mrs Suggitt's back but she wasn't warmed by it. The previous night's events still haunted her. She gazed into an imagined, distant horizon, and her naturally pale complexion had become insipid. Her right fingertips unconsciously touched their counterparts as she kept the heels of her hands upon the table.

Mr Maxwell, who had noticed she was looking over his shoulder, enquired, "Mrs Suggitt?" Her fingertips paused and, though she moved her head to squarely face him, her eyes didn't see him.

"Yes?" She half-whispered.

"She's not up to this, can't you see that?" Abraham stated, his voice hard.

Mrs Suggitt had taken the chair to the right of his while Mr Maxwell sat opposite her. Mr Snyder was facing Mr Roberts. Miss Dexter had chosen to join Lady Owston, Miss Webster, and Miss Roberts in the parlour.

Diana's hand pivoted upon its heel and she brushed her fingers against Abraham's. "No," she said, her voice trembling in its weakness. "I *must*; for Mother now as well as Maryanna." To Maxwell she added, "What is it you wish to ask me, sir?"

"Mr Maxwell," he reminded. There had been formal introductions when he'd first entered the room but, evidently, Diana's delicate emotional state had prevented her from recalling it.

"Oh yes, of course…" She forced a weak smile to her lips, "Mr Maxwell." No sooner had she uttered the words did her smile vanish without a trace.

Abraham meanwhile rubbed his mouth while leaning heavily upon his elbow. Occasionally, a frustrated or annoyed sigh would rise from him.

"You were at home all of last night, correct?" Joseph enquired.

Diana swallowed her emotion, "Yes… that is correct. Alone at first… then Clement came home after speaking with the Society at the *Turk's Head*. He brought Regina with him… and, much later, Abraham came."

"At what time did he come?" Joseph enquired.

Abraham jumped in with, "I've already told you that." The journalist looked to him, without speaking, and the dock worker gave another sigh. Nevertheless, he turned his head away and allowed Diana to answer.

"Half-past midnight, I believe. He was upset…" She watched her brother-in-law's bent form, "…Regina had argued with Mother—as your group witnessed, Mr Maxwell—and Clement had brought her here." She paused as she realised she'd already said that. She lightly touched her forehead, as if willing her fingertips to jog her memory. "Abraham wanted to take her home so she could apologise to Mother. Clement and I convinced him it was too late to do so as Regina had already gone to bed. We invited him to stay the night also…" She dropped her hand to her chest as she took in a sharp, deep breath. A soft cry escaped her lips after and she closed her eyes. Several moments passed in which only the sound of the fire popping could be heard. Eventually her hand closed to clutch the fabric of her dress while she released a deep, shuddering breath. Opening her eyes, she continued, "Abraham looked in on Regina and then retired to the second guest room. Clement and I retired to our own room."

"And no one left again until…" Joseph consulted his notebook.

"Mr Trowel called?" Diana nodded.

"Did you have any lemonade at the house, or did anyone bring some back?" Mr Maxwell enquired.

Diana frowned deeply but shook her head and replied, "I know how she was given the poison; none of us had any lemonade at all that night, either here or at the *Turk's Head*."

"The night of Maryanna's death, you were at home all evening, too?" Joseph enquired, "With your husband?"

"Clement left soon after dinner, around eight thirty, I believe. He returned home a little after eleven thirty—as you already know, Mr Maxwell." She rested her hand atop the other on the table, "He told me of the conversation about it which he'd had with your group last night. I…" She bowed her head, "Already knew the true nature of the business that had drawn him away from home that night, not on the night itself but afterward. He confessed it all to me and we later informed Inspector Woolfe of it also." She retrieved her handkerchief from her pocket and, momentarily pressing it against her nose, continued, "I don't condone my husband's actions, Mr Maxwell, but I understand why he felt he needed to do what he did."

"You lied for him when you were both first asked about your whereabouts by the police," Joseph stated. "Has he also lied on your behalf though?"

Diana looked up sharply, her lips parted. "I… I don't understand," she replied after a moment.

Abraham had also turned his gaze to the journalist who replied, "You went out as well on the night of your sister's murder, but not to find her as your husband had." Joseph turned his head toward the dock worker, "You went to see Mr Roberts." The two at once looked to one another in surprise.

"So it's true, then?" Mr Snyder enquired.

Diana and Abraham turned away from each other and, while she bowed her head, he sighed deeply and replied, "Yeah, it's true. Who told you?"

"Your daughter," Mr Maxwell replied. "Who you thought was sleeping at the time."

"I wanted to convince Abraham to allow Maryanna to return home." Diana tightly held her handkerchief and pulled at its corners. "Clement had agreed for her to live here awhile—to remove all temptation of the gin from her. I'd hoped, once he heard of our plans, Abraham would let her go home afterward."

"But he told you he loved you instead," Joseph stated.

Diana's head shot up and she stared at him, startled, before once again swallowing back her emotion. Her lips quivered but she couldn't bring herself to speak. Turning away, she pressed her handkerchief against her mouth to stifle another small cry of pain.

Mr Roberts attempted to put his hand on her shoulder, but she pulled away. Sighing deeply, he instead ran his hand through his hair and turned toward the Bow Streeters. His hands came to rest on the table as, leaning forward, he explained, "I did tell Diana I loved her—that I'd always loved her—but she told me she loved Clement. It was the answer she'd given me before and the answer I'd been expecting. The stuff with Maryanna…" He shook his head as he looked to his hands, "…It made me feel bad. When Diana came that night… I thought it was another chance at happiness." His tone hardened when he met Joseph and Sam's gazes, "I *loved* my wife; it was *her* I chose all them years ago, not Diana."

"But the drink made her into a monster," Mr Snyder replied.

"So you thought you might've chosen the wrong sister." Mr Maxwell added.

"No!" Abraham glared at them. "I don't know *what* you're trying to say but I didn't murder my wife!" A sob sounded from Mrs Suggitt, prompting Mr Roberts to try to calm down. Filling his lungs as, sitting back, he slid his arms off the table, he then sighed loudly. "Look, neither me nor Diana done in Maryanna; you've got to look elsewhere for that."

"What time did you ge' to Mr Roberts' place?" Mr Snyder enquired from the stricken woman.

Diana took several moments to reply. When she did, she'd lowered her handkerchief and turned toward the cabman once more. "I… I believe it was… nine thirty. I waited for half an hour after Clement had gone out before leaving." Her voice faltered and, again, she clutched her handkerchief to her mouth.

"You don't have to do this, Diana," Abraham urged, concern in both his face and voice.

"I do," Mrs Suggitt whispered. Taking another few moments to settle her emotions, she continued, "I knew Mother worked until eleven o'clock—when the pub closes—so was confident I could speak with Abraham without her influence. I was all the more thankful to find Regina was already asleep when I arrived." She kept her gaze fixed upon her handkerchief as she now held it on the table. "Abraham and I talked about… Well, you know what we talked about now. I told him it wouldn't be awkward between us, despite his repeated confession of love, and reassured him I would continue to help him and Regina in whatever way I could. We left the question of Maryanna returning home unanswered for it was growing late and I needed to return home before Clement got back. I left at around ten thirty, arrived home at eleven o'clock and found Clement hadn't yet arrived. I therefore hurried to change into my nightgown and slipped into bed. I must have lain awake for almost an hour before I heard the bedroom door opening. I turned my back to it and pretended I was asleep. I didn't want him to know I hadn't been at home all evening."

"And does he know now?" Joseph enquired.

Diana frowned deeply. Her lips trembled again, and she shook her head, "No… I knew how it would look and I didn't want him to think ill of Abraham." Her hands started to shake as

199

her voice became strained, "When Maryanna's body was discovered outside the bazaar, murdered, I thought the worst." She turned her head away so she couldn't see Abraham's reaction as she continued, "I thought Abraham had murdered her so he could be with me. *That* is why I went to the Bow Street Society. I hoped you would discover the truth before the police did so I could, somehow, protect Regina from the *awful, awful* truth."

"How could you think such a thing?" Abraham enquired, stunned. "I would *never*...!" He glared at his sister-in-law who'd flinched at his sudden yell.

Her whole body shook as she sobbed. "I'm sorry, Abraham."

Yet the dock worker's anger didn't dissipate. Clenching his jaw, he stood and looked down upon her. "I *loved* my wife, Diana. If you *think* I could do *that* to her—cut her up and abandon her body for all to gawk at—you don't *bloody* know me at all!"

He threw his chair aside—forcing Mr Snyder and Mr Maxwell to their feet—and stomped out the room. Sam had stepped between Abraham and the others in case the man wanted to start trouble while Joseph had cowered behind him. When the door slammed, both the journalist and Mrs Suggitt jumped on the spot. After, he swallowed hard and rested his sweaty palm on his chest, while her resolve broke down and she sobbed uncontrollably.

* * *

Rebecca felt the wind's cold caress, smelt the moss' sweet dankness, and listened to the gentle pitter-patter of rain as it landed upon her umbrella. Adorned in the colour of mourning, she stood alone at an aged grave. Its surface was blank, any memorial having been eroded long ago. No flowers graced its base and no mourners came to pay their respects. Alone in the cemetery's corner, it had been neglected in care and in memory. The clerk felt a pang of guilt for not having brought a dedication of some kind, despite having no connection whatsoever to the grave.

"Woolfe suspects Weeks is helping the Society," Chief Inspector Jones' voice stated beside her.

"Did he say why?" Rebecca enquired as she continued to gaze upon the grave.

"A discarded packet of Turkish cigarettes."

The clerk turned upon the policeman with an expression of annoyed disbelief. "That *careless* idiot!"

"You were all there when Inspector Woolfe noticed it in the Society's kitchen," Jones pointed out. "Why didn't you remove it before he could do so?"

"Weeks shouldn't have tossed it onto the floor in the first place," Rebecca retorted. She put her hand on her hip, sighed, and faced the grave. Jones parted his lips to speak but, despite her not looking at him, was prevented from doing so by her saying, "Don't say it, Richard."

"You don't know what I was going to say," the chief inspector replied, feigning offence. The clerk tilted her head toward him and lofted a brow in silent interrogation. Understanding the insinuation Jones retrieved his pipe from his pocket and enquired, "Well, I did, didn't I?" He hooked the pipe on his lower lip and, striking a match, ignited the tobacco in its bowl. "It's slender evidence to condemn a man on but Woolfe approached me personally, albeit off the record. That alone is enough to suggest he believes there's some truth in it." Jones puffed on his pipe and, holding it at his side, exhaled the smoke away from her. "I've told him to keep me abreast of any further developments in the matter."

"And Weeks?"

"His reputation and position have yet to be publicly compromised but you should expect a withdrawal of his services from the Society. Naturally, he hasn't stated such to me but, as long as Inspector Woolfe holds his suspicions, Doctor Weeks cannot afford to be seen, or even rumoured to be, anywhere near you, the other Society members, or its headquarters."

"They don't suspect your involvement with the Society, do they?" Rebecca enquired as she, again, turned toward him.

Jones again went to smoke his pipe but, in the moment before he placed it in his mouth, shook his head and replied, "Nevertheless, as I'm certain you've already guessed, this must be our last meeting for a while."

"I had," she replied with a distinct lack of her usual confidence and bolshiness. "But a part of me had hoped I was wrong." The clerk held her umbrella with both hands and, again, faced the grave. Suddenly its eroded surface signified something entirely different to her.

"Goodbye, Miss Trent," Richard's voice said and she heard his feet traipse through the wet grass. Purposefully choosing the opposite direction, she lifted her skirts with one hand, while still gripping the umbrella with her other, and began walking.

Without looking to him, she replied, "Goodbye, Chief Inspector."

EIGHTEEN

"It's you; I should've known," Rebecca said to the visitor standing on the porch. "I suppose you'd better come in." She went to the bottom of the stairs while the new arrival stepped inside and closed the door. A heavy silence fell between the two. The clerk folded her arms across her chest and waited. Her visitor kept close to the door, stealing small glances at the surroundings.

"You've done well for yourself, haven't you?"

"Don't," Rebecca said. "You've got no right to pass judgement on me." Allowing her arms to fall to her sides she walked toward her visitor with a cold expression. "Say whatever it is you've come to say and leave."

"Percy sent me," the visitor countered. "Told me to tell you he can't do it anymore—helping the Society, I mean. Some inspector at the Yard's on his back and Percy don't want him finding out." The visitor's voice softened as she moved forward a little, "I wouldn't have come here to stir up a hornet's nest, Rebecca. You know me more than that."

"Do I? You told me you loved me and, days later, confessed you loved *him* more. Weeks, Polly, *weeks* I've not heard so much as a *whisper* from you."

"I'm sorry, Rebecca." The barmaid replied, ashamed.

"You can tell Doctor Weeks I received his message and shan't be contacting him again." Rebecca walked past her former lover with the intention of opening the door—only to hear a knock from the other side. Upon peeking through the peephole, she discovered Lady Owston, Miss Dexter, Miss Webster, and Mr Maxwell standing on the porch. "You can't leave that way," she told Polly and headed toward the kitchen. "You'll have to go out the back door."

"Why?" Polly enquired, half-running to keep up.

"I don't want any of the other Bow Street Society members to know you were here," Rebecca replied. Entering, and crossing the kitchen, she unlocked the back door and held it open. Polly slowly approached, confused and hurt. At first, the clerk ignored this, gesturing for the barmaid to leave, but then sighed deeply. "Not because of our past, Polly," she explained.

"But because one of them may accidentally inform Inspector Woolfe of your visit and I don't want to see you in trouble."

Polly smiled and, stepping closer to the clerk, kissed her softly upon the cheek. "Thank you," she whispered and ducked out into the night.

Back in the hallway, the polite knocking had become urgent banging. "Miss Trent?!" Lady Owston called from beyond the door. The clerk, having secured the back, hurried past the stairs and opened the various locks at the front. Pulling the door open, she at once stepped aside to allow the Bow Streeters to enter. Already night had fallen upon London and, for a fleeting moment, Rebecca felt concerned for Polly's safety. Yet Lady Owston's sing-song voice dragged her back to the present moment.

"There are police constables absolutely *everywhere* at the Suggitt residence."

"There were a couple standing outside the front of the house," Miss Webster corrected. Unlike Miss Dexter and Lady Owston, she didn't remove her hat.

"Well, it certainly *felt* like they were everywhere," Katheryne retorted and led the way into the kitchen. Mr Maxwell followed but stood against the kitchen door to keep it open. Agnes and Georgina passed him and joined Lady Owston in sitting at the table. The artist hadn't attempted to make any eye contact with Joseph. He'd been looking at the stove, however, so hadn't noticed her lack of attention. Georgina took the second chair on the left while Lady Owston and Miss Webster sat in the two chairs on the right side. As was customary, Miss Trent sat in the chair closest to the door. She checked her pocket watch and put it down.

"I'm also expecting Mr Locke. Please, help yourselves to the tea." She indicted the teapot, sugar bowl, cream jug, and plethora of cups and saucers arranged in the table's centre. "I presume Mr Snyder will be along once he's settled the horses?"

"Yes," Mr Maxwell replied while reaching for the teapot. Recalling his shenanigans during their last meeting, Miss Webster blocked the teapot with her hand.

"Allow me to serve, Mr Maxwell," she stated rather than asked.

The *Gaslight Gazette* journalist straightened. "Oh… all right." He stepped away and, picking up the chair at the opposite end of the table, repositioned it to stand by the stove. He bent his knees and held his hands in front of the stove's door to warm them. Miss Dexter meanwhile busied herself with retrieving her sketchbook from her satchel. Once done, she opened it at the depiction of Mrs Yates' clothes and placed it in the middle of the table—safely away from the teapot—so everyone could study it.

"That will be Mr Locke," Miss Trent said as knocking sounded from the hallway. Rising, she left the room and went to let him in. When she returned, she was accompanied by not only the illusionist but also the cabman. The two men greeted the present company and promptly took their places, Locke on the vacant chair between Joseph and Agnes and Snyder beside Georgina.

Both new arrivals accepted offers of tea from the secretary but it was only Mr Locke who remarked to Agnes, "I see you have once again neglected to remove your hat this evening, Miss Webster."

Agnes' hand instantly slipped and poured tea onto the table. Putting both cup and pot down with a thud, she replied, obviously rattled, "I-I don't know what you mean, Mr Locke."

"HAT!" Lady Owston exclaimed as she shot to her feet. Everyone stared at her in utter confusion, Agnes included.

"Are you well, Milady!" She enquired.

"Yes, yes, child!" Katheryne replied with a dismissive movement of her hand. "I *just* recalled something I overheard at the *Writer's Club*. Two of the ladies were discussing how they'd never seen Mrs Gromwell without her bonnet."

"With all due respect, Lady Owston," Locke began, "I fail to understand the significance of such a conversation."

Miss Webster, on the other hand, understood her employer's intentions. Forgetting the spilt tea, she watched Katheryne with an uncharacteristic intensity.

"I *know* why Mrs Gromwell doesn't remove her bonnet indoors," Lady Owston continued.

"Please don't." Agnes at once added.

"I'm afraid I must," Katheryne replied, regretfully.

The secretary visibly stiffened and her hand gripped the table's edge. She said, in a voice unusually laced with fear, "I am asking you not to."

"What's going on?" Miss Trent questioned, her eyes narrowed, as she looked between the two women. Neither addressed her, however. Instead, Lady Owston gazed into the increasingly desperate eyes of her ward and felt her resolve waning.

"Miss Webster keeps her hat on when indoors because she bears scars from a fire," Mr Locke stated, calmly. Everyone looked at him as if he'd just performed a baffling trick. Miss Webster looked especially struck by his words.

"How did you…?" She whispered.

"If I am recalling this accurately—please correct me if I am not—when we three entered the library within the Holdens' residence you, Lady Owston, at once crossed the room and hid the lit fire behind a guard. Afterward, you went to Miss Webster's side and hushed words were exchanged, presumably to ensure your secretary was not too overwhelmed by the fire's presence." Mr Locke watched the ladies' reactions. Neither denied the truth of his words, however. His fingers incessantly scratched the back of his hand as he continued, "I did not remark upon it at the time as I considered it irrelevant. I was then reminded of it at the *Turk's Head Public House* last night when I saw you flinch out the corner of my eye. I had just struck a match. I therefore came to the, albeit assumed, conclusion you were afraid of fire. The majority of such fears arise from the aftermath of past events, specifically, ones which are particularly painful." He paused. "While I do not wish to go into detail presently, I too have personally experienced such an event in my own life." He smiled while his fingers finally ceased in their scratching of his hand. "Lady Owston's dramatic recollection of Mrs Gromwell's bonnet, and her stating she knew the reason for her not removing it, led me to suspect you wear your own hat constantly, Miss Webster, to hide scarring from the fire. A fact Lady Owston, as your employer and friend, would undoubtedly be aware of."

"You are a very observant man, Mr Locke," Lady Owston remarked with a heavy voice. Sitting down, she slipped her hand in Agnes' and squeezed. "Agnes' parents were killed in the fire; she came to live with me soon after. She was only twelve at the time."

The secretary slowly lowered herself onto her own chair but kept hold of Katheryne. She said, "I remember waking up to my bedroom filled with smoke. My governess' room was adjacent to mine, so I rushed to her door and opened it. The flames burst out over top of me and singed my head. I screamed and reeled backward." Agnes released her grip on the table as she realised she'd not done so. That hand soon joined the other in Katheryne's, however. "My parents' room was on the other side of my governess'. Miss Potter had fallen asleep whilst reading and knocked her kerosene lamp from her bedside table. She always took a sleeping draught at bedtime, for I wasn't in the habit of waking up during the night, so she didn't awaken." Agnes paused, her lips parted, as her mind's eye recalled that terrible night. "I was rescued by our butler. The fire had already taken a hold by then... there was nothing to be done for my parents."

"My sincerest condolences," Mr Locke replied, a sentiment echoed around the room.

"Ever since that night, I've suffered with a crippling fear of fire; the smallest of flames may send my heart racing and the world spinning," Miss Webster explained. She met Lady Owston's gaze and, upon seeing the soft twinkle of reassurance in her eyes, slipped her hands from her employer's. Reaching upward, she removed the pins keeping her hat in place and pulled it away. Beneath was a bare patch of flesh made rough by heavy scarring that could only have been made by a severe burn. "I'd always hoped my hair would return but it never did. I therefore took to wearing my hat and this." Agnes turned the hat over to reveal a circle of real hair stitched together and attached to the underside of the hat's brim.

Miss Dexter, quite saddened by Miss Webster's affliction, said, "You hide it quite well."

"But why wear false hair at all?" Joseph enquired, confused.

While Agnes replaced her hat and secured it with its pins, she explained, "It lessens the chances of anyone glimpsing my scars should my hat slip at all."

"And it is called a *postiche*," Lady Owston corrected. "Made from actual human hair to blend with Agnes' own."

Joseph hummed in understanding.

Mr Locke, addressing the secretary, said, "You were under no obligation to expose yourself in such a way, Miss Webster. Yet I admire your courage for doing so nonetheless."

"Unfortunately, not *all* men are as liberally minded as you, Mr Locke," Lady Owston replied. "During the last century, wigs, specifically the tall, powdered type, were *most* fashionable. Yet, even as our century dawned, their popularity waned. Nowadays, they are not only out of favour but considered positively *shameful*. Men who wear them are accused of preposterous vanity whilst the women's crime is to be intentionally deceptive to attract the eye of a potential husband. Given the fact Agnes is still yet to be married at her age, the prejudice against her wearing a *postiche* would be monstrous."

"As sympathetic as we all are to your plight, Miss Webster," Miss Trent said. "What significance does this have for the murders of Mrs Maryanna Roberts and Mrs Sarah Yates?"

"On account of the extreme disdain wigs, and the wearers of wigs, are held in by wider society, both the product and the wig-fitting service tend to be advertised in code. For example, women's wigs may be referred to as 'ladies' imperceptible hair coverings.' Furthermore, wig wearers strive to keep their secret at all costs. I've known ladies who have won a wig, won a husband, and then proceeded to conceal the truth of their follicle deception for the entirety of their marriage. Only their hairdressers know they wear a wig as it is usually the hairdresser who fits it. It is therefore my strong suspicion, Miss Trent, the room at the top of the stairs in the *Queshire Department Store* contains such a wig-fitting service. It would certainly explain why Mr Queshire continues to deny it is anything but a storeroom. Yet, more than this, it would explain why Miss Galway was so afraid of us discovering its true use. Such a revelation would undoubtedly expose the customers concerned to unbridled ridicule and the store itself to a scandal it may not survive."

"Um, Lady Owston?" Mr Maxwell began, his fingers twisting the small bow of his cravat. When she turned her gaze to him, he enquired, "If wigs are made from actual human hair, could it be possible for-for the scalps of Mrs Roberts and Mrs Yates to-to... to be made into one?"

Katheryne gasped sharply in utter horror and her hand shot up to cover her mouth. Reaching at the mere thought, she had to swallow the bile lest it be released upon the table. Everyone else in the room was equally as shocked as she. "I... I really couldn't say," Lady Owston finally managed to stammer. Taking a few moments to gather her thoughts, she continued, "The oldest method of wig making *I* am aware of is to make what is called a *weft,* a small, fringe-like thing which is sewn onto a foundation of net, silk, and other materials. More recently, however, a new method of wig-making was developed in France; strands of hair are sewn directly onto flexible, flesh-coloured netting using a needle much akin to those used in embroidery. The netting allows the wig to have a more precise fit on the wearer's head." She felt positively unwell as she considered *how* a scalp could be disguised as a wig; "Netting could be secured to the underside of the… the…" She swallowed, "…but the… you know what would have to be tanned into leather, I should think; a process which could take days *if* the wig-maker wanted to create a high-quality finish. Besides, as I understand it, the hair used in wigs is foraged from overseas."

"Where is Doctor Weeks? Surely, he could confirm if such a thing was possible," Mr Locke enquired, casting a cursory glance toward the back door.

Miss Trent frowned deeply and, clasping her hands together, rested them on the table in front of her. "Doctor Weeks shan't be joining us, either tonight or at any other time. Inspector Woolfe has grown suspicious of the doctor's assisting us and so Doctor Weeks has decided to cancel his membership of this Society entirely."

"But how shall we know for certain about the wigs?" Lady Owston enquired; a desperate edge to her tone.

Mr Locke smiled, however, and replied, "By examining the wigs at the *Queshire Department Store* ourselves."

"How? If Mr Queshire refuses to acknowledge the wig-fitting service even exists, how are we to convince him to let us see the wigs?" Mr Maxwell probed, his own voice one of annoyed frustration. Again, though the illusionist smiled, this time with a definite twinkle to his green eyes.

"By sending a lady in need of a wig, of course." He looked to Agnes who stiffened.

"I—I couldn't possibly," she protested.

"But you must," Locke countered. "Besides, the expectation would not be for you to approach Mr Queshire but for you to speak with the hairdresser who is, presumably, confined to the room." Percy slid Georgina's sketchbook closer to him. "Meanwhile, Lady Owston and I shall distract Mr Queshire by enquiring after Mrs Yates' missing clothes and jewellery. It shall also provide me with an opportunity to see the layout of the store for myself in case my… nocturnal talents are required."

"*Mr* Locke!" Lady Owston exclaimed, shocked.

"Letting myself into a property without a key," Locke clarified.

"Oh, I see…" Katheryne replied, moving her head back in surprise.

"It all comes back to that store," Mr Snyder remarked. For the entirety of the meeting thus far, the cabman had listened in silence. He'd already informed Lady Owston, Mr Maxwell, Miss Webster, and Miss Dexter of his findings from the conversation with Mr Trowel when they'd travelled to the Suggitts' residence. He could only assume Miss Trent had notified Mr Locke either in writing or using the do-dad on the wall she spoke into.

Lady Owston hummed and gave a sad sigh. "There is certainly a strong suggestion our murderer is *one* of the people connected to the store. Mrs Roberts' shawl was sold there after being deposited in a basket which, theoretically, all our suspects had physical access to. Then there is the arsenic Miss Galway claimed she purchased on Mr Suggitt's behalf. Arsenic *he* claimed was to rid the store of rats; if *that* was also in the storeroom then, again, they *all* had access to it." She frowned. "No hessian sacks, however. I asked Mr Queshire about them again this morning when we told him of Miss Galway's attempt to rouse him."

"Mrs Yates, though she didn't go to the store as far as we could tell, had access to arsenic too as she purchased some on behalf of the *Turk's Head's* landlord," Agnes explained. "Her being murdered does rather rule her out as a suspect, however."

"Unless she *did* murder Mrs Roberts and one of the others murdered her for revenge?" Mr Maxwell suggested.

"They were all together at Mr and Mrs Suggitt's house all night though." Georgina pointed out.

"They could be lying for each other; three out of the four have already done so," Mr Locke reminded her. "Of course, Miss Galway could have murdered Mrs Yates and created a fictitious stalker of Mr Roberts and Mrs Yates to give herself a reason to speak with Mr Queshire and thereby give herself an alibi."

"What would be her *motive* for murdering both women though?" Lady Owston questioned.

"She is keen to become a member of the Society and, by her own confession, she disliked Mrs Roberts," Mr Maxwell said.

Lady Owston shook her head, "No; I do not believe such a preposterous reason. Furthermore, Mr Locke, her ploy to provide herself with an alibi, as far as Mr Queshire was concerned, was unsuccessful for he didn't hear her knocking."

Mr Locke nodded, conceding to her reasoning, and said, "He is also a suspect though, is he not? Mrs Roberts caused a most undesirable scene in his store the day before she died and he, like all the others, had access to the storeroom wherein the donation basket was hidden—an initiative he personally manages—and the French Breakfast coffee was stored. I suggest we ask him to show us the batch of arsenic which was purchased from *Drummond's* when we speak with him tomorrow, Lady Owston."

"You have read my thoughts, Mr Locke. Regrettably, I must disagree with you with regards to Mr Queshire's position as a suspect. While I shall concede he *does* have access to the means of murder and, in Mrs Roberts' case, a possible motive, he does not have a motive for Mrs Yates' murder. I, for one, have also not seen any bottles of lemonade in his storeroom—though I shall also endeavour to enquire after it tomorrow."

"We cannot eliminate anyone as a suspect until we have completed our enquiries at the store tomorrow," Mr Locke pointed out.

Everyone made various noises of agreement before Mr Maxwell enquired, "Should I visit the docks tomorrow? Mr Roberts has told us he slept outside the gates after leaving home at the same time as Regina. Maybe someone saw him?"

"You could," Sam interjected. "But it won't do you any good. Blokes who're not on the Quay-Gangers' lists, like Mr Roberts, don't get much attention as long as they do the work. Any man who's not lame can go to the gates and get work with no questions asked. Mr Roberts not being on the Gangers' lists means 'e's not known enough by them; means 'e could've sent a mate instead and got him to tell the Ganger his name. But even then, the Ganger's gotta remember it."

Mr Maxwell frowned deeply in disappointment but, leaning back in his chair, nodded.

"You can speak with Mr Ratchett at the *Turk's Head* instead," Miss Trent said. "To see if he'll confirm Mrs Yates' story about the sailor and her explanation for the arsenic. He may have also seen Mr Roberts arriving to walk Mrs Yates home and, if she is telling the truth, Miss Galway leaving to follow them."

"Alone?" Mr Maxwell enquired with a hard swallow.

"No; Mr Snyder and Miss Dexter will go with you." Rebecca replied and closed her notebook, "I think that concludes our meeting, everyone. Be sure to tell me of your findings and have a good evening."

* * *

Mr Maxwell hadn't loitered after the meeting. Miss Dexter had invited him into the empty parlour, presumably for a discreet word, but the *Gaslight Gazette* journalist had mumbled an excuse and left. The pangs of guilt were still present in his chest as he unlocked the door to his room and stepped inside. It was one of many in a lodging house within walking distance of Fleet Street. Upon closing the door, he realised a lamp was lit behind him. Turning, he was stunned to see his father sitting in the armchair adjacent to the cold hearth. Oliver Maxwell removed the cigar he'd been smoking and exhaled a thick cloud of smoke in his son's direction, "Your landlady let me in, with a little monetary persuasion, of course."

"I wasn't expecting you this evening, Father—"

"Where have you been? I've waited for you for hours."

"I—I was at work."

"No, you weren't. I went there first."

"My work with the Bow Street Society," Joseph clarified while his hands loosely gripped the lapels of his frock coat and then dropped to his sides.

Oliver stood and, tossing his used cigar into the grate, said, "Just as long as you weren't with your whore." The journalist flinched at the last word. Parting his lips to reply, he found his voice wouldn't utter a single syllable; strangled as it was by the usual, yet extreme, nervousness he felt whenever he was in his father's presence.

If Oliver noticed his son's stricken state, he didn't comment upon it. Instead, he walked toward him and said, "You're to come to dinner again tomorrow night. Mr Lillithwaite and his daughter, Poppy, shall be in attendance. She's been unable to catch the eye of a suitor and her fading youth means she's increasingly becoming a burden to the family.

I've reassured Mr Lillithwaite that his daughter will find a suitor in you provided he honours his promise of a generous dowry."

"But Father—" Joseph began to protest in utter desperation. He was at once cut off, however, by a hard back-hand across his face. The force was enough to not only jerk his head to the side but to also send him off-balance. His left leg crossed over the right before he stumbled. Stopping his fall by taking hold of the mantelshelf, Joseph then gripped it tightly while he reeled from the shock. His face violently stung and his eyes watered. Half-bending over, he heard movement behind him and flinched.

"You will *not* answer me back again, Joseph, and you will *certainly* not question my orders. Do I make myself clear?"

"Y—Y—Yes, F—Father," Joseph stuttered, fighting against the tremble which had overtaken his body.

Oliver gave a soft grunt of acceptance and, retrieving his hat, said, "I'll expect you to arrive promptly at eight." He walked away, "And wear some decent clothes; I do not want to be embarrassed." The sound of the door closing was like music to the terrified journalist who at once collapsed to his knees in relief.

NINETEEN

Mr Locke held open The *Queshire Department Store's* door for Lady Owston and Miss Webster to enter ahead of him. Lifting the tip of his cane approximately an inch off the ground, he then swept it around to his front while silently pivoting on his heel. When he followed his fellow Bow Streeters inside, his was a far livelier reception than theirs. At once, he heard the excited mutterings of the millinery department's assistants to his left and a gasp from the haberdashery department's assistant to his right. Holding the edge of his top hat's brim between his leather-clad thumb and forefinger, he twisted his torso first to the right and then to the left. While facing each direction, he granted the young ladies with a graceful bowing of his head and a polite smile. The millinery ladies had clasped one another's hands in anticipation before remarking on the illusionist being "such a gent" and fanning their flushed faces with their hands. The haberdashery assistant, on the other hand, had stood stock still and finally curtsied once he walked away. The famous magician's presence hadn't failed to catch the eye of the store's customers, either. Most were ladies of a certain age, however, who literally frowned upon the assistants' vulgar behaviour. Yet this didn't prevent their smiling and returning Locke's "Good morning" when he gave it.

"You have caused quite the stir, Mr Locke," Edmund remarked when the illusionist joined him, Lady Owston, and Miss Webster at the perfumery department.

Percy smiled, "I can assure you it wasn't my intention to do so."

"Whether intentional or not, I would still like to thank you for it. I will undoubtedly witness an increase in customer numbers as soon as these ladies tell their friends the Great Locke shops here."

"As you know, my wife is already an avid supporter of your store; I am quite certain she shall be pleased my presence has assisted in its continued success."

"Indeed," Edmund replied. To the whole group, he enquired, "How may I be of assistance today?"

"I wish to purchase some leather gloves I saw the other day," Agnes said as she lifted a hand to her shoulder while still facing the store owner.

"And Mr Locke and I would like to steal just a *few* more minutes of your time, *Mr* Queshire—if it is convenient, that is?" Lady Owston added.

"But of course; I'm only too happy to help." He stepped back and, as Lady Owston walked toward the storeroom, fell into step beside her. When they reached the door, he opened it for her and waited while Mr Locke entered next. Agnes had meanwhile started to cross the store toward the haberdashery department. Naturally, Mr Queshire looked over, to ensure she was being served, before joining her associates and closing the door.

"Pardon my saying, miss, but was that truly the Great Locke I saw?" the assistant enquired. Agnes hummed but at once stepped away to approach the stairs.

The door to the hairdressing salon was left ajar, no doubt to keep the chill of the store from seeping within. The secretary was grateful for this small mercy for it lessened the chance of her being unable to execute her task. She did nevertheless take the precaution to listen at the door marked *Staff only* once she'd reached it. She heard absolutely nothing. Her attempt to turn the knob was successful but, as she eased the door open, its hinges squeaked. She flinched at the sound and waited for someone to emerge from the salon to confront her. Again, nothing happened and relief filled her.

Beyond was a windowless corridor. Brass brackets, each supporting a shaded gas lamp, were mounted on the near and far ends of the left-hand wall. In the light, she saw a bolt fixed to the inside of the door she'd just closed. Against her better judgement, she slid the bolt into place and, again, paused to listen; still no sounds reached her. A second closed door stood at the other end of the corridor. In the space between was a line of four vacant, ornately carved chairs with their backs against the left-hand wall. Their plush, burgundy-coloured armrests and seat cushions were of the highest quality while their frames were immaculately clean. Agnes' pace was cautious in its speed as she moved down the corridor. Upon nearing the chairs, she noticed several oil paintings mounted on the wall opposite. They depicted a variety of everyday objects arranged at different heights on a tablecloth. She unconsciously slowed as she came within a few feet of the other door. There were neither plaques upon it nor any other hint of its function. The corridor had evidently served as a sort of waiting room but for what?

"May I help you at all?" a man queried as the door unexpectedly swung open.

Agnes jolted backward with an unbridled gasp of surprise.

"Pardon moi, Mademoiselle," the man apologised with a distinct French accent. He was in his mid-to-late forties with ashen-coloured hair and dark-brown eyes flecked with gold. His attire consisted of an impeccably pressed, black frock coat, black trousers, crisp, white shirt with high, starched collar, a burgundy cravat, and a waistcoat. The last had gold-thread roses embroidered onto its two front panels fastened by brass buttons. He was fair skinned with a healthy amount of laughter lines around his eyes and mouth. Agnes needed a couple of moments to calm her racing heart, which she requested, but she was by no means a hysterical wreck. When he introduced himself therefore, she was entirely capable of returning the favour.

"A pleasure to meet you, Mr Vuitton. I'm Miss Agnes Webster; I'm here under the strong recommendation of my friend, Mrs Gromwell."

"Aaahh." Mr Vuitton smiled broadly. "Come in, s'il vous plaît?" Rather than simply move aside, however, the Frenchman stepped out into the corridor. Gazing through the open doorway, Agnes soon discovered why; the room beyond couldn't have been any larger than six feet long by six feet wide. It, like the corridor, was windowless. This time, however, only a single, large gas lamp, mounted on the wall in its back-right corner, illuminated the space. Agnes stepped inside and allowed her eyes to adjust to the gloom. When they did, she saw a rosewood, ladies' writing bureaux standing against the back wall. It had its shelf erected but all of its small, expertly constructed drawers were closed, and presumably locked. Standing on the left-hand corner of the bureaux's shelf was a free-standing mirror identical to those she'd seen on the millinery department's counter. The mirror was tilted to enable the customer, who would seat herself before it, to admire her reflection with ease. The gas lamp behind her would also fully illuminate her face by bouncing its light off the mirror's surface. Above the bureaux were three shelves, one above the other, with several solid, walnut 'heads' on cross-shaped stands lining them.

These 'heads' were smooth and devoid of any facial features. Resting atop every 'head' was a splendid wig which had been carefully combed and arranged. The wigs were of all shapes and sizes while being limited to natural hair colours. Lying on the polished, exposed oak floorboards was a Turkish-style rug whose floral design was rich in burgundies, creams, and golds. The walls meanwhile were adorned with a textured, burgundy, floral wallpaper, over which were mounted oak-framed bulletin boards. Pinned to these boards were advertisements, of varying sizes, for women's hair tonics, remedies, and "coverings." An immense, intricately drawn poster, advertising the breadth of goods available at the *Queshire Department Store,* had taken pride of place in the centre of the right-hand wall. Though it was the only decoration on that wall, the poster's sheer size meant it dominated it entirely.

Mr Vuitton indicated an oak chair standing about a foot away from the bureaux and invited Agnes to sit. The chair was identical to those in the corridor in that it had a balloon-shaped back and plush, burgundy velvet seat cushion, armrests, and back cushion. She therefore found it extremely comfortable.

Mr Vuitton closed the door and placed an identical chair, retrieved from another corner, behind Agnes'. While she was facing the bureaux, he faced the wall to her left. He'd positioned his chair in such a way that she could see his face over her shoulder in the mirror's reflection, though.

"Mademoiselle, pardon my saying, but it seems to me you do not require a covering?"

"I'm grateful for your saying so, sir," she replied. "But, alas, I have hidden my shame well." Dipping her head a little, she carefully removed the pins from her hat. Each one was added to a neat pile on the bureaux's shelf before she lifted her hat and placed it on top of it. Initially perplexed, Mr Vuitton rose to his feet to take a closer look. Agnes tensed in anticipation as she watched the Frenchman peer down at her ugly baldness.

"What is the cause of the scarring?" He finally enquired and lifted his hand, "May I touch it, mademoiselle?"

"You may," she replied. It was the first time anyone other than Katheryne or her maid had laid a finger upon her bare patch of mutilated flesh. Agnes had expected him to flinch or scoff in disgust but he did neither. Instead, his fingertips were light and unobtrusive as they traced the lines of scarring. Realising she had yet to answer his first question, she said, "I was involved in a fire at my home as a child. I opened a door and the flames burnt my scalp."

"Do you use hot crimping irons, hot pins, or any other means to make your hair wavy?" Agnes shook her head. Mr Vuitton indicated the posters on the bulletin board opposite, "And you have applied A.G. Edwards & Co.'s *Harlene* remedy for baldness and *Koko for the Hair* to no avail?"

"Nothing has worked; I'm deathly afraid of the rest falling out, too," she added, something Agnes was surprised she'd admitted to for not even Lady Owston was aware of that particular fear of hers.

"And you have used lemon juice rubbed into the scalp? Washed your hair, and rubbed it hard, every night with a teaspoonful of salt and one scruple of quinine added to a pint of brandy you have mixed well?"

Agnes nodded and said, "Both. Happily, my hair is still intact. It is only the patch of baldness that refuses to disappear."

"Oui, mademoiselle," Mr Vuitton agreed with her evaluation. Retaking his seat, he waited for Agnes to turn toward him and continued, "It is sometimes the practise of madames," he paused, "that is, how do you say? Married women... Err, pardon, non. Practice of older women to wear lace mantillas; I do not think such an accessoire would suit you, however. I can show you some *postiches* which match your colouring but the position of your baldness makes it difficult to cover without increasing the size of your head. An, err, bigger head is *most* unbecoming, oui?"

"Oui," Miss Webster replied with a weak smile. She had learnt a couple of French words from her employer who had spent some time in Paris some years ago. Mr Vuitton picked up Agnes' hat and, turning it over, stood to examine the attached false hair under the gaslight.

He enquired, "And you have tried to hide your baldness by brushing your remaining hair over?"

"Yes, but my hair isn't thick enough to hide it entirely," Agnes replied, her hope fading. When she'd agreed to investigate the mysterious room at the top of the stairs, she'd fully expected to find a charlatan of sorts. After discovering the opposite, she'd utterly forgotten her original reason for coming. "Is there *nothing* you can do?"

"Mais oui, mademoiselle," he said, smiling broadly. Passing her hat back to her, he added, "Stay here, s'il vous plaît, and I shall return."

Agnes felt lighter at both hearing and seeing his enthusiasm in wanting to help her. She utterly understood why Mrs Gromwell had come to him—*Mrs Gromwell!* She suddenly remembered what she was there to do. A momentary checking of her memory had her recall she was looking for mousey-brown and blond wigs. *If* Mrs Roberts' and Mrs Yates' scalps had been removed so they could be turned into wigs, that is. When she finally heard the door close behind the Frenchman, she stood and swiftly examined the wigs on the stands; none appeared unusual. Next, she opened a cupboard beneath the bureaux's shelf.

Within, she found box upon box of real human hair wigs. Without hesitation, she took out each box, lifted its lid to check the hair colour of the wig inside, and returned it to the cupboard when it didn't match her criteria. After checking numerous boxes in this way, she finally discovered her first mousey-brown wig. No sooner had she taken it from the box though did she hear Mr Vuitton walking down the corridor toward her. She at once replaced the now empty box in the cupboard, closed the door, and returned to her seat while depositing the wig into her coat's inside pocket.

"I have this *postiche* and this *postiche*," Mr Vuitton announced as he entered and presented her with two hairpieces: one a chocolate-brown and the other a dark, chestnut in colour. Miss Webster forced a smile to her usually emotionless face and, turning toward the mirror, inspected the reflection of each *postiche* as it was held over her bald patch.

"The first, I think," she said. The thought she may well have the scalp of a dead woman concealed on her person spurred her decision. Yet there were still questions which were left unanswered in her mind. While Mr Vuitton carefully wrapped and boxed her *postiche,* therefore she enquired, "For how long has Mr Queshire and Mr Suggitt been offering this service?"

"Monsieur Queshire, trois years. Monsieur Suggitt does not know it is done; he was angry when Monsieur Queshire and I told him about it, so Monsieur Queshire said for me to go on but not to tell Monsieur Suggitt."

"Do you make the coverings?"

"Non, Monsieur Queshire buys from mon amie, Monsieur LeGarde, in Paris. He is a wig maker of the first class. I, err, how do you say? Mend the wigs if they are broken after going on the ship."

"Have you had any new wigs delivered lately?"

"Non, we will get some at the end of this week," Mr Vuitton replied and held out a box sealed with an exquisite red ribbon tied into a bow. The box itself was plain and innocuous. Agnes accepted it and, enquiring after the price, gave him the necessary amount. A brief exchange of thanks was had before she left, thoroughly pleased with both her purchase and what she'd managed to find out and retrieve.

* * *

"How is Miss Galway? I wanted to find out from her personally but couldn't see her in the store," Lady Owston remarked. She, Mr Locke, and Mr Queshire had settled themselves at the storeroom's table.

The illusionist had intentionally taken the chair directly adjacent to the window, under which the table stood. His top hat, with his gloves tucked within, sat upon the table at his elbow. While the owner answered, Percy rested his cane upon the window ledge. In so doing, he brushed his fingers over its lock and, without looking to it, identified its mechanism—a swing arm, typical for the sash style. Comprised of two halves, screwed into the frame and sliding sash respectively, the lock had a rounded hook on a pivot. The hook would slide downward into the deep recess of the lock's other half attached to the frame. The point of the hook would then 'catch' the recess' edge to prevent a potential intruder sliding the window up from the outside. A simple yet effective security measure; most intruders wouldn't risk breaking a window's pane for fear the noise would wake the inhabitants. Mr Locke knew a method that didn't require such extreme measures, however; one which he wouldn't employ in this case unless he deemed it absolutely necessary.

"She didn't feel quite ready to return yet," Edmund explained to Katheryne, across from whom he sat. "The recollection of someone pursuing Mrs Yates, mere hours before her murder, has had a profound affect upon Miss Galway. Her fear that he may have seen her watching is practically crippling her; the sooner your group identifies the man the better."

"When did she tell you this?" Mr Locke queried. "If she has not returned?"

"This morning; I meant she hadn't returned to her duties. Naturally, I sent her back to the lodgings when I saw, how to such a great degree, the matter was still upsetting her."

"Alone?"

"Yes; why ever would I not? It isn't an unreasonable distance to walk in the daytime."

"Perhaps, if you were not 'crippled' by the fear a man suspected of murdering two women would seek you out," the illusionist countered with a triumphant smirk. With an ironic tone, he continued, "Though I am certain you considered such." He paused to watch the owner's reaction, "I presume she did not arrive for work yesterday?"

"She did not."

"Naturally; otherwise she would have informed you of her fear then. I am nonetheless intrigued by your waiting until this morning to speak with her, however. Given that Lady Owston, her secretary, Miss Webster, and Miss Dexter notified you of Miss Galway's attempt to rouse you from your sleep on the very morning of Mrs Yates' murder. Personally, my curiosity alone would have compelled me to leave my store at once to speak with the assistant concerned. For you did not tell Mr Queshire of Miss Galway's reason for wanting to speak to him at such an early hour, did you, Lady Owston?"

"No, I don't believe I did…" Katheryne rummaged through her memory, "…No, I didn't. And you didn't ask me why she wanted to speak with you either."

"I was still trying to digest the news of Mrs Yates' murder," Edmund stated. "And I was told yesterday morning, by Miss Annie Simkins—another of the store's assistants— Miss Galway was unwell. Due to Mr Suggitt being, predictably, unable to return to work, I was obliged to take on his duties in addition to my own. Put quite simply, Mr Locke, I could spare no time to visit Miss Galway, or even speak with her on the telephone, until this morning when she arrived for work."

"She purchased arsenic on Mr Suggitt's behalf, did she not?" the illusionist enquired, unfazed by the owner's growing irritability.

Edmund scowled at him, "She did, as Mr Suggitt has already confirmed."

"May I see it?"

"No," Edmund addressed Lady Owston next as he explained, "It was only a few grams and I've already exhausted them. I used two slices of buttered bread, to sprinkle the arsenic on, which I placed in the basement as bait for the mice."

"I thought it was an infestation of rats you had?" Mr Locke challenged before Lady Owston could even open her mouth.

Edmund turned hard eyes upon Percy, "Rats… mice, they are the same to me. Their specific biology is irrelevant when they are chewing through expensive silks."

"*Mr* Queshire." Katheryne smiled. "Have any further items been donated to your stock?"

"I've not personally taken receipt of any garments but there were some new ones in the basket." Edmund looked back to the illusionist. "You may check if you wish."

"I do," Locke replied. He stood and, silently stepping around Lady Owston in one fluid motion, went to the basket.

Though he stood at Edmund's back when he lifted the lid, he didn't notice any attempt by the owner to scrutinise his search. Instead, he heard him ask, "Have you sampled your soap yet, Lady Owston?"

"*Nooo!* I'm afraid I haven't," she confessed. The thud of the lid had her looking behind him, however. The fact Percy wasn't holding anything when he turned around told her all she needed to know.

"There are no clothes elsewhere, Mr Queshire?" Locke enquired. "You mentioned a basement; perhaps we should check if any of Mrs Yates,' or indeed Mrs Roberts', clothes were put there by mistake?"

"Absolutely not," Edmund snapped. "I've cooperated considerably more than I ought to have, and been exceptionally patient, with you and your associates, Mr Locke." He thrust his chair back, only narrowly missing the illusionist on account of his quick reflexes. Turning to him, he went on, "There are *no* donated garments aside from those in the basket. The fact I take in any at all has the potential to ruin me, which is why I was reluctant to tell Lady Owston of it in the first place. She, unlike you, had at least the decency to be fair with me. If you do wish to accuse me of anything, then I would suggest you do so now, Mr Locke. Yet, know you say it under risk of inviting a court case against you for slander."

"My good fellow." Percy smiled. "I can assure you that I have enough money to tie you and your store up in legal bureaucracy, appeals, and hearings for years to come. Since you have resorted to reselling subpar goods as new, thereby defrauding your trusting customers, I rather suspect your financial affairs are not so buoyant. I therefore suggest you refrain from threatening gentlemen with court proceedings unless a distant, rich relative suddenly dies and you inherit a substantial sum of money." His smile faded. "Besides, my request to see your basement came from a desire to fulfil a commission given to the Society by Mrs Diana Suggitt, not from a vindictive quest to ruin you. Do not misunderstand me, however. Should you feel obliged to commence such court proceedings against me, I would have no qualms in not only ruining you financially but also legally and morally. A man does not threaten such extreme measures unless he feels threatened himself. My question is inevitably this, therefore; what is the specific reason for you feeling threatened?"

"You are quite correct, Mr Locke; I *do* feel threatened but not because I'm hiding the stolen garments of two murdered women. As you've seen, the basket doesn't contain any—and neither does the basement, which you'll have to take my word for. Your persistent challenges to the answers I've freely given, though, have served to make me suspect that you think I had some part in these crimes. I did not. Yet when a man is shown the shadow of a hangman's noose, and he does not deserve to have his neck placed within it, he is apt to be defensive. I have told you the truth, despite your trying of my patience, Mr Locke, but now I must ask we end our conversation here. I'm still understaffed on account of Mr Suggitt's continued absence so I would appreciate the opportunity to return to the management of my store."

"Of course," Lady Owston agreed. Both men looked at her; Mr Locke with a lofted brow. "But first tell me why you think we are looking for Mrs Yates' clothes, Mr Queshire," she added, plainly.

The owner's mouth twitched but he replied, "An assumption on my part. I presumed the same man who murdered Mrs Roberts murdered her mother, ergo Mrs Yates' clothes would have been missing like her daughter's."

"Do you have any lemonade in the storeroom, or perhaps upstairs?"

"No, I don't like it; even with sugar I find it too bitter for my palette."

"*Thank* you, Mr Queshire," Katheryne beamed. She picked up her gloves and, as she was pulling them on, headed for the door. "I know how *valuable* your time is. I really *do* appreciate your sparing some of it for us."

"You're always welcome to it, Lady Owston." Edmund smiled, his usual charm returning. The illusionist wasn't graced with the same acknowledgement, however. Instead, the owner ignored him as he and Lady Owston left the storeroom ahead of him. Returning to the window to collect his cane, Locke reminded himself of its lock's mechanism with a brief glance, the earlier identification having already slipped his mind. Retrieving his gloves and hat also, he then loitered long enough to visually inspect the floorboards before vacating the room. He had found no indication of a trapdoor leading to the basement, so he could only presume it lay elsewhere. Catching up with the others past the perfumery department, Locke overheard Edmund ask Katheryne, "You *will* send my condolences to Mr and Mrs Suggitt and their family? I've not seen them since it happened."

"But of *course!*" she exclaimed. Catching sight of her secretary out the corner of her eye, she spun around, "There's Agnes." She lifted her hand to garner her attention before facing Mr Queshire again as he bid them good day. "Good *day* to you, too," she replied and watched him return to the storeroom.

Leaning upon his cane, Locke pondered an idea of his. When Katheryne then left his side to greet Miss Webster, the illusionist decided to put it to the test. He strolled over to the perfumery's counter and, waiting until its assistant was distracted by another customer, slipped past. With his back half turned toward the rest of the store, he eased the storeroom door open about an inch and peered inside. Mr Queshire was closing the window. It had been thus while they'd spoken, so Percy was intrigued as to why he'd decided to open and re-close it after they'd left. He was forced to abandon his thoughts and dart out of sight, however, when the owner turned toward his hiding place. Next hearing footsteps approaching, Percy silently abandoned the immediate vicinity and pretended to browse the central counter.

After allowing a few moments to pass, he lifted his gaze. Lady Owston and Miss Webster were deep in conversation beside the millinery counter, but Mr Queshire was nowhere to be seen. Percy contemplated whether to allow the ladies to return to Miss Trent while he searched the premises for the missing clothes. A cursory glance around him caused him to dismiss the notion, however; there were too many admiring customers and assistants for him to slip into, obviously restricted, rooms without being noticed. He therefore re-joined his fellow Bow Streeters.

"I didn't have time to inspect it properly," Miss Webster said to her employer in a hushed tone. "But I have it in my coat."

An unusual statement to enter a conversation on to be certain, Mr Locke thought. Yet his attention was distracted by a glint of gold among the hairpins. Given their highly decorative and ornate appearance, such a thing wouldn't usually be out of place. The *shape* the gold was in, however, piqued his interest. While the pins were long, straight, and narrow—even with additions—this was round and hollow. The gold item was difficult to fully identify though as it was nestled among the pile of pins within an open tray on the countertop.

The assistant was thankfully distracted by a demanding customer, so Locke took the opportunity to 'procure' the item. If it was indeed Mrs Yates', he didn't want Queshire to know he had it by purchasing it. He therefore slipped his hand over the exposed tray and, picking up a clump of pins positioned around the ring, lifted it away. While he transferred the pins in that hand to his other palm, he slipped the ring over his thumb. With the pins safely exposed, while he pretended to inspect them, he put his then freed hand into his trouser pocket. At first, the ring wouldn't slide from his thumb so he had to discreetly grip it with his index finger, through the material of his trousers, and slowly pull it down. When he felt the ring drop, he withdrew his hand and replaced the pins into the tray. The entire process had taken under a minute and no one had noticed a thing.

Turning to Miss Webster and Lady Owston, he said, "If you ladies would be so kind as to wait in my carriage outside, I shall be but a moment."

"Where are you going?" Agnes enquired, surprised.

"To investigate a most curious occurrence." He replied.

Both Lady Owston and Miss Webster reluctantly agreed and allowed the illusionist to leave the store. Once outside, Locke sought out the service alleyway at the rear and subsequently, the gate to the store's backyard. Given the storeroom window directly overlooked the yard, and thus the gate, Percy didn't want to risk being seen by the owner. He therefore didn't touch the gate or its lock. Nor did he even attempt to enter the yard. Instead, he gave a small jump and, gripping the wall's top edge, lifted his entire body weight from the ground. Stopping when he could see over the wall, he held himself there while he scrutinised every inch of the window ledge and yard.

Everything seemed normal and nothing was out of place. The illusionist became all the more intrigued. *What had Mr Queshire been doing at the window?* Lifting himself a little higher, he then saw the shuttered, wooden doors raised from the ground directly underneath the window. He could only assume they were the entrance to the basement. A momentary glance was cast back to the window. Seeing no one in the storeroom, Locke heaved himself up and over the wall. Being careful to place, rather than drop, his feet, onto the ground on the other side, he silently crept across the yard and crouched at the doors.

They were secured with a heavy chain and cast heart lock. Simply by looking at the rust, which had formed inside it, the illusionist knew the lock would be impossible to pick. Yet he knew it would be impossible to open with its original key, too. Clearly it had been many years since this entrance had been used. This, along with the unlikelihood he could uncover the internal entrance to the basement without being caught, led Locke to the unpleasant conclusion he'd have to abandon all hopes of doing so. Even returning at night held its own risks; should he gain access to the basement, Locke knew the only viable exit would be the suspected trapdoor. Mr Queshire could therefore easily contain him and, in the best-case scenario, summon a constable. No, the odds of success were not only far too small, but also greatly outweighed by the level of risk involved with such an endeavour.

Resigned to this fact, the illusionist stood and retraced his route across the yard—after ensuring no one was at the storeroom window, of course. Repeating his earlier technique of scaling the wall, he was soon in the service alleyway brushing down his frock coat. Since no one, either from the store or otherwise, had challenged him over his actions, Mr Locke strolled back to Oxford Street, this time to inform his fellow Bow Streeters of his discoveries and decision.

TWENTY

The *Turk's Head Public House* had an eerie atmosphere when closed to customers; the dilapidated tables and walls made it seem abandoned. The presence of a crackling fire in the hearth, unobstructed from view, increased Miss Webster's sense of uneasiness. Her fear's exposure at the meeting had brought comfort after her initial embarrassment, though. As, rather than ridicule or trivialise her irrational behaviour, Mr Maxwell and Miss Dexter had allowed her to sit with her back to the pub's fire. She could still hear its sounds but she didn't have to look into its flames and, as far as her anxiety was concerned, that's all she'd needed. The journalist and artist hadn't drawn attention to her precaution either; instead, they'd actively encouraged it by entering the pub first and taking the only other available seat Mr Ratchett had invited them to occupy. This being the bench positioned underneath the window, directly to the right of the door; the same they'd occupied two nights prior, in fact. The coincidence hadn't gone unnoticed by Miss Webster but, as both Joseph and Georgina hadn't been with her then, she chose not to remark upon it.

"Thank you for speaking to us, Mr Ratchett, at what must be a difficult time," Miss Dexter said with genuine sympathy.

The landlord was a man in his late fifties with a body half-crippled from years of pushing and lifting heavy barrels. Broad biceps, clothed by a cream shirt, were just one indication of his strength. Yet his shoulders were rounded and his back was a little hunched while he sat beside Miss Webster. His joints had seemed stiff when he'd lowered himself onto the stool, too. He also chose to push his stool away from the table, so he could rest his hands on his knees rather than fold them across his chest. His chestnut-brown, unkempt hair had flecks of grey to its edges while his sideburns, though closely cut, were more grey than brown. An old, crumpled apron hung about his waist but was nevertheless clean and unstained. When he spoke, his voice sounded like it came from the depths of his chest.

"Anything to help out the Roberts. Still can't believe what 'appened; wife's beside herself."

"Mrs Yates took care of your wife the night Mrs Roberts died, didn't she?" Mr Maxwell enquired, his pencil poised over his open notebook.

"Yeah," the landlord replied. "Jenny's got sickness of the lungs."

"Was Doctor Locke not with her?"

"Nah; I've not got much trust in women doctors but we can't afford a regular one. All she could do for Jenny was give her some tonic and tell her to rest up. So, Mrs Yates took over most of Jenny's care."

"But Mrs Yates finished work early that night?"

"Robbie McDonald came and collected her; them two went back a long way. We all did; I was a Merchant Seaman with Robbie until I met Jenny. He's always held a candle for Sarah."

"Mrs Yates told our associate, Mr Snyder, that Robbie sailed from London the day after Mrs Roberts' murder," Miss Webster stated. She too wrote a record of the conversation but purely for the purpose of providing an accurate report to Miss Trent and the others. Mr Ratchett merely nodded so she enquired, "Did he know Mrs Roberts at all?"

"Not that I know of, but I'll tell you who she *did* know—and who came looking for her the night she died, too. Sarah's other son-in-law, Mr Suggitt. Came in about a quarter past nine. I told him Maryanna was barred and she'd not come in besides. He got all het-up but then left. I told Sarah about it when she came down about fifteen or so minutes later. I let her leave early because she and Robbie wanted to make the most of their time. He's gonna be heartbroken when he gets back to port and finds out she's gone."

"Do you have any idea when that may be?"

"I'm afraid I don't; months, a year even? Depends if he decides to change ships when he gets to the other end."

"Arsenic," Joseph stated. Tapping the edge of his notebook with his pencil he enquired, "Mrs Yates bought you some for the mice from *Eastleigh's* chemists, didn't she?" Joseph leant his forearm on his book and, absentmindedly putting his pencil into his mouth, nibbled on the wood. The sudden and bitter taste soon after had him pull out the pencil and look at it in disgust, however.

"She did," Mr Ratchett responded, either not noticing the journalist's eccentric behaviour or choosing to ignore it.

Miss Webster on the other hand watched in half-disbelief as Joseph proceeded to wipe the spittle from his pencil on his trouser leg.

"Can we see it, please?" she finally enquired of the landlord when she'd pulled her attention back to him.

Mr Ratchett grimaced as he forced his reluctant joints into motion and stood. Without uttering a word to the Bow Streeters, he went behind the bar and retrieved something from the shelf underneath its top. When he'd returned to his stool, and sat with a sharp drop, he put a brown-paper packet on the table. It was clearly marked with the *Eastleigh's* name and, more importantly, was still sealed. "Police wanted to look at it, too," Mr Ratchett explained. "I've not had a chance to use it yet, what with Jenny's illness and then Mrs Yates' murder."

"What did the police say when you showed it to them?" Miss Dexter enquired.

"Not much, just thanked me for showing it to them. They came the day before Sarah was murdered, probably trying to say she killed her daughter. I showed it to them to make a point."

"You don't believe Mrs Yates was responsible for Maryanna's death, then? They weren't on speaking terms, after all," Joseph pointed out.

Mr Ratchett looked him square in the eyes as he replied, "Sarah loved her children—all of them. She talked harshly about Maryanna but that was her way of protecting herself. That girl hurt all of them in that family with her drinking; there was no need for it, either. Was just like her dad."

"The night Mrs Yates died," Georgina began after a small nod. "Did Mr Roberts walk her home at closing?"

"He did; got here at eleven o'clock and left with her."

"Did you see anyone watching them or, perhaps, following them when they left?"

"Now that you mention it, there was someone, a young woman who sat by the door. Soon as Abraham came in, she watched him. I'd caught her watching Sarah, too. Then, when they left, she got up and walked out after them."

"Can you remember what she looked like?"

Georgina opened up the sketchbook resting in her lap and began to draw while Mr Ratchett replied, "She was small, like the size of a twelve-year-old or something. She was older than that though; I could tell by looking in her face." Mr

Ratchett paused as he closed his eyes. "Wiry, blond hair she had, in a bun at the back." He gestured to the base of his skull with his large hand. "Wore a skirt and a blouse; can't remember what colours."

"Was there anything unusual about her face? A large nose, maybe? Distinctly coloured eyes?" the artist encouraged, attempting to spur the landlord's memory. The man clenched his eyes but, after a couple of moments, lifted his hands and dropped them again with a weary sigh. He opened his eyes and shook his head.

"Sorry, I can't remember. It was closing time and I was tired. I just wanted to get them out and check on Jenny."

Miss Dexter frowned; it wasn't the most accurate of descriptions but it certainly *sounded* like Miss Galway. She decided against showing him the sketch for what she'd done was faceless and lacking in any tangible detail. Instead, she smiled at him and closed her sketchbook while Joseph and Agnes completed their notes. Georgina said, "Thank you again, Mr Ratchett."

* * *

Miss Dexter scrutinised every minute muscle reflex on Abraham Roberts' face as he examined the ring in his hands. Sitting in one of the armchairs in the Suggitts' parlour, Abraham had his elbows on his knees with his back bent and his head bowed. Mr and Mrs Suggitt and Regina Roberts were in the library at the request of the Society. Aside from the artist in the room, Mr Locke, Mr Maxwell, Lady Owston, and Miss Webster were also in attendance. Mr Snyder, who had brought Georgina, Joseph, and Agnes to the house, had remained with his cab a couple of streets away. Locke, standing at the fireplace, enquired of Mr Roberts, "Do you recognise it?"

"Yes…" Abraham's voice was laden down with grief as he spoke. "…It's Sarah's. The initials engraved on the inside are her husband's." He lifted bloodshot eyes to the illusionist, "Where did you find it?"

"The *Queshire Department Store*," Locke replied.

Confusion at once descended upon Abraham's features. He looked from Percy to Georgina and then to Joseph and Agnes, who shared the sofa opposite with the artist. "What would it be doing there?"

"Mrs Yates didn't take it there?" Miss Webster enquired, her monotone causing the question to sound more confrontational than she'd intended.

Mr Roberts' face contorted with annoyance. "Nah. She never went near the place."

"Perhaps your daughter, then?" Joseph suggested. "Or Mr and Mrs Suggitt?"

"She was wearing the ring the last I saw her," Abraham said, his annoyance steadily metamorphosing into anger. "When're they supposed to have bloody done that?"

The Bow Streeters exchanged glances.

Lady Owston, who had chosen to sit in the other armchair, took in a deep breath. "Well," she began in a cautious voice. "There is the possibility one of them could have murdered your mother-in-law because they suspected she murdered Maryanna…" Katheryne paused. "If we are to examine such a possibility, then we must not only include *you* among our suspects, Mr Roberts, but also suggest the murderer deposited the ring at the store to direct suspicion away from them. As to the question of when, the only possible time would have been the morning after Mrs Yates' death, due to her being murdered so early in the day."

"Nah." Abraham shook his head. "Sarah didn't kill Maryanna; she hated the drink but she loved her daughter. Anyway, Diana, Clement, Regina, and me couldn't have killed Sarah because we was all here when she died. We told you that."

"Indeed, you have," Locke replied. "But more than one of your group has admitted to lying to us to protect another. Why would they, and others, not lie again for the same reason?"

"You want to know why?" Abraham stood and went to the parlour window. Upon opening it, he told the constable outside, "Get Inspector Woolfe here; tell him I want to talk to him." At first, the constable seemed reluctant but, after a moment's contemplation, left his post to carry out the request. Mr Roberts once more closed the window and, facing the room, said, "I want you to hear this from him." The Bow Streeters exchanged glances with mixed reactions; Joseph and Georgina were perturbed while Lady Owston and Mr Locke were curious—*very* curious indeed.

TWENTY-ONE

"Four days ago, the Bow Street Society was commissioned to investigate the murder of Mrs Maryanna Roberts," Lady Owston started as she stood before those gathered at the *Queshire Department Store.*

The owner, who was near to her, listened intently. Occupying chairs directly in front of the independent journalist were Mrs Ruth Holden, Mrs Diana Suggitt, Miss Regina Roberts, and Mr Abraham Roberts in that order. Father and daughter held one another's hand in the young woman's lap. Clement stood behind his wife, their intertwined fingers resting against her shoulder. Mrs Holden had segregated herself from her neighbours while her husband kept his distance from her. Standing behind, yet to the side, of her, he kept his hand on her chair's backrest purely to ease the weight from his tired legs

Behind Lady Owston was the counter located between the haberdashery and millinery departments. Miss Webster, who faced inwards on its right outer edge, recalled the gloves she'd admired there. The memory was vague and she couldn't identify the specific pair from the many still displayed. She wasn't perturbed, however, for her priority was to record this most important of events in her notebook. While her pencil glided across the page, writing shorthand notation, her concentration was halved between it and the words she heard. Mr Maxwell stood to the left of the secretary, at an angle to those sitting. Miss Dexter, Mr Snyder, and Mr Locke stood side by side on Lady Owston's right. Doctor Weeks had both elbows on the haberdashery department's glass countertop as he smoked, watching his ex-fellow Bow Streeters. Inspector Woolfe meanwhile observed everyone from his vantage point at Mr Maxwell's left side. Two constables stood on the street outside, their backs to the window. Beyond them one could see the small, yellow glow of the Black Maria's lamp cutting through the growing darkness.

"And now we are ready to reveal who we believe took her life," Katheryne stated and raised the thick file she held in both hands for the others to see. The drama in their collective reaction was equal to the soberness heard in her voice. Mrs Suggitt's fingers had tightened their grip on her husband's while she stifled a gasp with her handkerchief. Clement had straightened and put his free hand upon his wife's other shoulder. Nervous anticipation had descended upon Regina's face while she covered her father's hand with her second. Abraham had momentarily looked away from Katheryne, but otherwise kept his lips pursed and his gaze hard. Mrs Holden displayed a distinct lack of interest by tutting and rolling her eyes, and her husband sidestepped to grip her chair with both hands.

Woolfe, who had seen all these physical responses, said, with cynicism, "Here we go." He put a cigarette between his lips. "I told you what would happen if you carried on meddling." He exhaled the smoke and it drifted across the group, causing both Mrs Holden and Mrs Suggitt to waft it away with their hand and handkerchief respectively. Caleb said, "Perverting the course of justice by conspiracy; that's what this is."

"I thought you wanted to know the truth, too," Regina countered.

The inspector smiled, the vision of his face in so doing reminding many present of the wolf from the tale of Little Red Riding Hood. "I do, but we're not going to hear it from them." He pointed to the Bow Streeters, "They're bloody meddling civilians; they don't know anything about how a case *should* be investigated. There are proper rules to follow, strict methods when recording evidence, and ways suspects should be questioned."

"I still think we should hear what they've got to say," Regina replied, casting defiant eyes in Woolfe's direction.

"Can we *please* get on with this?" Mrs Holden enquired, annoyed. "We have a dinner engagement at eight."

"Two members of my family have been murdered and you're worried about dinner?" Abraham snapped.

Mrs Holden merely rolled her eyes for a second time, however. She said, "I couldn't ask someone like *you* to understand."

"You *what*?" Abraham barked as he leapt to his feet. Mrs Holden, startled, shot back in her chair.

Clement rose to stand between the two and, to his brother-in-law, said, "Ignore her, Abraham. You getting into trouble won't help anyone."

"Sit *down*!" Woolfe boomed over them all and every pair of eyes turned toward him. Maintaining the scowl he'd directed at Mr Roberts until that man returned to his seat, Inspector Woolfe shot a warning glare at Mrs Holden when he caught sound of her muttering a condescending remark under her breath. The elder woman was taken aback, upon realising she was overheard, but didn't speak anymore. Mr Suggitt meanwhile had resumed his prior position behind his wife.

"Right." Caleb shifted his attention back to Katheryne, "Let's hear it, then; your theory, before I'm obliged to arrest everyone for brawling."

"Thank you, Inspector," Katheryne replied. "Both Mrs Maryanna Roberts and Mrs Sarah Yates were poisoned with drinks laced with arsenic; French Breakfast coffee for Mrs Roberts and lemonade for Mrs Yates. The scalps and breasts of each victim were removed and taken by their murderer. Their clothes were also stolen and, in Mrs Yates' case, so too was her gold wedding ring. From descriptions given by Mr Suggitt and Mr Roberts, our artist, Miss Dexter, sketched Mrs Roberts' and Mrs Yates' missing clothes." Katheryne took the named drawings from the file and passed them to Georgina who held them aloft for all to see. Mrs Suggitt and Mr Roberts simultaneously averted their gaze while she gripped Clement's hand and he clasped Regina's. Meanwhile, Mr Holden stared at Maryanna's sketch with sorrowful eyes as his wife stifled a yawn. Mr Queshire, who'd not faltered in his stoicism, folded his arms and waited.

"Mrs Roberts' body was discovered in the doorway of the *London Crystal Palace Bazaar's* Oxford Street entrance," Katheryne continued. "Her body having been taken there in a hessian sack by her murderer." Woolfe's eyes narrowed and he looked to the Canadian who, conveniently, was scratching his neck with his head bowed. "Are you listening, Inspector?" Katheryne enquired.

Caleb grunted but, when she didn't continue, he added, "Yeah, I'm listening."

"Good." She smiled. "On account of where Mrs Roberts' body was found, we had to consider the likelihood of her murderer being a stranger. At that point in time, this was a more probable scenario than the alternative. Yet, when we later learned *how* she was killed, this probability decreased and the likelihood of her murderer being someone she knew strengthened.

"This was due to three reasons: a) She was poisoned, a weapon most frequently utilised in closed quarters, b) The poison was put in coffee, a beverage she would *certainly* not have chosen if gin was available, and c) If she hadn't known the person who gave her this drink, she wouldn't have accepted or drank it. On the surface, reason b may appear to support the stranger theory as it seems to demonstrate a lack of intimate knowledge about Mrs Roberts. Yet, given her public preference for gin, a stranger would've been more inclined to offer an arsenic-laced bottle of that drink than coffee. Reasons a) and c) may also be applied to Mrs Yates' murder. She, unlike her daughter, *was* given her preferred choice of beverage by her murderer—lemonade. This fact *does* demonstrate a more intimate knowledge of Mrs Yates so again, we suspected she, like her daughter, was murdered by someone she knew. The simple fact Mrs Yates was murdered *in* her *own* home strengthened our opinion. Her requirement that her son-in-law escort her home after work demonstrates an awareness of possible danger at night. It would've therefore been against her instincts to invite a stranger into her home when she was alone. As a result, we dismissed the possibility of our murderer being an unknown entirely. This dramatically decreased our circle of suspects for both murders. Due to the similarities between the two crimes, in terms of chosen weapon, corpse mutilation, and items stolen, we also quickly concluded we were seeking the same person, or persons, for *both* deaths."

Next taking receipt, and refreshing his memory, of the file, Mr Locke said, "Mrs Roberts' body was identified by Metropolitan Police Constable Fraser for two reasons. The first: she was a prostitute known to frequent the area. The second: she was the sister-in-law of the *Queshire Department Store's* assistant manager, Mr Clement Suggitt. It was to him notification of her murder was given by Constable Fraser. Mr Suggitt then broke this news to his wife, Diana, via telephone and told her not to travel to Oxford Street. She, in a state of great distress, at once went to Bow Street and commissioned the Society to investigate her sister's murder. The reason she cited, for wanting the Bow Street Society to accept her case, was a lack of confidence, on her part, that the Metropolitan Police would be willing to identify her sister's murderer on account of

Maryanna's 'fallen woman' status." He stayed Inspector Woolfe's inevitable protestation with a lift of his cane, "I am simply stating the facts, Inspector, and not attempting to sully anyone's reputation."

Caleb gave an unconvinced grunt and continued smoking.

"The experience of the Dorsey case compelled us to refrain from automatically believing our client's innocence. It also highlighted the need to consider *all* as suspects until evidence against their guilt could be uncovered; Mrs Suggitt was no exception to this." Mr Locke paused as he looked upon the woman in question, "She commissioned our services but she was not above our suspicions."

"I, my secretary Miss Agnes Webster, and Miss Georgina Dexter, were assigned to investigate the case by the Society's clerk, Miss Trent," Lady Owston said while the illusionist returned the file to her. "We travelled to Oxford Street with Mrs Suggitt in the Society's hansom cab. It was driven by Mr Samuel Snyder who, unbeknownst to our client, had also been assigned to investigate. Mrs Suggitt informed Agnes, Georgina, and me of an incident which had occurred at the *Queshire Department Store* the previous day, one which had an altercation between Mrs Roberts and another customer at its centre."

"I presume you are referring to *me*?" Ruth Holden cut in, disgusted.

"Indeed she is," Mr Locke replied. Temporarily reclaiming the file from Lady Owston, to reread the beginning of the next passage, he then idly scratched a red patch on his hand as he continued, "We were told by Mr Queshire and one of his assistants, Miss Rose Galway, that Mrs Roberts propositioned your husband." The illusionist shifted his gaze to the man in question but his address continued to be aimed at Mrs Holden, "You naturally took offence to such behaviour and threatened to leave the store. Mr Queshire intervened however and, despite Mrs Roberts' violence and verbal abuse, removed her from the store. When the request for your identities was made, Miss Galway was the one to grant the information. Mr Queshire, for the sake of propriety and reputation, had intended *not* to do so."

"As is only to be expected," Mrs Holden retorted.

"Under normal circumstances, I would be inclined to agree with you," Mr Locke replied with a smile. "However, we were investigating a murder and thus were obliged to question *anyone* who could, potentially, be involved. You and your husband were suspects because of your altercation with Mrs Roberts. If Miss Galway had *not* let slip your names, we may be still trying to track you down even now."

"When Agnes and I spoke to you at home," Lady Owston re-joined. "You made it *abundantly* clear you not only had a low opinion of Mrs Roberts, but you thought she was of the 'criminal class.' Furthermore, you stated her murder wasn't unfortunate."

Diana inhaled sharply and stared at the wealthier woman in disbelief.

Feeling eyes upon her, Ruth stated, "It *wasn't*."

"How could you *say* such a thing?" Diana enquired, dumbfounded. "Do you have *any* idea what was done to her?"

"She was a *foul* creature, Mrs Suggitt," Ruth countered. "Who squandered her God-given life in the gin houses."

"That doesn't mean her murder was a *good* thing!" Diana cried as her hand, clenched tightly about her handkerchief, trembled with rage.

Mrs Holden, witnessing this, sneered, "I now understand why your sister was as *foul* as she was; uncontrollable anger is evidently a family trait." If Clement hadn't been gripping her shoulder, Mrs Suggitt may have echoed Abraham in her reaction. Instead, she pressed her face against her husband's arm and gave a frustrated gasp. Mrs Holden smirked and, addressing Lady Owston, went on, "As I told you at the time, neither my husband nor I would slay another human being; it is against God's Commandments."

"You also told us you'd both visited the *Theatre Royal* on Drury Lane until nine thirty on the night of Mrs Roberts' murder," Katheryne replied. "Furthermore, that you both returned home at ten o'clock and, while your husband read in the library, you retired to bed."

"A story which your husband confirmed during my conversation with him at the *Royal Coachman Public House* on Hill Street," Mr Locke added.

"And *why* would he *not*?" Mrs Holden scoffed.

"Indeed." The illusionist smiled. While he accepted the file from Lady Owston, he looked to Bartholomew. Seeing trepidation in the man's eyes, Locke considered a non-disclosure of the facts he held in his hands. A glance at Mrs Holden, however, convinced him that such a revelation may be fortuitous to Bartholomew in the long term. He therefore said, "You did not remain in the library, Mr Holden. Instead, you left your home and sought out Mrs Roberts. She, by your own admission, was just one of the women who regularly satisfied your carnal needs in exchange for monetary payment. Needs which your wife could not, for propriety's sake, fulfil." He paused and, again, glanced at Mrs Holden. "You have my sympathies." Though she'd assumed he'd addressed her, Mr Locke had been looking at her husband when he'd spoken. A slight jolt of Bartholomew's head was the only sign of acknowledgement, however. "Yet you did not simply have 'services rendered;' you told her she would not receive any future coin should she approach you in such a manner, as she had earlier that day, again. You, in your own words, wanted to remind her 'of her place.' You also paid her only half the amount you usually would—*after* she had 'verbally' rendered her service to you— partly because she was inebriated at the time and partly because of her earlier behaviour. Am I recalling this correctly, Mr Holden, or would you like to make some amendments?"

"*Disgusting!*" Mrs Holden quipped.

To both her and everyone's amazement, Bartholomew ordered, "Be *quiet,* woman! *I* am your *husband*; I shall find my pleasure wherever *I* see fit."

"Maryanna was *sick*," Diana cut in, distressed. "She needed *help*, not for men like *you* to take advantage of her."

"I did *nothing* of the kind, Mrs Suggitt. I paid her for the pleasure she gave me. Besides," his expression softened and, when he continued, it was with a regretful voice, "I enjoyed warmth from her I couldn't ever hope to receive from my wife. Ruth and I married for convenience; it is a lonely and soul-destroying existence to be in a loveless marriage. I'm not ashamed to admit that, when I heard of Maryanna's death, I was sad beyond measure."

While Mrs Holden angrily chewed her tongue, Mrs Suggitt had managed to force a weak smile to her lips. She said, sadly, "I still can't condone your behaviour, Mr Holden, but... I'm nevertheless comforted by the knowledge her impact on others' lives wasn't entirely negative."

"It was your reaction to her death which convinced me you were not responsible for it," Mr Locke stated.

238

"And it was your vehement disgust and dislike of her, Mrs Holden, which had Agnes and I convinced *you'd* had no part in the poor woman's murder, either." Lady Owston added.

"Yet these were mere assumptions on our parts," Mr Locke said. "The evidence of your innocence would come when we scrutinised the practicalities of either of you committing the act. Doctor Weeks, we have a vague idea of when Mrs Roberts was murdered but could you clarify it for us, please?"

The Canadian straightened and looked to Inspector Woolfe. When he aired no objections, however, Weeks replied, "Were between midnight and four in the mornin'. She were then found by Constable Fraser at six."

"As I suspected. Thank you, Doctor." Locke smiled and, turning his attention back to Mr Holden, continued, "Even at midnight, the meeting you had with Mrs Roberts, at approximately ten forty-five, was over an hour before the earliest time at which she could have died. Furthermore, you only remained with her for a few minutes. You then returned home and climbed into bed at eleven forty-five where, as both you and she stated, your wife was asleep. On the surface, therefore, it would appear neither of you had any practical opportunity to murder Mrs Roberts. And yet," he lifted his cane, "you each had *motive* in the form of the earlier altercation. You had each been humiliated by it, if for different reasons. Could it be one, or perhaps both, of you murdered her because of this? You could have lied for each other and your servants, who dressed you the following morning, could have unwittingly provided you with an alibi. Why would an alibi be required? Because the murderer, having stolen her clothes, left Mrs Robert's shawl at the *Queshire Department Store*. You each could have risen early enough to return to Oxford Street, abandoned the shawl at the store, and returned home in good time to be 'awakened' by your servants.

"This scenario did not play out, however, for two reasons. As a regular customer of the department store, you, Mrs Holden, would have been aware of Mr Queshire's usual reluctance to discuss his customers with those who had no right to the information. You would assume, therefore, your name would not be uttered in connection with the altercation with Mrs Roberts. Why, then, would you go to the trouble of disposing of Mrs Roberts' shawl at the very establishment where the altercation took place? The answer is you would not. You had absolutely no reason to suspect anyone would visit you to ask after your altercation with Mrs Roberts. You could have therefore simply retained the shawl without fear of consequence. The presence of the shawl on one of the store's dummies the very morning *after* Mrs Roberts' murder, though, tells us this was *not* the case. Which leads me onto the second reason. It is my belief, Mr Holden, that despite you being unable to recall it when I asked you what Mrs Roberts was wearing the last you saw her, she *was* in fact in possession of her shawl at that time."

"It does look familiar, yes," Bartholomew admitted as he scrutinised the drawing.

Smiling, Mr Locke continued, "Mr Queshire adorned the dummy with the shawl on the *night* of Mrs Roberts' murder when he was alone in the store. Due to the fact she *was* wearing it during your meeting with her, and Mr Queshire did *not* mention he had received a late-night visit from you or your wife, it is our conclusion that neither of you had any practical opportunity to dispose of the shawl before our visit. As a result, regardless of any semblance of motive or practical opportunity to commit the deed, you are both innocent of Mrs Roberts' murder. Since there was no tangible connection between either of you and Mrs Yates, we also believe neither of you were responsible for her death."

"May we leave, then?" Mrs Holden enquired, frustrated. The Bow Streeters looked to Inspector Woolfe for a decision.

"Yeah." He gestured toward the door. "Go home."

"*Thank* you," Ruth replied and, getting to her feet, left the store in mere moments.

Her husband, for whom she had not even slowed her pace, offered his hand to Clement and said, "I *am* sorry about Maryanna's death."

"Thank you," Clement answered quietly.

A little of Mr Holden's sadness was eased by this this and he withdrew his hand. He then bade goodbye to the others and followed his wife into the night.

When the Harpy and her spouse were safely out of earshot, Mr Queshire commented to Mr Locke, "I appreciate you not revealing the existence of the second-hand basket to Mrs Holden."

"She had not placed the shawl *within* it so it was unnecessary for her to be made aware *of* it."

"But someone else here did," Mr Maxwell pointed out. "The storeroom, where the basket is kept, is never locked so, theoretically, any of you could've put the shawl there."

"Earlier, I stated Mrs Suggitt was not above our suspicions," Mr Locke began. "Once we had eliminated the Holdens as possible suspects, we turned our scrutiny to all those who were close to both victims, Mrs Suggitt included. Yet, before we explain our conclusions regarding our client's level of guilt, we must first explain those relating to her husband."

"As Maryanna's brother-in-law, it should have fallen to *you* to intervene when her behaviour around the Holdens became unpalatable," Lady Owston said. "Instead, it was Mr Queshire who felt obliged to confront her and, subsequently, remove her from his store." Clement swallowed hard but remained silent as Katheryne continued, "According to Mr Queshire, you would distance yourself from Maryanna whenever she visited the store, an allegation you have never denied. Your wife, on the other hand, would converse freely with her sister where all the customers could see. Thus, your behaviour couldn't have been born from a decision to disown Diana's family. During our conversation at the *Turk's Head Public House,* you admitted you'd never made a secret of your dislike for Maryanna. We must therefore assume you distanced yourself from her for the same reason. Regardless, however, Mr Queshire had felt unable to request your assistance *because* of your reaction to Maryanna's past visits to the store.

"Yet, your feelings toward your sister-in-law ran deeper than a simple dislike of her; you yourself told us you thought she was making the lives of her husband, her daughter, and even your wife a misery."

"She was," Clement replied and retook his wife's hand.

Seeing this unconscious action, Katheryne hummed and gave a weak smile. She then went on, "But it was your *wife's* pain specifically, caused by her being constantly disappointed by her sister, which compelled you to offer Maryanna two hundred pounds to leave London. An offer, though generous, she refused. She also threatened to tell your wife of it and it was this reason which, you believed, had brought her to the store."

"Yes," Clement confirmed through a sigh.

Lady Owston gave a small nod and, taking the file from Mr Locke, said, "You've already admitted to us this was the reason you decided to look for her on the night she died. In addition to her usual haunts, you visited the *Turk's Head Public House* where its landlord, Mr Ratchett, informed you she'd not been in all evening. You were reportedly agitated by this news but left regardless. It wasn't *you* who first informed us of your search, however. Mrs Yates, Maryanna's mother, had been informed of your visit, by Mr Ratchett, shortly after you'd left. *She* told us of it. Furthermore, Maryanna had been *barred* from that establishment on account of her having caused trouble there in the past. One must therefore wonder *why* you would even check the pub at all. Mrs Yates and her daughter hadn't been on speaking times prior to Maryanna's death so, surely, it would've been unlikely she'd have gone there. *Perhaps* you wanted everyone to *see* you *without* Maryanna so you could *prove* you hadn't seen her all evening when her body was eventually discovered?"

"Don't be ridiculous," Clement stated, annoyed. "I was at home in bed by a quarter to midnight; ask Diana."

"She's already lied for you once," Inspector Woolfe pointed out.

Mr Suggitt, wide-eyed, looked from him to Lady Owston and back again. He cried, "I didn't murder Maryanna!"

"Why not?" Mr Locke challenged. "You had the motive; you wished to ensure she held her tongue over your proposition. You had the opportunity: your wife, who has already lied for you by telling the inspector you were at home together all evening, could have lied about the time you came to bed. You had the means: there is a tin of the French Breakfast coffee, used to administer the arsenic to Mrs Roberts, both in the storeroom here and, in your own words, at your residence. Furthermore, you requested Miss Galway purchase some arsenic from *Drummond's Pharmaceutical Chemists* on your behalf. Though Mr Queshire confirmed it was indeed for a rat infestation in the basement here, you could have easily stolen the arsenic and given it to your sister-in-law. Then there is the shawl; as assistant manager, you could have placed it in the second-hand clothes basket without anyone's suspicions becoming aroused."

"Your guilt does *appear* certain, Mr Suggitt," Lady Owston said with a frown. "And yet the certainty wanes when one scrutinises whether you had the *capability* of not only murdering Maryanna, but also her mother and, in addition to their murders, mutilating their bodies. Yes, you initially lied about your whereabouts on the night Maryanna died. Yes, you failed to tell the police about the argument between your sister-in-law and the Holdens, and, yes, you told Miss Dexter you didn't want the Bow Street Society to investigate anymore. However—"

"What?" Diana interrupted, stunned. Turning in her chair to look up at her husband, she enquired, "Clement...? Is this true...? You asked them to stop...?"

"I did it for you, darling," Mr Suggitt replied, both his expression and voice laden down with intense sadness. "I could see how much pain you were in and I couldn't bear it. I thought... if we just let the *police* do their duty, it would be resolved sooner and this nightmare would be *over*."

"*Oh,* my darling," Diana replied through a half sigh of relief and sorrow. As he fell onto the chair beside hers and pressed her fingers to his lips, she trembled alongside him. Her hand lifted to briefly touch his cheek before the two collapsed into one another's arms. Unable to restrain his emotions any longer, Clement buried his face into his wife's shoulder and wept.

"I'm so sorry, Diana. I never meant to hurt you..."

"Shush," she soothed as she gently stroked his head. "It is done, my darling."

"However," Lady Owston slowly repeated. "As we have all just witnessed, you are sincere in your love and devotion to your wife. The murder of her sister, though enabling you to be rid of her once and for all, would have devastated your wife as it has now. The same consequence has been born from the death of your mother-in-law. Thus, while you *are* capable of lies and deception—uttered to protect your wife—you are *not* capable of murdering the two most important women in your wife's life. The love and devotion you feel for Diana simply wouldn't allow you to commit the deed."

"And so, we go back to Mrs Suggitt," Mr Maxwell announced once he was given the file. Putting it down on the countertop, Joseph then smoothed down his frock coat before picking up the document. He cleared his throat, coughed, and cleared his throat again while flipping through the pages until he reached the part he was after. "Wait a moment!" He turned toward Inspector Woolfe, "Was there any hessian sacks at the Suggitt home?"

"No."

"Thank you." Joseph smiled but the policeman's glare didn't budge. Feeling his cheeks becoming hot therefore, while he wiped his palms on his frock coat, Mr Maxwell swallowed and said, "Mrs Suggitt lied about being at home the night her sister died."

"*What*?" Clement hissed as he lifted his wet face from his wife's shoulder and looked to her.

Diana, with fresh tears of her own falling, whispered, "I was going to tell you…"

"While you were out looking for Maryanna," Mr Maxwell resumed. "She was visiting Mr Roberts." Clement at once cast a questioning gaze in Abraham's direction but his eyes were fixed firmly on the *Gaslight Gazette* journalist. "When she got there, at around nine thirty, she thought Regina was asleep behind the curtain, so did Mr Roberts. She already knew her mother wouldn't be there because she was working at the *Turk's Head Public House* until eleven o'clock like she did every night. Mrs Suggitt told Mr Roberts she wanted her sister to live with her so she wouldn't be tempted by the gin anymore. Rather than celebrate this good news though, Mr Roberts, again, confessed his love to Mrs Suggitt. Regina, who was *awake*, had overheard all of this."

"You did *what*?" Clement growled as he leapt to his feet.

Diana stood also and, blocking his path to Abraham, cried, "I didn't return his affection, darling! I reminded him, as I had so many times before, that I loved *you*!"

Clement's hands were clenched into fists as he glared at the dock worker, who had also risen to his feet. "Is that right, Abraham?"

"It is. I loved Maryanna, Clement, but the drinking… I was losing her to it. When Diana came to see me… I thought it was another chance at happiness, but I *respected* what she told me. *Nothing* happened between us."

"They're telling you the truth, Uncle," Regina said as, she too stood. Going to Clement's side though, she gently took hold of his arm and tried to coax him away from her father. "Please, Uncle. Aunt Diana *did* tell Dad she loved you. She also said she'd still help us before she left and Dad came to bed." Clement's jaw clenched but he tore his glare from Abraham to instead look upon his wife. Tears rolled freely down her cheeks as her lips trembled and her hands, gripping the lapels of his coat, shook.

Realising how terrified she was, Clement felt his anger at once fade. He put his arms about her and, pulling her into an embrace, said, "I believe you, my darling." His hand rubbed her back, "I believe you."

"When Mr Snyder and I spoke to Mrs Suggitt, after Miss Roberts had told Lady Owston of the overheard conversation, she said she'd left Mr Roberts' residence at ten thirty. She, um…" Joseph flicked back a couple of pages in the file but, discovering he'd gone in the wrong direction, flicked forward too far. He frowned and, turning back another page, was silent while his finger ran down the lines. "Ah! Here we are!" He smiled broadly at the others but, seeing their disconcerted expressions, dismissed the joy from his own and cast his eyes downward instead. "When she returned home, at approximately eleven o'clock, Mr Suggitt hadn't returned. She retired to bed and, after lying awake for almost an hour, heard the bedroom door open and she pretended to be sleeping." Joseph rested his hand on his cravat, "Mrs Suggitt had the same access to the French Breakfast coffee and arsenic as her husband, as well as the second-hand clothes basket *if* he had told her of its existence. Clement has already confirmed in his own account though that she was indeed asleep in bed at a quarter to midnight on the night her sister died. She therefore had *no* opportunity to commit the murder before her husband came home.

"She, like Mr Suggitt, *did* lie to us on several occasions. Firstly, to protect Regina: She hired the Bow Street Society because she suspected Mr Roberts of murdering her sister. She wanted *us* to discover the truth before the police did so she could protect Regina from it. Secondly, she lied on her husband's behalf about their being at home all evening. Thirdly, she lied to her husband about visiting Mr Roberts because she wanted to protect her brother-in-law. Lying and murdering are two *very* different things though and she had no motive for killing either victim. Thus, like with her husband, we have concluded she, too, is innocent of these crimes for these reasons."

"Mr Roberts," Sam said and accepted the file from Joseph. When the dock worker looked his way, Mr Snyder continued, "You tellin' Mrs Suggitt you loved her is a reason for you wantin' your wife dead. You got French Breakfast coffee at your house with no dust on the tin; everythin' else on that shelf woz covered in it so someone must've used the coffee. Miss Dexter asked 'bout the sacks and you told her you didn't have any, which we thought woz true as we couldn't see any either. There's loads of sacks at the docks though so you could've got one from there." The cabman sniffed and wiped the underside of his nose with his thumb. "Your daughter's just said you went to bed after Mrs Suggitt left. We know, from Regina, you woz both knocked up at four o'clock in the morning; you to go sleep outside the dock gates and she to go to Covent Garden. That doesn't give you any time to do in your wife between the two times Doctor Weeks said. We think you never got near the arsenic Mrs Yates had bought either because Mr Ratchett still had it when we asked him. We can't check with the Quay-Gangers at the docks, about you bein' there or not, as you're not a Royal but we don't think you ever had a sack at home either. So, even though you lied, too—about Mrs Yates livin' with you—and you left out bits—Mrs Yates not talkin' to your daughter—you didn't do in your wife. Mostly because the reason doesn't make sense: you'd do in Clement before you done in Maryanna if you wanted to be with Diana because Maryanna wozn't livin' at home. You'd tossed her out on her ear when you found out she'd been tea-leafin' the housekeepin' monies."

"He was the last person to see Mrs Yates alive though," Inspector Woolfe pointed out. "He walked her home, remember?"

"When was Mrs Yates murdered, please, Doctor Weeks?" Mr Locke enquired of the Canadian who, again, sought guidance from the inspector. This time a small nod and a grunt from him gave Weeks the permission he needed.

He replied, "Were between half past midnight and quarter past two in the mornin' when whatshisface found 'er."

"Mr Trowel," Caleb said.

"Yeah, 'im." Weeks replied with a nod.

"Mr and Mrs Suggitt said Mr Roberts got to their house at a half past midnight and he stayed the night," Mr Snyder explained. "So Mr Roberts didn't have any time to do in his mother-in-law either." The cabman rested his large hand on the file's open page. "But getting' back to his wife, there woz two hours when her body was put somewhere."

"Given the fact she was placed in a sack, a difficult feat at the best of times, with some ease, one must presume the process of," Lady Owston stepped across to Sam to refer to the file before she resumed, "*rigor mortis* had yet to take place. Therefore, one must be inclined toward the earlier time of midnight for when Mrs Roberts was murdered. Between the later hours of four o'clock and six o'clock, when the body was discovered, the sack, with body, would have had to have been stored somewhere safe."

"Mr Roberts wouldn't of been able to take it back home because Regina or Mrs Yates could've come back," Sam went on with a nod. "We've got no one sayin' 'e went to the *Queshire Department Store* to drop off the shawl either. So, Inspector, we don't think Mr Roberts done in either woman."

Inspector Woolfe glared at the cabman but he knew what he'd said had made sense, which angered Caleb all the more. Sighing deeply, though it sounded more like a growl, he said, Right, so if I agree with you—*if* I do—that Mr Roberts wasn't the one who murdered his wife, am I right in next assuming you think his daughter was responsible? Because she's the only one you haven't ruled out yet."

"No, I'm afraid not, Inspector," Miss Dexter replied with a meek smile. She thanked Mr Snyder for the file and, placing it on the countertop, quietly cleared her throat. "Once one assumes Mr Roberts is telling the truth about where he was the night Mrs Roberts died, one must further accept Miss Roberts' account. She couldn't have possibly murdered her mother, Inspector. Even if we were to consider the chance of her father and aunt lying to protect her, Regina had no reason to murder her mother; she loved her and wanted her back home."

"Pardon my interrupting," Mr Queshire began as he dropped his hands to his sides and moved toward the artist. "But isn't there a possibility you're *all* neglecting to consider?" His stoicism transformed into a frown, "It's a ghastly thought but, given the tragic circumstances, I feel it's my duty to draw attention to it."

"And what's that?" Inspector Woolfe enquired with equal measures of suspicion and curiosity.

"He is referring to the possibility they *all* murdered Mrs Yates because *she* murdered Mrs Roberts," Miss Webster spoke up. Straightening from where she had been bent over her notebook, she cast cold eyes across the gathering. Mr Queshire, though looking somewhat sheepish, nodded his agreement. Miss Webster, however, didn't respond. Instead, she continued, in her usual monotone, "She openly admitted to her feud with her daughter, when Mr Snyder conversed with her, and stated Maryanna had been barred from the pub. She also confirmed Mr Robert's story that he had been forced to ask his wife to leave the family home because he'd discovered she'd stolen the housekeeping money to pay for gin." Agnes calmly turned the page in her notebook. "Mrs Yates didn't deny living with her granddaughter and son-in-law, citing the reason she was doing Maryanna's job—taking care of the family—for her. According to Mr Ratchett, Mrs Yates was taking care of the unwell Mrs Ratchett when Mr Suggitt had come seeking Mrs Roberts.

"At half past ten, on the same night, a sailor by the name of Robbie MacDonald came to the pub to escort Mrs Yates away so they could spend some time together. An arrangement confirmed by Mr Roberts—who hadn't needed to escort his mother-in-law home that night because of it—and Mr Ratchett. The landlord and Mr MacDonald were old friends, so he would've at once recognised him when he'd arrived. According to Mrs Yates and Mr Ratchett, Robbie left London on the morning Maryanna's body was found. Though it *is* possible the sailor *could* have murdered Mrs Roberts and then left it is *highly* unlikely. As for Mrs Yates, we couldn't eliminate her as a suspect as she could have slipped away from the sailor's company and murdered her daughter. With Mr MacDonald out at sea, there was no immediate way we at the Society, with our limited resources, could confirm her story. When Mrs Yates was also murdered, we had to scrutinise this theory even more."

"Our murderer was arrogant; he, or she, brought his own lemonade to Mrs Yates' residence for, according to Mr Trowel's account, there was a bottle of it on the table and two glasses," Mr Locke explained. "Mrs Yates *did* know her murderer for reasons we outlined earlier. While Mr Roberts, Miss Roberts, and Mr and Mrs Suggitt *had* been eliminated as suspects for Maryanna's murder it does appear, at least in theory, one, or all of them, could have murdered Mrs Yates as revenge for murdering her daughter. Mr Roberts, Miss Roberts, and Mr Suggitt had *all* visited the *Turk's Head Public House*, where Mrs Yates had been drinking lemonade, the night of her murder, after all. Though unlikely, *one* of them *could* have stolen said lemonade to lace it with arsenic. Their subsequent answers to our enquiring after that beverage, in which they denied having ever possessed it, could have been simple lies."

"At this point, we must return to Mrs Roberts' shawl, deposited in the second-hand clothing basket in the storeroom here, however. Also, Mrs Yates' ring, identified by Mr Roberts, which was found, by Mr Locke, in a tray on the haberdashery department's countertop only today," Lady Owston re-joined. "Mrs Yates *could* have brought the shawl here and given it to the one of the assistants as a donation, though no account of that ever having taken place has emerged. Furthermore, Mr or Mrs Suggitt, Mr Roberts, or Regina Roberts *could* have deposited the ring into the tray *after* murdering Mrs Yates—and encouraged the others to lie to provide an alibi—except for one, very important detail. Inspector?"

"None of them have been allowed to leave the Suggitt place since we brought them back from Moore Street," Woolfe stated.

The corner of Mr Queshire's mouth twitched. "I see," he replied and forced a momentary smile. Turning away from the group then, he folded his arms and continued, "But… if they are all vindicated, you must inevitably return to your original supposition a stranger had killed both victims?"

"You are presuming we have exhausted our entire list of suspects," Mr Locke replied. Swinging his cane at his knee, he approached the department store owner. "Time and time again during the course of our investigation, we were brought back to here, the *Queshire Department Store.*"

"The altercation between Mrs Roberts and the Holdens, Mrs Roberts' shawl being displayed on a dummy the morning after her murder, the French Breakfast coffee in the storeroom, the arsenic purchased by a store assistant, Miss Galway, and then Mrs Yates' ring in the tray," Mr Maxwell reeled off at Edmund.

Lady Owston also moved toward the owner, saying, "From the moment I saw a customer entering the room marked *Staff only* at the top of the stairs, I have been plagued by the question of 'why.' *Why* was she going into that room? *Why* was Miss Galway so *deathly* afraid when I remarked upon it? *Why* did she refuse, time and time again, to divulge the room's true use? And *why* were you, Mr Queshire, so keen to make me believe it was nothing more than a storeroom? Finally, the answer came to me after Mr Locke remarked upon Miss Webster constantly wearing her hat indoors."

All eyes turned to the secretary as she stepped back from the counter. She reached upward and, after pulling free the numerous pins, lifted her hat to reveal the bald patch beneath. In a quieter, more intense tone, she explained, "I lost my hair as a child, during a fire at my home. The experience left me with a near-crippling fear of fires and flames." She gestured toward the illusionist, "When Mr Locke, Lady Owston, and I visited the Holdens' residence, we were invited to wait in their library. A fire was burning in the hearth and Lady Owston, knowing of my fear, shielded the fire from my view by a guard. Later, at the *Turk's Head Public House,* Mr Locke noticed me flinch when he lit a match. At our next Bow Street Society meeting, he made his comment, which prompted Lady Owston to recall a lady at the *Writers' Club,* Mrs Gromwell, who never removed her bonnet when indoors either. Lady Owston had overheard two fellow members remark upon the fact, while at the club, but its significance wasn't fully appreciated until Mr Locke's remark."

"I had seen Mrs Gromwell leaving the room at the top of the stairs earlier in the day," Lady Owston began, her eyes still on Mr Queshire. "When I enquired after her presence there, she, like Miss Galway, became extremely frightened. She spoke to me of shame and how she had lied to everyone. I was still in the dark until Mr Locke said what he did and then I made the comparison between Agnes and Mrs Gromwell. I realised each wore either a wig or a hairpiece, though Agnes' is attached to her hat. As you know, Mr Queshire, ladies who wear wigs are seen as deceptive by wider society. Yet they still have a requirement to be deemed beautiful by potential suitors. The wig-fitting service, which operates out of that room." She pointed upward. "Meets the demands of these ladies while still keeping their shame a closely guarded secret."

"I thought we'd agreed *not* to have such a service?" Mr Suggitt enquired of Edmund with a mixture of confusion and annoyance.

"*You* had decided it wouldn't be appropriate, Clement," Mr Queshire replied, his stoicism having fully returned. "But you forget this is *my* store and it shall provide whatever service *I* deem suitable."

"While Mr Locke and I were speaking with you in the storeroom today, Agnes snuck upstairs," Lady Owston told him.

Miss Webster, having replaced her hat and pinned it back in place, said, "I met a very lovely Frenchman called Mr Vuitton. He confirmed you had no knowledge of the service, Mr Suggitt, and even spoke to me of various treatments I could try to encourage the regrowth of my hair." She walked behind the counter and, reaching underneath it, pulled forth a small, cardboard box. "While he was out of the room, I searched the bureaux there; I found this." She retraced her route around the counter and, approaching the Canadian, enquired, "Doctor Weeks, can you identify if this wig is a tanned human scalp or not?"

Shocked gasps simultaneously escaped from Mrs Suggitt and Miss Roberts while Clement and Abraham exchanged startled glances. Weeks, agitated for far different reasons, frowned deeply and simply stared at the box for a moment. Sensing Woolfe drawing near, he tried to tame his curiosity but failed miserably. He therefore snatched the box from Agnes and emptied its contents onto the millinery department's counter. When Caleb stood at his side, Doctor Weeks glanced at him with a worried expression but the inspector indicated for him to continue.

"Thanks," Weeks said. Pulling a handheld magnifying glass from his pocket, he held the wig under the light of a chandelier and took several moments to scrutinise it using the glass. "Can't say for sure," he finally announced. "I can run some tests but I ain't gonna be able to say for sure if it's human or animal."

"It is *certainly* not the usual layer one would fine underneath the netting in a wig, even in the more modern ones," Lady Owston remarked. "Furthermore, one would expect to see small bumps where the individual strands had been threaded into the material. There are none here."

"So, this Mr Vuitton murdered Mrs Roberts for her scalp?" Woolfe enquired.

While Weeks put the wig back into the box, Mr Snyder shook his head and replied, "Nah, but it *was* someone connected to this store."

"*Who*?" Mrs Suggitt cried in desperation. When the Bow Streeters all shifted their gazes to one person in particular though, the colour drained from her face and she shook her head. She whispered, "No... it cannot be..." Swaying upon her chair a moment, she then fell forward in a faint. Fortunately, her husband was quick enough to catch her but he, too, was drawn with distress. Mr Roberts meanwhile had leapt to his feet and attempted to rush the person in question. Inspector Woolfe had darted in front of him, however, and grabbed his shoulders to easily lift him off the ground and place him elsewhere.

"Wait a minute," he growled at the dock worker. Miss Roberts, who had remained seated, was utterly speechless.

"And *why* would *I* murder Mrs Roberts and Mrs Yates? Neither of them visited the wig-fitting room," Edmund Queshire said without emotion.

Mr Locke, who stood directly before him, answered, "Because Mrs Roberts humiliated you in your own store and Mrs Yates humiliated Mr Suggitt in front of her customers. You admitted you had allowed your emotion to overwhelm you when you had removed Mrs Roberts following her altercation with the Holdens; a natural reaction given the fact she had verbally abused you and was violent toward you in front of your customers. She made you appear weak in an environment where you were not only respected but admired. Then, at the public house, when Mrs Yates scolded her son-in-law for his angry reaction to our questions, you made a remark, 'such unnecessary behaviour,' I believe it was. We had presumed, at the time, you were referring to Mr Suggitt's behaviour but you were not. You were, in actuality, referring to Mrs Yates'. She had belittled him into submitting to her, thereby painting him as a weak and feeble-willed man."

"Looking back on Miss Galway's behaviour whenever you were in the room, or she was talking about you," Lady Owston said, "I see now she was deathly afraid of you, too. When I confronted you over the selling of second-hand goods, too, your persona morphed into something very ugly indeed. I had never felt threatened in a man's presence until then."

"And then there was your other comment," Miss Webster began. "In which you spoke of keeping Mrs Roberts safe if she had returned to the store, even after it had closed. We thought you were speaking metaphorically. You were, in fact, admitting she *had* returned to the store *after* it had closed. She was, in all likelihood, looking for her sister. Seeing an opportunity to enact your revenge upon her, you invited her in, probably to the storeroom, and prepared her a cup of French Breakfast coffee."

"You used the arsenic which Miss Galway had purchased, and which you could not produce when we asked to see it today, to lace the coffee. Mrs Roberts drank it and died within minutes," Mr Locke explained. "You then proceeded to beat her body, remove her clothes, scalp her, take her breasts, and wrestle her remains into the sack." He paused to swallow back his nausea, a state he hadn't expected to find himself in. "Given you live above the store, a fact you have freely admitted, you would know when the servicemen would usually start their rounds. Therefore, you waited until you were certain no one would be around before carrying Mrs Roberts' body to the doorway of the *London Crystal Palace Bazaar,* an establishment you were already aware of on account of its second entrance being located opposite Argyll Street, which is, of course, where the lodgings for your assistants may be found. The shawl you mended and placed upon the dummy, as you described, in time for the store opening the next day. I must admit it was rather fortuitous my wife purchased it, otherwise we may not have been able to make the connection."

"Edmund, is this true?" Clement enquired, his still unconscious wife lying in his arms.

Mr Queshire ignored him, however. Instead, he maintained a rigid stoicism as Lady Owston said, "Miss Galway, keen to impress us to become a Bow Street Society member, followed Mrs Yates and Mr Roberts home. When they neared their destination, however, Miss Galway noticed a man lurking on the other side of the street. She couldn't see his face but was so frightened by his behaviour, she ran home and awoke her fellow lodger, Annie Simkins, to tell her what had happened. By the time Miss Webster, Miss Dexter, and I arrived to question her about what she'd seen at the pub after we'd left, Miss Galway was in *such* a state of distress. She explained how she and Annie had come here to try and rouse you from your sleep but could gain no answer. To belay her fears, we came here that night, too. You were fully dressed when you came to the door." Katheryne's expression became a terribly sad one. "You said you had been adding sodium hydroxide to the soap mixture you'd had simmering all night. In reality though, it was *you* Miss Galway had seen, *you* who had murdered Mrs Yates, and it was *you* who was... disposing of her flesh and... scalp."

"After leaving us at the *Turk's Head Public House,*" Mr Locke re-joined. "You returned here and laced a bottle of lemonade with arsenic; presumably you had seen her drinking it while she spoke to Mr Snyder. Taking it and two glasses, you went back to the pub but waited outside until Mrs Yates left with Mr Roberts. You could not loiter outside their home as you did not know where they lived. After following them back, you expected Mr Roberts to leave again once he had been informed of the incident with Regina you yourself had witnessed that evening. Several minutes later, Mr Roberts did indeed leave and you waited a little longer before going inside. You may have enquired of a passing neighbour which room was the Roberts'— that detail we can only assume—but eventually you found it and you knocked. Mrs Yates answered and your suspicion she would be alone was confirmed. She probably recognised you from earlier in the evening and you no doubt gained entry by lying about a message from Mr Suggitt. Once inside, you poured the lemonade for you both and killed her. Afterward, you did the same to her body as you did Mrs Roberts' with the exception of transporting it elsewhere. You took her clothes and ring and, upon returning here for a second time, dropped the ring into the tray."

A heavy silence descended upon the room. Everyone, in varying degrees of shock, kept their eyes fixed upon the man who they had considered employer or even friend. Mr Suggitt and Mr Roberts both expected Edmund to deny the horrific accusations at any moment. Yet, he didn't. Instead, a smile slowly lifted his mouth and he said, "I *do* hope you enjoyed lathering your foul body in the soap I gave you, Lady Owston. For it was Mrs Roberts' flesh you rubbed between your vile legs."

"Ugh!" Katheryne cried, covering her mouth in horror. Mr Locke, who was within arm's reach of her and looked rather sickened himself, took hold of her shoulder to keep her steady.

Edmund, however, was far from finished. "I could deny it, of course. Claim Miss Galway was the one who had murdered both women to garner the attention of the Bow Street Society but to give the credit of *my* work to a *woman* does *not* sit well with me.

"I overheard Rose telling Annie Simkins of the man she'd seen following Mrs Yates when the two tried to rouse me. I was covered in blood at the time so, naturally, I couldn't come to the door. I listened at the window and it was then I knew Rose had to be my next source of material. When she came in this morning, she told me all of what had happened. It was evident she hadn't seen me for she wouldn't have confessed it all to me if she had. Still, I had resolved to be rid of her—she was a liability anyway, as you saw when she blurted out the Holdens' name, Lady Owston. I convinced her to remain in the basement until this evening when I would notify the police a man was following her. I told her it was too dangerous to return to the lodgings, or to leave the store, for the man had probably followed her home and then here. She was so gullible she believed every word I said and trusted me entirely."

"I saw you at the window earlier," Locke said. "I thought you had put something on the outside ledge, but you were, in reality, making sure we had not left and gone straight to the external entrance to the basement. You had, undoubtedly, read the *Gaslight Gazette's* account of my nocturnal exploits during the Dorsey case and feared I could break the lock on the external basement doors."

"I am not concerned about being exposed, Mr Locke; I would do it all again. I merely wanted the opportunity to remind Lady Owston of *her* true place by putting Miss Galway's body on her front step. I knew Inspector Woolfe distrusted the Society and I hoped he would arrest and hang her."

"But *why*?" Regina pleaded as tears fell down her cheeks and onto her skirt. Mrs Suggitt, meanwhile, was slowly coming around to her husband's gentle soothing noises.

"You do not like women very much, do you?" Mr Locke questioned; his voice hard. "Your interrogation of my wife over her chosen profession was testament to that."

"Mrs Yates reminded me of my mother," Edmund calmly replied. "My mother had presumed to tell me what to do, had presumed she could control my life as she'd controlled my father's. Women are parasites to be stepped upon, Mr Locke. Yet we allow them to gain more and more control every day— *women* journalists, *women* doctors, *women* artists and writers. They shall never be satisfied until they have dominated us all." He paused, "But do not misunderstand me; I didn't kill Mrs Roberts and Mrs Yates to right a political injustice, far from it. You're correct in your assumptions about how I murdered Mrs Roberts and Mrs Yates and why. Yet I also wanted *revenge* for every wrong done to me by women. Those who visit my store are greedy, lecherous vermin who think it is their birth right to bark orders at me and scold me when things do not go their way.

I wanted them all to have a taste of their own foulness once they'd realised they'd been bathing in the flesh, and wearing the scalps and clothes, of their dead peers. The wig *is* Maryanna's scalp; you will find Mrs Yates' here, too. Lady Owston." He smirked. "The soap batch I said was gently simmering when you came to me about Rose's visit? Mrs Yates' flesh, naturally."

"Where is Miss Galway?" Lady Owston whispered as a terrible realisation came over her.

Edmund's smile grew and, with great relish, he replied, "In the basement, of course. I killed her over an hour ago."

EPILOGUE

DEPARTMENT STORE FROM HELL EXPOSED read the headline of Mr Maxwell's article in the *Gaslight Gazette's* evening edition. The event described within had unfurled several days prior but he, and the other Bow Street Society members, had been sworn to secrecy by Inspector Woolfe. The oath had eventually lifted after Mr Queshire had entered a guilty plea at his formal hearing the day the article was released. The remainder of Mr Maxwell's piece therefore read as follows:

> The owner of the *Queshire Department Store*, Mr Edmund Queshire, today pleaded guilty to two counts of murder at the Central Criminal Court, the Old Bailey. The sentence of death was passed by the black-cap wearing judge, the Right Honourable Sweet, and shall be carried out in a matter of days. Newgate Jail has already announced Mr Queshire's execution will be held away from the macabre curiosity of the public eye.
>
> Mr Queshire was arrested for the murders of Mrs Maryanna Roberts and Mrs Sarah Yates following an investigation by the Bow Street Society, the group having been commissioned by a relative of both victims, Mrs Diana Suggitt. Upon being identified as the person responsible, Mr Queshire readily confessed to his crimes with relish and even showed the Society, and Metropolitan Police Inspector Caleb Woolfe, the horrors which lay in the store's basement. To those of a sensitive disposition, your correspondent recommends you cease your reading now.
>
> The body of a third victim, Miss Rose Galway, who was a sales assistant at the department store, was found hanging, naked, from the

basement's beams. She had been mutilated in the same fashion as Mrs Roberts and Mrs Yates and, like they, had been poisoned with a cup of French Breakfast coffee laced with arsenic. The missing clothes of all three women were shown to the group by Mr Queshire, he having deposited them within a basket located in the basement's corner.

In Mr Queshire's rooms upstairs, Inspector Woolfe and the Bow Street Society discovered a large pot on the stove. It contained a heavy mixture, pale in colour, which the store owner identified as being the remains of Mrs Yates' missing flesh. It had been reduced in mass through the process of boiling and mixed with sodium hydroxide to create a soap preparation. Mr Queshire confirmed he had sold batches of such soap, containing the flesh of Mrs Roberts, within his store. Any ladies who have recently purchased soap from the *Queshire Department Store* are therefore requested to deposit it, sealed or otherwise, at their nearest police station. An additional request regarding ladies' head coverings, purchased from the same establishment, has also been made by Inspector Woolfe.

Rebecca lowered the newspaper at the sound of knocking on the front door and left her office to answer it. "May I help you?" she enquired of the flat-cap-wearing man who stood on the external porch.

Rather than answer, however, he posed a question of his own, "Is this the place for the Bow Street Society?"

"Yes, who are you?"

"Mr Daniel Holland, locksmith, come to fix a new lock to your front door. Mr Locke asked of me to come by."

"*Did* he?" The clerk's brow lofted. "This is the first *I've* known about such an arrangement. You're going to have to wait here while I telephone him."

Mr Holland doffed his hat to her, "Whatever you say, Miss Trent." Rebecca, who had turned away, paused at his use of her name. His smile seemed genuine though, so she continued on inside, ensured the door was secured behind her, and went to the telephone. After instructing the operator where she'd like her call to be placed, the clerk waited only a moment for the illusionist's voice to give its greeting in her ear.

"I have Mr Holland standing outside the Society's headquarters."

"Who? *Ah!* Was he scheduled for today?"

"I wouldn't know; *I* wasn't the one who organised his visit."

"My sincerest apologies, Miss Trent. I had every intention of informing you of my plans when I made the arrangement, but clearly my memory failed me on this occasion." Rebecca heard a faint rustling of papers before Locke continued, "I have supplied him with a lock of my own design to affix to your outer front door. It shan't prevent someone of *my* skill from entering the premises uninvited, but your average housebreaker would find it an impossible challenge. As agreed, I have put forth the capital for the lock's installation and provided Mr Holland with instructions as to the procurement of the monies. If you so wish, I may be able to attend Bow Street in…" He paused a moment. "An hour but, personally, I do not think my presence shall be necessary, do you?"

"I think it would be wise for you to confirm he is indeed the locksmith you arranged, Mr Locke, considering the safety of every Bow Street Society member, and myself, would be under threat if he isn't." She gave a sardonic smile so he could hear it in her voice when she added, "I'll see you in half an hour." The telephone's receiver was then replaced in its cradle before the illusionist had a chance to protest.

* * *

The hind legs of the hansom cab's dual horses went up and down but Maxwell didn't pay them much heed. Instead, his mind replayed the last dinner at his parents' house. Miss Lillithwaite, Oliver's choice for his son's bride-to-be, had been pleasant enough company. The meal itself had also been enjoyed without incident and, prior to Joseph's departure, his father had even *praised* his exemplary behaviour, a turn of events welcomed by the journalist. His article making the front page of the *Gaslight Gazette* had also pleased him. Yet both that fact and his positive paternal experience couldn't dispel the hollow feeling in his chest.

"Oi!" the driver suddenly bellowed from above, "Time to ge' out!"

"Apologies!" Joseph unhooked the doors and, scrambling from the vehicle, paid the amount agreed prior to his departure from Fleet Street. While the cab then pulled away, he crossed the pavement to his lodging house. Something familiar was seen in the corner of his eye, though, which compelled him to abandon his original plan. "Mr Snyder?" he enquired as he neared the second hansom cab parked a little way down the street.

"Evenin', Mr Maxwell," Sam replied with a smile and a touch of his hat.

"What are you doing here?" Joseph glanced into the vehicle but saw no one sitting there. "Is there another case for us to investigate?"

"There's more important things in life than murders and crime," Sam lifted his head toward Maxwell's lodging house. "Best to go on in, lad."

"Why?" Joseph enquired, confused. Yet the elder Bow Streeter wouldn't furnish him with anything more than a knowing smile. Returning to his residence therefore, Maxwell paused at its door to glance back at the cabman before going inside. He couldn't see anyone in the hallway beyond so he climbed the two flights of stairs to his floor. When he neared his destination, he looked through the balustrades and saw someone outside his door. It wasn't until he was on the landing itself that he recognised who it was, "Georgina?"

"Joseph," she beamed. "Where have you been?"

"I was at work; what are you doing here?" He watched as she approached, his heart urging him to wrap his arms about her when she did. Yet his hands continued to hang loose at his sides, refusing to heed the call.

"I had to speak with you," Miss Dexter's smile faded. "You were so startled at the Suggitts' house after our kiss…" She bowed her head, "…I'm not a woman like Mrs Roberts, Joseph. *Please* do not think ill of me."

"I don't," he replied as he closed the gap between them. Putting his hands on the sides of her shoulders, he added, "You could *never* be like Mrs Roberts or Mrs Yates, Georgina."

"Then why did you flee?" She looked up at him with desperate eyes and a sharp pain gripped his chest. How he wanted to kiss her… to hold her… but it was no longer as simple as following his heart's desire. As it had done so in the Suggitts' hallway, Oliver's voice addressed Joseph's mind, reminding him of his obligations to duty and reputation. The journalist also thought his cheek had begun to sting, a reminder of his father's punishment for disobedience. Suddenly, he realised *why* he'd felt so hollow these past few days.

The meal, Miss Lillithwaite, and his father's strictness all led him to one horrifying, yet seemingly inevitable, conclusion: "I must… break our engagement… Georgina…"

"No…" she whispered, yet his gaze was kept fixed to the wall behind her. At once, she withdrew from him and added, "You can't be sincere in your words."

"I'm sorry…" he said, unable to prevent the pain from breaking his voice. "…But this is how it must be."

"I don't understand… I thought you wanted us to be wed? You gave me your *word* all you had promised would come to pass, Joseph. You put your hand over your heart and you *promised* me!"

"*Please,* Georgina, don't make this any harder than it already is," he begged and finally met her gaze. Her eyes glistened with unshed tears but he knew he couldn't weaken, that he *must* not weaken. "It is ended, my love… I'm sorry."

"Sorry? Is that *all* you can say?" She sharply turned her back to prevent him from seeing her tears. She didn't fail to realise there were eerie echoes between then and the time at her parents' house. Again, she had opened her heart to him and, again, he had hurt her in a way she'd not thought possible. "Do not come to me again, Joseph; never did I think you would ever lie to me… or that you could be so *cruel*!" She picked up her skirts and flew down the stairs, her anguished sobbing growing quieter and quieter as she went.

* * *

"Saying thank you isn't sufficient to describe what I'm feeling, Miss Trent," Mrs Suggitt told the clerk. "But I shall do regardless, not only on my own behalf but also that of my sister and mother: thank you."

"We only did what you asked us to," Rebecca replied. "But your thanks are still gratefully received." Diana smiled with a small nod and took a sip of her tea. She and her husband had come to the Society's headquarters to pay the required fee for that group's services. Clement Suggitt sat beside his wife at the kitchen table while the clerk was opposite. "What are your plans, now that there is to be no trial?" the clerk enquired as she put down her own cup.

Both Suggitts looked at one another but it was Clement who said, "Mr Queshire has gifted the store to me."

"Surely you're not considering accepting his offer?" Rebecca enquired, stunned. Yet the reaction her words received from the two informed her they intended to do just that. "Your sister was murdered there, so too was Miss Galway."

"Which is even more of a reason to ensure some good emerges from this horror," Clement countered. "Naturally the store's name will have to change but, already, footfall has increased. The people of London wish to visit the place where such ghastly deeds were carried out."

"Abraham has agreed to help Clement with the refurbishment of the store's interior," Diana explained.

"*Minus* the salon, storeroom, and wig-making service, of course."

"And Regina is to become a sales assistant, while *I* take on the role of manageress to ensure the safety of the store's female employees."

"I can't say I follow your logic," Rebecca said with a slight frown. "But I can understand the reasons behind your decision." She offered a small smile, "And I wish you the very best of luck in your new endeavour."

"Thank you, Miss Trent," Diana replied with great relief. "This is something Clement and I simply must do."

"Forgive my intrusion but my husband said I could find you here," a voice said from the doorway. The three simultaneously looked toward its source and at once recognised its owner.

"Good afternoon, Doctor Locke," Rebecca greeted as both she and Mr Suggitt rose to their feet. Beyond Lynette, Percy Locke was supervising Mr Holland's installation of the front door's new lock. "You've already met Mr Suggitt, I believe?" Miss Trent first indicated the new department store owner and then his manageress. "This is his wife, Mrs Diana Suggitt. How may I help you?"

"A pleasure to make your acquaintance, Mrs Suggitt," Lynette said as she met that woman's gaze. Turning her attention back to the clerk, however, she continued, "I have been led to believe the Bow Street Society is in need of a member with medical expertise, is that correct?"

"It is," Rebecca confirmed. She watched her with more than a hint of suspicion as she wondered how she'd come by such information. The sound of Mr Locke's voice drifting from the hallway, however, furnished her with an excellent guess. Straightening her back while she glanced at her guests, she enquired, "May I enquire as to why you wish to know?"

"I had thought that obvious, Miss Trent," Doctor Locke replied with a curious tone. "I would like to apply for the position."

If you enjoyed the book, please leave a review on Amazon and/or a rating on Goodreads. Thank you!

www.bowstreetsociety.com

Notes from the author

*****Spoiler alert*****

I first came across the Whitechapel Murders case (aka Jack the Ripper) when I was around fifteen years old. I read a book—I don't recall if I'd borrowed it from the school's library or a public one—which was supposedly based upon a newly discovered diary of Sergeant George Godley. Godley was a Metropolitan Police officer who worked with Inspector Aberline on the case. I think it may have been *Jack the Ripper: The Final Solution* by Steven Knight. Regardless, it stayed with me long after I'd finished it. Even now, I can still envision a drunken Inspector Aberline being roused by Godley.

In the years since reading the book, I've discovered it has received mixed reviews from both Ripperologists and general readers. This hasn't stopped me, like most with an interest in true crime, from having a fascination with the Whitechapel Murders. I've watched several films & documentaries and read several books on the subject. At the time of the murders themselves, everyone had a theory, including Sherlock Holmes creator Sir Arthur Conan Doyle. He suggested it could've been *Jill* the Ripper, as midwives could walk the streets, covered in blood, and no one would've remarked upon it.

Obviously 'Jack' wasn't the murderer's actual name—at least as far as we know. Jack was simply a name attached to an otherwise unidentified man, in the same way John Doe is attributed to unidentified male corpses today. The reason why it became attached to the Whitechapel Murderer was largely because a letter—allegedly from the murderer—sent to the Central News Agency of London, was signed 'Jack the Ripper'. In November of 2016, I was lucky enough to look upon the actual 'Dear Boss' letter, as it's since become known, while attending a Victorian Crime evening at the National Archives in Kew, London. When one considers how much paper is simply thrown away these days, it's truly amazing the letter has survived the hundred-plus years since its creation.

In 2011, I read *Sweeney Todd – The Demon Barber of Fleet Street* by Thomas Peckett Prest, a prolific writer of Penny Dreadfuls in the nineteenth century. The very first time I learnt of Sweeney Todd was while watching an episode of *Coronation*

Street. One of the characters, while eating a pie, referred to the story. I remember asking my mother who Sweeney Todd was and she told me. Like the Whitechapel Murders, the story of Sweeney Todd has always intrigued me. I wanted to read the original story all the movies and books were based upon so I ended up buying, and reading, the above title.

The foundation of the idea behind the murders in *The Case of The Lonesome Lushington*, and the man responsible, is an attempt to combine the Jack the Ripper and Sweeney Todd crimes. This is why Edmund Queshire's first victim, Mrs Maryanna Roberts, is a prostitute fallen on hard times. It's also the reason why Queshire mutilates his victims' bodies, why he turns their flesh into soap and their hair into wigs, and why he tries to sell these items in his department store. According to Peckett Prest's story, Todd had the flesh of his victims baked into pies by Mrs Lovett who sold them in her shop, hence the reason behind the reference in the *Coronation Street* episode.

A Jack the Ripper victim partly inspired the domestic circumstances of Maryanna Roberts—Annie Chapman. While conducting research into the lives of the Ripper victims, for an unrelated project, I came across a photograph of Annie with her husband, John. She, like Maryanna, had been the victim of circumstance and alcoholism. The photograph of Annie, smartly attired in an impressive dress with neatly styled hair, and John standing beside her with his hand on her shoulder, reminded me Annie Chapman, like all the Ripper's victims, were real people. They'd had a life unrelated to the Ripper and people who cared for them. As far as I'm aware there hasn't yet been a television series or film focusing on the victims' lives alone. Personally, I think it's long overdue.

Maryanna Roberts, her family, and the second victim, Mrs Sarah Yates, are all members of the working social class. This was intentional on my part, along with the decision to involve the Society's cabman, Sam Snyder, in the investigation. Those familiar with the first book, *The Case of The Curious Client,* will know he didn't conduct any of the interviews like he does in *The Case of The Lonesome Lushington.* I wanted to show the reader this other side of London society without resorting to the clichés often associated with the Victorian Era, e.g. all poor people were criminals. I also didn't want to fall into the trap, as a writer, of only focusing on crimes among the middle or upper classes.

There is a strong theme of shopping and consumerism running through the book. While thinking of the title for the first book, I knew there were certain themes which ran through it. One of these themes was curiosity—both being curious oneself and being curious to others—which is why the book was given the title it was. When it came to *The Case of The Lonesome Lushington,* I wanted to take the concept of themes further. I therefore decided to have a predominant theme running throughout the book which helped highlight a particular aspect of Victorian society. In this instance, the themes became consumerism, Oxford Street, and the varieties of establishment one could expect to encounter, e.g. chemists, department stores, etc. I intend to continue in this vein with all future Bow Street Society books. Not only to create a sense of place, but also to give each book its own distinct identity.

Inspector Caleb Woolfe, the investigating officer for the Metropolitan Police, is far from happy about the Society's involvement in the case. His resistance to their efforts is more than simply his personal opinion, however. In *Sir Howard Vincent's Police Code 1889*, a constable is instructed to "on no account move it or anything surrounding it; or allow any other person to do so" (p.117) when first called upon to investigate the corpse of a victim of foul play. The much later *"Police-Duty" Catechism and Reports*, by H. Childs of 1903 gives further clarification to these orders:

> *Ques.* In the case of a death by violent means, what steps should be taken?
> *Ans.* Remain by the body until properly relieved; send messenger for inspector and divisional surgeon; not allow the body to be moved, or room or place or anything about it to be interfered with; exclude the public, [and] give no information to public except by permission of superior officer.

Obviously, the above was published after the year in which *The Case of The Lonesome Lushington* is set (1896). Nonetheless, "exclude the public" would've been covered by Vincent Howard Code's instruction of not allowing "any other person" to move a body. In short, Inspector Caleb Woolfe is merely doing his job.

As a result, the Society isn't revered by the police or given privileged access to evidence like other literary detectives, such as Sherlock Holmes and Hercule Poirot (the creation of Agatha Christie). It would've certainly made it easier for me, as the writer, to follow the tradition of the amateur detective who's unconditionally trusted by the police. Yet, at the same time, it wouldn't be realistic. Realism and accuracy are two things I strive for while researching, planning, and writing the Bow Street Society books and short stories. By putting the obstacles in the Society's way, in the form of the police's resistance etc, I also hope to show how resourceful and ingenious the Society members can be. They have to draw upon every skill and piece of knowledge they possess to solve the case. I think the Society's investigation in *The Case of The Lonesome Lushington* is a perfect example of exactly how the group goes about this.

~T.G. Campbell
August 2017

MORE BOW STREET SOCIETY

The Case of The Curious Client
(Bow Street Society Mystery, #1)
NOVEL

WINNER OF FRESH LIFESTYLE MAGAZINE BOOK AWARD APRIL 2017

In *The Case of The Curious Client,* the Bow Street Society is hired by Mr Thaddeus Dorsey to locate a missing friend he knows only as 'Palmer' after he fails to keep a late night appointment with him. With their client's own credibility cast into doubt mere minutes after they meet him though, the Society is forced to consider whether they've been sent on a wild goose chase. That is until events take a dark turn and the Society has to race against time not only to solve the case, but to also save the very life of their client...

EXTRACT

Parked directly outside the shop was a two-wheeler, highly varnished, hansom cab. It had both the inside and outside plates and stencilled certificate on its back, to show it had passed its examination by the inspectors at Clerkenwell. Furthermore, whomever owned it, in this case the Bow Street Society, had paid the two shillings for the licence to drive it around London. Further expense the Society had had to lay out, not obvious by merely looking at the vehicle itself, was the fifteen shillings carriage duty to Somerset House and five shillings to the Metropolitan Police for a licence and badge to drive. In this case, the driver's licence was currently at the Society's office, for the purposes of insurance, whilst he took the cab around London. Though the cab was inspected annually, a cabman's ability to drive was only assessed once. At the end of each year, the cabman took his current licence, complete with the length of time he'd served with his employer written on the back by the employer himself, to New Scotland Yard who would issue him with a clean licence for a further twelve months.

Pulling the cab was a single, brown horse, brown being the more fashionable colour and the one more preferred by cab customers. The wheels, meanwhile, were approximately four feet wide and consisted of a wooden ring with an iron sheet embedded on its outside, a centre attachment to the cab's axle and seventeen wooden spokes going from the centre to the outside. Between these wheels, and resting upon the axle, was the main body of the cab; a wooden bench within a two-sided box with a ceiling also doubled as a canopy over the heads of the passengers. The front edge of this canopy was carved into a curved arch whilst, attached to the edges of the left and right walls by hinges, were heavy, wooden doors with pointed middle sections to thus accommodate passengers' knees once they were seated inside. These, coupled with the wooden canopy overhead, provided some shelter from the elements and from any mud and spray the horse's hooves may kick up. Glassless windows in the sides of the cab enabled passengers to see where they passed, as well as providing the much-valued free flow of fresh air. Finally, candlelit lamps hanging from the top corners of the front of the cab enabled passengers to see when climbing into the cab at night.

"You wanna cab?" the driver's rough, East End voice enquired as he looked down upon Mr Eddows and Miss Johnson. He sat upon a narrow seat, attached to the outside of the cab's back wall, elevated enough so he could see over both the cab and horse. This seat also had iron railings on three sides to prevent him from toppling out when the cab was in motion. When the couple looked up, brown, beady eyes met their gazes, set deeply in the middle-aged driver's weathered, bushy, side-burned face. His broad shoulders slightly hunched over calloused hands, holding the ends of the horse's reins. These reins ran along the top of the cab, through the hollow tips of a V-shaped attachment mounted upon the canopy's front edge (to keep the reins in line) and down to the horse's harness. Aside from his face, the driver's hands were the only other parts of his body visible beneath a heavy, black cape. Even his scuffed, and slightly torn, black-leather boots were concealed, though they rested against the back of the cab.

Having pulled down the brim of his brown hat, to block the low, winter's sun, he now pushed it back up with a fat thumb as Weeks replied, "Yeah, we do."

"Hop in, then," the driver replied, pulling his hat down again and clearing his throat. "Plenty of room inside." Though a cab like this could only ever seat two persons comfortably, on this occasion, three would be a squeeze and four an absolute push. Five, therefore, was utterly out of the question. Thus, whilst Dr. Weeks perched his feet upon a considerably narrow step at the back of the cab—one hand gripping the side rail of the driver's seat, the other gripping the roof's edge—Miss Johnson climbed inside and sat down. Her young beau followed, Miss Dexter, and finally, Mr Maxwell, who had to hold his breath to place himself within the narrow space beside Miss Dexter.

In seating himself though, he accidentally touched her knee. "Oh!" he cried. "Please, forgive me." He felt his cheeks burn again and one look at Miss Dexter revealed hers did the same. Pressing his body against the side as much as possible, his hip wedged against Miss Dexter's. "Fortunately, the journey isn't a long one," he stated before clearing his throat. Pulling his door down, as Mr Eddows had, Mr Maxwell faced the problem of where to put his hands. Deciding the top edge of the door to be the most appropriate place, he clasped his hands together and rested them there. The sharp lurch forward, as the horse trotted, caused him to fall back slightly, however. One hand gripped the cab's window whilst the other unconsciously set down in an instinctual need to steady one's self. Upon feeling the material of Miss Dexter's dress beneath it, his eyes widened. Yet Miss Dexter's own hand came to rest upon it, and even gave it the gentlest of squeezes, as she smiled reassuringly at him. "Oh," Joseph glanced downwards, surprised. "Erm… thank you, Miss Dexter."

"How are you feeling, darling?" Mr Eddows enquired, his head tilted slightly as Miss Johnson pressed her fingers to her temple. She had as much seat space as Mr Maxwell, but her head was leant out the window slightly. At least she got the benefit of some fresh air.

"Foul, still," she complained. "I shall be relieved when we reach the hospital."

"We're taking them to the hospital?" Joseph enquired, looking to Miss Dexter in confusion.

"Yes, Mr Maxwell," she replied, trying to warn him with her eyes about saying anything further.

"Where else would you be taking us?" Mr Eddows enquired, leaning forward slightly and looking to Maxwell with those suspicious eyes again.

"Endell Street," Joseph said, matter-of-factly, only realising his error a half second after the words had left his lips.

"Endell Street?" Mr Eddows enquired, angrily.

"Yes… you see… erm…" Joseph stammered.

"What the bloody hell's going on?!" Eddows demanded. Striking the back wall of the cab, he shouted, "You said you were a doctor!"

Weeks, having heard it all, cursed sharply and replied, "I am! Maxwell, keep yer damned mouth shut!"

"But I—" Joseph began, deep regret in his face and eyes.

"Let us out!" Eddows demanded, reaching over the doors to unbolt them. The driver cracked the whip though and the horse galloped on ahead, the cab lurching violently this way and that as it weaved through the chaotic sea of London traffic; omnibuses, cabs, carriages, and vans all sped past in a blur of colours and smells. Faces of pedestrians rushed by the windows as they ran around the cab without warning. One stepped out in front of the horse, only to leap back again as they realised how dangerously close they were.

"Get off the bloody road!" their driver yelled above them. Both Miss Johnson and Miss Dexter had covered their mouths at the sight. Now, their hearts pounded with terror—Miss Dexter out of fear for the pedestrian, Miss Johnson out of fear for her own safety.

"Are you coppers or sumin'?!" Eddows shouted, his once refined accent now having degenerated into an East End one. "We've done nowt!" he added. Reaching over Miss Dexter, he grabbed the lapel of Joseph's coat and yanked him toward him as far as the still closed doors would allow. "Either you let us out, or I'll have to do sumin' stupid," Eddows warned, his other hand now holding a revolver as it emerged from under the door.

"Don't be thick, Toby," Miss Johnson shouted, her fear increasing upon seeing the gun. She gripped his arm with both hands and tried pulling it towards her.

"Oi, ge' off me, bitch!" Eddows growled, looking over his shoulder at her. The whole cab leapt up into the air slightly as it struck something in the road and, as it came down with a bump, Eddows' hand slammed upon the top edge of the door. He immediately lost his grip and the gun clattered down the door and, in a freak turn of events, struck the horse's hoof and fired. The horse gave a blood-curdling shriek as the bullet lodged itself in its thigh. Its leg collapsed, causing the animal to topple sideways whilst still galloping with its other legs. The cab, with no way of stopping, crashed immediately into the body of the stricken animal; its left wheel was lifted clean off the ground—still spinning—as the horse stopped the right in its tracks. Everyone within lifted their arms to shield themselves as the cab flipped and rolled into oncoming traffic. More horses shrieked as the other drivers fought to swerve out of the way.

Some even yelled "Look out!" whilst pedestrians on the pavement ran frantically out of the way of the approaching cab, screaming. The cab struck the curb but, as it had already rolled some distance, only tilted a little before falling back onto the road.

The Case of The Shrinking Shopkeeper
(The Bow Street Society Casebook, #1)
SHORT STORY

    The Bow Street Society Casebook is a sub-series of mini mysteries to read on the go by award winning author, T.G. Campbell. The Bow Street Society is a fictional group of amateur detectives operating in 1896 London. Each of its civilian members has been enlisted for their unique skill or exceptional knowledge in a particular field. They've previously been featured in *The Case of The Curious Client* and *The Case of The Lonesome Lushington* novels.

    In *The Case of The Shrinking Shopkeeper*, two members are called in by the Society's clerk, Miss Rebecca Trent, to assist a sweet-shop owner who believes he's losing

274

height at an alarming rate. Is he delusional or is there something more sinister going on? It's up to the Bow Street Society to find out-before it's too late…

EXTRACT

"I'm at my wit's end, Miss Trent."

"It *is* an unusual predicament you've found yourself in, Mr Foggity. When did you first notice something was amiss?"

"At the beginning of last week," he frowned. "No, one moment," he counted on his fingers. "Yes, it was the Tuesday before last." Mr Emmanuel Foggity was in his mid-fifties, but his youthful complexion and brilliant, chestnut-brown hair veiled this fact. Neat brows and strong cheekbones framed his lively, light-blue eyes. Pale lips, topped by a wax-coated moustache, were nibbled upon as he watched Miss Rebecca Trent write her notes.

The Bow Street Society clerk wore a light-weight jacket over a high-necked, plain-white shirt. A tie, secured into a large Eaton knot, rested between the broad lapels of the former. Both tie and jacket were forest-green to compliment the season. Though already slim, Rebecca's figure was nevertheless exaggerated by the synching of her clothes and the contours of her tight, corset undergarment. Her own brown hair had been tied into a neat French braid and hung between the excess fabrics of her jacket's mutton-chop sleeves. Mr Foggity's attire, on the other hand, was far less elaborate—a light-grey suit with matching waistcoat and tie over a pristine, white shirt. The collar of the last was broad and so heavily starched, his Adam's apple caught upon it each time he swallowed.

The sounds of birdsong and passing carriages drifted upon a light breeze through the half-raised sash window of the Society's parlour. Miss Trent's notebook, knees, and feet were bathed in golden sunlight as she wrote. Though a handful of furniture had recently been added—a sofa by the hearth, a dresser, and armchairs in which the two sat—the room remained cavernous.

"I've never been a tall man," Mr Foggity went on, "but to shrink as quickly as I have isn't natural, is it?" He simultaneously lifted his hands and shoulders for a moment. "Yet, my doctor has sworn to me on his reputation as a man of medicine that I'm *not* shrinking." Holding his knees, he leant forward. "Am I mad, Miss Trent?"

"I certainly believe you're convinced something is happening to you, Mr Foggity." She rested her hand upon the notebook and met his gaze. "Whether it's madness or not is something that remains to be seen by our members."

The Case of The Winchester Wife
(The Bow Street Society Casebook, #2)
SHORT STORY

In *The Case of The Winchester Wife,* Captain Bennett Winchester, a retired merchant seaman, seeks the Society's help following a most baffling incident with his wife at King's Cross railway station. Mr Samuel Snyder, a Hansom cab driver by profession, and Miss Georgina Dexter, an artist, are asked to investigate by the Society's clerk, Miss Rebecca Trent. It soon becomes apparent, however, that their commission is not as simple as it seems…

EXTRACT

"It's preposterous, expecting a man to unburden himself to a woman," Bennett Winchester slurred as the mantel clock chimed. Though it was midmorning the Bow Street Society's parlour had neither daylight nor gaslight to soften the retired captain's pointed profile. Bloodshot, brown eyes looked beyond the wall as he approached, turned, and retraced his route, each thump of his boot succeeded by the heavy thud of his peg-leg.

Miss Trent's gaze tracked him during each pass of her armchair yet she remained seated. "Captain Winchester," she began, "you weren't obligated to come here and I wasn't obligated to receive you, yet here we are. Putting aside my disinclination to beg your pardon for my gender, I instead ask you to observe your surroundings. You and I are the only ones here. Therefore, your choice is clear—either swallow your masculine pride and tell me why you're here, or leave and put your trust in those at Bow Street Police Station."

"Don't speak such impertinence to *me!*" Captain Winchester barked, drawing Miss Trent to her feet.

She countered, "I shall speak whatever I want, Captain, when you are in *my* domain." His lips repeatedly furled and unfurled against gritted teeth while calloused hands, which had previously rested within his greatcoat's deep pockets, balled at his sides. Starting at his neck, his already pink face steadily flushed as if port had spilt under his skin.

He snarled, "How *daare* you, you uncouth *wretch.*"

"Continue as you are, Captain Winchester, and *I* will be calling upon the officers at Bow Street," Miss Trent promised despite his stale-rum-drenched breath turning her stomach. Whether it was the tone of her voice, her fixed gaze, the words themselves, or a combination of all three which cooled Bennett Winchester's rage was unclear. Regardless the result was the same. After some aggressive chewing of his anger, the captain plonked himself in the vacant armchair. The clerk wasn't naïve enough to think it ended, however. Instead, she enabled additional calming time by fetching tea from the kitchen. Coffee would've been more sobering for him but, alas, she suspected such a blatant assumption wouldn't have been welcomed by his volatile temper.

The Case of The Perilous Pet
(The Bow Street Society Casebook, #3)
SHORT STORY

In *The Case of The Perilous Pet,* the Bow Street
Society is hired by solicitor Mr Treaves following the death of
his friend, Sir Thomas Russell. Though considered an accident
by most, Sir Russell's son believes otherwise. It's therefore up to
Society members Dr Rupert Alexander, a veterinary surgeon,
and Mr Bertram Heath, an architect, to test the feasibility of a
bizarre accusation and finally uncover the truth…

EXTRACT

"For over thirty years, I've been retained by Sir
Thomas Russell as his solicitor," Treaves began, when he'd
savoured a morsel of cake. "Delicious," he added with a smile.

Switching the cake for his tea, he continued, "We'd also become good friends during that time." He took a quiet slurp and replaced the cup upon its saucer. "As you can imagine, then, it came as quite the shock to receive news of his sudden passing."

Miss Trent's hand, lifting her own teacup, halted. Meeting his gaze with a loft of her brow, she replied, "Indeed."

"It was a month ago now," Treaves went on.

The clerk, having taken her intended sip, put down her drink to commence taking short-hand notes of the discussion. Waiting a moment, Mr Treaves said, "Mr Appleby, Sir Russell's manservant, found him on the floor at the foot of the stairs. He'd heard a cry and the sound of something heavy tumbling down them. It took only a few moments to reach him but, by the time Mr Appleby had, Sir Russell was dead—his neck broken."

"Was a doctor called?"

"Yes. He confirmed the cause of death. He explained a younger man may have survived the fall, but Sir Russell's frail bones had sealed his fate. Eighty years old, he was. Much older than I or even Mr Appleby." Mr Treaves frowned. "Doctor said he wouldn't have felt a thing—even after his neck had snapped. A small mercy." Another morsel of cake, clasped between thumb and forefinger, was deposited into his mouth. Smacking his lips together as he sucked—not chewed—the sponge, he added, "One reads about heads still showing life after being cut from the body. Speaking, blushing, and the like."

"There was no question it was an accident?" Miss Trent enquired to sharpen his focus.

Swallowing, Mr Treaves shook his head and had another slurp of tea. "None at all. Not in my mind, Mr Appleby's, the doctor's, or even the coroner's. Sir Russell's son, Stephen, was a different matter entirely, however." The solicitor gathered up the remaining crumbs and, still gripping them, slipped both thumb and forefinger into his mouth to their knuckles.

"He has accused Sir Russell's Staffordshire bull terrier of murder," Mr Treaves added, putting the plate down.

SOURCES OF REFERENCE

A great deal of time was spent researching the historical setting of *The Case of The Lonesome Lushington*. This research covered not only the physical setting of London in 1896 but also communication technology (such as typewriters and telephones), medicine, the Metropolitan Police, Pharmaceutical chemists, and ladies' fashions to name but a few. Thus, a great deal of information about the period has been gathered, so as to inform me of the historical boundaries of my characters' professions and lives, which hasn't been directly referenced in this book. Where a fact, or source, has been used as to inform the basis of in-book descriptions of interiors, street names, items, and geographical locations *et cetera* I've strived to cite said source here. Each citation includes the source's origin, the source's author, and which part of *The Case of The Lonesome Lushington* the source is connected to. All rights connected to the following sources remain with their respective authors and/or publishers.

BOOKS

1897 Sears Roebuck & Co. Catalogue: Introduction by Nick Lyons (Skyhorse Publishing, 2007)
The following citations are from the above book:

"Millinery Department" section, specifically entries No. 23484 (*The Murray Hill Ladies' Leghora Flat Straw Hat*) & No. 23494 (*The Olympia*) p.320
The Murray Hill Ladies' Leghora flat straw hat and The Olympia in the millinery department at the Queshire Department Store.

"Millinery Department" section, pp.319-321
Materials adorning the decorated hats, and their varying heights, sold in the millinery department at the Queshire Department Store.

"Corset Department" section, specifically entry No. 23639, p.324
Nursing Corset in the hosiery department of the Queshire Department Store.

"Rubber Hair Pins" section, p.334
Rubber hair pins sold in the Queshire Department Store.

"library and Office Furniture" section, specifically entry No. 9250 "A $25.00 Book Case for $16.75," p.593
Mr Holden's bookcases.

"library and Office Furniture" section, specifically entry No. 9266 "A $16.00 Desk for $10.75," p.593
Mr Holden's desk

"Furniture Department" section, specifically entry No. 9179 "A $15.00 Table for $10.00," p.589
Suggitt's dining room table

*****

Stevens, Serita Deborah with Klarner, Anne The Howdunnit Series: Deadly Doses: A Writer's Guide to Poisons, (Writer's Digest Books, Cincinnati and Ohio, 1990)
The following citations were taken from the above book:

"Two: The Classic Poisons: Arsenic, Cyanide, and Strychnine," p.11
Doctor Weeks' findings, specifically Maryanna's Roberts' stomach being inflamed and arsenic being present in her throat.

"Appendix D: Poisons by the Time in Which They React," p.274
Doctor Weeks' statement that arsenic can start working in as a little as one minute.

*****

Stratmann, Linda <u>The Secret Poisoner: A Century of</u>
<u>Murder</u> (Yale University Press, New Haven and London,
2016)
The following citations were taken from the above book:

"CHAPTER FIVE: The Suspicions of Mr Marsh," pp.66-67,
specifically the suggestion that Marsh had applied heat to
produce the odour of Garlic to detect the presence of arsenic.
Doctor Weeks' statement that arsenic smells like garlic when
heated and that he got this smell after he had executed the
Marsh Test.

"CHAPTER FIVE: The Suspicions of Mr Marsh," p.70,
specifically the explanation of how, in 1837, Swedish chemist,
Jöns Jacob Berzelius, modified the Marsh Test apparatus to
weigh any resulting arsenic.
Doctor Weeks' statement regarding his having weighed the
arsenic to determine there were about three teaspoons' worth.

"CHAPTER FIVE: The Suspicions of Mr Marsh," p.74,
specifically the explanation that arsenic was so widely used
in the nineteenth century that it could be in the material
used to make a chemist's apparatus.
Doctor Weeks' explanation of the widespread use of arsenic and
how it's in the apparatus the Marsh Test relies upon.

"CHAPTER FIVE: The Suspicions of Mr Marsh," pp.72-73,
specifically the explanation of Orfila suggesting ways of
ensuring sulphuric acid and zinc were free of impurities, the
explanation of how Professor Orfila and physician and
chemist, Jean-Pierre Couerbe, discovered arsenic in the
bones and flesh of corpses, they'd not considered to have
been poisoned with arsenic, and the explanation of 'normal
arsenic' and Orfila's announcement of how 'normal arsenic'
could be easily identified compared to ingested arsenic due
to 'normal arsenic' not being water soluble.
Doctor's Weeks' explanation that sulphuric acid and zinc could
have arsenic in them, too, if one doesn't make sure they're free
of impurities first, Doctor Weeks' description of the story of
Professor Orfila and Physician and chemist, Jean-Pierre
Couerbe, and Doctor Weeks' explanation of 'normal arsenic'

and how it's not soluble in boiling water where a poisoner's arsenic is.

"CHAPTER FOURTEEN: Expert Witnesses," p.197, specifically the description of a discovery by veteran chemistry professor at the Royal Institution, William Brande, that the arsenic found by a Reinsch Test used by Professor Taylor to prove a woman by the name of Miss Bankes had been murdered by a Dr Smethurst, had been introduced by the copper gauze used in the Reinsch Test.
Doctor Weeks' statement that one must ensure the copper one uses is pure otherwise it can mess up the test.

"CHAPTER SIXTEEN: MATRIMONIAL CAUSES," p.217, specifically the explanation of the Pharmacy and Sales of Poisons Act coming into force in 1869 and how, because of it, the following applied: no one could sell, compound or dispense poisons unless they were a pharmaceutical chemist, no one could buy a poison unless they were known to the chemist or were introduced by someone known to the chemist, and all sales had to be recorded in a book, together with the buyer's name and address.
Doctor Weeks' explanation of the same Act and of the above criteria it imposed. Also Doctor Weeks' statement that buyers have to give their name and address, and the descriptions of the poison books at Drummond's Pharmaceutical Chemist's and Eastleigh's

Illustration "10 James Marsh's apparatus for the separation of arsenic"
The Marsh Test apparatus in Doctor Week's mortuary.

*****

Baren, Maurice <u>Victorian Shopping</u> (Michael O'Mara Books Limited, London, 1998)
The following citations were taken from the above book:

"The Chemist's Shop" chapter, pp.81-89
PURE DRUGS ONLY sign in the window of Drummond's Pharmaceutical Chemists, that shop's exterior, and the products

featured in the advertisements pinned to that shop's interior wall.

"Fireside Shopping" chapter, pp.105-108
Fireside shopping and how orders worked, the publication, contents and cost of the Exchange, and Mart, The Journal of the Household.

*****

Chapter Three: Details of Death's subsection Examining a Body at the Scene. Crime Investigation: The Ultimate Guide to Forensic Science, (Parragon, Bath, 2007) p.47, specifically the Rigor Mortis section.
Doctor Weeks' explanation of the rigor mortis process.

Gordon, Peter & Doughan, David DICTIONARY OF BRITISH WOMEN'S ORGANISATIONS 1825-1960 (Foreword by Sheila Rowbotham) (Taylor & Francis Group) (London and New York, 2013)
Lady Owston's Writers' Club.

* * *

INFORMATION SHEETS

Museum of the Royal Pharmaceutical Society Information Sheets
The following citations are from the above source. The sheets were downloaded as free PDFs from the Royal Pharmaceutical Society's Museum information sheets webpage:
http://www.rpharms.com/learning-resources/information-sheets.asp

"INFORMATION SHEET 15: DISPLAY GLASSWARE"
Glass bottles containing varying amounts of coloured water in the window display of Drummond's Pharmaceutical Chemists, the names and descriptions of the onion, swan neck and pear carboys, and the name and description of the Specie Jar (including its label).

"INFORMATION SHEET 12: DISPENSARY BOTTLES"

The origins of the "carboy" name, their original contents and purpose, the nineteenth century use of carboys, the alternative name of "Shop Round," the potential reasons behind the use of specific colours for the liquids in window display bottles, the cylindrical jars on counter containing lozenges, and the various bottles on the shelves behind the counter at Drummond's Pharmaceutical Chemists.

"INFORMATION SHEET 11: BALANCES, WEIGHTS AND MEASURES"

The scales on the counter at Drummond's Pharmaceutical Chemists and of the specific use of Troy weights for prescribing and dispensing of medicines despite the Avoirdupois weights and measures being favoured in the Medicinal Act of 1858.

* * *

MAPS

Booth, Charles <u>Booth's Maps of London Poverty East and West 1889</u> (reproduced by Old House Books) *purchased from* **Shire Books http://www.shirebooks.co.uk/old_house_books/** *Where the Head of the Mob Squad, Inspector John Conway, had been born in the East End of London (Stepney), the locating of the Holdens' residence on Hill Street in Mayfair (number 200, Hill Street is a fictional address), the locating of the Suggitts' residence on Reeves Mews, and the location of Reeves Mews and its surrounding areas. Also, the direct quoting of the names of Booth's social class classifications in reference to the households on Reeves Mews and its surrounding areas, Moore Street, Edgware Road, Nutford Place, and the lane to the rear of Molyneux Street and south of John Street. Also the locating of Mr Roberts' residence on Moore Street, and the locations of Moore Street, Queen Street, Edgware Road, Nutford Place, and the lane. Also, the locating of the fictitious Turk's Head Public House on the corner of Edgware Road and Queen Street and of its clientele consisting of the residents of Moore Street and the lane.*

* * *

MUSEUMS

The Museum of London
Timeline on wall of the Museum of London.
Thames Embankment having electrical street lamps since 1878.

The Old Operating Theatre & Herb Garret Museum
Online Surgical Instrument Collection, specifically a
Surgical Tourniquet, c. 1870. (2002:028H)
http://www.thegarret.org.uk/collectionsurgical.htm#1990002
The Surgical Tourniquet Locke uses.
.

* * *

VIDEOS

Magneto Era (1876-1900) by PHONECOinc
Published on 23rd August 2013 on www.youtube.com
Basic description of the telephone in the Bow Street Society's
Headquarters.

* * *

WALKS

The Alleyways and Shadows Old City Ghost Walk with
Richard Jones
Attended: Saturday 16th July 2016
http://www.london-walking-tours.co.uk/
Spiked window attachments as burglar deterrents.

* * *

WEBSITES

Lee Jackson's *The Victorian Dictionary*
http://www.victorianlondon.org/index-2012.htm
The following sources are all taken from The Victorian
Dictionary website

Jackson, Lee Chronology 1801-1901
*The location of the first public lavatory for ladies in 1884
(Regent Circus).*

Cassell & Company Limited, The Queen's London. A Pictorial
and Descriptive Record of the Streets, Buildings, Parks and
Scenery of the Great Metropolis in the Fifty-Ninth year of the
reign of Her Majesty Queen Victoria, 1896

*Photograph of the Victoria Embankment, from Charing Cross
Station and accompanying description used as historical
reference sources for basis of the in-book descriptions, history
and location of the Victoria Embankment, the Victoria
Embankment's Promenade, Albert Embankment, and the third
Thames Embankment division running Millbank to Battersea
Bridge.*

*Photograph of Regent Circus and Oxford Street, looking east
and accompanying description used as historical reference
sources for the basis of the in-book description and locations of
Oxford Street and Regent Circus. The description accompanying
this photograph was also used as an historical reference source,
in conjunction with* Dickens, Jr., Charles "Police Force" entry
Dickens' Dictionary of London, 1879, *for the basis of Inspector
Woolfe belonging to the E Division of the Metropolitan Police.*

*Photographs of the Water-Lily House, Kew Gardens and The
Palm House, Kew Gardens and their accompanying descriptions
used as historical reference sources for basis of the in-book
descriptions and history of each location.*

The Pocket Atlas and Guide to London, 1899
The location of the London Crystal Palace Bazaar.

Dickens, Jr., Charles "London Crystal Palace" entry Dickens'
Dictionary of London, 1879
*The location of the London Crystal Palace Bazaar and direct
source of the quote "cheaper kind of fancy goods" in Chapter
Two.*

"BAZAARS AND ARCADES" Routledge's Popular Guide to
London, [c.1873]

288

The location of the London Crystal Palace Bazaar.

Black's Guide to London and Its Environs, (8th ed.), 1882
Name, construction and Architect of the London Crystal Palace Bazaar.

Dickens, Jr., Charles "Police Force" entry Dickens' Dictionary of London, 1879
Used as an historical reference source, in conjunction with the description accompanying the photograph of Regent Circus and Oxford Street, looking East from Cassell and Company Limited, The Queen's London. A Pictorial and Descriptive Record of the Streets, Buildings, Parks and Scenery of the Great Metropolis in the Fifty-Ninth year of the reign of Her Majesty Queen Victoria, 1896, *for the basis of Inspector Woolfe belonging to the E Division of the Metropolitan Police.*

Punch: "DIRECTIONS TO LADIES FOR SHOPPING," Jul-Dec. 1844
Ladies waiting in private carriages for store employees to come to them.

"How to Make Tea and Coffee" entry Cassells Household Guide, New and Revised Edition (4 Vol.) c.1880s [no date]
The coffee in The Queshire Department Store's *storeroom having been prepared twice weekly, left to cool, heated on the stove when required, and drunk mid-morning and lunchtime. Also concurrent reference to this being the habit of the English middle classes at the time.*

"Income and Management" Chapter, Cassells Household Guide, New and Revised Edition (4 Vol.) c.1880s [no date]
Miss Webster's statement regarding Lady Owston's household taking in deliveries of sacks of potatoes every month.

Bell's Life in London and Sporting Chronicle, 27 January, 1883
Maryanna Robert's Convict Supervision Office photograph, specifically Locke's identification of the photograph's origin, Maryanna's fingers being spread across her chest, and her shoulders being held by the hands of unseen men.

Phillips, Watts, <u>Chapter III Rag Fair. The Wild Tribes of London,</u> 1855
Lady Owston's description of the Rag Fair's location, its methods of business, and its clientele.

"OMNIBUSES" – <u>Reynolds' Shilling Map of London,</u> 1895
Oxford Street being included as a stop on many of the omnibus routes.

Wynter, Andrew, <u>Chapter 12 – A Chapter on Shop-Windows. Our Social Bees; or, Pictures of Town and Country Life, and other papers,</u> 1865
Lovely hues being formed in the coloured liquids filling the window display bottles at Drummond's Pharmaceutical Chemists on account of the gaslight shining through from the shop's interior. Also the use of polished mahogany.

Sims, George R., <u>How the Poor Live – Chapter 12,</u> 1883
Dock Labourers sleeping at the dock gates in the hopes of being picked for work the next morning, Royals, Quay-Gangers, and Dock Labourers waiting around for late ships.

Krout, Mary H. <u>A Looker-On in London. Chapter 9: Women's Clubs (1896),</u> 1899
Lady Owston's Writers' Club, the bulletin board, and the club's Presidents and Vice Presidents.

Greenwood, James, <u>Toilers in London, by One of the Crowd [James Greenwood], Umbrellas to Mend,</u> [1883]
The job of a Knocker-Up, specifically the times written in chalk on walls and doors by customers, constables taking jobs, and the requirement to allow oneself enough time to get to one's patch before the first customer needs waking up.

Staffe, Baroness <u>How to take care of the hair: The Lady's Dressing Room, trans. Lady Colin Campbell,</u> 1893 - Part II (cont.)
Hair used in wig making foraged from overseas, use of hot pins and hot crimping irons to make hair wavy, lace mantillas being worn by old ladies, advice to not increase size of head by applying false hair, and recipes for preventing hair loss.

A.G. Edwards & Co.'s "Harlene" World-Renowned Hair Producer and Restorer advertisement, 1891
Mr Vuitton's reference to this product.

Koko for the Hair advertisement, 1891
Mr Vuitton's reference to this product.

*****

The Victoria & Albert Museum
http://www.vam.ac.uk/
The following two citations come from the above website:

Article: History of Fashion 1840-1900
http://www.vam.ac.uk/content/articles/h/history-of-fashion-1840-1900/
Miss Webster's attire, specifically her "leg-of-mutton" sleeves and the angle she wears her hat (according to this source hats were generally worn squarely on the top of the head. Also, Mr Edmund Queshire's appearance, specifically his clean-shaven face and his three-piece suit. Also, frock coats having become more associated with the older, or more conservative, gentleman.

Online Collection: Pair of Wedding Shoes
http://collections.vam.ac.uk/item/O146173/pair-of-wedding-unknown/
Lady's Owston Court (or 'Louis') shoes.

*****

The Tudor Links Article: 1896 Winter Blouses
http://www.tudorlinks.com/treasury/articles/1896winterblouse.html
References to blouses as a 'waist' or 'waists.'

Elizabeth Montague Letters' Article: Bluestocking Circle
http://www.elizabethmontaguletters.co.uk/the-project
Elizabeth Montague and the origins of the Bluestocking Circle's name.

A Victorian.com's Article: <u>Servants and the Servant Question: The butler</u>
http://www.avictorian.com/servants_butler.html
The Holdens' butler's attire.

NYP Corporation - National Burlap Manufacturer's Nursery Supply Blog Entry: <u>The History and Uses of Burlap</u> Posted on Tuesday, May 3rd, 2011 at 4:51 pm
http://nyp-corp.com/blog/the-history-and-uses-of-burlap/
Doctor Weeks' statement that hessian fibres were found in Maryanna's hair and that her body was transported in a hessian sack.

Vale and Downland Museum – Local History Series
Downloadable PDF: <u>Sacks for Hire by Reg Wilkinson</u>, downloaded from *the Wantage Museum's* website.
http://wantage-museum.com/wp-content/uploads/2013/04/Sacks-for-Hire.pdf
Hessian sacks being used for the transportation of bushels by farmers, Sack Hire Companies and their depots, and sacks' links with coal.

Tlucretius.net's Article: <u>Victorian Slang</u>
http://www.tlucretius.net/Sophie/Castle/victorian_slang.html
The use of the slang term "Lushington" to denote a drunken person.

Sunset Times website
http://www.sunsettimes.co.uk/
The first signs of dusk at four thirty in the afternoon.

UCL Bloomsbury Project's website's article: <u>London School of Medicine for Women</u>
http://www.ucl.ac.uk/bloomsbury-project/institutions/london_school_medicine_women.htm
The existence and legality of the London School of Medicine for Women.

Historic England's website article: <u>Oxford Circus Underground Station entrance on north-west corner of Argyll Street and Oxford Street</u>
https://historicengland.org.uk/listing/the-list/list-entry/1401022
Construction of the Oxford Circus Underground Station and by whom

British Medical Journal website, specifically item **Br Med J 1896;1:267** from the online archive: <u>TREATMENT OF ASEPTIC WOUNDS WITHOUT BANDAGES OR DRESSINGS</u> by James Mackenzie, M.D
http://www.bmj.com/content/1/1831/267
Reference to the name of this article, and its author, in Chapter Fifteen

Creative Review website's article: <u>Under the Skin: the evolution of Gray's Anatomy</u>
https://www.creativereview.co.uk/under-the-skin-the-evolution-of-grays-anatomy/
Background, name and interior of the thirteenth edition of Anatomy, Descriptive and Surgical from 1893.

BBC News website's article: <u>How The Lancet made medical history</u> by Martin Hutchinson, BBC News Online staff
http://news.bbc.co.uk/1/hi/health/3168608.stm
The Lancet was controversial in 1896.

Printed in Great Britain
by Amazon